Knickelpede Knight

Knickelpede Knight

A XANTH NOVEL

Piers Anthony

ISBN: 978-1-5040-9681-2

Published in 2026 by Open Road Integrated Media, Inc.
180 Maiden Lane
New York, NY 10038
www.openroadmedia.com

Knickelpede Knight

Chapter 1

NIKIPEDIA

Nicolas Nickelpede's clairvoyance made him aware of the approaching human young woman, whose hair and eyes were the color of hope. That was unusual for that species, but was only a trace of her significance. There was an aura of special importance about her that made his awareness resonate. What was her business here? His antennae quivered. He was aware of things in his vicinity, but sometimes needed more information to grasp their meaning.

As she knelt down beside his apartment entry she extended her delicate hand to touch the ground before it. There was a fire ant riding her left shoulder. And the Baton of Protagonism appeared in the air just above them.

At that point Nik knew this was more than important. Human visitors came and went, and there was a fire ant hill here in the Bug Section of the Queendom of Thanx, where all creatures lived in peace. Nickelpedes did not pinch nickel sized scoops of flesh from local humans, and humans did not stomp nickelpedes flat, and fire ants did not jet fire at humans or other bugs. Neither did nickelpedes and fire ants go to war against each other; each was satisfied with their own territory and treated each other with respect. It was an ongoing truce that benefited them all. There were even some friendships between bugs and humans. Some women carried spiders in their hair to nab marauding mosquitoes, and human food leftovers were regularly put out for bugs to feast on. Ghosts and sewer monsters put on scary shows for human children, and of course werewolves, vampires, and harpies behaved, sometimes even rescuing small children who got lost. It was suspected that some men preferred such creature ladies to normal women, and some women took spooks as lovers. It was their own private business, as long as it was voluntary. If any threat came to the queendom as a whole, they would all fight together for their homeland, each according to its ability. On rare occasion some stupid predator tried, and quickly regretted it. Even rogue dragons would suffer when baskets full of angry nickelpedes and fire ants got dumped on their tails.

But this was different. The presence of the Baton meant that a significant episode in the ongoing History of Xanth was commencing. Few folk could see that instrument, or were even aware of it, but his clairvoyance acquainted him with anything crucial within range. This was important. In fact, now that he focused on it, it was overwhelming. His life was about to change phenomenally. How could an insignificant nickelpede, however scholarly he might be, ever aspire to becoming a Protagonist in his wildest dreams, let alone actually become one? Nik was the distant offspring of a sphinx and a lady nickelpede who accidentally drank together from a love spring and used an accommodation spell to satisfy their passion. Other nickelpedes held him in contempt, for he had never gouged flesh from any fleshly creature. They had no respect for intellectual pursuit. He was a nothing creature. Yet here was the Baton. Something huge was happening.

Nik quickly emerged from his apartment and boarded the waiting hand. The girl stood, carrying him aloft, and touched her own right shoulder so that he could ride her in comfort on that perch. They had not encountered each other before, but the truce guaranteed that they could trust each other.

A melodic voice sounded in his mind. "Hello, Nicolas. I am Anthem Ant. You are clairvoyant. I am contact telepathic. We are aboard the human girl Noe, whose magic talent is Anonymity; she usually gets ignored in plain sight, but is a nice person and can be quite persuasive when she tries. We need to work together." Anthem was of a different species, but her mental voice was delightfully feminine. In fact there was a musical chord in the background as she spoke, enhancing her voice. He liked her immediately.

"I know this is important," he replied mentally. "I saw the Baton." He felt immensely more intelligent than ever before. "What is the larger situation?" Because he already knew it was tremendous.

"You saw the Baton! Yes, now I see it too, via your mind." The Baton bobbed, acknowledging the recognition. "First Noe must speak for herself, so we can know her personally. She grasps the larger picture, which can be challenging for us smaller creatures. I will translate her thoughts to your mind. Your turn, Noe." The chord played Voila!

The girl spoke in the human sonic language, the thought content coming to him apart from that noise. "Thank you, Anthem. I am noe the prettiest, smartest, naughtiest, or luckiest girl extant, thus my name. I function largely on hope. You may conveniently ignore me. My job is to carry you whenever you need to go, a beast of burden as it were."

"Noe," Anthem protested with a descending chord. "you are no beast! Neither are you the ugly, stupid, prudish, or unlucky one you imply. Not at all!" Then she corrected herself. "Oh, you were speaking figuratively, with a slant of humor. My minuscule ant mind forgot to invoke the vastly superior human intellect now available to it. Continue."

Which helped to explain his own suddenly expanded mental facility. He had always been scholarly, but now he was super-scholarly, aware of aspects that had never occurred to him before. It was the ambiance of the human mind, connected by the telepathy. And something more he had yet to fathom.

"Humor," the girl agreed with a mental smile. Nik found himself liking her, too. Humor was not normally a nickelpede trait, but the surrounding telepathy enabled him to appreciate it. It was what in human society was known as a social lubricant, enabling diverse folk to get along with each other with pleasure. "A human nuance. Nik, we are to associate closely with two capital D Demons, married to each other. As you may know, the ratio of a Demon to an ordinary demon or indeed any mortal person is roughly that of a galaxy to a grain of sand." She allowed her mind to expand momentarily to the scale of galaxies, which were well beyond the knowledge of ordinary Xanth dwellers, who thought that puns and panties were most of what was important in life. Bugs normally did not even know, let alone care, about p's and p's. It was a wondrous flash of perspective, showing among other things that her mind was not at all limited to such incidental things. "These two Demons are not closely familiar with the minor details of mortal interactions, so wish to accompany an insignificant exploratory mission as anonymous observers, attracting no attention to themselves. That mission, should you choose to accept it, is to map all the settlements of the Land of Xanth. Your clairvoyance and Anthem's telepathy, augmented by accompanying human minds, should enable you to fashion an authoritative representation. Are you interested?"

So that was the Something More! Two Capital D Demons. Interested? Nik felt as if he were a human male who had been kissed by a human female wearing lip bomb: he was blown away. His inclination was scholarly, not violent; this was beyond any dreams he might have thought to have, had nickelpedes had dreams. To map the whole of Xanth! What a project!

But he was cautious. Could there be a catch? "By settlements, do you mean the nickelpede mounds, ant hills, quarterpede quarters, dollarpede vaults, and such?"

She made a cute frown. Connected as he now was, he was able to recognize and appreciate the expression. She was noe the prettiest, but still far from the ugliest girl. "Think wider."

"Dragon nests, centaur stalls, mermaid pools, elf elms, ogre smashes, harpy aeries, roc rooks, ghost haunts, demon lamps, troll highways—"

"Where the sign says STOP—PAY TROLL," she agreed with another appealing trace of a grin. "Think broader."

Then it came to him. "You mean to include human towns?"

"Exactly. Humans may be minor, but they're part of Xanth too." The humor was rising.

He shared the mood. Human emotions were fun. "Amazing! But for the sake of completion, yes, they probably should be included, distasteful as the notion may be." His expanded mentality was sheer delight to use. "However, it will be tedious to cover the whole of Xanth, even with human assistance. It could take a lifetime."

"My friend Princess Hilda's talent is sewing. I'm sure she would let us borrow a couple of her flying carpets, so that traveling will be fast and efficient."

"Even so—"

"The mere presence of the Demons will enhance your clairvoyance. You will be able to scout all the settlements in a given vicinity without having to visit them individually. Anthem's telepathy will be similarly augmented, so she can get their names and natures from a distance, not limited to physical contact. That should multiply your efficiency a hundredfold."

So it should. "Oh, I could kiss you!" Then he remembered that she was of a completely different species. The fond clicking of claws was not for her. "My apology. I meant—"

"I know what you meant. Mental rapport tends to blur physical distinctions. But apart from that, it would be possible with an Accommodation Spell. Divergent species can even generate stork signals to create new cross species. That's how centaurs, werewolves, naga, harpies, and mermaids came to be. We can kiss if you wish."

Could she be serious? "Uh—"

"Relax, nickelpede. I'm teasing. My romantic interest is in my companion the Magician Santo, though he is gay."

"He is jolly? Why is that a problem?"

"Gay. It is slang for one who prefers his own gender for romance. We are friends, not lovers, though we are now coming of age for legitimate stork signaling."

This was new to him. She loved one who could not love her back in the manner she desired. The ant's telepathy carried emotion as well as meaning. Noe was privately hurting. "I'm sorry."

She laughed, with a tinge of regret. "Not your problem. There's always hope, per my hair and eyes."

The hovering Baton bobbed, its version of a nod. Did it know something they did not? How could there be realistic hope in such a situation?

Noe changed the subject, hiding the hurt. "Now it is time to meet the Demons who will appear in mortal form for this occasion. It is merely a simulation, a picture without substance, but can be taken literally for convenience. Herewith Andromeda, Demoness of Change." There was another Voila! chord.

A most attractive female nickelpede appeared before him. The very air shimmered around her, evincing her enormous power. "A greeting, Nik. I am glad to make your acquaintance."

Suddenly he had stage fright. This was a capital D Demoness! A galaxy to a grain of sand, manifesting to another grain of sand. "Uh—"

"I am the Demoness of Change," she reminded him. "With your approval, I will change your reticence so we may more readily converse."

What did she have in mind? "Uh, s-sure," he stammered.

"Done."

And his awe of her faded to camaraderie. “That is amazing, Andromeda! Suddenly you are an associate rather than a, well, galaxy.” A galaxy was a huge cluster of stars, and a star was a vast ball of burning gas, both of them concepts formerly beyond his awareness. He was just a bug on a chunk of matter orbiting a star.

“We are indeed associates in the exploration of the mortal realm of the Land of Xanth. All I ask is that you honor my privacy by not publicizing my presence or my nature. Demon Bang and I prefer to be anonymous. Our presence, even as mere observers, will enhance your capacities, but apart from that we may be ignored.”

“Which is why you chose to be with Noe!” he said, catching on. “Her talent is anonymity.”

“Indeed. But to clarify the nature of ambiance. The Demon Xanth, whose power is magic, came to this isolated planetoid to rest, perchance to sleep, and from his still body leaked the essence that came to imbue this little world with magic. He became intrigued by the mortal realm and let it be. That indicates the inherent power of a Demon. My power is equivalent, but I prefer to stifle it in your presence. Even so, it will affect you. My associate and now husband Demon Bang is almost infinitely more powerful. He generated the universe by causing what the Mundanes call the Big Bang. He is to a normal Demon as a Demon is to you. He too will stifle his power, but his mere ambiance is formidable. So we can’t be entirely anonymous, but it will help if you mortal folk cover for us.”

“Understood,” Nik said. “Thanks to the mental amplification your own ambiance provides. I will do my best.”

“Now you need to transfer to Noe’s friend Santo, a male human. For reasons we immortals are laboring to assimilate, mortals seem to prefer that female Demons associate with female mortals, and males with males. So Anthem is with Noe and with me, while you will be with Santo and with Bang.”

Nik wasn’t quite certain of the rationale either, but it seemed best to go along. There was too much else to absorb already. “I am amenable,” he agreed uncertainly.

Noe put her hand to her shoulder next to him, and he boarded it. The hand carried him to another hand, and he hopped onto that. “Hello Nik. I am Santo,” the new mind said.

Nik's enlarged intellect raised a question. "How can I be in touch with you when I am no longer touching Noe? Your talent is not telepathy."

Santo laughed. "Indeed it is not. I am the Magician of Holes. I make holes in anything, small or large. Some facetiously call me holy. Others suggest I have a hole in my head. But the proximity of two Demons has the incidental effect of broadening Anthem's talent to become fully telepathic, so she remains connected to you, and to me. We can all freely speak to each other, and fathom our several underlying personalities. You need have no concern on that score."

Meanwhile the hand had carried Nik to the man's right shoulder. Nik jumped to it and took firm hold of the cloth of the man's shirt as the hand departed.

Something else came to him. "Is it feasible to commune privately?"

"That is difficult in the circumstance. Anthem could cut you out of the circuit, but then you would be unable to dialogueue with me. We have no real privacy here. Fortunately we are all compatible folk, and can understand each other reasonably well despite our differences in gender, species, and status. The Demons are aware of everything; remember, they are observers, assimilating the whole of the mortal realm as they encounter its details. That is the ultimate purpose of this excursion. You are nominally mapping Xanth, and that is a good and worthy enterprise, but it is superficial. We mortals are all like ants under the microscope of Demon cynosure."

Nik was taken aback. "Oh. Surely true."

"However, I am aware of your concern, as it is a common one, a Noe is long familiar with it, so spot privacy is unnecessary. You wonder about my relationship with Noe, who loves me in a manner I am unable to return. That seems unfair."

Nik could only agree. "Unfair to her."

"I agree too. But there are two modifying aspects. One is that it is her choice. She would rather be with me on this partial basis than with a normal human man, in significant part because we truly understand each other. Our friendship is more important than prospective romance. The other is that she possesses a gender portal that enables her to transform to a male body at will. I can also use it to change to a female body. So we can romance as two males or two females when we choose, and sometimes we do, now that we, at ages eighteen and seventeen respectively, are parties to the secrets of the Adult Conspiracy."

Nik was momentarily baffled. "The what?"

"The full title is 'The Adult Conspiracy to Keep Interesting Things from Children.' It is largely limited to the human occupants of Xanth and Mundania, though some other species, such as centaurs, werewolves, elves, and related crossbreeds are coming to honor it as they interact with humans; that is why it is new to you. Suggestive words are changed or bleeped out, and the details of signaling the stork to request delivery of a baby human are suppressed. Children hate it, and swear to eliminate it when they come of age and have more power, but they invariably join it, to the dismay of their younger acquaintances. Crossbreeds like centaurs, mermaids, and harpies are amused by it, and bypass the stork works, but don't betray it lest they incur the dangerous wrath of normal humans. It is an uneasy truce, like that of the occupants of the Queendom of Thanx with respect to their natural combative urges, but it suffices. It is a foible of the human species."

Nik was learning a good deal more than he had anticipated. "Anthem, Noe, and Andromeda are party to this dialogueue?"

"We are," the ant, human, and Demoness said together in his mind, startling him. There truly was no privacy here.

The three females laughed in unison, and faded out, mentally, leaving only the physical figure of the girl with the ant on her shoulder, standing beside the young man with the nickelpede on his shoulder. Two humans, two bugs.

"However, I am studying the art of private communication," Anthem said. "With the Demonic enhancement I may be able to establish individual lines, as it were, so that we can confer without bothering others in the larger circuit."

"That will be nice," Nik said.

"Now it is time for you to meet Bang," Santo said. "He is by far the most powerful Demon in the universe. In fact he made the universe by causing its initial explosion, the so-called Big Bang. Before that there was nothing."

The overwhelming awe returned. "Uh—"

"Be at ease, nickelpede," a phenomenally potent mental voice said. "We chose you to be our expediter here in the Land of Xanth, because of your talent for clairvoyance, which nicely contributes to our purpose. Tune us into the background and go about your business." And the presence faded into that background, still present but ignorable. Bang had done what Andromeda had done, enabling him to function normally in the Demon presence. Bang was now just another associate. He knew intellectually that this was far from the case, but he no longer was awed by it.

Nik focused on that business, feeling the new quality of his enhanced psyche. "First I will need a map. Not a physical one so much as a magic one, that can be evoked and modified at will. Simple on the surface, but capable of encyclopedic data storage, so that a mere touch of its surface will evoke desired information about that spot in Xanth." He paused. "I will need a name for it."

"The Nikipedia," Noe said. "The masterwork of a nickelpede."

He focused his mind to dismiss that as humor, but discovered that he liked it. Because she had suggested it, he couldn't be accused of naming it after himself. "Nikipedia," he agreed. "And two of Princess Hilda's carpets, so we can travel freely."

Noe spread her arms forward, and two carpets fell onto them, looking entirely ordinary. She must have come prepared. "Invoke," she said. The carpets straightened out to float flat in the air on either side of her. "Down." They lowered to half their prior height. She put her hand on one, lifted a leg high so that her underwear flashed under her skirt, and sat on it. It bobbed slightly, taking her weight.

Nik suffered a momentary siege of fascination. "At ease," Santo murmured. "Your physical and mental association with me has caused you to identify psychologically with my male human body. Unlike me, you are intimately attracted to the female gender. So you freaked out at the glimpse of her panty."

"Sorry," Noe said. "Panties make no difference to Santo, and I have gotten careless. I will try to be more decorous." But there was an undercurrent of satisfaction; she liked proving her new female power.

Nik was silent. This was yet another example of the new state he was in. Nickelpedes did not freak out at the sight of underpants; bugs did not wear them. But the enormously mighty human mind evidently brought with it some of the human liabilities, such as foolish cultural reactions.

Still, it had been an amazing moment. Noe was blossoming into a really appealing girl, panties and all.

She smiled. "Thank you."

Which made him blush. That was another weirdity, because nickelpedes did not blush. He was identifying almost too closely with the human form and foible. To cover up his awkwardness, he refocused. "The map."

"The Nikipedia," Noe said as the form of the map appeared before him, with little patches marking all manner of geographic features.

"Voila!" Anthem said, with a resounding chord, just as she had when introducing Noe. It was evidently a flair she liked. "Courtesy of an anonymous observer." Such as a Demon. Slowly it filled in with an outline of the Land of Xanth.

"And we are here," Noe said. The outline of the Queendom of Thanx appeared in the southern portion, with an inset map of the Bug section, and a glowing dot marked their position within that.

Santo got on the other carpet, which bobbed similarly as it took his weight. "Now to officially commence the Quest."

"Quest? All we are doing is making a map."

"The map is the Quest," Santo explained. "All Quests start with a visit to the Good Magician's Castle. We must follow the forms, so there is no suspicion that there is an alternate purpose."

Oh, of course. To show the Demons the details of the mortal realm.

Nik took hold. "Now, if I understand the situation correctly, we must go to the Castle of the Good Human Magician. Do we know the way there?" But already his enhanced clairvoyance had the answer. "The carpets will take us there, following the directives of our minds."

"I've got it," Noe said. She focused.

Both carpets abruptly moved. Nik suffered no imbalance, as the carpet had a magic field to keep its riders secure, but the breeze of the motion flicked up Noe's skirt again. Santo averted his gaze just in time to spare Nik the embarrassment of another freak. They zoomed up at a steep angle until they were above the tops of the trees, then soared across the relatively level land, startling a flock of harpies. These were ugly fowls with the heads and bosoms of women, and the bodies, legs, and tails of birds.

"Hey, watch where you're going, bleepheads!" one swore.

Noe saluted them with one hand with the middle finger extended. She was evidently noe the most polite person when annoyed.

"That is an insulting gesture," Santo explained. "It expresses open contempt of the recipient." He smiled. "She is a nice girl, but she has an ornery streak I admire."

The harpies reacted with fury. "Oh yeah, carpet baggers?" one demanded insolently. "We'll poop on your stupid heads!" The flock flapped its wings vigorously to rise above the level of the carpets. "Bombs away!" They oriented, ready to strafe with their droppings.

Whereupon the carpets veered to intercept the flock, accelerating so that the creatures were knocked tumbling all directions in the air. In barely two moments the harpies were left behind in disarray, their swearing soiling the air around them with a filthy yellow cloud.

"That wasn't nice of me," Noe said with an unapologetic smile. "I don't like foul fowl."

"Nobody does," Santo agreed with perfect understanding.

The scenery of Xanth spread out below them, forests and fields, rivers and ponds, hills and dales. There were occasional clusters of human houses, villages that they would soon be adding to the map. Then came a classic castle surrounded by a moat. They flew down to land in a glade near it. They were there at the residence of the Good Magician. Nik knew it would have taken them at least a day by foot, even on enchanted paths.

"We'll have to park the carpets," Noe said as they dismounted. She snapped her fingers and the carpets flew to her like tame birds and draped themselves on her outstretched arms. She folded them and they disappeared into a small bag she produced that Nik realized was larger on the inside than the outside. Magic, of course. "No outside magic is permitted in the Challenges. We have to navigate them ourselves." She glanced at Santo. "I think that means Nik and Anthem, identifying with our human bodies, as they are the nominal leaders of the Quest. Santo and I will batten down and leave it to you two. Ready, bugs?" It was no insult, but a way to place Nik and Anthem in one category.

"Ready," Anthem said through Noe's mouth.

Nik found himself standing as a human man. "Uh," he said with a familiar uncertainty. Clairvoyance hardly helped with such social situations.

Anthem took his hand and squeezed it reassuringly. “You’ll get used to it.” Then she pulled him close and kissed his cheek.

He stood bemused. Suddenly she was the essence of femininity, enchanting him by her very nearness. Male and female nickelpedes came together mainly to mate, not even liking each other very much, but this was a different universe. An entire social spectrum was spreading out where he had known of none before. And, to his bemused surprise, he was discovering that he liked it. She was an ant borrowing a human body, but she was all female. Their near association with human bodies made it feasible to relate emotionally as well as physically. Realistically it was illusion, but still compelling.

“Thank you,” Anthem said, with a romantic chord. “I am sorry you aren’t an ant.”

“Or you a nickelpede,” he agreed.

“Sometimes I almost wish I could appreciate her as you do,” Santo said internally. “As either ant or human. Both are deserving. But I must settle for friendship.”

There it was. They were beset by physical and social obstructions, and could only glimpse the joys of more normal folk. It was glorious and sad. Even the Baton looked pensive, and there was a melancholy cast to the background Demons’ mood. The Demons, too, were learning.

“Now the Challenges,” Anthem said, happy to change the subject. “There are always three, and you have to be smart and a bit off-center to figure them out and make it through to the castle proper. Otherwise we won’t make it, which would be a shame.”

“A shame,” he agreed. Their mission evidently depended on getting through.

“Choose a path. I will follow you.”

“I will choose a path, but you must come beside me,” he said, taking her hand.

“Beside you,” she agreed, stepping forward with him. It was clear she was pleased.

He saw a path leading from the glade toward the castle, so he walked along it, Anthem beside him as if they were a human couple holding hands on a date. It wound around an acorn tree, considered half a moment, and headed for another glade.

There stood a halfway handsome woman beside a pretty girl of about half her age. Nik realized when he considered it that humans, who as a general rule lived far longer than bugs, slowly deteriorated as they aged.

"Yes," Anthem murmured. "Noe is just coming to the most appealing age for a human woman, newly nubile and relatively innocent. These must be mother and daughter."

"You don't know for sure, with your telepathy?"

"My telepathy is damped, here in the Castle environs."

Oh, of course. He was no longer directly aware of her ant mind despite being in physical contract with her human host. They had to depend on their physical observations and sharp minds.

"Hello, strangers!" the woman called as they approached. "I am Helena Handbasket, and this is my daughter Helen A. Handbasket. We are here to be helpful." She gestured, and a street appeared, leading toward the castle. "This is the Road of Good Intentions. We shall be happy to guide you along it."

This was wa-a-ay too convenient. It had to be a trap.

"I have heard that the way to Hell is paved with good intentions," Anthem said. "Also that it is easy to go to Hell in a handbasket."

Helena looked appalled. "Oh, my dear, however could you even think such a thing? We insist that you trust us!" She gestured again. "See, everywhere else is impassable." And indeed, on one side of the Road was a tangle of briers and thorny plants, the thorns just quivering to stab any passers-by. On the other was a flowing stream with black and white horses running on its surface.

Nik bent to pick up a stick. He tossed it into the stream. A huge toothy fish leaped out of the water to catch it in the air before splashing back down. The liquid of the splash struck a stream-side plant, which instantly withered. Acid or worse. There was no safe venue here.

"You are here to divert us from the castle," Noe said to Helena.

The woman's smile turned nasty. "And what are you going to do about it, my dear?"

Nik spied a large cone lying at the edge of the glade. It looked like a pining cone, but wasn't. His clairvoyance had been damped out, but he recognized it from prior experience. It was a cone of privacy. He picked it up and held it aloft. A soft light fell from it, surrounding them both. "We must talk," he told Anthem. "This guarantees we will not be overheard."

"True," she agreed. "But I have no idea how to get past this witch."

"I do. That is a Stream of Consciousness, and those are Night and Day Mares running along it. You are presently a human girl, which means you get along well with horses. See if you can persuade them to carry us across that deadly river, as they plainly use it as their highway. I will distract the Helens while you do."

"Distract the Helens? But we have to get away from them!"

"Not necessarily. When you make the deal with the mares, signal me, and we'll jump on them together and escape."

"We can but try," she agreed doubtfully. "How will you distract them?"

"I will make a feint at the elder, then kiss the younger Helen."

"But she's right at the age of enticement! She'll seduce you into love and you'll be lost."

"I will have Santo do the kiss."

She stared at him. Then she burst out laughing. "And he's immune to female attraction! What a devious ploy!"

"The kind that will maybe get us through the Challenge."

She shook her head. "You intrigue me."

"Ditto here."

"We'll have more to discuss, in due course. Now let's do it."

He set down the cone. They faced the Helens. "We have business," Nik said. Then he strode forward and took Helena in his arms. He quickly kissed her on the mouth.

"What are you doing, wretch?!" she exclaimed, shaking him off. "Get away from me!"

But he was already moving on to the young Helen. He kissed her, and not only did she accept it, she kissed him back with all the power of her gender. It would have been deadly, as she intended, except that he turned the body over to Santo as the contact was made. Helen put her all into it, not realizing that it was useless. Santo could not be ensorcelled by a woman. Meanwhile Helena was expostulating, furious about his attempt on her.

"Ready!" Anthem called.

Nik broke the kiss, leaving Helen halfway stunned by her failure; then he turned, and leaped onto the back of the waiting daymare. Anthem vaulted onto a nightmare at the same time. In half a moment they were galloping across the river, accompanied by the angry screeching of both Helena and Helen, who realized that they had been outmaneuvered. Soon they stopped at a new glade, closer to the castle.

They slid off their mounts. "Thank you so much," Anthem said to her mount, hugging her. Nik took the hint and hugged his daymare. Both horses whinnied their appreciation. They liked being recognized for more than dreams.

They had navigated the first Challenge.

But the second one was already upon them. A fierce dragon barred their way forward. It opened its mouth the blast them with fire—and sneezed, blowing out a ball of smoke. But it still blocked the way. It might have sniffles, but they could not get safely past it. Neither could they go around it, because a lake surrounded them, and more dangerous fish were in it; they could see them lurking.

Nik looked around. There were little bottles growing on stems. They were cold; there was snow on them. What did this have to do with the dragon?

Then Anthem caught on. "Cold medicine!"

Of course. Nik harvested a bottle, opened it, and tossed it at the dragon. The dragon automatically snapped it up, swallowed it whole, then froze in place. Literally. It lay across the path with ice chipping off its head.

So they had nullified the dragon. But the path ended beyond it. In fact this was an island. The dragon had not been the real threat.

Nik had an inspiration. "The cold medicine!"

"We don't want to take that," Anthem said. "It would just freeze us here."

"Watch this." He picked another bottle. He opened it, then poured it out into the water. A plate of ice formed. A toothy fish came, crunched the ice, and quickly retreated; this was not for it.

"Oho!" Anthem exclaimed. She ran to fetch more bottles. Soon they were pouring them out ahead of them, walking on the ice ramp as it formed. Soon they made it back to land.

Second Challenge navigated.

Only to encounter the third. The path was buried in the worst ever tangle of noxious weeds, including constrictor vines, poisonous fruits, and viciously slicing blades of grass. Before it was a little stand with a sign:

"A-LOT-A, delicious creamy drink enhancer." There were several mugs of it on the counter.

"It might be luscious," Anthem said. "But what we need is a way through the wasteland."

Nik considered, drawing on Santo's broad knowledge. "It seems to be a pun on latte, a kind of drink. But what we need is a way through that jungle, as you say. The sign says it's an enhancer. Could there be a hint there?"

She laughed. "Could the weeds be thirsty?"

"If there's been a drought."

They paused, considering. Then Nik slowly poured the drink on the ground, in the middle of the weeds.

After a moment and a half, the weeds lay down, relaxing. The ground cleared in an expanding circle.

"It's enhancing the ground itself," Noe said, amazed.

They poured more, and the whole path ahead cleared. They walked along it, and in no more than three and a half moments were at the moat. They had navigated the Third Challenge.

The drawbridge was down and the moat monster nonthreatening. They crossed over to the castle. The front gate was open.

A small cloud appeared before them. It extended arms, legs, and a head. It was demonic. "Hello, Nik and Anthem," it said. "I am Dara Demoness, Designated Wife of the month. Wira usually handles the introduction, but it's her day off. Follow me." She walked into the castle, her gait suggesting immense feminine appeal.

Nik was taken aback. "Designated Wife?"

Noe opened her mouth, but Dara stayed her with a gesture. "In a nutshell, Good Magician Humfrey outlived half a dozen wives. When he went to Hell to recover one, it messed him up by returning all six. Since a man is allowed only one wife at a time in Xanth, we arranged to take turns, one wife a month. He tends to be grumpy, so one month on and five months off is comfortable. We get along well with each other in a separate home. I was his first wife, and now it is my privilege to handle your visit."

They had reached a comfortable internal room. Dara gestured them to seats, and resumed her discussion. "We demons have a network, so we know what's what. I know who is with you, observing. We shall make no further reference to that. Except this: I am in awe of the immense power radiating, and am daunted, so hope that—ah, thank you. The awe is gone, for me and the Good Magician. Now, according to the protocol, you need to have a Question, and perform a Service for your Answer."

"Oops!" Noe exclaimed. "We forgot about that."

"I suggest that your Question be 'How can we best proceed with the mapping?' and that the Service be to add to your party two artifacts who would like to participate."

"Uh—"

"I will introduce them to you now." Dara lifted one hand, and a wand appeared in it. "This is Wanda, left over from the prior adventure, as the Baton of Protagonism knows." The Baton bobbed acknowledgment. "She can be used to conjure a spirit into a body, which can be useful. She can also manifest as an illusory woman. Wanda?"

She flipped the wand into the air. It fell toward the floor, but before it landed a mist surrounded it. The mist shaped into the figure of a lovely young woman with midnight black hair and eyes. "Illusion," she agreed. Then she faced Noe. "I know you from before. Please take me now."

Noe nodded. "Nydia Nymph carried you." She reached out, put her hand through the woman, and grasped the wand inside. She tucked it into her belt.

"And Knight Knife," Dara said. A knife appeared in her hand. It expanded into a full sword, then retracted back to the knife. "He can be useful in combat as a self-guided weapon. He is deadly when required to be; otherwise he just bluffs."

"I'll take him too," Noe said, taking the knife.

Thus simply it had been decided.

"Now with the formalities handled, I will take you to see the Good Magician," Dara said. She led the way to a coiled flight of steps that exited at a cramped office largely filled by a vast tome. Nik was aware that this was the fabulous Book of Answers. His clairvoyance had returned, now that the Challenges were done.

Dara faded out. Her role had been performed.

The Good Magician Humfrey rather resembled a century-old gnome. This was hardly surprising, as it was known that he used measured doses of youth elixir to maintain his age at that level, and it was suspected that he had some hidden gnomic ancestry. But nobody said anything, lest it aggravate his legendary grumpiness.

He gazed at them, his expression hinting that he knew more than he was saying. Even the two Demons were impressed; their background awareness leaked into Nik and Anthem's augmented minds as muted admiration. He truly was the Magician of Information. "Your map will indicate your preferred route," he said. "In fairness I must warn you that there will be a complication when you come to the site marked with an asterisk, that will involve your anonymous observers. More need not be said." His gaze dropped to the book before him. They had been dismissed.

Dara reappeared. "I will show you to your room for the night. Tomorrow you will embark on your Quest."

And that, it seemed, was it.

Chapter 2

ZOMBIE LIPS

They got to know Wanda Wand and Knife Knight overnight. Santo and Noe already knew them, but it was best to acquaint the two watching Demons with them in a routine manner. They were a couple, and had traveled widely with Nydia Nymph, who was now a full woman widely hailed for saving the universe, among other things. Wanda had survived the Magician who made her, and been rescued from solitary oblivion by Nydia. Knife was an enchanted sword who had also survived his master and had been similarly rescued. Both were ready to assist the Quest in whatever ways they could, in return for the adventure and companionship surely coming. Wands and knives could get lonely too; they preferred to be in use and active.

"Why did the Good Magician want you with us?" Noe asked. She and Santo were back in charge of their bodies, the bugs satisfied to ride their shoulders as before. Anthem's telepathy enabled the wand and blade to speak to the others in the party, though outsiders would not be aware of it. "You're both quite useful in your places, but we're just making a map. I doubt we'll need conjuring or combat."

"He knows something we don't," Knife answered. "We can surely demonstrate our usefulness in due course."

"He surely does, and we surely will," Wanda agreed, flashing him a smile as she made an illusion face. "Meanwhile we can enjoy being treated like people instead of objects."

"Of course you're people!" Noe said. "We all know that."

"Exactly. There are those who don't."

Anthem laughed with a musical background. "Even bugs appreciate being treated like people."

"Even anonymous Demons," Andromeda's quiet thought came.

Nik spread out the map in the air before them, guiding it by his thought. This, too, was apparent only to the members of the Quest. It showed a meandering route back to the Queendom of Thanx, and on beyond. That made sense, as there were settlements of assorted species everywhere, including in Thanx itself. The asterisk was at the end of the route, in an unremarkable region. What could be so significant about that? Along the way were two lesser markers, rather like stickpins. One of them was at Thanx. What did that mean?

"We'll find out soon enough," Anthem said with a foreboding chord.

They bid farewell to Dara, treating her as a person, and marched out to officially begin the Quest. Noe wore Wanda, tucked into her waistband, and Santo wore Knife, who resembled a hunting knife when not in action. Nik spread his clairvoyant awareness, which was indeed dimensionally stronger than it had been before this adventure. He picked up on half a myriad of ant hills, including some fire ants, and a smaller number of pede mounds, including some nickelpedes, and assorted other bug species, mainly bee hives and fly clusters. A butterfly cocoon was next to a breadfruit tree, available for those hungry for bread and butter. Each settlement had its name and its government and its limited territory, which he picked up on as he focused. The map pinged as he added them to it, including their populations, specializations, and recent histories. They didn't even have to dismount from the carpets. This was easy and satisfying. So far.

By the end of the day they were at the queendom. Demesne Demoness, Queen of Thanx, came out to greet them. "Dara told me via the demon net. You're on a Quest!"

"We're mapping all the settlements of the Land of Xanth," Santo said, speaking for Nik.

"It's so good to have a real live Quest originating here. It will do wonders for our notoriety. But I am also instructed to have you talk with Apoca, Queen of the Lips tribe. She's married to a naga prince, but vacations here."

"We'll put the Lips tribe on the map," Noe said.

"This is more than that. You will need to talk with her privately."

"We shall do that," Nik said. Could this relate to the stickpin?

The demoness vanished. They followed the map to the Lips section, a kind of inset queendom in the larger fabric of Thanx. Then to the residence of Queen Apoca.

Apoca met them at her door. She was about thirty-four and had a pretty face, a shapely figure and the broad lips of her kind, which could kiss a man into abject love slavery if she willed it. But it was her hair that transformed her. It was translucent, conducting the colors of her scalp. It was yellow, which Anthem and Noe recognized as doubt, until she recognized them and it turned green for welcome. "Hello Santo, Noe," she said. "And Nik and Anthem. And Knife and Wanda. And anonymous observers." She had evidently been well advised. Actually both Nik and Anthem had been residents here, but beneath the notice of royalty.

"We are listing your tribe on the Nikipedia Map," Noe said for Anthem. "But there's a curious mark right here at this spot. Do you know anything about it?"

The hair turned plaid, evincing mixed emotions. "Oh, that would be Aura. She's one of my Lips women, but she experienced an unfortunate mishap. She suffers from migraine headaches, which are horrendous. When one starts it makes an aura, hence her name, which scintillates outside her body and can on occasion set fire to loose straw. So she was not popular, and volunteered for night watch duly, guarding our precious spice garden. One night the ground shook with the measured thuds of an invisible giant, evidently coming to raid the garden. He intersected her aura as he squatted down, and she saw his outline as a disturbance in it. So she hurled herself forward and kissed him on his monstrous mouth, exerting her full power, love enslaving him." Her hair turned red. "But she discovered two things too late. One was that he was a zombie giant. The other was that he carried some reverse wood. So in some respects they both reversed. He became visible and alive, while she became a zombie." The hair turned black. "Worse, now her kisses zombify the recipient, so her isolation is much worse than it was before. She let the giant go, but she can't reverse the change, not even with more reverse wood. It was a weird fluke." The hair turned yellow. "She went to the Good Magician for advice, and he told her to join the Quest that was about to initiate. That would be yours." The hair was green again.

"But—" Noe protested, horrified. "We can't have a zombie!"

"Tell her that," Apoca said, gesturing as her hair turned yellow/green for passing humor. There behind her was a zombie woman, crying rancid zombie tears. It seemed that the Quest was her only hope. She obviously felt rotten, though her freshness made her well preserved.

They had a quick consultation. "There must be a reason," Noe said.

"There's always a reason," Santo agreed. "Generally more than what's on the surface."

Anthem reached into the woman's mind, which was still reasonably intact. "She's desperate, and we are her only hope. The longer she is a zombie, the worse her condition will get, until she rots away entirely. But she fears we will reject her. She can't blame us for that. *Everyone* rejects her. That's why she's crying. She feels doomed."

The others glanced at Nik. It was his decision to make. His clairvoyance, even enhanced as it was, could not tell him how a zombie could possibly help a mapping mission. His pincers crackled at the thought of even touching a zombie. But this was a person in pain, and the nice thing to do was to help her if they could. The Good Magician just might have a reason for adding her to the Quest, apart from her benefit. Maybe she could after all somehow help them. There was only one way to find out. "She can join us," he decided.

"Oh, zhank you!" Aura said, her zombie slurring evident. She did have the wit not to try to hug any of them. She merely approached and stood somewhat apart from the group, evidently a familiar pose.

Noe spread out a carpet in the air and sat on one end. "Sit on the edge, across from me," she told Aura. "So we don't have to touch. You understand why. But we can talk; Anthem's telepathy will clarify your voice."

"Thank you," Aura said, her voice now clear in their minds. She climbed onto the carpet and sat there. Her tears still flowed, but now they were sweet. "I will not touch anyone."

"Here's a mental hug," Noe said, sending it. Then the others sent her their mental hugs.

"Oh! That feels so good!"

Of course it did. Aura had been starved for human contact ever since the disaster with the giant, and maybe before that, to a lesser degree. Objects and bugs might resent being ignored, but zombies were actively avoided.

Santo and Nik boarded the other carpet. Apoca's hair was brilliant green as they floated away. She was pleased. She cared for her Lips women.

Nik guided the carpet in the direction indicated by the map. That took them to the Visitor's Subdivision. "But this is where royalty and Demons hang out," Noe protested. "There was even a Demon marriage ceremony here." Then she reconsidered, remembering their observers. "Oh. Of course." They felt Andromeda's amusement.

A sumptuous meal was served by magically floating plates, with fresh steaks from beefsteak tomato plants, boot rear drinks, and eye scream for dessert for the two humans. Nik and Anthem got toasted seeds and spider eggs, and Aura some suitably spoiled fruit, all she could eat now. Wanda and Knife did not need to eat, and spent the time chatting with Aura, as they had no fear of zombies. Bang and Andromeda tuned out, not needing to observe this familiar process; the others felt their absence. The two Demons surely had private business with each other, as newly married couples did.

In the morning, the observers back, the Quest resumed, following the route indicated on the map. They started with the assorted human, animal, bug, spook, and other settlements, listing them all. Then they moved out across the terrain. It was routine, until they came within range of an ornery ogre colony. It was amidst a grove of psychiatrees, hopelessly complicated, so that no mental sense could be made of it. The ogres were of course too dull to notice. Ogres were justifiably proud of their stupidity. They would have to check it personally for the map.

Rather than show the carpets and humans, Nik and Anthem went out by themselves, expecting not to be noticed. Nik, being a larger bug, carried Anthem on his back. He found that he liked this direct personal contact. Her contact telepathy was super strong, carrying with it her alluring musical femininity.

"Thank you," she said mentally, responding to his thought compliment. Both laughed, a mannerism they had picked up from the humans. It meant they enjoyed each other's company.

They came into sight of the colony. It was ordinary for ogres, with trees bent into obscure shapes, and splintered wood everywhere. No other creatures were near, of course; they knew better than to mess with ogres.

"Plug bug!" It was an ogre who had spied them.

Nik tried to scramble out of the way, but the ogre's massive foot was already smashing down to stomp them into thin jelly. There was no hope of reasoning with the creature; even if it had been smart, it wouldn't have cared. Ogres liked smashing things. In futile desperation Nik lifted a pincer in a pinching reflex.

"'Gain pain!" the ogre cried and hopped away.

Confused, Nik looked. What had happened? There was only a huge ugly ogre foot lying there.

"You pinched off his foot!" Anthem said, amazed.

"But I couldn't possibly have—"

"The Demon enhancement," she said, working it out. "You pinched beyond anything any ordinary nickelpede could ever even think of doing."

He gazed at the severed foot. "That must be it. I'm glad you weren't squished to paste."

"And I'm glad you weren't. Here's a human-type kiss." She threw it mentally.

The kiss struck him on his mouthpart. It knocked him into the air, then let him float slowly back down to the ground, accompanied by the music of the chord. It was way more potent than the other kisses had been. He stood bemused.

"I think I shouldn't have done that," Anthem said. "I'm sorry."

"Don't be," he said dizzily. "I will remember it the rest of my life."

"But we're two different species, neither of which kiss," she reminded him.

"We are," he agreed sadly. "But it was still a great experience. Now I know why humans value it."

"I liked it too. But bugs don't love, so it can't mean anything."

There was a pause as they tried to assess the situation. But it was beyond understanding at the moment. An ant and a nickelpede?

He entered the ogre colony on the map, and they returned to the carpets. "What a phenomenon!" Noe exclaimed.

"The ogre pinch?"

"The kiss. It smacked all of us. Even Santo was impressed."

"So was I," Aura said. She was becoming more sociable as their association continued.

"So were Knife and me," Wanda said. "The accompanying love music was wonderful as well. We're glad you didn't get squished, too."

Oh. The enhancement, again.

"But the pinch was impressive enough," Santo said. "That enhancement effect is far more potent than we knew."

It was indeed.

The landscape became barren. No animals lurked, and there was no brush, with trees widely spaced. Something had cleaned it out. But there was no sign of anything unusual. Areas varied, and this was part of the patchwork of Xanth.

They resumed the mapping. Before long they came to another complication. Several termite nests were jammed together so tightly they seemed to overlap. Where did one settlement end and another begin? That needed to be clarified for the map.

"I think we'll have to ask," Nik said.

"We'll go out alone together, again," Anthem said. She seemed almost eager. He liked the notion too, foolish as any idea of romance between them was. "I will try to signal the queen termites."

They rode out alone together, again. Anthem's very touch on his back felt magical. The intensity of her contact telepathy was compelling. He loved being so close to her.

"Me too," she murmured. "You feel my telepathy, I feel your clairvoyance. We have similar powers, distinguishing us from our species. I love it."

Indeed, he felt closer to her than to another member of his own species, mad as that might be. This adventure was turning out to be weird in ways he never would have anticipated, had he ever even seen it coming.

They came in sight of the termite settlement. It was like a wall of super-hardened mud, buttressed by a rocky foundation, reaching up toward the treetops. Little windows showed several stories up, with guard termites watching from them. A formidable fortress. It was now clear what had cleaned out the neighborhood: such a termite city required a lot of food and digested construction material. Everything was grist for a termite colony.

Anthem sent out an introductory salute chord, enhanced to penetrate to every chamber. "We must talk with your queens. We are on a Quest."

The response was not what they had expected. "Capture the intruders! We'll eat them for lunch." Termite soldiers poured out of the windows, running down the wall and across the ground, intent on mayhem. It was evident in their thoughts. Anything that came within range was marked for a meal. There would be no dialogueue, no negotiation; the decision had been made long before the visitors came on the scene.

There were way too many termites for Nik to fight. He might take out two or three by pinching off their heads, but the rest would chomp them both up in a fraction of a moment.

"Maybe I can burn them back a bit," Anthem said. "Long enough for us to retreat."

A fire ant's jet of fire could burn up one termite or scorch several. Regular bugs knew not to mess with this species. But hundreds were coming at them. They were doomed. Yet that fire was all that was offered. The enhancement effect might make the jet more like a little blowtorch, maybe making the termites pause. It was what they had to try. "Do it," he agreed as the vicious horde closed in.

Anthem fired her jet. Blowtorch? It was more like a flamethrower! The fire speared out in a widening cone, incinerating everything in its path. It struck the wall and blasted a hole in it. The foundation rocks melted. The wall collapsed into rubble mixed with smoking termite corpses.

But there were more termites that had been outside the cone of fire. Anthem grimly readied her fire for a second blast.

"We yield!" a queen called. "Only spare what's left." the remaining soldiers withdrew.

It seemed they had impressed the termites.

After that, negotiation was easy. They soon had information for the map, and chances were that no termite would ever again attack them. Word did tend to spread. Soon they were back on their way.

"That," Santo said with bemused satisfaction, "is what I call enhancement."

No one argued.

They settled back into the routine, and made good progress, thanks to the enhancement. Between settlements they chatted. Aura was increasingly interested in the Quest, and not just because they were accepting her. "This seems really worth doing. When I was a normal Lips woman I dreamed of traveling, but wouldn't have been safe without a companion. Oh, I know, the enchanted paths are safe, but I wouldn't have wanted to confine myself to them. I wanted to see centaurs and dragons and roc birds, but for those I would have had to be part of a touring group with magic wards, but my chronic headaches made me unwelcome. So this is really like my dream."

Nik, through Santo's human mind, recognized Aura as a most attractive woman, especially as she sat on the edge of the carpet swinging her legs forth and back, the breeze playing with the hem of her skirt. Santo had no romantic interest, but could objectively judge such appeal. He knew that the Lips ladies didn't have to kiss with power, so she could have had a normal boyfriend, and kissed him into submission if he got too pushy. Why would a headache make her unpopular?

Aura laughed, picking up his thought in this telepathic environment. "My headaches have become chronic, even with the zombieism, so the auras are always there, though usually not too bright. Now I will focus and show you one."

A scintillating band of light appeared before them, hovering at about head height. To the side, where it intersected some foliage, the leaves withered and curled as if caught in a fire. "Folk don't like to get toasted," Aura explained. "I wish I could abolish it entirely, but I can't, and it's unpredictable. All I can do is mute it, usually. The same is true for my zombifying kisses. My powered kiss won't enslave you, anymore, but it will make you a zombie. The rest of you are safe as long as you keep your distance." She made a gesture of gloom. "I don't have to kiss with power, but who wants to kiss a zombie, no matter how amenable she may be?"

"Only another zombie," Noe said sadly.

"Yes, if they are not too rotten. I don't want to half-live as a zombie; I want to return to full life, flirt with normal men, marry one, and have normal Lips children. I can live with the headaches, but the zombie aspect has to go."

Now Nik understood. It occurred to him that the Demoness of Change could probably abolish the auras and the kisses, but she was observing, not intervening. It was surely best to keep it that way, lest the anonymity of the Demons be compromised.

Surely, Andromeda agreed with a tinge of regret.

They came to a section where the recent pundemic lingered. Puns were everywhere, generating pundemonium as they gave people pundigestion and caused them to emit such foul puns that nobody else could stand to be near them. The stench was smearing the tree trunks and causing the foliage to droop. Unfortunately there were assorted settlements there that had to be mapped. They would have to forge on through, enduring the punishment.

They passed a cute little punda bear. "Did you hear about the moist towelette that wasn't picked in time?" it asked. "It became an old and soggy sheet."

Noe groaned. "That's the proper response to a bad pun," she explained. "A groan."

Nik hadn't known that. He would remember.

Next was a little showcase where a comic couple joked. It was labeled The Puns & Judy Show. Nik's clairvoyance indicated that there had once been something like that in Mundania. They sailed past before they could get smeared by any of the puns.

Only to get caught by a type of anteater, a pungolin. It spied Aura. "Hey, zombie, want to take a dirt nap?"

Aura groaned appropriately and sailed on.

Next came a group of people sitting along a table: a punel. "What's flu medicine for?" one cracked. "Clogged chimneys." Another spied Nik. "Hey, learn all about Xanth in the Nickelpedia, or at least about nickelpedes."

There was a scaled pungolin. "Hey, did you know that wormwood is an aphrodisiac? Absinthe makes the heart grow fonder."

Santo and Noe groaned. It was clear that this was becoming wearisome.

A tanklike punzer cruised past. Its pilot peered out of the top. "Did you know that when zombies fall in love, it's necromance?"

Nik could see that Aura was getting tired of being a target for bad puns. He didn't blame her. But she seemed to be stuck for it.

Then came a pundit. Naturally he spied Aura. "Hey, zombie lady! Do you need a death support system?"

That did it, Aura jumped off the carpet, grabbed the pundit, and kissed him with power. He immediately turned zombie, while she turned alive.

"It won't last," she said as she jumped back on the carpet. "They slowly recover, while I slowly re-zombify."

"But you sure look good now," Noe said.

"I feel good. But I know better. For that limited time, my normal love-slave kiss power returns, instead of the zombifictation power. At least that's an improvement."

"That's sad," Noe said sympathetically.

Then they saw a bull charging toward them. "That's a humbull," Anthem said, reading its mind. "Anyone who hears its constant humming sees their own arrogance and are irreversibly changed. We've got to avoid it, lest our Quest be taken as unjustified pride and be demoted."

But it was too late. The bull would run into them in moments.

Aura jumped down and ran to intercept it. She flung her arms around its neck, hauled her face into place, and kissed it firmly on the mouth. Then she let go, rolling clear.

Nik and Anthem exchanged a direct glance. Aura had risked her health, possibly her life, on their behalf. "She is trying to help us," Anthem said.

"And succeeding," Nik said. "That bull is trouble."

Their attention returned to the action. The bull turned zombie. It slowed to a halt, confused. Then it turned away and wandered into the brush. It now had other things on its rotting mind.

"That's odd," Aura said as she returned to the carpet. "I'm well, at the moment, but my kiss still zombied it. I meant to pacify it."

"Let me deep-read your mind," Anthem said.

"Have at it, friend. I have nothing to hide, alas."

Anthem focused. "You're not a latent zombie," she said, surprised. "You are completely alive."

"But I've been through this before. I always revert in day or so."

"Not this time. Your zombie kiss is all that remains of your zombieism. Your brain has no zombie rot."

"This is downright weird," Aura said. "I don't understand it."

Nik got half a notion. "Have you ever kissed a pun before?"

"Of course not! But that bull had to be stopped."

"Here is what my clairvoyance vaguely suggests: puns are opposite to zombies. They can't coexist in the same person. When you exerted your power on a pun creature, there was feedback that blew away your zombie infection."

"Zombies really don't understand puns," Aura said. "The only reason I did was because I have not been zombied long." Then she did a double take. "Are you saying I'm cured? I mean, permanently?"

"You may be, except for your change in kissing. Somehow that remained."

"I'll take it! This must be what the Good Magician saw."

"Yes. So if you want to go your own way now, you can do so. You don't need us anymore."

"And leave the rest of you to struggle with the puns and nasty creatures? I wouldn't do that. I owe you infinitely more than that."

Nik was not surprised. She had come across as a good person even when a zombie. "Then stay, and welcome. We are glad to have helped you, even accidentally."

Aura looked at Anthem. "This all right with you?"

"Of course," the Ant replied. "And with Noe and Santo. I feel it in their minds."

"And with Knife and me," Wanda said. "We know what it's like to be different."

Aura's tears returned, this time flowing joy. "May I hug you? Physically? All of you?"

"Yes!" they said together.

They hugged, Nik and Anthem sharing Santo and Noe's physical ones. It was wonderful.

The work continued, as Nik added the local settlements to the map, fending off the constant barrage of puns. Even the map wavered at times as if it were groaning.

They finally floated out of the pun zone, to their relief. Yet it had been worthwhile, because it had not only saved Aura, it had given them a weapon against zombies, should they ever need it. Simply hit them with bags of awful puns.

They came to something odd. It was a pool of darkness. Not water, not fog, just a valley filled with black as if there were no sunlight.

They hesitated. With magic, anything was possible, but was this safe to enter? "I sense no hostile minds," Anthem said.

"And there are settlements within it," Nik said, "but that darkness is total. We could float into a tree trunk."

"I can help," Aura said. "With my aura." She got off the carpet and waded into the pool. Her sparkly aura appeared, illuminating the region before her.

Well, why not? This did solve the problem.

They came to a cross between a tangle tree and an elf elm. The other trees in the vicinity were still, but this one was waving slightly as if there were a breeze, which there wasn't. That was the tangle effect; the predatory vines were never completely quiescent. "Hail, floaters!" an elf called. "Do you have business in the Pool?"

"Yes," Santo answered. "We are mapping Xanth, and your tree is a settlement. What is it called?" Anthem could read that information, but it was polite to ask.

"We are the Tangle Elf tribe. I am Elmer Elf, lookout for the day."

"Thank you. Is there a reason for the darkness?"

"A long-ago Magician wanted privacy, so he made a pool of darkness. Then he moved on, forgetting to turn it off. So now those of us who prefer privacy use it. We elves, for example, go out to forage without worrying about the security of our special tree, because no one else can find it if they even know it's here." He smiled. "We use reverse wood to make ourselves stronger the farther we get from our tree, instead of getting weaker in the usual manner of elves. So we can range quite far, knowing that our tree is safe. We plant new tangle elms where we go. We travel in pairs so that one can take the chip when the other needs to be normal."

"But won't our map give it away?"

"Not unless you mark it to call attention to it. There are hundreds of elf elms, and only one mature tangle elm so far. That's why it could be at risk; some folk are wary of tanglers."

To be sure, Nik thought. Tangle trees were notorious for luring creatures close, then grabbing and eating them. Any that tried to grow near human villages were attacked with fire and magic. The elves must have made a special deal. Maybe to seed the trees wide and far, in exchange for tolerance and protection. It was their business.

"We'll leave it anonymous," Santo promised, picking up on Nik's reassurance. On the map it was just another elf community.

They moved on, noting assorted bug settlements. Then they came to an ugly herd of bulls that nobody wanted to associate with, so they had settled here in the darkness. They were the unspeaka bulls.

In due course they emerged from the pool. Aura doused the light of her aura and returned to the carpet. They were making fair progress.

Then they came to a rogue tribe of Amazons. Anthem picked up their nature from a distance. They did not want to be mapped, because they were an illicit settlement engaged in raids and thievery. If they caught on to the nature of the Quest, they would attack it in an effort to destroy it, rather than have the local kingdom know about them. Anthem's enhanced fire and Aura's electrically scintillating aura could drive them back, but it would be an ugly scene. They had control of the local area that needed to be mapped, thus could not be avoided. So instead the Quest tried for distraction.

"I can talk tough when I need to," Aura said. "I'm a Lips woman. We have the vocabulary."

"Take us along," Wanda said.

Aura put on Knife, who quickly armed her in a formidable manner. He was a self-powered weapon needing no skill by the one who held him. Wanda exerted her illusion to make her resemble another warrior lass as she floated beside her. Meanwhile, Noe enhanced the unnoticeability of the other Quest members so that only a person peering directly at the two carpets would even notice them.

Aura marched up to the nearest Amazon squad leader, a formidable creature whose name, Anthem read in her mid, was Amber. Her opponents were reputed to be preserved in amber as telling examples. "Out of my way, hussy!" Aura snapped insolently. "I don't want to soil my clean blade on your stinky blood."

"And don't try to stab my friend in the back as she passes, coward," Wanda said fiercely. She knew how to play a part too.

Hoo! The other Amazons gathered round, eager to see their leader slaughter this arrogant stranger. None were watching the quietly passing carpets.

"How's that again, interloper?" Amber inquired dangerously as her hand went to her sword.

"You hard of hearing, pig face? I said stand clear so I don't have to waste my time brushing you back."

That did it. Amber's sword ripped out of its sheath.

Only to be blocked by Aura's sword, the self-powered Knife, moving more swiftly than any human hand could direct. In fact, it had dragged Aura's hand along with it. "You eager to die, cretin?" Aura asked around a sneer. "Put that toy away before you annoy me."

The watching Amazons drew in an amazed breath. They had never seen anyone outdraw Amber.

But the Amazon was not a timid girl. She wrenched her sword around, trying to bash the opposing sword back.

Aura's weapon did a clever maneuver and wrenched Amber's sword out of her hand. It tumbled ignominiously to the ground. Then with blurring speed it snapped up against the Amazon's throat. "You're obviously too stupid to deserve beheading," Aura said. "So I'm just going to let you go with a warning spank." The sword whipped around and the flat of it loudly smacked the Amazon's bottom. As insults went, that was potent.

Then the two of them walked on, leaving the Amazons staring in mixed awe, wonder, and disbelief, with here and there a suppressed smile of admiration. Had this really happened? Amber's stifled rage suggested that it had. She would probably lose her status.

Meanwhile the two carpets had sailed on beyond, unobserved.

"That was nasty fun," Aura said. "Thanks to you, Knife"

"You're welcome," the sword replied, satisfied. "It's good to see a bit of harmless action. Nice dialogueue, too."

"Thank you." They both laughed.

They caught up to the main party and boarded the carpets. "Good show, girls," Santo said. "The Amazons never saw us."

Was he patronizing them? Aura and Wanda jumped off their carpet, came at him from either side, and kissed him simultaneously on the cheeks. They were teasing him, knowing that he had no romantic use for ladies, not even warrior women.

Nik saw that Aura had become an integral part of the Quest. She was really helping! He was glad for her, and glad for them all.

The mapping resumed as they passed half a myriad anthills and nickelpede mounds. It was good to be back in the dull routine.

Then another un-dull incident threatened. "There's a zombie graveyard ahead," Nik said. "That's a settlement, so we'll have to list it. But I can't get all the specifics from a distance. The zombie minds are too far gone for that; they're not well organized. We'll have to approach them directly."

"Be cautious," Aura said. "I speak as a recent zombie. You can never be quite sure how a rotten mind will react."

"Let's scout them first," Anthem suggested. "You and I can get close without alerting them."

"We're just bugs," he agreed, knowing she had something in mind.

"We'll park the carpets out of sight and see to natural functions," Noe said. "We're about due for a break anyway."

Anthem got on Nik, and he dropped off the edge of the carpet to land on the ground. He started walking toward the graveyard while the carpets quietly floated past the foliage to the side and disappeared.

Anthem then dropped off him. "I will walk beside you."

He glanced at her—and she no longer looked like an ant. She was a lovely lady nickelpede. So that was what she had in mind! She was generating a mental picture of herself as she would look as a female of his kind. Her every step generated music.

"You are beautiful," he said. "I wish—"

"So do I. Be we can't touch. It would spoil the illusion." A downward chord.

Indeed it would. But was wonderful being with her in this manner. "Are we falling in love?"

"I think we are, foolish as it may be. It's crazy, but I like it."

"Crazy love," he said.

The music played a bit of the human wedding march. They basked in it.

"But we have scouting to do." She reverted to ant mode and climbed back on his back. She had confessed her developing passion, and confirmed his.

"Now we are touching," he said. "It still feels marvelous."

"Marvelous," she agreed with another upbeat chord.

They scouted the zombie graveyard. "I can't tell how many are buried here," he said. "There are too many fragments. We'll still have to talk with the functioning ones."

"Their half-dead state makes their minds messy for me too. We're stuck for open contact." She played a desolate chord.

They returned to the carpets. The others had picked up on their conclusion. "Ride me," Aura said. "I can defend myself, with the help of Knife and Wanda." It was evident that those three had become friends.

They boarded Aura, who walked toward the graveyard. "That was nice illusion," Wanda told Anthem. "The music too. We were listening."

"Thank you." The chord was tinged with mixed feeling.

Wanda walked beside Aura again. Actually her wand essence floated, and her illusion clothed it with the appearance of an ordinary pretty girl. She was moral support. If anything happened to Aura, Wanda could zip back to the carpets to acquaint them with the situation, if by any chance they weren't tuning in. Of course they were.

The graves were in bad repair, probably because the zombies were in and out of them so much. They evidently preferred to emerge at night, when the harsh sunlight was gone. This was late in the day, making it easier to rouse them.

One grave site was fancier than the others, with an elaborate headstone. That had to be the leader. The name on it was Zoltan.

"Hey, Zoltan!" Wanda called. "We want to talk with you!" She took Knife, extended him to sword length, and slapped the ground near that tombstone.

The ground rippled. An icky arm flung out, followed by the gaunt head and cadaverous body. In three unsightly moments the zombie leader stood before them. He smelled rank. "Who callz mee?" he demanded.

"I do. I need information."

His sunken eyeballs oriented. "You musht be really new," he said. "I don't shee or schmell any decay."

"I'm not a zombie," Aura said. "I'm an ex-zombie."

"Imposhible. Zombieshm is a terminal condishion."

"Not so. I encountered special magic." She paused, thinking of something. "Would you be interested in that?"

Zoltan was horrified. "Neverr!"

She took it in stride. "Regardless, we are here to list your settlement for our new map. What is its name, and how many of you are here?"

Meanwhile the other graves were stirring. There would soon be a number of zombies joining them. The odor was strengthening.

"You wanth to lisst uss? Sso as to be able to wiipe uss out? We canth have that!"

"Not so. We just want to have all the settlements of Xanth entered. Just give us your information and we'll move on."

"Aand then will come the flaming dragonz to exterminath uss!"

The other zombies were shambling to form a messy circle around them. This was becoming awkward. Zombies, like ogres, were hard to reason with.

"Not so," Aura repeated. "We just want you to be duly listed."

"We have to sstop you!" He looked around at the clustered zombies. "Grab them! We musst be rid of them!"

This was going to be messy indeed. They would have to fight their way clear of the mob, and they wouldn't get the information they sought.

Aura stepped into the zombie leader and kissed him on the mouth. Nik wasn't sure what good that would do, as he was already a zombie.

Aura finished the kiss and stepped back. The zombie stood for a moment. He did not turn increasingly zombiefied. Neither did he become fully alive. "I love you," he said. "How can I sserve you?"

The love slave kiss was back! At least for zombies.

"Call off your minions," Aura said evenly as she wiped off her soiled mouth. "Give us your information. Then we'll go."

The leader waved his arms. "Gho away," he ordered. The zombies dispersed. Then he gave the name of the graveyard and its population. It was that simple.

"Thank you," Aura said. "Now go about your business." She turned away.

They returned to the carpets. "Now we know the other side of your condition," Anthem said. "Your kiss zombifies living folk, and love slaves zombies."

"So it seems," Aura agreed. "I had thought it would worsen his condition, but this is better. We were able to get the mapping done without a messy fight."

"So we were," Nik agreed. "We couldn't have done it without your help."

"I would not be fully alive without this Quest. We're more than even."

So it seemed.

Chapter 3

SHAMEFUL CENTAUR

They camped for the night on the carpets. Santo and Noe simply treated them like floating beds, pulling blankets over them and sleeping. They parked them high enough to avoid any disturbance by animals, and trusted that Noe's anonymity would make them uninteresting to flying creatures like aaas beees ceees, harpies, rocs, or dragons. Nik and Anthem settled down on the underside of Noe's carpet, having no trouble clinging to the fabric, and slept side by side, sharing dreams. He assumed the dream semblance of a handsome fire ant, while she was beautiful in her natural form. It was wonderful, and the background musical chords were lovely. Even the Baton of Protagonism, which followed his perspective, seemed cheered.

The next day's travel took them to Centaur Island, where they properly entered the centaur community on the map. From there they went to a lesser island where talented centaurs dwelt. Centaurs were not supposed to have talents, being magical creatures themselves, but some did, and were duly exiled. The members of the Quest, including Aura, agreed that this was foolish; magic was everywhere in Xanth, and no one could dictate where it might appear. But the centaurs were adamant: they were magical crossbreeds, a defined species, and that was that. Even the winged ones were frowned upon, though they were slowly gaining grudging acceptance as a subspecies.

The map led them to the stall of a centaur filly who looked perfectly ordinary for her species. She had fair features, brown eyes, long brown hair that merged with her mane, neat shiny hoofs, and a lovely brown tail. "Hello," Noe said. "We are a mapping Quest that may have something to do with you, but we don't know what it is."

"You don't want me with you," the filly replied. "I am Shameful Centaur, with the talent of giving people what they don't want, including truths they are in denial about. That really aggravates folk. Even the talented exiles here don't like me." She sighed. "I'd go live elsewhere, but nobody else wants me either."

This evidently intrigued Santo. "Tell me what truth I am in denial about."

Shameful gazed at him. "You have a girlfriend you say you don't want, that she's actually only for show, what the mundanes call a 'beard,' but you actually like her and wish you could hold her and kiss her the way other couples do."

Noe straightened up as if in shock, but said nothing.

Santo nodded. "You have scored. I have no romantic interest in women, but do wish I could be romantically involved with Noe when I am male and she is female. She is a fully worthy person, a perfect companion for me. But I can't. My nature won't let me."

Noe closed her eyes, but a tear got loose anyway.

"True," Shameful said. "Your denial was that you didn't want it. You are an honest man. That much I can say, even if you do want to hear it."

"Thank you," Santo said with a wry expression. He glanced at Noe. "I'm sorry,"

"That's all right." But a second tear welled.

Nik realized that this was similar to the case with him and Anthem. They could love each other, but not do anything about it.

"So what do you want of me?" Shameful asked. "Now that I have shown you how uncomfortable I make normal folk."

"The last time we had a challenging indication like this," Noe said, "she joined our Quest."

"She did," Aura agreed. "And benefited greatly by it."

"As did the Quest," Santo said.

Shameful seemed perplexed. "Are you suggesting that you might actually want me with you as you travel? I find that hard to believe." She shrugged. "But then I find any positive thing hard to believe. I am locked into ugly reality. Other folk have nice dreams of success and popularity. I don't. That's a truth I don't want."

The others looked at Nik. "We deal in truth," he said. "Shameful, if you care to join our Mapping Quest and travel with us, you may do so, truth and all. It is possible that we will be able to help each other. The fact that you are marked on our map suggests this is the case."

"Gladly," the filly said. "Anything's better than what I face here and elsewhere, and your Quest strikes me as considerably better than nothing."

"We should hope so," Aura said. "If you care to carry me, I will bring you up to date on our situation as we go. It has complicated features."

"Get on," Shameful said. "I see you have a zombie aspect, but you're not a zombie. That's bound to be an interesting history. Surely more interesting than my own sorry state."

It was apparent to Nik and Anthem that the centaur was depressive. But of course some folk were, and she did have reason.

Aura got on, and began talking, acquainting her with the folk of the Quest and the nature of their mission. Then she hesitated.

"We have two observers along," Anthem said, picking up on the reason. "They are anonymous Demons. We do not mention them to others, but their presence has the effect of magnifying our powers. You as a member of the Quest need to know this."

"That's why I suddenly feel so much stronger," Shameful said, catching on. "Not happier, but stronger."

"Yes. But there may be complications you never anticipated."

"Bring them on!"

That was foolhardy, but they let it be. They recorded the centaur exile community on the map and moved on.

The map led them next to the border of the Neverglades, so called because it was said that those entering them never got out of them. But if there were settlements there, they had to be recorded.

Nik glanced at Aura and Shameful. "You don't have to risk it."

"Yes we do," Aura said, speaking for them both.

"It's par for my course," Shameful said. "Lead and we'll follow."

The two carpets paused so they could harvest some pies and boot rear for future meals, then accelerated along the straight path leading into the glades. Shameless galloped behind, thrilled with her enhanced physical speed and strength. Soon they were in terrain never seen by ordinary Xanthians. They passed a section lined by terrified trees, their branches lifted in fear, their leaves quivering. A sign said Petrified Forest. Some of the trees were so frightened they had frozen into stone, and some had fallen and broken into many fragments, as if sawed up for boards.

"They appreciate reality," Shameful said. "We all hope to live, but we all die, including trees. It's terrifying."

Another section was labeled The Painted Desert. Huge buckets of paint had evidently been splashed across the landscape, making it bright red, blue, green, yellow, white, black, polka dot, and plaid. Maybe if seen from far enough above it would have been a picture. Then there was the Giddy Canyon, evidently an arm of the Gap Chasm extending here where no one knew. The path went right up to the crevasse before losing its nerve and veering aside. They felt slightly giddy, unsurprisingly.

Finally they came to a giant invisible city. They could tell because it was drenched in smog that showed the buildings as gaps in the fuzziness. There was even a huge invisible sign: Giantopolis.

"This must be where the invisible giants live," Noe said, amazed as they paused. "The smog is why no one has seen their city."

"One reason," Aura agreed. "Its invisibility would be another."

"Something's wrong," Anthem said with a worried chord. "Not with us, but with them." She turned to Nik. "Maybe if we combine our talents we can figure it out."

Nik was glad to join her on any basis. He extended his clairvoyance while she extended her telepathy. In barely two thirds of a moment they oriented on a particular giant building, where a giant little boy was crying as he explained his problem.

Anthem focused Nik's mind on the boy. He was Gil Giant; all the boys were named Giant. Then Anthem focused herself on the girl. She was Gigi Giantess; all the girls were Giantess. Both Nik and Anthem became the giants, mentally; that way they could get the full background.

"I was chasing Gigi," Gil was saying woefully. "I like her. All I wanted to do was kiss her, but she thought I was going to hit her, and she ran, so I chased her."

Nik saw the scene via the giant's eyes. Gigi was a pretty little humanoid giant girl with streaming yellow hair and a nice summer dress. She ran over a ridge and he lost sight of her for much of a moment. Then she screamed. In barely two instants he crested the ridge himself—and the girl was gone. There had not been time for her to run out of sight beyond the ridge. Something must have grabbed her and hauled her away. That was why she had screamed.

So he came back home, knowing that something had to be done. His folks took him to Gigi's folks, where he was now explaining.

"We can help," Nik said through Gil's mouth. Anthem had expanded their minds and sounded a chord so that the giants felt their presence and believed them.

Astonished, the Giant parents looked at him.

"We are visiting members of a Quest to map all the settlements of Xanth," he explained quickly. "We have clairvoyance and telepathy. We happened to tune in on this scene. We can locate Gigi so you can rescue her."

The giants were about to argue, but then Anthem brought Gigi to all their minds. She was trapped in a dark cell, crying. Then they saw through her mind what had happened. A mean giant had wanted a little girl without all the fuss and bother of marrying a woman, putting up with her foibles, signaling the stork, and waiting tedious months for delivery, so when he saw one he had simply lassoed her from a distance, hauled her in, and taken her to his cellar to cry herself out of tears so he could dress her up without wetting the new clothing, and present her as his own. If she didn't cooperate, well, he could always tie her to a rock and dump her in the sea. That would clear the cell so he could try again. Later or sooner he was bound to get a good one.

The parents were horrified and outraged. Anthem, in Gigi's mind, got her to peer out the small upper window where she spied a field with a colony of giant invisible field mice. They were, of course, visible to her, as invisibles could see each other, and the mental image made them visible to them all.

"We know that field!" Gigi's father said.

With that information, the giants notified the constabulary, quickly went to the house, captured the abductor, and rescued the girl. They told her how Gil had helped, and why, and she, relieved, caught hold of him and kissed him. A sweet chord sounded and a giant little heart flung out. Now they knew they were meant for each other, when they grew up. And Nik entered the mouse field on the map, along with the giant city.

Then the visitors realized that they had, in effect, kissed each other physically, because Nik was identifying with Gil and Anthem with Gigi.

What an experience that had been! They relived it repeatedly as they rested that night, parked in an invisible city park.

"That was something to see and feel," Aura said. So it was more than Nik and Anthem who had felt the kiss.

"Yes," Shameful agreed. "I wish I could meet a nice stallion who liked truth."

"Maybe one whose worst desire was to be with a talented filly, then discovered that he liked you after all."

"What are the chances?"

That ended that fantasy, as they both knew the chances were somewhere between zero and minus one. Males of any species were notorious for their superficiality.

The next day they moved out of Giantopolis and into a more rugged section of the Neverglades. This was labeled Volcanova.

"It's where volcanoes meet privately," Nik said, extending his clairvoyance.

"I didn't know they did that," Shameless said.

"Nobody did. It seems they kept it private by meeting here in the Neverglades where nobody would know."

"A lot seems to happen in the Neverglades that nobody knows about," Aura said.

"Surely by no coincidence," Noe said.

"But once our map is complete, folk will know," Nik said. "Can you tune in on them, Anthem?"

"Yes. I see they haven't actually moved here. It seems that moving is complicated for volcanoes, so they don't do it often. They are having a mental meeting, which is why I can read them. They are planning something."

Anthem was able to put the intercepted dialogueue on mental speaker sound so they all could hear it. The different volcanoes had different tones, and the physical background of each was visible, so it was clear which one was speaking.

"I am tired of us being avoided or ignored," Mount Thera complained. "In my day we generated tsunamis that flooded lowlands and devastated the shores and wiped out whole civilizations. Maybe we should do that again."

"Yes," Mount Pinatuba um-pahed. "We even filled in a big valley some time ago so that the folk there thought the whole world was drowned, and one boat landed on a mountain, where it seeded back all the animals. They didn't forget that in a hurry! It's even in one of their religious books."

"I tried for a big blast," Mount St. Helens said. "But my throat clogged and it came out sideways, only blowing over a few thousand trees. That was embarrassing."

"It's overtime for a big one," Mount Yellowstone said. "Every million years or so I bury Mundane 'Merica in ash, but creatures survive elsewhere and return. More is needed to make our point."

"So why don't we all erupt everywhere all at once?" Thera asked. "So they have nowhere to hide?"

"Beautiful," Pinatuba honked musically. "Let's do it."

"We can spread the molten word," St. Helens said. "Enlist all the lesser cones so that no region is spared."

"Set the date a week hence," Thera said. "That will give us time to spread the word to all the vents and coordinate."

"And to build up our magma," Yellowstone said. "I've got a second pool of it I don't want to waste."

So it was decided, and the meeting adjourned.

"This is mischief," Santo said.

"Really bad news," Noe agreed.

"The kind that comes when I'm around," Shameful said. "None of us welcome this information."

"We have to stop it," Aura said. "But how?"

Nik extended his awareness. "There is a Demoness of Volcanoes, Vulcanova, after whom this region was named. We might appeal to her to stop this plot. She would have the power to prevent it."

"And we can reach her from here," Anthem said with a happy chord. "Because this is her hideaway."

"The Neverglades do seem to be popular with obscure powers," Noe said. "If I had reason to be more anonymous than I am, I'd consider living here."

"Let's do it," Nik said.

Anthem extended her telepathy, enhanced by more powerful Demons than any found here, and soon discovered Volcanova's mind. She had been observing their progress, as she did everyone who passed through her retreat, just in case there was anything interesting. "Please, we need your help. The local volcanoes are going to erupt together and maybe destroy Xanth. You could make them stop."

"What is that to me?" the Demoness asked, manifesting as a fierce woman with molten hair. "I like eruptions." She tuned out, and her image faded. Grains of sand were not very interesting.

"We're in trouble," Nik said.

"I have a thought you may not much like," Shameful said. "Multiple eruptions would be a disaster, but the hot mountains might be intimidated by the prospect of a worse disaster, and back off."

"Worse?" Aura asked.

"A meteor strike. A big one could wipe out all the volcanoes."

"So it might," he agreed thoughtfully. He extended his awareness, and lo! There was Meteoro, the Demon of Meteors, also had a hideout here in the Neverglades. It seemed it was a popular private hidden resort. He looked like a streak of light with a ball at one end.

Anthem reached out again and found the snoozing mind of Meteoro. She put the dialogueue on speaker. "Please, the Land of Xanth is about to be ravaged by volcano eruptions. We need to save our home."

"Volcanoes are the department of Volcanova," he responded. "We try not to interfere too much in each other's business."

Nik got a notion. "But it will destroy your retreat here in the Neverglades. That would be her interfering in your business."

"So it would," he agreed thoughtfully. "But she has a volcanic temper. It may be easier just to let it go."

This was not the answer Nik, or any of them, wanted to hear. He glanced at Shameful. But in fairness he recognized that she was not the cause of it, merely the messenger, as it were. The volcano problem would have occurred regardless. It was better to know it, so they could at least try to handle it.

"Let me try," Aura murmured. "Lips women know how to handle men."

Did they really? The game, as it were, appeared to be lost anyway, so she was worth a gamble. Nik gestured her to go ahead, waving a pincer.

"Hot tempered women can be passionate," Aura said to Meteoro. "If you know how to handle them."

The Demon was interested. "Mortals can have insights, perhaps because their lives are so brief and earthy. They have to score quickly if they are going to. What is your approach?"

"Stick and carrot. The stick is that you could divert a large meteor to crash into Xanth, taking out all the volcanoes, and she knows it. The carrot is that you could assume the form of a handsome male and evince personal interest in her. The deal for her cooperation would be to spare Xanth."

"I approached her once. She had no interest."

Now Shameful spoke. "I understand that on occasion Demons indulge in the pleasures of the mortal form. The two of you could animate human bodies so as to feel their intense mortal feelings. She might like your attention in this new guise, at least for the fleeting moment that is the compass of the living form."

"That could be. But locating suitable human bodies would be a chore."

"Suppose we provide them?"

What? Nik saw that this was going wrong. The only purely human bodies here were Santo, Noe, and Aura. None of them would do anything like this on their own.

Shameful looked at him. "You and Anthem could identify with Santo and Noe, as you did before, and follow the will of the Demons. I know you don't want to hear this, but it could work. Consider it."

It was true. Nik and Anthem were straight male and female. Given human bodies, they could do romance. In fact the prospect was tempting.

Now Nik looked at Santo. The man looked grim, but knew the stakes were high. There was also that in him that wanted something like this, as Shameful knew. He nodded.

Santo suppressed his mind, and Noe suppressed hers, as they had before. Nik and Anthem took over. Now they were in essence a human couple. They quickly changed clothing so as to wear their finest for this occasion.

"Demon Meteoro!" Shameful said. "Here is your mortal human host for this incident. Engage with him."

The Demon did. Nik felt the immense presence as it oriented on the grain of sand that was Santo, and the microscopic fragment that was Nik. Nik had felt the enhancement of the presence of the Demons Bang and

Andromeda, and the huge increase in mental capacity when he borrowed Santos' brain. Now he was a magnitude larger again.

"Demoness Volcanova!" Shameful called. "Demon Meteoro has the capacity to destroy all the volcanoes and the whole of Xanth, but he will relent if you will negotiate in human form. We have a mortal body waiting for your use."

"Why should I bother?" she replied, the heat of her irritation blasting at them all like a wave of roiling smoke.

"Because not only can you save your hideaway, you may have an interesting vicarious romantic experience."

Now the Demoness was intrigued. Worlds were nothing to Demons, but novel experiences were a prime way to relieve the boredom of absolute power and endless existence. "I will consider." She oriented on the body.

Now Nik also felt Anthem's similar increases as she went through the stages of becoming a human woman animated by a Demoness.

The two composite entities stood and faced each other. Noe was her human self, but in a lovely dress and slippers and a pretend flower tucked by her ear, with a nimbus of flaming red hair and a wonderfully developed body. Santo was similarly himself, in a handsome suit and halo of muscularity and confidence.

"You are glorious," Meteoro said.

"And you are splendid," Volcanova answered.

Both Demons were taken by the intensity of living feelings.

They came together and kissed. Light flared. There was an eruption of meteors flying in all directions, plus a few.

"Let's get private," he said urgently. "Mortal bodies can't handle Demon passions."

"Agreed. With no eruptions or meteor strikes."

Then the Demon presences faded, leaving only Nik and Anthem, then Santo and Noe.

"I always wanted to do that," Santo admitted.

"So did I," Noe breathed.

"So did we," Anthem said with a feeling chord.

"And we saved Xanth from the volcanoes," Shameless said.

They had indeed. The centaur had engineered it, using her power.

They moved on, by carpet and by foot. The land was level, with brush growing in large patches. There were modest looking flowers.

"There's something amiss here," Shameless said. "But I don't know what it is."

"Nothing I can see," Aura said, looking around. "Just wasteland."

Nik thought to check for anything significant, but this area had no settlements. The further they went, the better he felt. Maybe it was because they had stopped the volcanoes.

"I feel it too," Anthem said. "In fact everyone does, except for Shameful. She doesn't trust it."

"It's her curse of a talent. She's locked into the ugly side of reality."

So it seemed. But for the rest of them it just kept getting better. The landscape was dull, yet the mood was phenomenal. They were positively delirious with joy.

"Folk, stop," Shameful said. "We've got to go back."

"What are you talking about?" Noe asked. "This is the best excursion we've been on."

"Uplifting," Santo agreed.

"No," the centaur said. "I have it now. It's swamp gas that's intoxicating you."

"Ludicrous."

Shameful turned her fore-section around to face Aura, who was riding on her back. "Do you feel it?"

"I feel great," Aura said. "If it's gas, I want more of it."

The centaur tried Santo. "How about you?"

"I have no problem. It's a pleasant day."

"And you, Nik and Anthem?"

"We're fine," Anthem answered for them both. "The local air is invigorating."

Shameless pondered briefly, then turned back to Santo. "I understand that you can make holes, including tunnels to far places."

"Yes."

"Humor me. I'd like to see a tunnel. One made just for me to see."

Santo was pleasantly perplexed. "I can make one here, but everyone would see it."

"Then let me take you to a separate spot, so it is private."

"Okay," he agreed amiably.

Aura got off, took Nik, and Santo got on. They walked away. Nik realized that Santo was intrigued both by the prospect of riding a centaur and the minor mystery of her purpose. He had a good mind, and liked to understand things.

"Now," Aura whispered, "We follow. Catch them in their weird tryst. Keep your minds damped."

"Tryst?" Noe asked. "Santo's not interested in ladies, not even centaur ones."

"How do we know? It might be that crossbreeds are different."

Noe made a silent whistle. "Could it be?"

"That Demon kiss might have tuned him in to what heterosexuality offers," Aura said. "Enough to make him really curious. He can't admit to any such interest, so he's going along with Shameless just in case she has a notion."

Oho! This could be fun indeed.

Santo and Shameless went to a small grove of coventrees and disappeared within. The others walked soundlessly there. When they reached the grove, there was no sign of the man and centaur. There was only the mouth of a tunnel big enough to hold a mounted centaur.

"They must really want privacy," Aura said. "I wonder where it leads?"

"His tunnels can go anywhere, even other worlds," Noe said. "They stay in place until he abolishes them."

"So it should be safe to follow," Aura said. She perched on the carpet Santo had vacated.

"Why not?" Noe asked. Was there a trace of jealousy? Who could blame her? She wanted Santo for herself, but knew that he would first have to come to better terms with male-female relationships. The devious contours of the landscape were simple compared to those of the emotions.

They guided the carpets into the tunnel and floated through to its exit. There were Santo and Shameless, facing away. "That's impressive," the centaur was saying. "But where are we?"

"I don't know. I meant to have it outlet in another copse, but I must have misjudged. This isn't any place I've seen before."

Now they all gazed. They stood before what appeared to be a volcanic vent that was issuing multicolored fumes. Beyond it was a blue mist, above which in the distance was a blue mountain.

"How could Santo have misjudged so badly?" Anthem asked with a perplexed chord. "He always knows exactly where his holes go."

That was another mystery. Unless Santo had wanted far more privacy than any copse of trees could offer.

A woman walked out of the mist. She was ordinary except for two things: she was quite pretty, and she was solid blue, from head to toe, literally. Her nicely coiffed hair was blue, her face was blue, her arms and hands were blue, her dress was blue, and so were her legs, feet, and shoes. She was in fact monochrome. "Be careful of that vent," she said. "It's a fluke with all colors of magic. You could get dizzy or sick."

"Colors of magic?" Santo asked.

She gazed at him appraisingly. "You're not local, are you. Your steed is amazing."

"I am Santo, from the Land of Xanth, and this my associate, Shameful Centaur. What land is this?"

"This is Chroma, of course. I know not of Xanth. It must be far from here." She focused on Shameful. "A centaur! I thought they were mythological creatures."

"We are a crossbreed species," Shameful said. "Xanth is a world where many types exist." She eyed the woman back, not at all shy. "May I inquire your name?"

"Bluette, of course. All folk are known by their colors, outside of their home chroma. If you are from another world, how did you get here? Our planetary colony has been lost for centuries."

"We took the tube," Shameful said, turning to indicate it. In the process she saw Aura and Noe on their carpets. She shrugged, taking it in stride. "We are a party of eight, mapping our land."

"You have floating carpets outside of the colors? Surely you're not Glamors."

"We are hardly glamorous," the centaur said, laughing.

Bluette shook her head. "The Glamors are flukes who can perform magic outside of the colors, in the zones between the volcanoes. I see you really are not of this world, but you are capable of magic in interim space. Those flying carpets show that." She paused, taking stock. "Where are you going?"

"Nowhere," Santo said. "I was merely demonstrating my magic talent for Shameful, and it seems it went awry. We regret intruding on your space."

"You made a tunnel between worlds?" Bluette asked. "This is beyond even Glamor capacity. Otherwise we would have contacted Earth long ago."

"He's Magician class," Shamelful said. "Magicians and Sorcerers are extremely potent with magic."

"Evidently so." Bluette considered. "On this world, most folk can perform magic only within their home chroma. I am embarking on a brief journey to visit a friend in a green zone. I must travel along a route between colors, for limited safety, as I have no magic outside of the blue zone. It occurs to me that we can do each other some good. Suppose I ride with you on one of your carpets? I'll tell you all about Planet Chroma, and you tell me about your world. That exchange of information should help us pass the dull time traveling."

Dull? Hardly! Anthem's survey showed that they all were amenable. They were in an extremely curious place, and wanted to know more about it before going home.

Bluette got on the carpet with Noe, and Santo returned to his carpet with Aura, relieving Shameful of the burden of his weight. They started following the curvaceous route around the blue zone.

"The planet Chroma is riddled with volcanoes," she said. "Each erupts its own color of magic. From space it resembles a multicolored ball." The image in her mind reminded them of the painted desert they had seen, only this was planetary wide. "The folk who live near a given volcano soon imbibe its essence and become that color, and can do the full range of magic. Everything from conjuring items to flying to making themselves handsome or beautiful, as I have. But only in their own color, as I mentioned, so they are largely helpless outside it. I can do only blue magic; in any other chroma, or between chroma, I am without magic, like the nonchroma folk. That makes me nervous, as there are dangers in the nonmagic areas. I feel unclothed without my magic. But I am an excellent judge of character, which is why I trust the group of you." She glanced at her carpet companion. "How is it with you?"

"In the Land of Xanth," Noe said, "each person has one magic talent, or very rarely two. These range from the ability to make a spot appear on a wall, to full Magician or Sorceress level, such as transforming people or creatures to other living forms, or crafting powerful illusions." She smiled. "Or making tunnels between worlds. But most folk have simple talents. Mine, for example is being largely anonymous. Aura, on the other carpet, can love-slave a man with her kiss, or render him into zombie status. Shameful Centaur's is to give people what they don't want. That's why they gave her that name; they don't like her, though she is a perfectly decent person. Santo is a Magician, with a talent of making holes of all sizes and kinds; that makes him one of very few. We have four additional members: Nik and Anthem, who are highly talented insects, and Knife and Wanda, who are highly talented objects. All of us are people on our own terms, and we respect each other. Our plants, too, are largely magical, but generally don't bother people who don't bother them. Some plants even cater to us, such as the pie plants, whose fruits are many varieties of pie, ready to eat when ripe, and beer-barrel trees whose copious sap is mildly intoxicating. Some plants produce boot rear, a drink with a real kick."

"Fascinating. That reminds me. You are doing me a favor, providing this convenient transport. Would you like something to eat?"

Anthem's thought spoke for them all. "We have not eaten in a while, but don't want to be a burden."

"No burden. Steer into the blue, where I can work my routine magic, and I will conjure food for you. Will fresh fruits do?"

"That's fine."

They moved into the blue zone. Bluette get off, held her arms forward, and a big basket of blue fruit appeared in them. She brought it back to the carpets. "These are all types, despite their monochrome. Try them."

They did. Noe bit into a blue apple, Santo a blue banana, Aura a blue peach, and Shameful a cluster of blue grapes. Nik and Anthem settled for blue seeds. Knife and Wanda didn't have to eat, being objects, but they admired the assortment. All were delicious, tasting exactly like their types.

"You conjured this out of nothing?" Noe asked, amazed.

"Not exactly. Fruits are grown in gardens, and items are made in workshops by hand labor. There are markets for all manner of things. I have accounts at several. When I conjure things to me, it goes on my monthly bill, and in due course I pay in service."

That almost sounded like playing nymph, especially for a woman as sightly as she was. "In service?"

"I'm a supplies accountant for a construction company. I know how to track things. Magic can facilitate material things, but can't make a person smart or educated. I have a good mind. I go and help the market proprietors tally their supplies so they know what's what. It's part of the necessary brute-work for civilization. Nothing is truly free, regardless of the benefits of magic."

"One service in exchange for another," Santo said. "Xanth is similar." He was clearly impressed with the blue woman.

They moved back out while eating. Bluette was consuming a blue pear. "I suppose I could have showed off a bit, done my sexy somersault dance in the air, conjured my tambourine for a musical accompaniment, changed to my scant party clothes, but you get the idea. Life is easy in the zone, once you are proficient with essential magic, though some are more proficient than others. I do have my touch. At times I wonder why the nonchroma folk don't move into zones. But that's their choice."

"They can't do any magic?" Noe asked. "Not even personal talents?"

"None. It's a wonder they persist."

"Maybe they aren't good at magic, so avoid it. They surely have ways to cope."

"Actually they rule the planet, perhaps because we of the chroma zones are not unified." Bluette laughed. "We are largely helpless outside our zones, but they can be unmagical anywhere."

The path curved away from the blue, veering toward a lake between a purple zone and a white one. "That white one looks almost like Mundania," Noe said.

"Mundania?"

"That's a realm bordering Xanth, or maybe a separate world, where there is no magic. It seems horribly dreary to us. But they are clever with gadgets."

“That sounds like the world from which we were colonized. Earth, where science rules. In fact that may be why it seems halfway familiar to you: white magic is what they call science. I understand it is fairly common in the larger universe.”

“Science,” Noe agreed. “They do use that in Mundania.”

Their dialogue continued. Nik found it fascinating. There was so much more to the universe than he had known or imagined.

The avenue widened, forming a tree-bordered plane between four of the magic zones. Now the volcanoes could be seen in the distance. A red one was erupting its red plume, the color slowly settling around it. The folk there would be red, and do red magic. This was an interesting realm.

“My curse is striking again,” Shameful said grimly. “What we least want is about to appear.”

Then men emerged from the cover of the trees and walked purposefully toward the members of the Quest. Distracted by the dialogueue, Nik had not thought to use his clairvoyance to check their immediate surroundings.

“Oops, this is mischief,” Bluette said, alarmed. “That’s a criminal band that preys on zone folk they catch between zones. We need to get out of here before they catch us, or there’ll be real trouble. I didn’t know they were in this region.”

Shameful turned around, then paused. “Too late.”

Now Nik saw that there were more men cutting off their retreat. They were coming in from all sides. This was a closing trap.

“They do mean mischief,” Anthem said with a dismayed chord. “They plan to rob us, take advantage of the women, and let us go when they tire of us. If we resist, they’ll beat us up and do it anyway.”

Bluette heard the ant’s voice in her mind, as they all did. “It is best not to resist. They will be relatively gentle if we cooperate, pretending it’s friendly, but they can be brutal if annoyed.”

“Quick vote,” Anthem said. “Fight or accept?”

The consensus coalesced quickly. “We fight.”

“I hope you know what you are doing,” the blue lady said, worried.

Nik organized it. “Aura, take Knife and Wanda, as before. Warn, disarm, rather than kiss, unless you have to. Santo, be ready to hole any man that threatens violence; hurt warningly rather than kill. Noe, get closer to

Bluette and be unnoticeable. Put away the carpets; we don't want them to be at risk of theft. Shameful, take Anthem and me and keep a careful eye out so we can alert Santo about what's needed. Don't start the violence; we want to back them off instead, if we can."

"You do seem to know your business," Bluette said. "I confess I would rather not be coerced or raped."

They organized as directed and waited for the spokesman of the band to approach. He came to stand before Santo, the evident leader of their group. The others stood in a circle around them, their hands on their weapons.

"We are the Badass Band," he said. "You are travelers between chroma. There are two ways this encounter can play out: You can freely give us your valuables, including those floating carpets you're hiding, and your women can have a good time with our men. Then we can go our separate ways with no regrets. Or you can decline to be friendly, in which case we shall batter you and take your valuables anyway, and rape your women, the more screaming the better. Then we will part company, while you recover from your battering and meditate upon the benefits of future cooperation."

"We have a counter offer, BB," Santo said. "We each go our ways with no further interaction, no exchange of goods or services or mischief. Or you can decline, and discover what you are up against, to your regret."

The BB leader smiled. "So it's like that, eh? You're trying to bluff us out. You'll be sorry." He raised a hand. "Do it, Badasses,"

The surrounding men eagerly converged. Whereupon Aura, a prime target, stepped into her first would-be rapist and kissed him smartly on the mouth. He wilted, lost in the throes of new zombieism, and she immediately tackled the next. When two men tried to grab her arms, her sword came out and sliced their waistbands so that their pants dropped. This embarrassed them. It also showed how efficient that sword was, a clear warning.

Meanwhile, three men came at Santo with their clubs swinging for his head. Holes appeared in their hands so that they dropped the clubs as they howled in pain. More men charged in, and got similar holes. Then Santo turned to face the spokesman, who hadn't moved, though he looked shaken. "Got the message, BB, or do you prefer holes in your feet?"

"Message received," the man said grimly. He had seen the action on two fronts and was no fool. He signaled the band to retreat. They helped the wounded and the zombied to organize themselves, gather up their weapons, and depart.

"Spread the word," Shameful called. "Banditry is no longer safe here."

They surely did get that message.

Soon Noe brought out the carpets and they rode on.

"I must confess I am impressed," Bluette said. "I did not realize how effective your talents could be. I suspect you saved me from a raping."

"We prefer peace," Santo said. "But we are equipped for violence if that can't be avoided."

"You certainly are!"

In due course they arrived at the green zone where there was a green woman waiting for Bluette. "These are my friends from Xanth," Bluette said. "Absolutely fascinating folk, and they protected me from the BB robbers. They have flying carpets that operate between zones."

"Fabulous! Are they going back to your blue zone?"

Bluette looked at Noe. "We are," Noe said. "We're just visiting here."

"I have a friend going to blue," the woman said. "Could Greene ride with you? I guarantee he's a good person."

Noe put out a mental query. The others had found Bluette interesting, and were curious about Greene. "Sure."

The green man soon joined them. He got on the carpet with Noe. He was tall, handsome, and of course monochrome green. "The word is that you bashed the BBs. You're heroes!"

"We did what we had to," Noe said. "We tried to warn them."

"The BBs don't take warnings as well as they give them." They all laughed. Greene was turning out to be fun. He continued to be fun as they traveled. These Chroma folks were every bit as easy to be with as regular Xanthians.

They returned to the blue zone, where Greene got off, thanking them for the favor and the delightful company. He had more than paid his way in that respect, as had Bluette.

Now they returned to the tunnel. This led not to the gas infested section they had left, but to a region beyond the Neverglades. What had happened?

"I made a deal with Santo," Shameful said. "We needed to get out of the gas."

And their minds were clearing. "That Chroma adventure," Noe asked. "Did it even happen?"

"It did and it didn't" Shameful said seriously. "I was not affected by the gas, as my nature is contrary to pleasant flights of fantasy, but I picked it up from the ambiance Anthem provided and played along until I could get you out of it. The Chroma world may exist somewhere, and Santo's tunnel could have taken us there, but I'm not sure. It may be that the gas enabled the rest of you to commune with the folk of Chroma, so the interaction did take place, but it was mental rather than physical. It certainly was real enough on your terms."

Nik hadn't thought of that. They had spoken with the inhabitants of Chroma without difficulty, when the languages should have been different. Magic made all Xanthians understand each other, but Chroma was a different realm with different magic. There should have been a communication problem. That argued for imagination rather than reality.

"This deal you made with Santo," Noe said. "Exactly what was it?"

"She had me make two tunnels," Santo said. "One to somewhere else, the other to Xanth, outside of the Neverglades. She was desperate to get us out of there, any way she could. Since we had already mapped the settlements in the glades, I humored her, or so I thought. My mind, too, was largely zonked out by the gas. We departed via one tunnel, and returned via the other."

"We didn't want to leave the gas," Noe said. "You gave us what we wanted least." She smiled ruefully. "Including revealing some awkward personal relations."

"Yet it was best to bring them into the open," Santo said. "I think I do love you, Noe, in my fashion."

The girl actually blushed. She wanted to be with him so much, but only with complete acceptance on his part.

"I think you saved us from intoxicated ruin," Aura told Shameful. "Even if you did have to fool us to do it."

And that was the general consensus. Shameful, like Aura, had demonstrated her value to the Quest.

Chapter 4

DANCE

They had landed at the edge of the Gold Coast of Xanth, where much of the landscape was golden. The nearby beach was gold, the sand was gold—even the waves of the surf were golden. The passing people had a golden tan. But this was not Chroma; they were not monochrome, and were not displaying copious magic.

They got to work adding the various settlements to the map: human, crab, and golden ants. They were back in the routine, which was a relief, after the near mischief of the Neverglades.

A male centaur trotted up. His hide was paisley patterned, with colorful figures throughout. He spied Shameful and approached her. "Hello. I heard there was a talented centaur filly in this vicinity that nobody liked. I know how that is! Nobody likes me either. I'm Shameless Centaur. Let's date." A figure on his fur waved.

Shameful thought he was playing her; Anthem picked up her distrust. "Go kiss Aura," she snapped, indicating the woman. "She turns folk into zombies." She was telling him what he surely did not want to do.

"Sure." He clearly did not believe her. He walked to Aura, put his hands on her shoulders, drew her in to his face, and kissed her smartly on the mouth.

Aura, surprised and annoyed, kissed back with power.

Shameless became a zombie centaur. He stumbled back, stunned.

"Oh, no!" Shameful cried, seeing it happen before she could react. "I didn't mean it literally! I'm sorry!"

"We need a pun in a hurry," Noe said. She looked around. "There's a muddle puddle. It really confuses people who walk through it."

"Go splash in that puddle!" Shameful called to Shameless. "Now! I'm serious."

Confused, he walked to the puddle and splashed it with his front hooves. The water sprayed out to land on the nearby ground, and on him.

And the zombie aspect faded out. He was alive again.

“What happened?” Shameless asked, taken aback. “I just had a rotten feeling. Did I imagine it?” Even his hide figures looked dismayed.

Noe answered. “Shameful thought you were playing her, trying to make her think you liked her when you were just cruelly teasing. So she told you to go zombie yourself, meaning to stop bothering her. She never thought you'd actually do it. But you did, so we had to dezombify you. Puns destroy zombies, leaving living folk. The interaction also nullifies the pun. So you are normal again, and that puddle is now just ordinary mud. You did not imagine it.”

“I'm sorry” Shameful repeated, mortified. “My talent of bringing people what they don't want makes more than enough mischief; I don't want to add to it.”

He regrouped, emotionally. “I'm sorry too. I certainly didn't want to be a zombie. I'm pretty wild, and I come across as a chronic liar when I'm not one. I just can't stop making things up. So I really am not popular. No filly will date me, partly because of my magic hide, partly because of my talent of bringing folk what they think they want but that isn't good for them, like a kid in a candy patch who will make himself sick, but mostly because I'm just so wild. I thought I could make it with an unpopular filly with another messy talent, because she would understand. But I guess I had better leave you alone. I shouldn't have come at you like that. I will go.” He walked away.

Shameful almost galloped to intercept him. “No, no! I misunderstood. Maybe it can work if we get to know each other better. Let's find out.”

He eyed her. “You mean it? You're a pretty filly. You're not trying to play me back?”

“I am not. I am sorry I misunderstood you.”

“Then let's give it a chance. Let's go for a trot and dialogue. If it turns out negative, I will depart and leave you alone.”

“Let's trot,” she agreed. She turned to face the group. “We'll be back soon.”

They trotted off.

"They do seem hot to trot," Noe remarked, a smile hovering not far from her face.

"I'm already sorry I zombified him," Aura said. "He caught me off guard."

"It happens," Noe agreed. "I think we're about to have a new member of the Quest."

They did. Before long the centaurs trotted back. "We liked our dialogue," Shameful said. "Now we shall discover whether it can work out in the longer term. We centaurs are rational creatures who take time to form relationships." Then she officially introduced Shameless to the others. She had already told him about the Quest in general terms.

They resumed the mapping. It turned out that Shameless was willing to carry one of them if there should be a need, especially since he felt so much stronger in the Demon ambiance. That could be handy on occasion.

Then they came to another pun region, with mouse and insect settlements within it. There was no help for it but to grit their teeth and tackle it.

The puns came at them like swarms of biting flies. A fairy flew up to Aura holding an envelope. "Have you seen any lady fee here? I have a letter for them." The fee were small fairy-like folk.

Aura groaned. "Fee mail? Get away from me!"

A pun on Female, Nik realized.

A robot staggered by, scratching his backside. "I've got ticks," it explained. "They'll be the death of me."

Robot tics. To be sure.

Then a little flying machine buzzed by. "Hi!" it said. "I am a drone. I have endlessly boring news of no consequence whatever. I can talk for hours, droning on until you fall asleep." It proceeded to do so.

Shameless went to Aura. "Kiss me," he murmured.

She looked surprised, then caught on. She kissed him with power, turning him zombie. Then he went to the drone, caught hold of it, and kissed it on the front grill. It immediately went dead, and he returned to full life. He had nullified the pun.

They came to a pan full of tea bags. Shameless paused. "Pan teas," he said. "Good thing I'm not full human; I could have freaked out." He went to get another kiss from Aura, then as a zombie went to grab the pan and hurl the tea bags away. Actually the only other males here, Santo and Nik, were not affected by pan teas, but it was best to play it safe.

After that, Shameless led the way, intercepting and nullifying the puns before they could torment the others. He disposed of Mun Danes, Tues Danes, etc; flip pants that went with flip flops; Liber Tea and Democra Sea; Lesson and his sibling Lessdaughter; a peace of cake together with a war of cake; Zom A and his companions Zom B and Zom C; and others. Soon Nik was tuning them out, as were the other members of the Quest. One pun was a groaner, but endless puns were worse.

Then Shameful Centaur paused. She approached Santo and Nik. "I have private news that may be quintessentially important. I need Quest approval before I can take it further, but it must remain secret to all others. Can we dally in a thicket of puns for privacy while I make my case?"

Something secret but deadly serious here in the tediously unserious pundemic pool? It surely did not relate to mapping, yet Shameful was not one to waste their time. Whatever could that be? They needed to find out.

"Yes we do," Anthem agreed. "I can't read her mind on this, but it is quivering with relevancy."

Nik got in touch with Shameless, whom Shameful had been watching kiss Aura repeatedly, but understood why, so wasn't jealous. "Please hollow out the center of that thicket and thin-et grove so we can have a private dialogue surrounded by a hedge of puns. Then join us inside. Something has come up that may be important."

The centaur didn't question it. He went to Aura, spoke briefly to her, and she climbed onto his back. Then on to the thick/thin grove as he started cleaning out the interior puns, turning his fore-section around to kiss her between-times. Soon the center was clear, while a noxious ring of puns enclosed it, seeming to shimmer in its eagerness to torment them.

They gathered there in a tight group. "Shameful has something to say to us," Nik said. "Speak, centaur, or open your mind to us."

Shameful spoke. "I yield the floor and my voice to a mental visitor I have."

Then she spoke again in an eerily different voice. "Thank you, Shameful, for allowing me to draw on your body, brain, and background information so that I may effectively communicate with your companions. Quest, I am the Demoness Entropy, so called because my role in existence is to encourage disorder. When energy is expended, I cause it to dissipate, returning to a neutral state. When matter is organized, I cause it to disintegrate in the course of time and return to disorganization. What other Demons accomplish, I tend to slowly destroy. For this reason I am not popular among other Demons, and have little contact with them. However, I am friends with Demon Chaos; we do understand each other, as the end product of my process is his domain. He learned of your mapping mission via mortal word of mouth, as he has a mortal girlfriend, and encouraged me to verify whether you and I can work together to accomplish our purposes."

She paused to let it clarify. A Demon wanted to work with them! A friend of Demon Chaos, who was perhaps the second strongest of all the Demons. This was different from mere observation. Bang and Andromeda of course knew of this, and Nik had the distinct feeling that they did not object. What could that mean?

Andromeda sent a quiet impression: yes, they knew, and no, they did not object. They knew Entropy from eons ago, and she was legitimate. It meant that this was indeed important, in ways that none of the mortals could completely understand until certain other factors came into play.

Entropy resumed. "My boyfriend, to put it in inadequate mortal terms, is the Demon of Puns. He is even less popular than I am, as he degrades serious matters to the basest form of humor, making Demons groan. He has been confined by a Demon stricture to this undistinguished world, to keep his wretched humor in bounds, far from them, and is now a resident of what you call Hell. The purpose is twofold: to punish me for loving him, and to clear the universe of his dreadful humor. His power radiates; that is the source of the puns that infest your world, including the recent pundemic. I propose to rescue him, but must do so surreptitiously, lest my action attract the baleful attention of the Demons." She smiled briefly, a strangely mixed expression. "And no, your two watching Demons will not betray the secret, because they are only observers, not participants, and also incidentally because it just might save the universe from overwhelming horror."

She paused again, letting them absorb more clarification. This continued amazing! The Demon of Puns! That explained a lot. And the universe was threatened with overwhelming horror? What could that be? Surely not more abysmal puns. But if their mission somehow saved it, that was surely worthwhile.

Entropy resumed again. "This is the reason I come to you. I need the cover of a legitimate mortal mission to conceal my rescue effort from the Demons. It will be best if they never know of my effort, or of its success if that is the case. I will spirit Pun away so that only the slowly fading humor miasma eventually reveals it, too late for them to prevent. As for the threat to the universe—there is an obscurity that even I can't fathom, but the implication is that it certainly needs to be stopped if that is possible. You are the agency that can stop it. In effect, you help me save Pun from confinement; I help you save the universe from revulsion. This seems more than fair to me."

Something that even a Demoness couldn't detect? But awful.

Anthem surveyed the members of the Quest. They considered: puns versus the universe. It was a fair deal.

So they were agreed. They would try to help her rescue Demon Pun. "But how?" Nik asked the Demoness.

Entropy smiled again, this time with a larger share of warmth. "There may be a way. In the mortal stories of figures they see as gods, there are narratives of rescue from Hell, Hades, the Inferno, the Nether Realm, or other supernatural domain. For example, the story of Tammuz and Ishtar. He is a young very handsome fertility god, also known as Adonis; she a beautiful goddess of erotic love and war, known by many names including Venus, but always highly seductive and fractious. She accidentally kills him, sending him to the underworld, so in severe remorse she goes to rescue him. She must pass through seven gates, at each of which she loses an ornament or item of clothing, so that she finally arrives naked and is imprisoned herself. But with the help of another god she finally succeeds in escaping with him. As it happens, there is an annual human dance competition commemorating that legend, and it is about to start not far from here. I propose that you enter that contest, and with that cover, make it literal, going to Hell to rescue Pun. That way there will be no overt indication of your real purpose, and the Demons, who have other concerns to take their attention, won't notice."

"Who enters the contest?" Nik asked. "We have only one human man and two human women in our party, and the man is not romantically interested in them."

Now her smile was bright, with glints of savvy. She was indeed drawing on the knowledge of Shameful Centaur. "A dance is a script, a performance not necessarily relating to the private natures of the dancers. But if your humans do not love in the manner of Tammuz and Ishtar, and feel that such love would facilitate their interaction, they need not pretend; Nik and Anthem, who do love in that manner, can animate their bodies, as they have before. They can do the passionate dance and rescue trek, if they are amenable."

"I'd love to be sexy Ishtar," Anthem said. "With you, beloved."

She called him beloved! Nik was whelmed. To be with Anthem again, for perhaps an extended period, in host bodies that made them effectively the same species! To dance with her. To hold her and kiss her, knowing that his hopeless desire was returned. Even on the trail to Hell, that would be Heaven.

Santo and Noe were amenable, as they had their own convoluted desires and barriers to negotiate. They could not be fully coupled by themselves, but as spectators of their own bodies in action they could share it.

"We'll do it," Nik said for them all.

"This way," Shameful said as the Demoness faded into the background. Entropy's ambiance was muted, as befitted her nature of diminishment; indeed her presence would not be noticed. She was like Noe in this respect, only more so.

Shameless and Aura resumed clearing puns, and the group made its way toward the dance hall.

"Why do they have the contest in a pun zone?" Noe asked as they went. "They won't get much of an audience there."

"For privacy," Shameful replied. "Ishtar arrives in Hell naked after showing her panties, so the dancing girls do too. That would freak out an audience."

Nik had a problem. "Staying in a dance hall in a pun zone is fine, but we have to actually get to Hell. We can't do both at once."

"Yes you can," Shameful said, cued by Entropy. "Physically you will be on the stage, but spiritually you will be making the actual journey. That's how it is concealed. The other dancers will do it only in imagination, but you will do it literally. Your human companions' souls will be traveling to Hell. Coordination may be tricky in sections, as you do need to maintain awareness of your bodies in the dance hall, but the enhancement provided by the ambiance of two or three Demons should enable you to manage it."

"So it should," Nik agreed, impressed. That ambiance had enabled him to pinch off an ogre's foot, and Anthem to incinerate a termite gang.

They reached the hall. Massed puns crowded close to its outer walls, but inside some degroaning magic had been used to scour it clean. The centaurs and Aura, together with her passengers Wanda Wand and Knife Knight, went to the small audience section, while Nik and Anthem, in the form of Santo and Noe, went to the center.

There were five other couples already there. "Welcome, contestants," the dance master said. "I shall call out the rules, in case any of you are not already familiar with them. Essentially, we are reenacting the story of Tammuz and Ishtar. Not perfectly, as mythology differs in details, but we have the essence. Our judge for the performances this year is the notorious Com Pewter, and the prize for the winner is a new Genius Phone he has crafted." He glanced to the side, where a robot body with a head made of pewter stood. Pewter could magically change things in his vicinity; his phone might have similar properties. That could make it extremely valuable. It was a prize well worth dancing for.

He proceeded to announce the rules and sequences while they all paid close attention. One was that each lady was limited to seven items of ornament or apparel. This was so each would be suitably naked at the conclusion. They would really be feeling the goddess's shame. Um no, the right body could make it glorious. Maybe that was part of the point of the dance: to show off what the ladies had, in the name of authenticity. "There's a certain muted appeal to that, among humans," Santo said mentally. "Especially when they have a pretext to flash their panties and freak out men." He and Noe being an exception in that respect; she could flash but he would not freak.

Then the music commenced, rendered by an orchestra of self-playing instruments, and they started dancing. The actual steps were not defined, but they did have to be graceful in the manner of a dance. Indeed they were; the men were all handsome and fit, and the women comely, in flowing outfits that showed off their appealing features. When the men walked, they evinced balance, power, and purpose. When the women walked, they were poetry in motion, not to mention sex appeal. Nik had not been aware of that quality until he associated with humans. Now he was coming to sincerely appreciate it. It was a joy to see an attractive human woman.

The opening sequence was the presentation of the lovers. The couples sashayed past the judge, evincing their great love for each other, pausing to hug and kiss, then moving on around the circle. Nik and Anthem were the last, and they put their all into it, trusting that their very real passion would be taken as a simulation. It was glorious. The enhancement was potent, and the human Santo was indeed more handsome than in real life, and the human Noe, normally not the prettiest girl, was now so lovely that the very air around her shimmered when she smiled. The demonstration kiss made their feet lift slightly off the floor, and two little hearts sailed out and orbited their heads. Their dance steps, too, were precise and telling. They were indeed ready to compete.

Then came the death sequence. The first couple took the spot before the judge while the others danced gracefully in place, waiting their turns. Ishtar was the goddess of erotic love and war, and her garb was both sexy and violent, with an armored bodice that flexed to show the contours of her fine breasts, and a mail skirt that caressed her tight waist, broad hips, and contoured butt, yet ended high enough to display her evocative thighs. She did a pirouette that made the thin metal skirt flare, artfully unveiling her legs to just barely below the panty line in a finely-tuned tease. She drew her sword, whirled, and stabbed an imagined enemy in the gut.

Only it wasn't imaginary and it wasn't an enemy. It was Tammuz, coming in close to kiss her, not realizing that she was about to thrust. The blade pierced his heart, and he fell toward the floor, his arms reaching out dramatically.

A handbasket swooshed in and caught him before he landed, carrying him away. The large print on the side of it said hell, just in case someone didn't know where it was going.

Ishtar went into dramatic raptures of grief. She had accidentally killed her beloved! She sashayed mournfully on around the circle, vacating the prime spot for the next couple.

"It's going to be hard to match that drama," Anthem murmured.

"We don't need to win the contest," Nik reminded her. "In fact we're best off just being an also-danced."

“That’s right,” she agreed, remembering. “We really are going to Hell, secretly. We don’t want to attract too much attention here.”

The second couple took the judgment spot. This Ishtar was so buxom she was almost bursting out of her straining halter. The two kissed. Then she clapped her hands behind Tammuz’s head and drew his eager face down into her formidable cleavage, smothering him with love. She held him tight so that he could not slip out and spoil the effect.

Then he slid down and fell to the floor. The Handbasket swooped him up. He had accidentally been smothered to death. Ishtar commenced her histrionics.

Noe almost laughed, mentally. *Now I’m glad I don’t have bigger breasts.*

The third couple had Ishtar unveil a huge chocolate cake she had harvested, complete with icing that radiated wicked fattening taste. Tammuz took a bite, went into a dance of pure rapture, and shoved his whole face into it, gobbling it down. Then he did a dance of desperation, choking on his gorge. He had gulped too much, and it stuck in his throat and killed him. The Basket carried him away.

The fourth couple had Ishtar slowly undress for Tammuz’s inspection, starting with her glittery blouse. When her splendid bare breasts came into sight, his heart pounded so wildly that it exploded from his chest in a shower of heartlets, and he fell into the Basket.

The fifth couple had Ishtar stand before Tammuz and breathe deeply, so that her blouse animated compellingly. He was so fascinated that he as he stepped forward he didn’t see an object on the floor, tripped, and fell, striking his head so hard it seemed to split open, a nice cosmetic effect. The Basket got him.

Then it was their turn. Noe was in a ballet costume provided by the dance supplier, which showed off her current beauty wonderfully. They smiled at each other, then kissed marvelously, reveling in the joy of same-species interaction. Then she did an arabesque, with one delicate arm pointing forward and one lovely leg pointing back, perfectly balanced. But she was unaware that Tammuz, who didn’t know the position, was coming up behind her, arms outstretched to embrace her from behind. The point of her toe caught him right in the chest. He fell, imaginary blood staining his belly; the shoe had stabbed his heart, and he was dead. The Basket swept him away. Ishtar went into her paroxysm of grief.

The limited audience applauded the performances of all the dancers. This was an outstanding group. Pewter merely stood there, apparently unmoved. He was of course a machine. He would render his verdict when the full dance was done.

The opening sequence was through. It was time for the rescue.

The spotlight now focused on Ishtar, who girded her lush loin and set off for Hell, intent on rescuing her lover. She was grim and lovely. Tammuz could be seen on a magic screen, caught in Hell, able to see Ishtar but not to show himself to her. She had to make this excursion alone. Each dancer had her approach, but what counted for Nik and Anthem was her own. Now she was not only dancing in the hall, but also making her way through the spiritual realm, as the original goddess had. She was garbed in six pieces of clothing and one ornate bracelet.

The road to Hell was of course paved with good intentions. In the dance hall the path was marked, leading to one colored gate after another, symbolically. But now their main attention went to the spiritual journey, which was another matter. The paved path was narrow, and horrendous spooks of many kinds lined it, reaching for Anthem/Noe without quite touching them. The point was to scare Ishtar, to make her flinch, not to actually catch her. After all, she was going to Hell anyway. She did flinch, evocatively, dancing her fear and her relief at escaping their clutches.

Nik, watching from the screen, wished he could help them. But this was an excursion only they could do. He did a little dance of frustration; all actions had to be danced. Anthem's chords served as background music. Meanwhile, in the real Hell, where he and Santo had gone spiritually, he also watched. They shared a sparse chamber with the Demon Pun, who was of course interested in the proceedings. The Demon was vastly larger than this chamber, or indeed this world, but he was locked into the semblance of a human form for this confinement. He was also gagged, to prevent him from uttering any groanable puns. There was a sink to wash in and a toilet to poop in, not that they needed to perform any such actions here. It was a makeshift prison, adapted from an old establishment that mortals had used. Its very make-do nature was part of the Demon's humiliation; he was being confined with contempt. Entropy was seething.

Ishtar came to the first gate. It was bright red with a barred entry and a red lock. She put her hand on the lock, but it would not release the gate.

Ironically, it was barring her way into Hell, not away from it. Surely the great majority of those passing here were going the other way. How could she open it?

Oh. She took off her decorative blouse, exposing her silky bra, in what ignorant mundanes would call a strip tease. Nothing could be simply done; it had to be performed in elegant gestures. She was no longer in her ballet costume, this being her spiritual trip, the clothing imagined but nevertheless essential for the dance. She set it on the lock with a flair, and both it and the lock puffed into red smoke and drifted away. She had paid her toll. The gate swung open.

"I feel exposed," Noe confessed as they pranced through. "Bras are supposed to be concealed."

"That's the point," Anthem reminded her with a reassuring chord. "Ishtar has to be diminished as she approaches Hell."

"True. At least now I am gloriously exposed, instead of inadequately exposed. Some women can even freak out men with their bras; I have seen it happen."

"Enhanced as you are, could probably do it, if you tried."

Noe laughed. "Oh, that would be wicked fun!"

Ishtar resumed her trek. Now the spooks were not scary, but appealing. Handsome men, svelte women, beckoning her to join them in their picnic. They had her favorite cookies and drinks, nice gardens and pools to admire, and the scenery was gorgeous. These folk were having a wonderful time, and promised to be excellent companions. The ladies were even wearing bras matching hers, sharing her exposure, making it socially correct, at least for this setting. But she knew that if she ever stepped off the path, she would never be able to step back onto it, and would be forever lost in this wonderland of pleasant distractions, assuming it really was as it looked. Her lover would never be rescued. That was the horror behind the temptation.

Nik, watching, did a dance of appreciation for her constancy. She wanted him more than a dreamy life. Just as Ishtar wanted Tammuz, and Entropy wanted Pun.

She forged on, refusing to yield to the offerings. The folk to the sides looked disappointed, as if her company was what they most desired. Some were children, looking for a compatible adult to guide them. They cried when she passed them by. That hurt worse.

Ishtar reached the second gate. This one was blue, through and through, and firmly locked. She considered, and decided to sacrifice one slipper. The path was not thorny, so she could walk barefoot. Nik nodded; she would not want to expose her panties any sooner than she had to. Feet were fine.

She lifted her sleek leg, made a dancing turn, and slipped off her right slipper with a suitable flair. If anyone saw up her leg in the process, and freaked out, so much the better. She made a production of placing the slipper on the lock.

Slipper and lock puffed into blue haze and dissipated. She passed through and continued her trek.

This time there were neither spooks nor people. The path wound through increasingly hilly but ordinary terrain, with no threats or temptations. This was suspicious.

Then she came to a daunting crevasse. It was so deep that darkness shrouded its depth. Cold air gusted up out of it, carrying the faint smell of carrion. No, she did not want to descend into that, even if it was all in spirit.

Fortunately there was a bridge. It arched up over the pit to land safely on the far side, a marvelous feat of dexterity. All she had to do was cross it.

Anthem set foot on it. Now she wished she had her normal six legs with the capacity to cling firmly to any object, instead of just two relatively clumsy ones. "Sorry, Noe," she thought with an apologetic chord. "No offense intended. Your body is fine for your realm."

"None taken," Noe replied. "This is a formidable structure."

She got fairly out over the void. Then the handrails ended. There was only the basic trestle. Well, she would just have to handle it.

As she went, the span narrowed, until it was barely wide enough to walk on. Another flavored gust brushed her, making her tilt perilously before she could recover her balance. She paused nervously, her chord in a jangle. Should she turn back while she still could, and give it up? This was too scary!

No! She would forge on. If she fell, she fell. She couldn't actually be hurt, in this immaterial form, regardless how it seemed. She would move on until she found a way to get across. She had a life to save from Hell.

With that decision she gained emotional strength. Her sense of balance was also enhanced, so that she could tackle the precarious beam competently. She accelerated, her chord sounding resolutely, reaching the peak of the arch and starting down the other side. At the narrowest point she had to swing one leg in front of the other, as the span was only wide enough for one foot at a time. More gusts came, but she danced on, daring them to dislodge her. Now it was the wind that faltered and lost force, unable to bluff out its target. That made it moan.

Nik smiled. The enhancement had extended to her equilibrium, yes, but also to her attitude, directed by her courage. What a worthy creature Anthem was! If only she matched his species, so they could be together in real life. That was the building tragedy of their love.

Soon Ishtar came to the third gate. It was solid green.

She spun about in a kind of pirouette she never could have managed without the enhancement, flipped off her left slipper, caught it midair, and presented it to the green lock with a flourish. There was a whiff of green smoke as the two objects disappeared. "I wonder if they're dating?" Noe said. "It's a handsome lock and a pretty slipper."

"But he's green and she's white."

"Sometimes opposites attract."

"Or different species," Anthem added sadly.

True words, Nik thought, as sadly.

The path led to a scenic castle. A bold knight in shining golden armor stood before it. "I am Sir Cumspect," he announced as Ishtar approached. So the puns were not entirely gone. "I have been waiting years for a decorous barefoot woman to share my estate and my life, and lo! I have found her. You are as comely as a goddess. I want to kiss your dainty feet and work my way up delight by delight. Come to me, you breath of Heaven, and make me deliriously happy."

"He looks a little like Santo," Noe said. "Only handsomer."

"Ouch!" Santo said to Nik. "So he does. And I'll bet he's hetero. He's not fooling about the feet."

But the knight was not aware that the maidenly body was only a shell governed by an ant. Anthem was not wowed into using those evocative feet and stepping into Cumspect's eager arms; he was neither ant nor nickelpede. "Maybe the next goddess is the one looking for you," she said, and moved on.

"Namndation!" he swore, and dissolved into his original state, a horrendous troll. Rejection had made the illusion fail.

Anthem heard something and glanced back. Coming up behind her was a fearsome lady troll, a goddess among her kind. Lady trolls were almost as ugly as ogresses—and just as justifiably proud of it. "Now you are mine!" she exulted as she stepped off the path and enfolded Cumspect in an unsubtle possessive clinch.

"Namn," he muttered just before she smothered his face with a toothy kiss.

"Dation," she agreed as she dragged him into the castle, which now looked more like a horror house. "Your first feat will be to fete my feet. Then we'll get down and dirty."

Well, this was the pun zone, Nik thought, mentally smiling. Hell had to use the actors available, trusting illusion to make them briefly presentable. This seemed to be outside the domain of the Adult Conspiracy, so that the evocative language had not been stifled. If it couldn't be used near Hell, where could it be?

The fourth gate was bright gold, like the troll's illusion armor, surly not coincidentally. Ishtar considered briefly, then gracefully removed her skirt. There were, after all, no males here to freak out with her panty.

But Santo, watching, rocked back, his gaze briefly locking. "You are a normal male of your species, affecting my perception," he said to Nik. "Even though it's not human. Suddenly I appreciate the effect of panty magic. It's amazing."

"Noe is now super enhanced," Nik said. "She really is goddess-sightly. Her panties have power they never had before. Enough, it seems, to affect even a gay man or an insect."

"True." They were both bemused and impressed.

They settled back to watch, managing with effort to appreciate the flexing panties without quite freaking, though it was a close call. Ishtar/Noe/Anthem grandly laid her skirt on the gold lock and watched the objects become golden smoke and float away. Then she pushed the gate open and danced—what motion!—into the next section of the route to Hell.

This was like a mundane city street. Mundane cars tooled along it, ignoring stop signs and pondering before reluctantly obeying stop lights. Pedestrians walked along the sidewalks, their cute little yappy dogs on leashes as they pooped passing lawns and pissed power poles. It was evening here, and as the light gradually dimmed the people faded out, leaving only a few on the walks.

Ishtar's path paralleled the right side sidewalk, where a single young woman walked. Her dress was patchy, her shoes old and worn. Her hair hung limply behind her ears, bereft of any ribbons or ornaments. She was one of the rejected poor folk no one wanted to be near. She looked nervous, glancing back over her shoulder as if fearing some pursuit. Indeed, now a rough looking man was coming up behind her, as if ready to rob, rape, or kill her, or all three, not necessarily in that order. Not that she looked to have much money, sex appeal, or life. She was plainly plain, a leftover nobody.

So what was the temptation here? Anthem recognized it: sympathy. This woman needed help.

"We can't let her be mugged," Noe said. "Even if she is an illusion."

"No we can't," Anthem agreed with a mixed chord. "But neither can we afford to step off the path."

"Are we going to have to watch her get cruelly abused?"

The brute man was almost upon the cringing victim.

Then Anthem got a notion. "Panties! They work on humans."

So they did. "Ma'am!" they called. "Flash him with your panties!"

The woman tried. But when she pulled up her skirt to display them, the panties were shown to be old, dirty, and torn, no good for this. The man hardly paused. "You think those rags will stop me? Your bleep is mine!" He reached out, about to grab her.

Her bleep? So the Conspiracy did function here, at least on occasion.

Anthem got another notion. "We've got goddess level panties."

"Oooh, naughty!" Noe agreed, smiling.

"Hey, nasty man!" they called. "Get a glimpse of this!" And they bent forward, away from him, accenting their beatifically pantied butt.

The man looked. And froze. He had freaked out. How could he have done otherwise?

"Thank you!" the woman called as she fled. In barely a moment and a half she was gone. They had saved her.

They left the man where he was, staring at nothing. Which was exactly what he deserved.

"That may be illusion," Noe said. "But the outcome is highly satisfying, in more than one way."

"We saved the woman, and proved that goddess panties do work here," Anthem said.

"And wiped out a bad man."

"You bet," Santo agreed silently. Nik, too, was satisfied to see the panties used for a good purpose.

The girls walked on. Soon they came to the fifth gate, which was orange. "Which item this time?" Anthem asked Noe."

"The bra. It's a classic torture device anyway. They never fit properly, and make women miserable, but they have to use them to make their upper torsos look younger and firmer than they ever are in reality."

"The bra," Anthem agreed. She removed it and set it delicately on the orange lock. Actually her goddess torso really was younger and firmer than reality; the bra made no difference. But not every human woman could share the ambiance of two or three Demons. "Orange you glad to have this?" she inquired of the lock with three fifths of a smile.

The lock didn't deign to answer. It puffed into orange smoke along with the bra. They moved on.

The path led past a dragon's lair. The creature lay lightly smoking on his nest of coins and gems. He was big enough to toast and eat a human person. This could be mischief. They needed to pass him promptly by.

The dragon spied them. He mewled. Then he laid his head on the edge of the nest and gazed at them sadly.

What? They paused, confused. Dragons roared, or chomped, or blasted fire, smoke, or steam; they didn't whimper. What was wrong?

Anthem, being a fire-jetting animal, was the first to catch on. "He's lonely!"

Noe was surprised. "Dragons get lonely?"

"Dogs and cats and parakeets and mice and horses and goldfish can be pets, with constant appreciative human company. But suppose a dragon wants the same? What of it?"

"Minuscule chance," Noe said. "Nobody pets a dragon."

"But don't dragons and maidens get along?"

Noe reconsidered. "They do, if it's the right dragon and the right maiden. I thought that was mainly a fable, but maybe it's true in some cases. I'm a maiden, and this is a dragon. But there's a problem. I'd have to step off the safe path to pet it."

And there it was. Yet another ruse to trick them into leaving the path. It might be all make-believe here, but the path was serious.

"We can't step off the path," Anthem said with a negative twang. "And flashing panties won't help."

"Yet now that I realize about the dragon, I hate to hurt him, even if it is an act. Maybe it's because I *am* a maiden."

Then Anthem had an inspiration. "We don't have to touch him physically. We can do it emotionally. By telling him a nice story."

"A story? What do dragons care about stories?"

"One about dragons and maidens. It's worth a try, isn't it?"

Noe shrugged. "If you have a story, tell it. It can't do any harm, at least."

Anthem thought rapidly, discovering that her enhanced mind could generate an appealing story, even for a dragon, then started in. "Oh Dragon, I am the maiden Anthem," she said with a chord of introduction. "I am a fire ant borrowing a human form for this occasion. So I know about shooting fire."

The dragon's near eye oriented on her. A mini whiff of smoke emerged from one nostril, forming into a question mark. She had captured his attention. He understood her, because she was actually speaking telepathically. A fiery female was something of interest to him, regardless of her species, as she had suspected would be the case. She was even able to invent spot character names.

"One day Drogo Dragon was out about his usual round, toasting the tails of impertinent harpies and foraging for a fat sheep to roast for his next meal, when he spied something unusual. A human maiden was out playing her dulcimer, and the sound was so beautiful that he just had to land quietly and listen. She noticed him. 'Oh, you like my music!' she said, pleased. He nodded. There was something about the notice of a maiden that he liked, apart from the music. 'My neighbors think it's too violent,' she continued, strumming a violent chord that Anthem rendered perfectly. 'But I prefer resonance and power to transmit mighty emotions, like those a dragon should have. Would you like to hear more?'

"Drogo nodded his snout slightly. He did find her music enchanting.

"'I am Dacia Damsel. Here are my favorites.' She proceeded to play several violent melodies, thrilled to have an appreciative audience. Drogo was transported; never had he heard such evocative music."

Anthem used her enhanced chord power to render the pieces directly. They were captivating. She was as thrilled as Dacia to have them appreciated, even by an apparition lurking to lure her off the path.

"After a while Dacia paused. She stood before the dragon's hot head, unafraid of his fire or teeth. 'Did you like it?' she asked, knowing that he did.

"In answer, Drogo lifted his snout and kissed her face. She shied away not at all. They had the camaraderie of music.

"Then something surprising happened. There was a transformation. Not dragon to human prince, but damsel to lady dragon. The kiss had broken the curse. 'Now I can be with you completely,' Dacia Dragon said in dragon talk. She spread her wings, lifted into the air, shot out a breath of fire, and flew with him to his lair, where they got really hotly friendly."

The story was done. The dragon lay on his nest, eyes closed. "Did you like my story?" Anthem asked, knowing as Dacia had that he did. In fact he blew a fiery smoke ring in the shape of a heart. He was more than satisfied.

They walked on. "That was amazing," Noe said. "I felt hot tears in my eyes." Indeed, they were wet with mild firewater.

"Maybe my storytelling ability is enhanced too."

"That must be it." They laughed together.

The sixth gate was purple. Noe removed her devastating panties and grandiosely laid them on the lock. In half a moment the resulting cloud was departing. They stepped through and entered what they trusted was the next to last challenge.

This time the landscape looked almost familiar. They paused, assessing it. Then they got it. "It's the region near the Queendom of Thanx," Noe said. "We passed through it, mapping the bee hives and bug settlements."

"That's right," Anthem agreed with a chord of recognition. "There's a deep swift narrow river at the boundary."

Nik recognized it too. Why was this background scenery here on the route to Hell? There was nothing Hellish about it. Had the path guardians run out of ideas?

A man was in a circular pi field, harvesting 3.1416 pies for dinner. He looked up as they passed. Then he sat down, an expression of surprised bliss scurrying to catch up with his face. His mind was suffused with wonder and desire.

Oh, yes. They were goddess shaped and completely nude. Noe wasn't sure whether to feel embarrassed or satisfied. Anthem was content with the latter. Appearance was power, especially here in the realm of illusions.

Soon they saw the river. There was narrow bridge across it, more of a plank span than a real effort. Maybe someday the queendom would get around to upgrading it. There wasn't much foot traffic, here in nowhere.

A woman ran toward it. She was well formed, and had large lips. She was a Lips woman, like Aura, evidently a resident of their enclave here. She would reach the makeshift bridge about the same time they did, from the opposite side. They would have to pause to let each other cross.

"Noe!" the woman called, spying her. "I have vitally important news!"

News? Here beside Hell? What on or below Earth could that be?

"I know that voice," Anthem said. "That's Queen Apoca!"

Curiouser and curiouser. Apoca did not belong anywhere near Hell. She was a good woman.

Then she tripped and fell forward, missing the bridge and plunging into the water with an ugly splash. "Help!" she cried. "I can't swi—"

Noe leaped to intercept her. But Anthem overrode her, causing her to stop short of the river. "That's not Apoca," she said. "Her mind is blank"

They watched the woman get swept downriver, her arms helplessly flailing. It was heart-wrenching.

"Not Apoca?" Noe asked. "You mean it's another phantasm?"

"Yes. Designed to make us leap involuntarily off the path to try to save her. But the script didn't reckon with my telepathy. Otherwise we would have been lost."

"Lost," Noe echoed faintly. "It almost happened."

"One more to go. It's bound to be a bad one. Brace yourself."

"I am not liking this dance as well as I did."

"The dance is fine. It's our detour to the real Hell that's evil."

"Oh, yes. I forgot."

"But in a necessary cause." Or so they hoped.

Nik and Santo hoped too. There were those who surely felt that the Demon of Puns should remain in Hell indefinitely. The loss of clothing at the gates was actually not too bad, but the incidents between gates were dangerous.

They crossed the span and walked on toward Thanx. But it turned out instead to be the final gate. It was death black.

Noe took off the bracelet, her last item of apparel. Now she was totally nude. She touched it to the lock, and the two fused into black smoke and dissipated. The gate swung open.

Anthem thought of something. "We have survived seven interim challenges and passed seven gates. Shouldn't that be the end of it?"

"Maybe. But this is Hell. It may have Hellish pranks remaining to torment us."

She had a point. "Agreed. We can afford to take nothing for granted."

"They're right," Santo said. "Hell is not evil so much as it is devious. That's one reason for the paving with good intentions. They make folk let down their guard so they can more readily be damned."

"And there's a bad challenge coming up that we can't warn them against," Nik said. "It will be painful to watch."

"In more than one way," Santo agreed grimly. "But we will watch anyway."

The girls walked on along the path as daylight declined. They came to a building with a number of shuttered rooms, but one remained open, the shuttering evidently forgotten or undesired, so that the light radiated out. They paused by that one, curious, though they knew that it was bound to show them something they didn't want to see, like one of Shameful Centaur's curses. But of course they could move on whenever they wanted to, theoretically.

Concealed by the outside darkness, they gazed into the room. It contained a lamp, a table, a chair, and a bed, like an ordinary bedroom. That was all. This was Hell?

Then its door opened and a man entered. They froze in shock. It was Santo! He looked perfectly ordinary. This must be his cell in Hell. It seemed more like a rented room than a torture chamber. He paused to gaze out into the night, but Anthem couldn't read his mind. That was blocked off, as probably was his talent for making holes, otherwise he'd have been out of Hell long ago.

Oh. He was here as part of the dance. As Tammuz. He wasn't even trying to escape. He was waiting to be rescued. That part was up to Ishtar/

Anthem/Noe. But it couldn't be as easy as just opening the window and spiriting him home. There had to be a trap, maybe to make them give themselves away. So they waited and watched.

Another person entered the room, a woman. She was shapely and had large lips, and a scintillating aura hovered near her head. It was Aura! What was she doing in Hell? Oh, again. The same thing as Apoca, a spook playing a role. Whatever could it be?

Santo heard her and turned to face her. "Aura! What are you doing here? You can't be real."

Exactly.

"I am in Hell too, the same as you," she replied. "As part of my punishment I am compelled to tell you my most passionate secret."

"Your secret?"

"You welcomed me to the Quest, when no one else wanted me. I truly appreciate that."

"We all welcomed you. I am merely a member, not the leader." The nominal leader, of course, was Nik.

"You are the only purely human man in the Quest," she said warmly. "Therein lies my guilty secret."

"I don't understand."

"I love you, Santo. Now that we are alone together, I mean to have you."

He was taken aback. "I have a girlfriend,"

"A pretend girlfriend. And she's not here."

"But I am gay!"

"That may change. You have not felt the power of a Lips kiss."

"That would not make any difference."

"We shall see." She stepped into him and kissed him on the mouth with power. It visibly coruscated from her to him, momentarily illuminating their merged faces.

She broke the kiss and stepped back. "I'm a zombie!" Santo exclaimed, horrified. Indeed, the first signs of rot were upon him, chipping off his mouth.

"My kiss of a normal man does that now, as you know," Aura said. "But my kiss of a zombie man makes him my love slave. It is time for that second kiss."

"But—"

She drew him in again and kissed him with power. It crackled, lighting their faces again. Then she broke, and he, dizzy, sat down on the bed.

"Now you are mine," Aura said with satisfaction.

"I am yours," Santo agreed, gazing at her with adoration.

"The hell he is!" Noe swore. "I'll break that up right now!" She lurched toward the window.

But Anthem was ready, and held her back. "They are spooks, both of them. They have no minds. It's just another trap to pull us off the path."

"No minds?"

"No minds. It's all an act, a little play, like the others. The real Santo has to be elsewhere in Hell; I feel his faint ambiance. The real Aura isn't in Hell at all; she's in the pun zone watching the dance."

"A little play," Noe said, relieved. "And I fell for it."

"It was pitched at you. But again Hell forgot that I am not human, and I am telepathic. Now we must get on with the business of rescuing Tammuz."

"Of course," Noe agreed weakly.

They walked on, then paused to glance back. Two hideous ghosts looked back at them, knowing they had failed. Then they faded out, and the room went dark.

"They made it!" Nik said, relieved. Pun looked relieved too. It was after all his rescue they were attempting, masked by the dance.

Anthem and Noe came to the prison door, which was far less fancy than any of the gates. It looked like a renovated rundown mundane structure. They pulled it open and entered.

Inside was a chamber with a desk where a bored mundane officer sat. He looked up as he heard them. His eyes glazed and his jaw went slack. It was as if he was surprised to see a nude woman with a goddess figure here in his office in Hell.

"I'm the cleaning lady," Noe said quickly, while Anthem projected a melodic reassurance that this was routine. Also the semblance of clothing. And a mop and bucket.

"Oh." The man waved them on into the main prison section.

And there was Santo, with Nik. And a determinedly ordinary man with a gagged mouth.

No introductions were needed or desired. They had to maintain the pretense that this was nothing out of the ordinary. The point was to avoid attracting the attention of whatever Demon was supposed to be supervising the prison.

Noe went to the toilet corner of the room. She set down the imaginary bucket and rested the mop against the wall. Then she turned and silently beckoned the gagged man. He came to stand before her.

"Entropy," she murmured. The Demoness came to imbue her body.

"Entropy will dissolve your physical body to its component cells," Noe murmured to Pun. "Which we will then flush into the sewer. The sewer pipe leads directly to Shameless Centaur, who will be your host for this area, masking your escape. Stifle your ambiance so that there will be no tangible evidence of your presence among us. Welcome to the Quest."

Then Pun sat on the toilet, clothed. Noe put one hand on his head, and the Demoness did her thing. It was like Aura's power kiss, only dimensionally magnified, one Demon acting on another. The head dissolved into protoplasm, followed by the rest of the body. It all plopped into the toilet, leaving the clothing empty. She flushed the toilet, and the thick liquid gurgled down the tube.

"Our job here is done," Noe said.

They tuned out Hell and tuned in the dance contest, which had been in their background awareness throughout. Their turn was just finishing.

"The winner is Santo and Noe," Com Pewter announced. "Here is your award." He handed the Genius Phone to Santo and departed.

They had won? They hadn't even been trying to, just wanting to do it well enough to mask their real mission.

The others applauded. It seemed that they had danced quite well during the distraction of their literal trek to Hell. Some of that realism must have rubbed off, enhancing their presentation.

Meanwhile, both Shameful and Shameless looked specially animated. Only the members of the Quest knew why.

Chapter 5

GENIUS PHONE

The dance contest was done, the Demon of Puns had been rescued though still maintaining a subterranean profile, and they were back in the pun zone. Because Shameless Centaur now hosted the Demon, they decided not to zombie him to eliminate puns, lest it mess up that hosting. So they had to face the puns head on, or maybe head into them face first. Even their thoughts tended to get punned up.

"It shouldn't take long to get out," Noe said. She remained outstandingly sightly, which interfered with her normal anonymity, but no one objected, her least of all. "We've recorded the settlements here. We can just teeth our grits and do it." She paused, annoyed. "Did I just make a pun?"

"In this zone it can happen," Santo said, a smile hovering. "Not your fault."

They teethed their grits and headed out. Only to encounter an odd creature with toads where foot digits normally were. Then Aura groaned. "A three toad sloth."

Yet it made a kind of sense. The toads were snapping up flies, evidently feeding the creature.

They rounded a bend. There was a ball of smoke. It extended arms, legs, and a head. It hovered, the limbs and body gradually shaping into a curvaceous female form. "What is this?" Aura asked.

A mouth formed in the head. "Devil, fiend, monster, spook, daemon—"

"Demon?"

"Whatever," it said curtly.

"Demoness Metria!" Noe exclaimed. "What are you doing here?"

"I went around the bend, looking for my alternate aspect Mentia's lost marbles. I found them." She held up a handful of small colored glass spheres, then pressed them into her forming hairdo. "They'll be here when she takes over the individuality."

"The what?" Nik asked.

"Commonality, social class, ethnic, example, representation—"

"Identity?"

"Whatever," she agreed, irritated.

Nik realized that he had fallen into her verbal trap, playing her game.

"I thought you were locked into your child aspect," Noe said. "Woe Betide."

"She finished her adventure and vacated. A child her age needs to rest. She was exposed to entirely too much adult material. These three nymphs should have been more careful." She looked around. "You've got the Baton of Protagonism with you. You must be having an adventure. Is it interesting?"

Oops. Nik knew from his enhanced awareness that this small D demoness was a pain in the posterior, always messing in with anything she found interesting so as to relieve her boredom. It was better to discourage her, so he spoke the truth via Santo. "We are on a mission to map all the settlements of Xanth."

"Boring," Metria said, fading out.

"But she's still here," Anthem said quietly. "Don't say anything about our larger situation."

"It's a dull chore, but somebody has to do it," he said for the benefit of the hidden listener.

They passed a patch of furry plants. They purred. "Pussy willows," Noe said. The plants purred.

A man approached them. "Avoid him!" Anthem warned with a sharp chord. "That's Hal E Tosis, who gives people bad breath."

They swerved, and were abruptly out of the pun zone. What a relief!

"And Metria is all the way gone," Anthem added. "Even she can get punned out."

"Anyone can," Noe agreed.

They resumed mapping. It really was dull. The two new Demons had become additional silent observers. That made good sense.

Then Noe spoke. "Is this a good time to learn about the Genius Phone we won, in case it turns out to be useful? I mean during the dull spaces between settlements?"

"That does seem smart," Santo agreed. He brought it out. It was a simple looking flat oblong. "How does it work?"

Nik extended his clairvoyance. "Tap the surface. It will give you a menu."

Santo tapped. "Ah. The first item is instructions for use." He looked at them. "There's a lot here. One says 'Virtual Clones.' What can that mean?"

Nik extended again. "Immaterial copies that connect to the material unit. Everyone can have a copy of the phone."

"Then we all can figure it out together," Santo said. "Let's do it." He tapped the entry.

Copies appeared before each member of the Quest. The ones for Nik and Anthem were proportionally small, hovering before them without needing to be held or carried. This was an accommodating device!

Nik looked at the Menu. His eye fell on the entry games. What kind of game could such an object play? He poked a claw at it. The claw passed right through the apparent screen, but a sub-menu appeared, listing games. One was pinch. He was a nickelpede; pinching was his specialty. Could this actually relate? He poked that, and a picture of a row of human folk appeared, about to tread on a nickelpede nest. He poked one, a female. She screamed and jumped right off the screen, her bare legs kicking prettily in air. A score appeared in a corner: the number one.

He poked at another before he could tread the nest, a booted man. "Bleep!" the man cried, and jumped away. The score was now two.

Well now. Nik poked rapidly at other figures, as they neared the nest, and the score mounted accordingly. He liked this game, and would be playing more of it.

Meanwhile the others were trying other games on their virtual units. Aura found one titled kiss, and her pokes caused the handsome little man figures to swoon dreamily love-slaved as the score mounted. Wanda and Knife, with her, also enjoyed the show. Noe found one called flash, that made panties flash visibly and men froze in place, freaked out in funny positions. Anthem found one called fire that made jets of fire streak out to scorch attacking insects that whirled and fluttered delightfully as they succumbed. Santo had one titled hole that allowed him to make holes through multiple objects. "Holey moley!" the phone exclaimed as he made the wining hole-in-one, and the holed objects did a little dance in air. Even the two centaurs found compatible games, trot and canter. Nik wasn't sure how those were scored, but they seemed to be entertaining.

After a while they got to exploring other features of the phones. "Nik!" Anthem spoke, her telepathy rendered into sound from the phone.

"Yes," he answered.

A picture of a gorgeous lady nickelpede appeared on his screen. "I love you, pincer legs." A romantic chord sounded in the background.

This made him pause. "Anthem, you don't need to assume a nickelpede avatar. I know you for what you are, and love you as you are. No revised image can improve you."

"That's so nice of you! I feel the same." The image became Anthem herself. "Our love is independent of our species."

"Yes. But it was nice to share a species when we were human."

"It was."

They gazed at each other in their screens, the mutual adoration forming a pink heart behind them. Yet they knew that their love could never be truly complete. That was the painful lurking reality.

Then Aura spoke through all their phones. "Please, I have a problem I hope someone can help me with. When there is time."

Anthem sent out her reading: it was important.

"There is time now," Nik said. "Speak, as much as you need to."

Aura didn't hesitate. "I experimented with my phone to see if I could contact my brother, August. I succeeded. He's in trouble. The Lips women can kiss with power, rendering men and sometimes women into love slaves. The Lips men have a common talent too, less spectacular but useful in its place. It is that of conjuring coats of any kind, whether jackets to wear, battle outfits, or coats of paint or other substance, like rust or mold. Some specialize in a particular variant. August's variant is magic polka dot paint that repels touch, whether human, animal, or bug. A coat of this on a roof will keep the bugs from infesting it, no offense to present company. A coat on a wall will keep people from smearing it with dirty hands. A coat on a floor will stop folk from walking on it, even if they wear heavy shoes or boots. It even stops him from treading on it, though he conjures it. It's very effective." She grimaced. "That's the problem."

"The problem?" Nik asked. "It strikes me as an excellent talent."

"He is working on an isolated island estate, painting it for an absent friend. This room is supposed to be for storing valuable things, like air looms, that weave delicate cloths out of air, so they don't want anybody or anything getting in there who doesn't belong. He made a really stupid mistake and painted himself into a corner. He can't get out. It will be days before his friend returns. He's embarrassed and mad at himself and hungry. If I hadn't called he would have been in a bad way. I sent him a clone phone so we could talk, thinking it would just be social." She took a breath. "Do you think we could rescue him with the carpets? And keep our mouths shut about his mistake?"

"We can," Anthem said with a reassuring chord, having spot surveyed the members of the Quest. "There may even be a settlement there to map."

"Um, we centaurs are not good at crossing deep water," Shameful said. "And riding a carpet would be awkward. Suppose we stay here while you visit the island, and you can rejoin us when you're through?"

Also, Nik realized, the centaurs were a dating couple, and hosting two dating Demons. They would not be bored by the delay. "That seems feasible," he agreed.

They headed out over the sea at dusk. The phones had an appetite, known for short as an app, for addresses. When they described the island, the phones oriented and zeroed right in on it. The members of the Quest zoomed over the waves, admiring the fish below, while the fish tried to see up under the two skirts, to the girls' annoyance. Soon the isle hove into view.

There was a single building on it, made of solid wallflowers with the blossoms forming the roof. Bees were happily servicing them, and Nik recorded their hive on the map. It was a very nice dwelling, well worth protecting with magic paint. They floated up to the front door, opened it wide, and Aura took one of the carpets while Noe joined Santo on his. They flew over the polka dot painted floor to the back.

There was August standing in his corner, relieved to see them. He was indeed a Lips man, with the big mouth and nice physique typical of his tribe. "We're here to help you, August," Aura said. "Me and my friends Wanda Wand and Knife Knight." She showed him the wand and knife.

"Glad to meet you," August said politely. He climbed onto the end of Aura's carpet, then lay on it to reach down to paint the vacated corner, making the job complete. He was, after all, a craftsman. After that they took him outside, where he got off the rug, kissed Aura, harvested a pineapple pie from a pie plant, gobbled it down, went to his boat and waved happily as he set sail back toward the mainland. Nik was reminded that the Lips woman didn't have to kiss with power. She was highly kissable without it. Anyway, her brother already loved her.

Then mischief struck, as if fate were annoyed by the escape of a victim. A passing grade school of nasty fish spied them and sailed out of the water to attack. They were flying purple piranha, flesh eating creatures hungry for fresh meat. They could not be escaped by boat or carpet; they flew magically without wings and were intent on their assorted prey. The schoolteacher fish was instructing them exactly how to do it.

Nik got a notion. He checked his phone's list of functions. Sure enough, there was a listing for repel—fish. He poked that.

Suddenly there was blaring sound and flashing light. Both speared out to intercept the fish. The piranhas were struck by the interference pattern. They became hopelessly confused, lost orientation and elevation, and crashed into trees near the shore, onto the ground, and even the water, where they flailed as if drowning. But for the people and bugs the effects were only mildly annoying.

Soon the area was cleared of fish. Nik turned off the repeller and the commotion died.

"That's some phone you got!" August called as he resumed sailing.

"We won it in a dance contest," Aura called back.

"Dang! I don't dance."

She laughed. "Learn, brother."

A piranha leaped out of the water, orienting on them, now that the repel was gone. Santo made a gesture as of touching a phone setting, and the fish quickly dived back below. It wasn't stupid.

"I am getting to like this phone," Aura said.

So were they all. They continued back across the sea as night closed in.

In due course they rejoined the centaurs, who seemed not at all dismayed by the delay. The party found a suitable spot and settled down for the night.

"I'm hungry," Noe said, discovering no food plants in the vicinity. "I wonder." She studied her phone, then punched the picture of a meal delivery service, Pied Piper Pies. She ordered assorted pies and boot rear for them all. "All we have to do is kiss the delivery folk." Kissing was a regular trade item in some businesses.

Soon a man and a woman arrived, Pied and Piper, brother and sister, carrying pies and drinks. They dismounted their horses and presented their wares. Then Aura and Noe kissed Pie, and Santo emulated his move in the dance and kissed Piper. He could kiss a woman; it just wasn't romantic for him. That seemed almost too bad, because Anthem picked up how well Piper liked it. The pair returned to their steeds, obviously satisfied. The enhancement made all the kisses marvelous.

"He didn't zombify," Noe said, realizing.

"Neither did my brother," Aura said. "A non-power kiss is just a kiss. You know that."

"So I do. I forgot."

The pies and drinks were good. They had discovered yet another feature of the Genius Phone.

"It has been quite a day," Aura said. "I am not yet ready to sleep. I need a diversion so I can relax. I wish I had a magic mirror to give me something interesting to watch."

"Magic mirror," Noe said. "I wonder." She checked the menu on her phone. "Here's an entry for ogre history." She touched it.

Two brutish ogres appeared on the screen, facing off. One swung his hamfist and bopped the other on the top of the head, driving his whole body down into the ground somewhat. The other just stood there, evidently too dull to realize he'd been challenged. Ogres were justifiably proud of their stupidity.

"I wonder," Noe said again. Then she touched magnify. Suddenly the picture expanded so that the ogres were life size. Now they stood twice the height of a human man, and four times as ugly.

The challenger struck again, driving the victim further into the ground, as if pounding a pylon into bedrock. Still he didn't react.

The blows continued, until the victim was entirely buried except for his head. At that point his human girlfriend became concerned. Ogre/

human romances were rare, but did occur. She dashed up and put her hand on his head, lending him her human soul.

That transformed him. He got smart enough to realize his predicament. Power surged through his interred body. One arm burst out of the ground, grabbed the other ogre by the ankle, heaved him up vertically, and held him there without seeming effort.

The buried ogre looked up at his opponent, still held vertical. "Now," he said calmly. "Shall we begin?" The human soul seemed to enable him to talk like a human. At that point the other ogre might have realized he was in trouble.

Then the grounded ogre flexed his arm, tilting the other ogre to horizontal, and heaved him like a thrown spear headfirst into the trunk of a nearby acorn tree. This did not hurt the ogre, but the tree was timbered, with a corns and b corns showering down. The buried ogre surged out of the ground and went after the other. After that the fight got violent.

"I didn't realize that souls made such a difference," Noe said. "I thought they were just spirits."

"Humans have souls," Santo said. "Human crossbreeds have partial souls. Souls do seem to add mental, physical, emotional, and ethical strength. So an ogre with a soul is stronger than one without."

"So it seems," she agreed, wincing as the mayhem intensified.

"Um, how about a more human adventure?" Aura asked. "Endless violence is not my thing for relaxation."

"Check your clone phone," Noe said. "Maybe it lists what the mundanes call movies."

Aura checked. "It does! Dozens! Fresh from Mundania. Here's one titled *Memory Mystery*. That intrigues me. Surely memory is the opposite of mystery."

"Put it on. We can all watch it."

Soon they were all watching the movie on the large projected 3D screen. It showed a pretty mundane woman of about thirty pacing the floor of her house, as if bothered by something. Then her companion, another woman roughly her age, showed up.

"Whatever is the matter, Doris?" she asked, concerned. "You look weird."

"Oh, Deirdre, I just remembered something I can't remember."

Her roommate shook her head. "Am I confused, or are you?"

Doris laughed somewhat ruefully. "Neither. It's that I just realized that there's a year missing from my life. I have no record of it, and no memory of it. But I must have lived it, or I wouldn't be here now."

"I've known you for the three years we've been roomies. You've been here, physically and mentally, throughout. We've even double dated. The men didn't mind because we're both curvy dumb blondes." Now Deirdre laughed. "It's a neat cover for the brains that turn men off. Remember the time we switched dates? Because he wanted intimacy, and I'm a virgin? I didn't want to mess it up."

"I remember. Experience counts. I handled him just fine, using my female condom, and he was a good lover. But this is something else. It's an actual missing year, ending shortly before we got together. I remember my life up to a year before that, and from then on, but there's a gap of a year I can't account for. It's as if I never lived it."

Deirdre considered. "Don't you keep a diary? A physical one, so nobody can hack it and snoop."

"I do. It goes back fifteen years, to my teenhood. Only you know about it." Then she paused. "The diary! Why didn't I think of that?"

"Because you're even more absent-minded than I am?"

"For sure!" Doris dived for her desk. She opened a hidden recess and brought out a compact booklet. She leafed through it. "I've been making daily entries, and never thought to look back. It's got to be here." She paused. "Uh-oh."

"Dor, if it's too private, I'll leave you alone. You know we keep each other's secrets."

"It's not that, Dei. It's that there's a section missing. The section."

"Damn! I was hoping that wouldn't happen. You know I didn't mess with your private book."

"I know. I did it myself. I initialed where the pages are gone. But why?"

The movie paused in place, the two young women frozen in their scene. "Is this worthwhile?" Aura asked. "I like it, as an insight to the odd mundane culture, though I don't understand all the references, like condom, but I don't want to bore the rest of you."

"I understand that a condominium is where some mundanes live," Santo said. "Maybe a condom is a larger one."

"That must be it. But apart from that, is this movie worthwhile?"

Anthem was current with the attitudes of the others. "We're okay with it. It's better than ogre violence. We're curious about her lost year too. Let it play."

The movie resumed.

"You cut out part of your own diary?" Deidre was saying. "This is weird."

"It is indeed. I can't think why I would ever do a thing like that. I value my record. It is after all my life. I write about the things that are important to me."

"There must have been something really critical you had to hide, even from yourself. Maybe you should just leave it alone."

"Oh, Dei, you know me. Once I get hold of something, I can't let it go. I've got to know!"

"Yes, I know you, Dor. You're one sensible savvy nervy woman. You wouldn't just erase something on a whim. There had to be good reason. That diary gap is you telling yourself to stay the hell out or you'll be sorry,"

Doris sighed. "Yes, I will be sorry. But I can't help it. I need those pages."

"I'm curious too. So let's be sorry together. Those pages have to be around here somewhere. You wouldn't have destroyed them. Where could they be?"

Doris considered. "Once as a child I had a naughty picture I didn't want my mom to find. I rolled it up and put it in an old sock and hid the sock in the back of a drawer we used for junk, where she'd never look. That worked." She grimaced. "Then Dad was cleaning up and threw it out, never knowing. So I lost it. I was half relieved and half mortified. From my adult perspective the picture wasn't so bad, just a naked man with a, you know."

"I don't know," Deidre said with a knowing smile. "I'm a virgin, remember? You can get such pictures on the Net,"

"I can get the reality, when I trade dates with you."

They both laughed naughtily. Then they started searching Doris's drawers. And there it was, hidden in an old sock.

"Before we take this farther," Deidre said, "One question. Your memory of removing the pages must have been erased with the missing year itself. But how did you get it erased? Memory is not the kind of thing you can just will out of existence."

"There are clinics where they help people with mental problems, like Post Traumatic Stress Disorder, PTSD. I think they use electroshock therapy. To make them forget, at least for a while. I must have gone to one of those."

"That makes sense, I suppose," Deidre said. "Though it reminds me of The Charge of the Light Brigade, an act of utter folly. That was when a military blunder sent the brigade changing right into the enemy guns, a suicidal maneuver. I have heard it said that Electroshock is like hitting a watch with a hammer to make it run better."

"A hammer," Doris agreed thoughtfully. "I must have been really desperate." She was not joking.

"Next question: can reading the entries bring the memories back?"

"With electro, the effect usually isn't permanent. The memories gradually return, and they have to dose the patient again. Three years should be enough to give me some hints."

Deidre smiled grimly. "Then we have a fighting chance. Third question: do you want me with you or the hell away from you when you read those entries?"

Doris's mouth quirked. "With you, friend. I may need immoral support."

The quirk crossed to Deidre's mouth. "Then let's do it."

They sat on the bed, side by side, as Doris opened the pamphlet-like sheath of papers to read the first entry.

Doris was in a new city where elites were relatively common. It fazed her somewhat, but she was determined to make the most of whatever offered. She got a job as a waitress to sustain her while shopping for a better position, such as personal assistant for an illustrious executive. Her superior potential was on standby at the moment.

Meanwhile, she dated. The Net was chancy, but about the only resource for a girl not properly familiar with the local scene. She didn't really like being alone, and hoped to find a good and malleable man to settle in with. She did not put up a site of her own, fearing it would attract predators. Instead she perused indirect evidences of available men. They were there for those who knew how to ferret them out.

And she came across what just might be both projects together: a top exec who was single. He was Hunk Honors, surely a nickname, but his credits seemed excellent. Why wasn't he married? Maybe he was extremely choosy. Maybe he just had not found the right woman: smart, savvy, shapely, romantically competent. Maybe she was that woman.

She contacted him at his site, honestly describing herself, as she knew he would verify it if interested. And to her muted amazement, she got a date with him.

Hunk picked her up at her apartment. He drove a quality foreign car, and was every bit as handsome and courtly as his reputation indicated. She liked him immediately, and hoped the sentiment was mutual. He took her to a fine restaurant, fortunately not the one she worked at, though she had not concealed her temporary profession. They took their seats, and she set about impressing him with her appearance, manner, and mind. He surely was looking for a superior woman, and she hoped to fill the role.

The waitress brought their order, which was fancier food than Doris could afford on her own. She was just putting the plates before them when something happened. A rough looking man cruised in holding a multi-shot firearm, the kind that was banned in some states.

"Oh!" the waitress said faintly. "That's my ex! He's a bad loser. He's come here to kill me. I don't know what to do."

Doris acted almost without thinking. "Honey, give me your cap, apron, and tray. Take my hat and shawl. Sit down and make like a customer. Keep your face out of his sight. I'm a waitress at another restaurant; I know how to do it. I will cover for you until he quits in disgust or gets arrested." She glanced at Hunk to make sure he didn't object. He didn't. In fact his return glance was appraising.

The waitress numbly obeyed. She took Doris' place at the table, while Doris took the tray back to the front counter. On the way she passed the armed ex, blocking his view of the table where she had been. "Sir, you should put that weapon away. The management does not encourage such displays here."

"Get out of my way, bitch!" he snapped, pushing her aside as he searched for his target. But there were only alarmed patrons, including one in a shawl who was obviously too frightened to look his way. None of the waitresses matched.

Then the police siren sounded. The management had called the moment the man entered with his rifle. The man hurried out before they could catch him. He had been successfully balked.

When the commotion settled down, Doris returned to her table and exchanged with the waitress. The manager appeared. "Lady, I think you just saved a life," he said tersely. "Your meal is free." He turned to the waitress. "Go home, Nellie. Wait till you're sure they've got him. Don't worry about your pay or your tip." He handed her a large denomination bill. Nellie departed gratefully.

They settled back to their untouched meal. "I'm sorry I messed up our date," she told Hunk. "I just had to act in the crisis."

"Beauty is as beauty does," he replied. "You are a fine and nervy woman."

So she had scored after all, apart from doing what she had to.

After the meal he took her home, and stayed long enough for a highly satisfying culmination. She knew she had really impressed him, in and out of bed. Then he went home. "Tomorrow you will have dinner at my house, after we tour the town."

Thus swiftly she became his open girlfriend. She had succeeded far better than expected, thanks to the restaurant incident. Soon she was living at his house, waited on by his servants, admired by his associates. She never returned to her waitressing job. She had arrived.

Then, slowly, things changed. Hunk remained attentive, but his job was demanding and he was often also out by night. The servants were invariably polite and discreet, and saw to her every physical need, but she became aware that there was something they were not telling her. There were also some rooms she could not enter. When she inquired, the servants made excuses, like delayed cleanups or broken furniture, but did not produce the necessary keys. Doris was skilled at interpreting evasions, but that did not yield answers. Mysteries really got to her; she just had to solve them.

Finally she acted. When Hunk was out, and the servants thought her safely asleep in the master bedroom and had retired themselves, she sneaked out and used a skeleton key to force the lock to one of the forbidden rooms. This one was on the third floor, where the master bedroom was. She was determined to solve the mystery, and she was not a female to be balked.

She nervously gripped her kerambit, which was an L shaped hard plastic defensive weapon a girl could use to bash a man's hand or face if she had to. Doris believed in being prepared, regardless of the situation, and knew a number of useful techniques. She opened the door, slid in, and closed it silently behind her. She did not turn on the lights; she used the flashlight built into her phone.

It was a nice enough room. There were pretty flowers by the curtained window, and a row of pictures of women. The women were not pretty; in fact some looked gaunt. But they were in decent outfits, with good makeup and nicely done hair, and smiling for the camera. But one thing was off: each had one lock of hair obviously missing. It was as if the point of the pictures was to show that one thing they had in common. This was distinctly odd.

Capacious closets contained lady outfits galore, for every size and shape of woman. These were what the pictured ladies wore. Surely finer outfits than they could afford on their own.

And a board in another section contained the hair locks, each carefully pinned below her printed name. But there were no women here, and no evidence that this room had ever been occupied by them. They had been here only for the dressing, the lock cutting, and the picture. The main mystery remained complete: what was the point? Surely not just the locks of hair on display.

Bemused, Doris quietly exited the room and made her way to the second mystery chamber, on the second floor. She used her skeleton key and phone light again, so that there could be no evidence of her visit. She was not a total novice at sneaking in or out.

This one was different. It was completely soundproofed; the quilted baffles were on floor, ceiling, and every wall. But there was no phonograph or other sound equipment; no one listened to loud music here. There did seem to be a sound recorder. Was this a recording studio? Not likely; there was only a kind of alcove with a padded chair set in a kind of plastic rim as if to prevent undue splashing. There was a drain beneath the chair. But it wasn't a shower; there was no shower nozzle above.

Doris played her light across it, peered closely, and found a faint stain as of old food on the drain guard, or—

Or blood. Now she saw that the chair was designed to clamp on arms and legs, holding them firmly in place, like the dread electric chair for executions. But why? It was not electrified.

She checked around, and found a nearby console with a flash drive. She turned it on.

It shrieked. The piercing sound of a woman screaming as hard as she could through her sobs. Doris quickly turned it off, flinching.

Now it came to her. Suppose a woman were locked into that chair, a vein of her leg pierced so that the blood poured out, and she could do nothing to stop that deadly flow? Nothing but scream, knowing that her life was draining? Until finally there was not enough blood left in her, and she went silent and expired. At which point the recording stopped.

What was the blood used for? Feeding the pretty flowers in the other room?

Doris felt sick. Maybe she was misinterpreting. She hoped so. For one thing, if women were dying here, where were the bodies? They could not simply be tossed out into the street for the garbage collector. There would be determined police investigations. The local news had nothing like that for this neighborhood; she had checked. So the story remained incomplete.

She exited the room and went to the third chamber, which was on the cellar floor. That one was spare, with no furniture. Only what looked like a well in the center. It was about four feet across, with a wide circular aluminum rim about two feet high and a smooth interior wall.

She peered into it, shining her light down inside. It showed nothing. No water, only endless depth. She fished out a penny and dropped it in. It disappeared into the darkness with no sound of landing. There seemed to be no bottom.

Where could such a featureless hole go? To the center of the planet? Hardly! It would fill in when it reached the depth where burning magma reigned. But assuming that it went that deep, what was the point? Anything descending into it would be destroyed by the magma.

Then it came to her. The bodies! Drop them in this hole, and they would never emerge. They would dissolve in the melted rock and be carried wherever it went. The perfect corpse disposal. Clean and easy and quiet.

Now the full picture came to her. Lure hungry homeless women in, feed them, prettify them for their pictures, save souvenir locks of their hair, then bleed them to death as they screamed and dump them in the disposal hole.

Yet why? Maybe because Hunk was an addict not of sex but of death. He listened to their shrieks of dying, recording them for replays, getting his jollies that way, as it seemed some warped men did. Then, their usefulness to him ended, he dumped them, literally.

Now she knew. What was she to do? She couldn't abide it, but neither could she stop it. If she even tried, she would be the next victim, lock, blood, and all. The household staff obviously knew and abetted it, covering for him. Cleaning up any evidence of the temporary presence of the doomed women. Doing the necessary paperwork to erase any indication that the women had even existed. Who would ever believe that such an outstanding man had such a nefarious secret? The staff members evidently had good lives for their loyalty.

Doris was in a quandary. Could she flee? Not likely, because she was not homeless. She had a history. Hunk's minions could soon enough locate her and disappear her. She might be more complicated to erase, as she had lived here briefly, but they surely knew how to do it. Maybe there had even been prior girlfriends who got too noisy and had to be silenced. She thought of the story of Bluebeard, the killer of six maidens, which was suddenly painfully relevant. She was the seventh maiden.

Could she stay here, pretending that she had never entered the forbidden chambers? Maybe, but there would surely be suspicion, and that would doom her. Neither could she tolerate the touch of the man hereafter, knowing his awful hidden nature. What she really needed was for this whole dreadful thing to unhappen. She made a wry grunt. Lotsa luck, there, girl.

The lights came on. "Hello Doris," Hunk said.

She almost fainted. He had caught her. Maybe he had even trapped her, waiting patiently for her to enter the three rooms and discover their dreadful secrets. He must have had a hidden closet. And prior experience.

Doris marshaled her nerve and played it cool. What else could she do? She was surely doomed, so she had nothing to lose. "And hello, Hunk. It seems I have fathomed your secret life." There was no point in pretending ignorance.

"It seems you have," he agreed. "Now you have a decision to make. Will you join my staff and support me as they do, benefiting as they do, or will you oppose me? I admit I would far prefer to have you with me, as you are the most appealing woman I have encountered."

"Thank you." She inhaled, attracting his gaze while her hand slid into her pocket to grasp the kerambit. "You seemed to be the ideal man for me. But I'm not into killing homeless women. So I'm sorry, but I must oppose you."

"I'm sorry too." He stepped toward her, reaching out to take hold of her shoulder.

She drew the kerambit and smashed the flat of the L down on his hand. Then before he could react, she reversed course and smashed the dull point of the L hard into his face, almost into an eye. It was a combination she had rehearsed many times alone, but had never actually performed before.

She danced to the side so that he was between her and the well. She shoved him forcefully while he was distracted by the pain of the blows, pushing him back against the rim so that his legs caught and he fell backwards across it. She grabbed his legs and heaved them up so that he plunged headfirst into the well. In a moment he was gone.

She paused, catching her breath and calming her pounding pulse. He had thought she would scream helplessly and try to flee? That was the point of her action, to catch him by surprise by attacking instead of cowering. Offense instead of defense. Assailant instead of victim. Ferocious change. It had worked. Fortunately.

Now she had to get out of here, with no dithering. She didn't return to her room; she went swiftly and silently directly to her car. In barely a minute she was on the night street, driving without lights, getting clear of the neighborhood and then the city.

What of the staff? They would soon enough discover that the reigning couple was missing, and figure out that one or both of them had exited via the well. They would cover up what they could, then scatter to points unknown before the scandal hit the press. The reign of Bluebeard was over. The seventh maiden had fought back.

Doris did not drive home. She went to a new city, made up a new identity, and stayed at a cheap rental place that did not inquire about backgrounds. She used only cash she had saved in case of emergency, destroying her credit card and hiding her ID cards. She was anonymous. When she thought it was halfway safe, she went for illicit memory erasure treatment.

"And that's my secret story," she told Deirdre. "I think I want to keep it that way. I don't like discovering I'm a murderess. Do you support me or oppose me?"

Her friend laughed nervously. "It was self-defense. I support you. Don't dump me in the well."

The movie ended, going into interminable credits. Aura shut it off. "I think I am not a fan of mundane movies. They're all violence or horror."

"I liked it just fine," Knife said.

"You're a weapon," Wanda said. "You don't count."

"If that girl had been carrying me, she wouldn't have had to worry about any man hurting her."

"I'm carrying you," Aura said. "But I'm not in a movie."

"Mundania is so dreary they must need such ugly stuff to relieve their boredom," Noe said. The others agreed.

They slept. In the morning they resumed mapping. Between settlements they continued to experiment with the phones. Nik and Santo succeeded in placing a call to Bluette, who was happy to chat with them. This indicated that it could reach other realms. That might be useful someday.

Meanwhile they were satisfied to tune out the movie, like cutting out a section of a diary.

Chapter 6

GHOST TOWN

They had just mapped a minor human village and a major ant hill when a petite young woman approached them. Her hair and eyes were green. "Yes, I dye my hair, in my fashion," she said when they glanced. "My boyfriend is a fan of green. I am Xenia, a local seamstress. Dresses from dress trees don't always fit perfectly, so I make them fit. That's how I get along."

"Fair enough," Noe said. She, as a girl, seemed the best one of them to interact with another young female. "I am Noe, and I am part of a Quest. These are my companions. What can we do for you, Xenia?"

"My boyfriend Gyles likes people, but they don't like him, which makes him lonely. I see you have magic carpets obviously sewn by a seamstress with way more magic than I have. My talent is to change the colors of things, such as my own hair. That helps my business, as some folk want different colored clothing. Regardless, I'd be happy to adjust all your outfits in exchange for your letting Gyles travel with you. I know he'd like that, and I know he could be useful to you too."

"There's a kicker," Anthem warned mentally. "Something weird."

"We're on a mission to map all the settlements of Xanth," Noe said. "Human, animal, and other. It consists mostly of traveling and amending our map. It can get tedious. Gyles might get bored."

"No he wouldn't."

"That kicker, again," Anthem said.

"Why don't people like him?" Aura asked.

"He's a ghost."

That set them all back. "You are dating a ghost?" Santo asked. "There must be a story there."

"A fascinating one, I'm sure," Wanda said. "I like ghosts, being ghostly myself when I am clothed with illusion."

"You don't count," Knife said. "You're an object."

"Oh? You seem to like me well enough when I dance for you."

"That's different. Then you're a stork signaling object."

Wanda sighed. "If only I could do it for real, instead of just in imagination."

Fortunately their dialogue was inaudible to Xenia.

"There is a story," the girl agreed, "but I didn't want to bore you with it."

"Bore us," Santo said. They were all getting into it now.

Xenia made a so be it gesture. "You asked for it. Gyles needed a shirt adjusted, a decade ago, and I smiled when I returned it to him, and something happened. You know how little hearts fly out when people kiss, if they're right for each other? A heart formed between us. Then we kissed, to verify it, and more hearts flew. We were in instant love. It does happen. But he was a bit older than I. In fact he was a young eighty, and I was an old fifteen. So we couldn't be open about our love; our families and friends would not have understood such a Mayhem/Dismember association. They would have thought he was too old and I was too young. We weren't. We dated secretly for five years and it was divine. He taught me everything about the physical side of love, which I hadn't known. He said that my influence took decades off his age. I loved that! His influence added years to mine. Then he faded away, or in Mundane idiom, died. But we didn't let that interfere. Death did not us part. We're still dating, secretly, kissing and holding hands in our fashion, and when I get old and fade out, I will join him as a ghost and we'll be open and happy together at last."

They considered that. "That's a rare love story," Aura said.

Xenia smiled with a rueful tinge. "There are rarer ones hereabout."

"We really don't need another member of our party," Santo said. "Not even a ghost."

Xenia teared up. "Please. He can really help you, I know he can, if you just give him a chance. His talent is to be helpful, and he still has it. He is still helping me, because he knows so much about anything."

Nik extended his clairvoyance. It hinted that the ghost could indeed be useful. "There may be a way," he said. "We have a machine."

The others looked at him blankly.

"He can be the ghost in our machine." He glanced at his hovering Genius Phone. "Machines need ghosts to be complete."

"He always did like machines," Xenia said dubiously. "He was friendly with the robots. Once one got a screw loose, and was acting crazy, but Gyles fixed it."

It was decision time. Anthem's spot survey indicated they were agreed. "Phone, give Xenia a clone," Nik said.

A virtual phone appeared in the woman's hand, startling her.

"That's a copy of a phone we share. Call your boyfriend," Nik said. "Just speak his name into the phone."

"Gyles," she said uncertainly.

"Yes, my love," his voice came from the phone, startling her so that she dropped it. But it didn't fall, being virtual. His face was on its screen, a man of a young eighty-five years, his age at death. She fetched in her nerve, thread by thread, and spoke again. "Dear, this—this person wants to speak with you."

Gyles smiled. "Sure. Talking is fun with this magic phone."

They had just verified that the Genius Phone could communicate with ghosts.

"Gyles, I am Nik Nickelpede, leader of this Quest. We are mapping all the settlements of Xanth, including the ghosts, if we can find them. You could serve as interpreter, if you care to. Simply enter the phone and be the ghost in the machine. You will then be able to talk with any of us at any time. Also with Xenia, via her clone, even if you are no longer near her physically."

The ghost didn't hesitate. He dived into the phone. "This machine is great," he told Xenia via the phone. "The best I've seen. I love it here."

"But I am obliged to warn you," Nik continued, "there may be complications in our Quest. There are hints that something unusual may occur along the way."

"I'll help you handle it," Gyles said confidently. "This is almost like living again, being able to speak aloud and being accepted by a group of living folk."

"Oh, Gyles!" Xenia breathed. "I'm so glad!" She turned to the others. "Now my shop is in town. Any clothing you want repaired—"

"No need," Santo said. "Our clothing is fine. Go home and relax. When you talk with Gyles, say 'private line,' and it will be just the two of you without the rest of us listening."

"Oh, there's no need for that," she protested. "We're not that private, at least to you."

"That's what you think, honey," Gyles said. "Private line."

His voice ceased. But they knew he was still talking to Xenia, because as she listened she blushed almost purple. But she was smiling. He might be a ghost, but he still knew how to romance a woman. In two and a half moments she turned about and headed for home, breathing deeply.

The party moved on, mapping the several settlements in the neighborhood, human, ant, termite, nickelpede, elf, and others. Then they came to the ghost town.

This was no ordinary haunted house. It was an entire ghost community that had taken over the site of a deserted town. It seemed there had been a cache of magic crystals that could enhance folk somewhat the way the ambiance of Demons did, but less so. When every crystal had been eagerly mined, the town faded out and the ghosts faded in. Spooky lights flickered in the cobwebbed windows, and spooky sounds animated the eerie air. No living person was here; ghosts were generally frightening to that kind.

"But that's just the impression of ignorant living folk," Anthem said with a downbeat chord.

"And there's something here we need," Nik said as his clairvoyance tuned in. "I don't know what, but it's here."

They listened. Now it came clearer, not moaning so much as singing, as if the wind was being harnessed to become almost tuneful.

Then Gyles spoke from the phone. "That's Dane and Rhonda. Their life story was sad. We ghosts all feel for them."

"That song," Noe said. "It seems vaguely familiar. What is it?"

"That is 'In the Gloaming.' Gloaming means twilight or dusk, in this case not the end of a day, but the end of a long life. I'll shape it into full living sound, as the phone can do what ghosts are not good at."

And from phones came the lovely melody and word:

In the gloaming, oh my darling, when the lights are dim and low
And the quiet shadows falling, softly come and softly go

When the wind is sobbing faintly with a gentle unknown woe,
Will you think of me and love me, as you did once long ago?

"Ooh," Noe murmured. "That is so *feeling*."

"And lovely." Aura agreed, her aura flickering.

Then the second verse.

In the gloaming, oh my darling, think not bitterly of me.
Though I went away in silence, left you lonely, set you free.
For my heart was crushed with longing; what had been could
never be.
It was best to leave you thus dear, best for you and best for me.

And one additional line with a variant melody:

It was best to leave you thus, best for you and best for me."

"Sometimes what is best is not what is fun," Santo said. He plainly knew.

"What happened to them?" Noe asked.

"That is more of a story, a sad one. I can animate it on the screen if you wish."

"We just saw an ugly mundane story," Santo said. "We're not sure we want more of that type."

"This a story of interrupted love. The sadness is that so much of their lives was wasted because of the interference of others. Otherwise, it's happy."

The group considered, then decided to eat and retire for the night and watch the story in the evening. In the gloaming of the day, as it were.

And in that gloaming, the two ghosts Dane and Rhonda came to them. They were disembodied souls, and bugs did not have souls, so were available to serve as temporary hosts. Nik and Anthem both found it enormously fulfilling. They remembered the difference a borrowed soul had made to the ogre in the ogre history story. Now they were coming to understand the nature of the soul more fully. It was so much more than strength. It was conscience, morality, motivation, and appreciation for existence; a person with a soul was infinitely more than one without.

Nik, joined by Dane, became him for this history, and Anthem, joined by Rhonda, became her. It was as though they were living in past times Mundania, where the couple had dwelt. Nik was now a poor weaver's son, age twenty, and Anthem was a rich heiress, age eighteen. They knew each other, as he had woven items for her father, and they both belonged to the village choral group, being the best singers there, but had never interacted closely, being in different societal classes.

Then came the party. It was a holiday free for all and everyone was there. One event was an open dance with a change partners feature. Nik found himself dancing with Anthem for a minute. He was a tall, husky, dark haired lad, and she was a shiningly platinum blonde with an hourglass figure. They strutted together, swung, smiled, and briefly kissed, per the flirtatious protocol of that particular dance; they were both good dancers too. Then it was time to change, and she was gone, and he was with another girl doing the same routine.

When the dance was done he went to the adjacent garden, bemused. That fleeting kiss had transformed his awareness of Anthem. Other girls were just girls, but what a maiden she was! His perfect partner. But of course she was leagues out of his reach. He would have to stifle his burgeoning passion.

There was a touch at his elbow. He turned to look. It was Anthem! "Did the earth move for you too?" she whispered.

She was interested in him? For answer he took her in his arms and kissed her with all the warmth he had thought to suppress. She returned it fully.

"I think we liked each other before," he said.

"Yes. But circumstances kept us apart."

After that they were a couple. They attended events regularly and held hands between times. Their love broadened and deepened. It didn't matter that they were of different social classes; they were incomplete without each other. For all their difference in status, they discovered common interests beyond dancing and music. They sang together, sometimes harmonizing, sometimes two different songs that somehow unified like two different people when done together. His favorite song was "In the Gloaming"; hers was "Long, Long Ago." There was a special joy in shared songs.

Then her father came to him one evening when he was weaving alone.

"I have other plans for my daughter," he said bluntly. "She is an attractive girl who can make an excellent economic liaison, perhaps even a royal one. She can have the kind of public prestige you could never provide. So you have a choice: marry her and let her be a humble weaver's wife, or depart for another country and set up your own business, never seeing her again, so that she can achieve her full potential."

Nik, stunned but not completely surprised, focused on a detail. "I have no money to travel, let alone establish a business. I am indeed a humble weaver."

The man produced a small bag. He opened it and poured out a handful of bright gold coins. They were worth more than Nik could fathom. Such a fortune could enable him to set up the best of shops with the best of equipment in a distant city! To become successful businessman, a dream formerly out of reach. "Would this help?" He put the coins back in the bag and set it down within easy reach. It was a tacit offer.

Nik didn't need to ponder what a negative response would mean. The man had made no threat, but he didn't need to. Nik could get anonymously waylaid. Anthem could disappear into nunnery. His options were to get out of Anthem's life positively or negatively. He really had no wider choice.

He was a realist. His romance was not to be. He picked up the bag and walked away, out of Anthem's life and his own local life. His heart was hurting, but he knew it was best for them both. Because her father had spoken truth. Nik would indeed have been a drag on her. Class was everything. This really was better for her. And, perhaps, for him. He belonged in his own, familiar class.

He became a successful weaver in another country. He met an appealing young woman, married her, had a family and a good life, for a peon. But he never forgot Anthem. In fact he knew of her, because she did marry a man with royal ancestry and became a popular socialite. Though always with a tinge of sadness in her demeanor, which actually added to her public appeal. Nik believed he knew the cause.

Decades later his wife died of natural causes. He missed her, as she had been a good woman, but not the way he still missed Anthem. His children were off and married. He turned his business over to the capable hands of his eldest son and retired.

Then he set off for his original home. He knew Anthem was now a wealthy widow. He could at least talk to her. She might curse him for leaving her, but at least there would be closure. *In the gloaming, oh my darling, think not bitterly of me . . .*

He went to her door and knocked. She opened it and stood there, beautifully aged. Her platinum hair was now gray, but she had kept her face and figure, as he had his own.

They didn't speak. Her eyes widened. She recognized him. Would she accept him, or banish him? He would have to abide by her choice. He was, after all, the one who had left her, with no provocation on her part. She would be well justified in cursing him. Yet he hoped she would forgive. The uncertainty was awful.

Surprising himself, he started singing. "In the gloaming, oh my darling, when the lights are dim and low . . ."

And she joined him, so that they sang their two songs together. She still had her voice, too.

Tell me the tales I delighted to hear, long, long ago, long long ago
Sing me the songs that to me were so dear, long long ago, long ago
Now you are come, all my grief is removed
Let me forget that so long you have roved
Let me believe that you love as you loved
Long, long ago, long ago.

In her animation she looked as she had before, long, long ago, absolutely lovely, her face shining with love.

Their impromptu duet was glorious.

Then she stepped forward, embraced him, and kissed him. "I know what happened," she murmured. "I found out when I inherited his papers, confirming what I had suspected. He forced you with the carrot and stick. I couldn't blame you. You had to go. I would far rather have you gone than dead. But I longed for your return, if it ever happened. Then I would know you felt the same."

His return had proved his constancy. He was no longer a peon but a moderately wealthy man who could now associate with her without great scandal.

They sang again, different yet together.

For my heart was crushed with longing
What had been could never be . . .
Then to all others my smile you preferred
Love, when you spoke, gave a charm to each word
Still my heart treasures the phrases I heard . . .

Then she cried. So did he. The relief was phenomenal.

They were happily together five years. Then he had a heart attack and died at age eighty-two. She was so distressed that she died too, within hours. Their ghosts, unsatisfied with the brevity of their reunion, considered options, then went to a peninsular fantasy land called Santh or Zanth, something like that, and settled in a ghost town there. But it wasn't enough. Insubstantial ghosts could not interact the way living folk did. They wanted the impossible: life together. But living humans already had souls, so were not available for more, and robots were not alive. They were stuck with unsatisfiable longing. Hence their mournful song.

Nik suffered an inspiration. "Anthem and I are bugs, but we are alive and responsible creatures, with potent talents. Suppose the two of you stay with us? Anthem and I are of different species, so can't interact the way other couples do, but we do love each other and do associate. It might be a half step for you, but better than nothing."

The ghosts considered. "Can you kiss?" Rhonda asked.

"We can touch antennae. Does that count?"

"Do it."

Anthem came across to join Nik on Santo. They touched antennae.

Suddenly they were kissing, human style. They knew, because they had done it in the dance with human bodies. Now they had their own bodies, but the effect was the same. Lips or antennae hardly mattered. There were even little hearts.

"It's the touch that counts," Rhonda said dreamily. "It's physical contact of the most sensitive parts of the body. That's what we're longing for."

"We can kiss!" Anthem cried deliriously. "We never thought of that before."

"This is wonderful," Nik agreed.

"This will do," Rhonda said. "It's vastly better than nothing. We will share with you. We will be alive again and you will have us as spirits."

"I think you are the first insects to have souls," Noe said. Because with Anthem's telepathy uniting them, and the tuning in of the phones, the whole Quest had been following their dialogue. "And yes, it was a real kiss. The touch of love."

"It was indeed," Aura agreed.

"There is something else," Nik said, sensing more than their breakthrough. "Let me extend my awareness." He extended it, and felt two other ghosts. "Clay and Octavia."

"I know them," Gyles said. "I will call them here." He made what sounded like a mournful howl. "And here they are."

"Hello Clay and Octavia," Nik said.

"Call me Tav," Octavia said via the phone. "It's less cumbersome."

"There is something about you that relates to our mission," Nik said. "We are a Quest in the process of mapping all the settlements of Xanth."

"So that's how it's spelled," Dane said. "With an X. I knew I had it wrong, but never thought of that."

"What has that to do with us?" Clay asked.

"I don't know," Nik said honestly. "But if you share your story with us, we hope to find out. There is something."

"What's in it for us?" Dane asked. He was obviously a practical type.

"You can re-live your story, sharing living human minds and bodies. In effect you'll be alive again, for a while."

"That's still not—"

"Dear," Tav said.

"a bad idea," he concluded hastily. His beloved had Spoken.

Nik and Anthem were taken. "I will be the male for the reenactment," Santo said.

"And I the female," Aura said. She glanced at Noe. "You have no objection, because it's not your story. You can observe and learn from a more objective perspective."

"So I can," Noe agreed, surprised. If Aura should succeed in evoking any romantic interest by Santo, Noe would pick up on exactly how it was done. The skit done by the two ghosts in the dance didn't count; the real Santo and Aura had not been involved. "Play it."

The ghosts joined Santo and Aura as visitors, and the living folk then, somehow, looked different. Aura remained dark haired and shapely, but assumed a youthful princess-like presence.

A picture appeared on the big phone screen. It was of a lovely young woman entering an ornate garden. She looked just a bit like Aura.

"This is Octavia," Gyles' voice came, as narrator. "She is a voluntary hostage at a neighboring kingdom. The kingdoms are at war, but have made a truce for negotiations, and have exchanged royal hostages for the duration, as safeguards against betrayal. The hostages are treated like valued visitors, and behave like them, but can't go home until negotiations are complete. Tav is the youngest of eight royal children, also the prettiest. She is just sixteen, smart, dedicated, motivated, and savvy about real life, so there is considerable interest in her hand in marriage, but for some reason her father has held off placing her. Maybe he is waiting for a better prospect. It's a mystery."

Tav paused to admire an elegant orange flower with purple highlights. "Bird of paradise," she murmured. She had an interest in gardening, especially exotic flowers.

"Hello, Princess." It was a handsome man of about twenty-five, appearing on the path ahead.

"Oh!" Surprised, she stepped back. One foot caught in a vine and she fell, her ornate slipper pulling off as her dress went askew.

The man hurried to help her. He caught hold of the vine and drew her dainty foot clear. "Fortunately you aren't injured," he said. "Let me introduce myself. I am Prince Clay, first son and heir of this kingdom. I maintain this garden as an avocation, feeling that wealth and power should not be the whole of a ruler's ambition. I'm glad you like it." Then he paused, gazing at her bare foot.

"Oh, bleep!" she said, uttering an unprincess-like word. "You have seen it. I am ruined."

"You have webbed toes," he said.

"Yes, it runs in some royal families. I refused to let them cut my feet to make them appear normal. My father the King said I would regret it, but he did not force me to take the cut. He was right; my foolishness has just undone his plan to have me charm and seduce you and merge our kingdoms so the war would end." She wiped her face with a royal hankie, as she was crying with disappointment. "Bleep!"

Clay silently let go of her foot and sat down on the ground. He pulled off one boot, exposing his own foot.

Tav stared. "You have webbed toes!"

"As you pointed out, it runs in some royal families. We surely have distant common ancestry. I, too, declined to mutilate my feet. I, too, feared mischief therefrom. What royal maiden would want deformed toes in bed with her? I wonder if your father knew?"

"I strongly suspect he did. He is one canny sovereign. I like to think I take after him. So you are not repulsed, I suspect."

He smiled. "I am not. In fact I am gratified. I confess that when I cleared that vine I saw more of your leg than your foot, and it gave me a masculine idea. If you remain interested in seducing me, you have an excellent chance of succeeding."

"I remain more than interested," she said, relieved. "Here, or in bed?"

"Here. I feel urgent. Our clothes are already messed up,"

"Here," she agreed, removing the rest of her clothing. So did he.

They kissed and had at it, each more interested than the other. The Adult Conspiracy fogged out the details, just in case there was a child or maiden aunt in the vicinity, but it was clear that more than feet were active.

In time they rested, each breathing pleasantly hard. "We will marry, of course," Tav said.

"Of course," Clay agreed. "Soon." They kissed again, then made their way back into the palace. If any servants happened to be watching, they discreetly faded out.

"We shall have to make up a suitable story of our formal meeting and falling into virginal love," Tav said as they bathed together to clear the last of the dirt.

"We shall indeed," he agreed, his gaze locked on her wetly glistening body somewhere below the head. Maybe there was a speck of dirt remaining there to be cleaned off.

"Perhaps you kissed my hand."

"And savored your smile."

She laughed. “That’s the first time I’ve heard that action described that way.”

“I would be happy to have more of it.”

“Oh? Will this do?” Then she sat on his lap in the water, twisted around to kiss him once more, lifted her leg, and the scene got fogged out again. Why should the Conspiracy care that they were helping each other wash? They were obviously doing a very thorough job of it. Feet, oddly, were never mentioned, though they plainly needed cleaning too.

“Soon” turned out to be an understatement for the timing of their wedding. The ceremony was barely over before they adjourned for more hand kissing and smile savoring. Folk were amazed by the constancy of their caring for each other, considering that everyone knew it was an arranged marriage for political expediency. He had no harem, no mistresses and she had no secret lovers. The palace staff would have known. They seemed to be mutually satisfied to keep constant company with each other. That was almost unheard of in royal relations.

Surprisingly, the stork brought their first baby so soon it must have been an expedited delivery. Normally it took at least nine months for the Stork Works to get its act together; it was notoriously inefficient. Other babies followed rapidly. It was apparent that Octavia, the eighth child in her family, was set to have at least that many children, and in fewer than eight years. They were to be seen all over the palace, wearing their closely fitting slippers. There were no bare feet to be viewed. Maybe the tykes had tender toes in need of protection from the elements or floor splinters. The palace staff was determinedly silent on the topic.

In due course, Clay ascended to the throne of the merged kingdoms, accompanied closely by his lovely and discerning wife, and a golden age of peace, prosperity and gardening commenced.

Then something unpleasant happened. Zombies appeared in several regions, sliming fences, sickening dogs, and scaring children. When soldiers tried to brush them back with swords, they just sliced apart, spreading stinking rot across the ground.

Clay and Tav got on the case in a hurry, as they were not fans of rotten folk and did not like to see gardens get slimed. They traced the source to what appeared to be a portal to another universe. They got this sealed off, physically and magically, and the influx ceased. Then they got the zombies picked up by rented garbage robots and buried them so deep it would take them decades to dig out, if they even tried. The siege was over. They did not advertise this awkward incident, as it might have reflected adversely on an otherwise splendid society and affected tourism negatively.

"I wonder how it would be to make love to a zombie woman," Clay said teasingly as they retired for the night.

"Not much fun," Tav said. "If you kissed her frontside, her cones would fall off and go splat! on the floor. The same for her backside."

"And you'd have similar trouble with a zombie man. His apparatus would break off and leave rot on or in you."

"Yuck! We'd better settle for our own equipment,"

"Maybe we should try it out now, to be sure we have no zombie infection."

"Good idea."

They did, vigorously, several times, and concluded that there was no rot. That was a relief.

There were other challenges, as were inevitable in governance, but they handled them. Eventually they got old. They retired, turning the kingdom over to their competent children, and finally faded out. Their spirits did not go to heaven, but lingered together in the vicinity, as they were not sure how much interpersonal loving actually occurred in Heaven. They took up residence in the nearby ghost town, where there were kindred spirits.

"That was a nice reliving," Tav said.

"But we weren't quite satisfied," Clay concluded. "It's as if we left something unfinished. We're not sure what, but we can't rest until it is."

"I may have a notion," Aura said, speaking for herself now that the history had been concluded. "I once kissed a zombie giant, and became zombified myself. I am over that now, but my powered kisses still zombify men. I wonder whether that giant could have come from that other universe, via your portal, escaped your kingdom, and come to make mischief at the Queendom of Thanx? He did seem to have unusual magic. That could explain some things."

Nik's talent twinged. "That could indeed. We can't be sure that all the zombies were eliminated."

"We were lucky we caught the invasion early," Clay said. "But it might occur again elsewhere. There could be other portals."

"So there could," Nik agreed. So did his clairvoyance. That could be the message in this interview.

Then something odd happened. "A Demon approaches," Gyles said. "The phone picked up the waves in the fabric of the universe. A powerful one."

Nik was surprised. "The universe has waves?"

Now Andromeda's confirming impression came. It did have waves. The motion of Demons caused them.

"A capital D Demon?" Anthem asked with a chord of surprise. "Which one?"

"The Demon Chaos," Squid said as she appeared before them. Then she introduced herself. "Hello, Quest. I am Squid, an alien cuttlefish who identifies as a human girl, from a future alternate timeline. I have essential news for you, and for the four Demons who accompany you."

"You know about the Demons?" Nik asked. The Demons, as observers, had been careful not to advertise their presence.

"I am the mortal girlfriend of the Demon Chaos, who is maybe the second strongest Demon in the universe. He knows things. He brought me here together with my father, who is a ghost from the future." She blinked away a tear. "He must tell you his story."

"Hello, Quest," the phones said. "I am Cuttle, Squid's father, now a ghost. My daughter and her friend, the Demon Chaos, have enabled me to come here and speak to you about a matter of pressing importance. In my natural state I look like this." The screen showed a creature with eight tentacles and two facial appendages, as well as two large eyes. Its hide rippled with colors. "I brought my family to visit a tourist world fifty years in the future, for fun and learning. We assumed human forms so as not to startle the natives unduly, as is common practice. This is my human simulation." The creature shifted colors and shape, the tentacles pairing off to become four limbs and the appendages became a human head. The colors blended into a face and clothing. Now he looked like a man. "Before I continue, are there questions?"

Santo spoke. "You said fifty years in the future. I come from that time, and so does my sibling Squid. But you may want to clarify for the others how you can be here, even as a ghost, since true time travel is known to be awkward because of potential paradox."

"I will answer that," Squid said. "Two wonderful women, a Demoness and a mortal, traveled across multiple frames to rescue five children, two of which were Santo and me. This was not exactly time travel. There are perhaps an infinite number of alternate frames of reality, like ridges in the sand of a desert, each very slightly different from its closest neighbors. One difference is time. One will be perhaps a second behind this frame of ours, here and now, while another is a second ahead. The farther you go, the greater the details diverge, until one can be, well, fifty years ahead of us. Thus it seems like our future, but it's not, exactly. It's a parallel realm that resembles our likely future. So when we five children were brought here, saving our lives from the destruction of our world, we were not traveling backward in time, but across similar tracks. We were adopted by local-frame families, and have done well enough. We are not actually related, but regard ourselves as siblings because of our common origin." She smiled at Santo. "I love you, brother, though you are a Magician and I am an alien creature." She morphed briefly into her natural form, that of a land-going cuttlefish.

"And I love you, sister," Santo said with feeling Nik had not seen in him before. He really did love her, regardless of her nature. That just might bode well for his association with Noe. "I am glad to see you here."

Squid turned her gaze to her father. "Back to you, daddy."

"Thank you, angel fish." Cuttle said. "And I thank you too, Demon Chaos, for bringing us here. Without your help, I could not have addressed this Quest."

A human face appeared in the air next to the screen, vibrating with hidden power. "What you have to say is important." It faded out.

Nik could feel the awareness of the four Demons with the Quest. This was not their doing, and they were intensely interested. They knew that the Demon Chaos was not doing this as a stunt. He cared about their world, because he cared about his mortal girlfriend, and exerted his colossal power on her behalf. The Demons knew that.

"With the formalities out of the way, here is my history," Cuttle said. "We thought our visit was merely entertainment, an unusual diversion. The odd human worlds were remarkably distinct from the norm, especially those with magic.

"Then it changed. We did not tell our child the larger situation, we just put her on a cable car to safety and hoped for the best. She, at least, might be saved. Then we faced the awful reality. This world was suffering an invasion by alien zombies. They had so disrupted communications and travel that we were unable to escape. We had to face the horror of it with the natives. It seemed that the zombies could not be fought off. Their very touch was lethal, because it conveyed a virus that infected living flesh and slowly converted it to zombie rot. Any bite or scratch sufficed, and they seemed determined to do exactly that. The only safe course was to avoid them.

"But they were everywhere. My wife tripped and fell, and a zombie bit her ankle." He smiled briefly. "She was emulating the human form, as I was. It didn't matter. The virus infected her skin, and she started to rot. I sought to help her, but she waved me off. 'Get away from me, my love,' she cried. 'Now my touch will infect you. Save yourself.' I tried to argue, but she threw herself into cuttlefish suffocation mode and perished."

Nik saw Squid freeze. It seemed she had not known this detail. Her mother was dead.

"Her spirit went straight to our Heaven, as she was and had always been a good creature. At least I knew she would be reasonably happy there. I expected to join her there in due course, endlessly chasing and eating tasty fish.

"And so I found myself alone, fleeing the zombies, as were the humans and other visitors. But I had one resource they did not: I went to the nearest harbor, flung myself into the sea and reverted to my natural form. There, the zombies could not catch me; the salty water would have washed out their gruesome animation. I swam to an island and rested there, mourning my wife and hoping for my daughter. But in a few days the zombies crossed the water in boats, coming to claim me. I dove back into the sea and swam for another island. But as I shaped my tentacles into legs and walked on it, a zombie rose out of a pit where it had been hiding and scratched my leg. Leg or tentacle, it didn't matter; I was infected, and doomed. So I went into suffocation mode myself, and died there, rather than slowly rot to pieces.

"But my spirit remained restless. I did not go immediately to Heaven to join my wife; that had to wait on other business. I needed to learn more about the zombie invasion, and inform others, in other lands, so that they could perhaps prepare themselves for defense. I flew around the planet, zeroing in on the source, and located it. It was an aperture to another universe. Not another track in this one, but a completely different realm. I was amazed. They had found a portal between the universes and used it to stage their invasion. Our entire universe was in peril.

"But there was another problem. I was now a ghost, and living folk could not see or hear me, and if any did, they would likely abhor me. How could I get my warning out? I was immured in limbo, unable to complete my self-imposed mission, but unwilling to go to heaven until I did. So I lingered unhappily, stymied."

Then he smiled. "Until my wonderful daughter found me. Now at last I have given the warning. Beware the zombie invasion! It is surely coming here. You must locate the portal before they do, and seal it, or there will surely be disaster."

Clay appeared on the screen. "There surely will. We saw it in our kingdom, and stopped it, but who can guarantee that is the only such portal? We need to be sure."

"You have not addressed one key question," Santo said. "Why? Why are the zombies, who have rotten brains pretty much by definition, invading another universe? Their normal course should be to decay away in peace, as normal zombies do. Even thinking is a sickening effort for them, let alone acting. Zombies simply are not the conquering type."

"Amen," Aura said.

"I learned that answer in the course of my investigation," Cuttle said. "These are not ordinary zombies, but a slightly different type; they have been imbued with the need to eliminate normal living creatures. That is why they attack and scratch or bite or get into food so that living folk take them in when they eat. My guess, based on a decade of unpleasant observation, is that some power, possibly a Magician or Demon of zombieism, made that change. Living folk live because of their instinct of self-preservation; they *care* about living. These zombies have been made to care about their own survival and that of their type. They know that some living folk have found a way to nullify their state. So they must eliminate the living folk before the living folk eliminate them. Only by accomplishing that, throughout the universe, can they finally rot in peace."

"Or in pieces," Aura said, not smiling.

"As long as any zombie exists, you are in mortal peril," Cuttle concluded. "You must eliminate them all, throughout the universe, or living life is doomed."

They digested that. Suddenly their mission was far more than mapping living settlements. It was saving life itself.

"Thank you, Cuttle," Nik said. "We shall take this most seriously." It was coming clear to him why the Demon of Puns was so important. Puns destroyed zombies.

Amen, Demoness Andromeda quietly agreed.

"I leave it in your hands, Quest and Demons," Cuttle said. "You are the ones who can stop it, if anyone can. Now at last I feel free to rejoin my dear wife."

"Bye, Daddy!" Squid called tearfully as the ghost faded out. Then she and Chaos faded out too, returning to their normal business, whatever and wherever that might be.

What a visit that had been! But now it was their problem. How were they to handle the likely zombie invasion? The universe itself might be at stake. Yes, they had the knowledge of puns as a crucial weapon, and they had the Demon of Puns along. But the universe was huge, and the source of the revised zombies was in another universe. That made just the attempt an awful challenge, even with Demon help. Where could they possibly start?

"The map," Aura said. "That marked place. That must be the portal to our version of reality."

That seemed likely. Nik checked the map. That was their next stop.

Anthem surveyed the prevailing mood. All the members of the Quest agreed. They would tackle the zombie threat. For whatever little that might be worth, considering the magnitude of the challenge.

Chapter 7

ALTERNATES

In the morning they moved on from the ghost town, mapping incidental settlements and getting to know their new companions. All of them halfway dreaded their critical next stop, so they avoided the subject as they traveled. Gyles chatted with Santo, Noe, Aura, Wanda, Knife, and the two centaurs, while Nik and Anthem got to know their companion spirits.

"It may be irrelevant to your mission," Dane said. "But when we came to Xanth and learned that living folk have magic talents, we were intrigued. We wondered if ghosts can have talents."

"It is my understanding that some talents attach to the body, and some to the soul," Nik said. "So yes, since ghosts are spirits, they can have talents too. They inherit the talents of their prior living selves, if the attachment is right."

"That was our conclusion," Rhonda said. They were in a compatible four-way dialogue. "But we were mundane ghosts, so inherited no talents. But we learned that living mundanes who come to Zanth, I mean Xanth, can develop talents in the ambiance of its magic. So we wandered if ghosts could do the same."

Anthem considered. "If some talents attach to the souls, then maybe ghosts can do it. It makes sense."

"I understand that the Dwarf Demon of Talents makes them and distributes them to the Stork Works for newly ordered babies," Nik said. "Once he got behind, and all new babies got the same talent."

"We didn't know about that," Rhonda said. "We bypassed that system by doing it ourselves."

"So we tried," Dane said. "We selected simple talents and focused, trying to make them our own. And we may have succeeded, though we aren't sure. They are sort of weak."

"What talents did you try for?" Nik asked, interested.

"I tried for dropping the other shoe," Rhonda said. "But living folk seldom drop the first shoe, so I couldn't try to make the second one drop. When it did happen, we couldn't be sure it wouldn't have dropped anyway."

"And I tried for scaring the living daylights out of people," Dane said. "But just the sight of a ghost can do that, so it could be coincidence."

"It could be," Nik agreed. "It might also be that your association with living creatures would enhance it. Especially being with us."

"Why is that?"

"As you now know, we are traveling with four Demons. They try to remain in the background, observing, but their ambiance tends to enhance our qualities, physical, mental, and talental. It might enhance yours too, now that you are with us."

"That intrigues me," Dane said. "I wonder if we could test it."

"Try to scare something. That passing tree, for example."

"Boo!" Dane yelled at the tree.

The tree drew back its branches in attitude of petrification.

"I think it's teasing me," Dane said. "It picked up our dialogue."

"Let me try," Rhonda said. "Mine has to make a physical sound, so teasing won't work."

"Try it, dear."

"Somebody drop a shoe."

Noe took off one of her slippers and dropped it on the carpet with a faint clatter. There was a pause of most of a moment. Then there was a clunk, as of a boot landing hard. "Ouch!" Noe exclaimed. "That yanked my whole leg!"

It seemed the talents were working.

"Will they work if we change hosts?" Rhonda asked, pleased.

"Let's try it," Dane said.

Nik felt an intangible withdrawal as his spirit departed. Then a fulfillment as the other spirit arrived. "Hello, Rhonda," he said.

"Hello, Nik," she replied with a nice little kiss on the top of his brain. Her female presence suffused him. He loved it.

"I'd be jealous," Anthem said with a downbeat chord. "If I didn't feel the same way about Dane's male presence."

"This is maybe out of turn," Nik said. "But could we kiss each other, as we did before? To see what feels like, reversed?"

"I'm curious too," Anthem said.

Noe brought her over, and she joined him again. They touched antennae. They kissed.

The result was weirdly phenomenal. In one way it felt like their prior antenna kiss. In another, it was oddly softer and sweeter, a kind of yielding power. He liked it, but didn't understand it.

"Females stoop to conquer," Rhonda explained. "Males only think they are in control. Now you know."

"That was some experience," Anthem said.

"I agree," Dane said. "Let's do it again."

They all laughed. Then they kissed again. It was just as wonderfully strange as before.

Then they returned to the testing of talents. This time Santo dropped a shoe on the carpet, and kicked his other foot wildly as the other shoe tore off and fell.

They passed a snoozing ogre. "Boo!" Dane yelled from his spot with Anthem.

The ogre jolted awake, then charged away, terrified. That left them all staring, as ogres were notorious for scaring rather than being scared. They were too stupid to get scared. Until this moment.

Yes, the talents worked.

"We should return to our proper hosts," Rhonda said.

"Do you have to?" Nik asked. "I really like your presence. There's something, well, comfortable about it."

"Your companion and mine might object."

"Speak for yourselves," Anthem said. "We like this mixed association too. It's as if we are for the first time complete, emotionally. It confirms what I feel with my telepathy: each person is a composite of male and female aspects, with one or the other gender dominating. We think of ourselves as one or the other, but that's only approximately true."

"Let's let it be, for now," Rhonda said. "It is enlightening to tune on the feelings of the opposite gender, regardless. It will surely help us relate, in future." She smiled, mentally. "I do indeed feel complete in a way I never did before."

"Me too," Nik agreed.

"We all do," Dane agreed.

It seemed that they had accomplished more than the verification of talents. They were coming to understand each other in new and better ways.

They came, if not in due course, some other course, to the spot on the map. It was just a very slightly discolored patch of air hovering slightly above the ground. Of course a portal to another universe didn't have to rest firmly on the ground. Around it sat three zombies and a living boy.

Nik's clairvoyance and Anthem's telepathy cried alarm together. The Quest halted, then backed off before the zombies and boy spied them.

"Two things," Santo said. "The portal is guarded. The zombies have living collaborators."

"Traitors," Aura said angrily.

"Or hostages," Dane said. "Like the other ghost romance we shared, where a hostage fell in love with her nominal captor."

Noe nodded. "If the zombies made a deal to spare that boy's family, he'd cooperate. That's not the same thing as traitoring."

"So what do we do?" Santo asked. "We could take out the zombies with makeshift pun bombs, but more would come through the portal. If we block that, they'll know we know and turn on us."

"I think we need to stop the invasion at its source," Aura said. "But a surprise attack would be best. That means we can't use that portal."

"But how can we get through, without a portal?" Noe asked.

Now Gyles spoke. "Two things, as Santo put it. There are many portals, and we ghosts can find them and pass through them. We generally don't, because living folk on the other sides are just as spooked about ghosts as the ones here. But there is another avenue. Santo makes tunnels to anywhere. He doesn't need a natural portal. He can make one to another universe."

"He can?" Aura asked.

"I believe I can," Santo said. "Now that I know that other universes exist. If I know exactly where to drill."

"We ghosts can tell you that. We can go through the existing one unobserved, scope out the terrain, and give exact coordinates."

"True," Rhonda said.

Nik's enhanced clairvoyance focused on an intangible aspect. "I think it's time for a Quest conference," he said. "We are considering entering not merely another village or forest or even parallel track, but another universe. Some of us did not even know that alternate universes existed. We need to consider all the aspects we can. This is not just mapping Xanth, it is trying to save it from ugly destruction."

"Along with the universe," Anthem agreed.

Dane chuckled without mirth. "I did not expect the gloaming to be infested with aggressive zombies."

"Or populated with highly talented bugs," Rhonda agreed. "Anthem's telepathy is a marvel to me. I can feel the life force of every living member of the Quest, and a couple of nonliving members."

"Thank you," Wanda said. "Some of us are conscious and feeling despite being unalive. Magic makes us possible."

Shameless Centaur spoke. "As you know, my talent is bringing folk what they want, but isn't good for them. My companion's is to give people what they don't want. I think our talents are merging on this matter. Here is our question: is it time to invite our four Demons to move from mere observation to open participation? They are conscious and feeling despite being unalive, as are the bugs, only rather more powerful, to say the least. Because they are as much affected by the interaction of universes as we are, and have as much to lose as we do. Namely, the continued existence of reality as we know it."

"I will speak for Bang and myself," Andromeda said via the phone, her image on the screen a constantly changing human female face. The features ranged from fair to ugly, and the hair from black to blue to green to pink to plaid, from a massive bun to sinuously curving locks. She was after all the Demoness of Change. "What threatens is a change not of our making or desiring. We need to visit the other universe to discover why it is sending these zombies here. Are we considered a dumping place for creatures they don't want, such as zombies, or is it an actual invasion using expendable troops? We need information before we can act. It is best to conceal both our visit and the involvement of Demons, so we will continue quiescent for now. But when the need arises, we will act openly. We thank you for your continued discretion." The face faded out.

There it was. The Demons were very much in the picture, but required continued anonymity. “We can tunnel to the other universe,” Nik said. “But where in that frame? My sensing is that it is very similar to our home universe, in the manner of the parallel tracks of Xanth Santo and Squid have visited or escaped, but not identical.”

“Could there be parallel versions of ourselves?” Anthem asked. “As also in the manner of the tracks. If so, those other selves might have relevant advice. They would not be our enemies.”

Santo smiled grimly. “Perhaps there is a parallel me who is attracted to women. Noe would like that.”

“Now cut that out!” Noe flared. “You’re the one I want, as you are, not a clone, even if you aren’t available.”

“It would be as likely to find a parallel Noe who orients on women,” Aura said. “Anything is possible. But I suspect that parallels to us will have similar orientations and attitudes to ours.”

“Another question,” Shameful said. “Will they be zombies?”

All of them froze in horror. The centaur, per her talent, had given them the thought they didn’t want. “A zombie universe!” Noe whispered, shuddering.

“We need to be prepared for that,” Nik said. “It would explain much.”

“Such as why they are coming here,” Shameful said. “Their bodies will not last long, so to continue their kind, they need a supply of fresh living bodies to infect. Their way of reproduction.”

“That’s an alternate to the theory that their purpose is simply the destruction of life,” Shameful said. “Either way it’s bad news for us.”

“If they are parallel to us, but zombified,” Shameless said, “we have the means to cure them. Demon Pun is in our camp, by no coincidence.”

Demon Pun remained silent, per the Demon policy, though he surely agreed.

“But until we get to those other selves,” Aura said, “we may need to mask ourselves as zombies, to avoid attracting attention as intruders.”

“How can we do that?” Noe asked. She grimaced. “Smear rot all over us?”

Now Wanda spoke. “My magic is to be able to float my core wand where I choose, and clothe it with illusion to make me appear human. The enhancement provided by the Demon ambiance affects me too. I can make Knife assume the semblance of a living man, and I could give all of you the semblance of zombies.”

"Let's hope there is no need," Aura said with a mental shudder.

"Allow us ghosts to investigate," Gyles said on the screen. "Ghosts are souls deprived of our bodies. Our separation has enabled us to travel in a manner normal souls can't. We can pop through the existing portal without being observed, look about, and return promptly to report."

"Do it!" Nik said gratefully.

He felt the departure of Rhonda, saddening him. He felt incomplete.

"Me too," Anthem said. "Now that we have experienced living with souls, we feel empty without them."

"But what they are doing is invaluable."

"It is."

Fortunately the absence was not long. In barely three moments Rhonda was back. "Bad news. It is indeed a zombie universe. Even the Demons, it appears."

They felt the horror of the Demons. Indeed, they were no longer just observers.

"Then when we go, Wanda," Nik said, "make us resemble early zombies. Not too much rot." Then he thought of something else. "The local folk—are they us? On our Quest?"

"No," Gyles said from the screen. "There was no sign of them here, or of any Quest. We think the zombie crisis preempted any such project."

Nik wasn't sure what to make of that. Why indeed mount a mapping mission when all settlements would soon be piles of rot? But then how were they to find their counterparts?

"I can make a tunnel to the vicinity of your home mound," Santo suggested. "Or Anthem's anthill. Or any of the others. So you can investigate."

"That makes sense," Nik said. "Anthem and I did not live far apart, though we did not know each other. Both are in the Queendom of Thanx. One tunnel to the general vicinity could enable us both to check."

"And we ghosts can facilitate the checking," Gyles said.

They decided to spend the night in the home universe, then tackle the zombie universe next day. None of them were too confident. Not even the Demons.

In the morning they located a suitably private glade in a dense copse on a river island. Sell fish swam in the water there, perpetually trying to make deals that benefited only themselves, so nobody much liked the area. In fact the river constantly groaned. They set up a temporary camp, the ghosts explored, and Santo made a tunnel to a private section of the queendom in the zombie universe, verifying that he could do it. Wanda made them all look slightly zombiefied, and the Demon Pun armed them with puns. They did not try to contact Zombie Queen Demesne there, for the sake of their privacy, but settled down to wait on the investigation.

"Um, a thought," Aura said. "Are there ghost alignments too? Do our ghosts have opposite numbers?"

"Oh, I like you," Gyles said. "If I didn't already have a living girlfriend, I'd want you. We need to check the ghost town right now."

"Um, thank you," Aura said with an amused flicker of her aura. "But you're a bit old for me."

"Dane and I are old too," Rhonda said. "But age doesn't matter much to ghosts."

It certainly didn't, Nik thought. Rhonda was ageless in her gloaming.

All three ghosts vanished, popping off to check their opposites. In half a moment, plus a couple of instants, they were back. "They are there," Gyles reported. "They are not infected, of course, but hate what they see among the living folk. They want to help. Dane and Rhonda want to tag along, hoping they can find hosts like ours."

"Why not," Nik said. "If my spirit is amenable." Dane was now back with him.

"Hello, clone," the new Dane said.

"Hello," Dane said. "Sure, come along."

Meanwhile the two Rhonda ghosts were similarly meeting and getting along.

"I'm almost sorry I don't have a ghost," Aura said.

"Hello Aura. I am Gyles clone. I don't have a machine to occupy. I'll be happy to accompany you for the nonce. I can't be your soul as you already have one, but I can tag along with yours."

Aura laughed. "I'm sure the two of you ghost souls will get along. Just don't flirt up such a storm that Xenia gets jealous. She'd change your color from invisible to polka dot."

"She would," he agreed.

Then Noe carried Nik and Anthem, together with their ghosts, to

Anthem's anthill. Noe had her enhanced obscurity on max, so that others could see her but not notice her. She squatted near the hill and extended her arm to let them drop to the ground and approach the entrance to Anthem's cell, where the ghosts had ascertained she was at this moment. Indeed, her telepathy was centered there, though the fully living Anthem could tell that zombie Anthem was not nearly up to par. Nik waited in a patch of weeds while Anthem entered the structure. Her telepathy kept him informed.

She came in sight of her zombie self. "Hello, Anthem," she said mentally. "I am yourself from a different universe. We need to converse."

"I am hardly up tzo converzing," the zombie replied with a rotten accent. "Go away."

It was time for a stronger measure. The Zombie Anthem, whom Anthem now thought of as Z, needed to be cured. "Have you heard about the blood vessel?"

"About the whaz?" Z asked dully.

"It's made of blood, or it sails on blood."

Z groaned. "That's an awful pun! Go farther away." But her coating of rot was flaking off, and her accent was fading.

"Look at yourself," Anthem ordered with a strong mental nudge.

Z did. "The rot is gone!"

"You are so longer a zombie. The pun cured you."

Z-nulled, now ZN, was amazed. "It did? But some fog remains in my mind."

Anthem tried another dose. "Have you ever raided a human kitchen and tasted a bun? If the pun is the lowest form of humor, the bun is the lowest form of bread."

ZN groaned again. "That's awful!" Her mind had cleared. "But I do seem to be fully alive again."

"You are. But don't advertise it, because the zombies might attack you so as to make you one of them again."

"I won't," ZN agreed, scraping up some mud to dirty her body so that it looked halfway rotten. "I feel so much better now!" She focused on Anthem. "But you are a zombie yourself. How can you function well?"

"I am not a zombie. Check my mind to verify its clarity. I am merely clothed with illusion to make me resemble a zombie ant. So I can go among the zombies without attracting attention."

ZN's attention focused further. "You say you are me, from another universe? Your mind verifies it, but how can that be?"

"The zombies are raiding my universe, or at least preparing to. A small party of us came to your universe to find out why."

"They are merely extending their conquest of this universe," ZN said. "They came through a portal, with us unaware, and soon converted all of us to their state. All it takes is a bite or scratch or even some infected food. We did not know that puns could reverse it. We abhor puns. Had we but known, we might have averted disaster."

"We learned recently," Anthem said. "It seems that the appreciation of puns requires some ability to comprehend verbal wit, and full zombies lack that ability, having rotten minds. So early converts still have that power, as their brains have not yet decayed far. I caught you in time."

"I am glad you did! But I am only one ant in a universe. I can't reverse all the others, even if they were fresh enough, even if I knew more puns,"

"True. But my party has stronger methods. We will help your universe if we can. But we need more information. You say the zombie invasion came from another universe, a third one? How many universes are there?"

"We don't know, but we think there are a considerable number. The plague must have originated in one of them and is spreading to others. We don't know why."

Anthem pondered, and decided to do something else. "Do you have a love life?"

"Me? I'm an ant. Ants don't have loves."

"I do. Only he's not an ant. He's a nickelpede."

ZN was astonished. "A nickelpede! How could such a thing happen? They're a completely different species of bug. We hardly ever interact, as they are mostly hunters and we are mostly gatherers. Our sizes differ too. One nickelpede might weigh as much as a hundred ants."

"They are different." Anthem agreed. "But not all nickpedes are alike, just as not all fire ants are alike. You and I differ from other ants in that we have the talent of telepathy. I encountered a nickelpede who has the talent of clairvoyance. We are working together, we appreciate each other's talents and personalities, and we fell in love. We can't consummate, at least not without an accommodation spell, but can and do adore each other. Would you like to meet the equivalent nickelpede in this universe? You might love him too."

ZN considered, interested. "What does love feel like?"

Anthem focused on Nik, letting her love range free.

"Oh my flickering flame!" ZN exclaimed. "I read minds, but never really picked up on this aspect. It was just a mental bypath. I am intrigued beyond measure. Yes, I would like to meet him."

"Then come with me." Then Anthem hesitated as another thought paused her. "One other thing. Would you like to have a soul?"

"A soul? Ants don't have souls."

"They can if a soul is interested."

"What does a soul feel like?"

"Rhonda clone?" Anthem asked mentally.

"Got it."

There was a scant third of a pause. "Oh my yes!" ZA breathed, which was interesting because ants didn't breathe. "My existence has been transformed. What a beautiful melody. I never appreciated music before, beyond simple chords."

Anthem heard "Long, Long Ago" playing in the background. Rhonda was doing her thing. It was working out.

"It is," Dane agreed. "I hope it does for me too."

They departed the cell and the hill. They joined Nik physically, as they had mentally. He was bemused to encounter two Anthem Ants in person, but knew their minds apart. "Hello, Anthem and ZN," he said formally.

"Hello, Nik," they chimed together. Then they got on his back, and he took them to Noe, where there were more introductions, making formal what they already knew mentally. Then Noe took them to the nickelpede mound.

Nicholas had a separate cell, because of his special talent, as did Nik, so avoiding other nickelpedes was not a problem. Anthem stayed with Noe separately, while Nik carried the clones, ant and ghost, to that cell. ZA now served as his contact with Noe and Anthem.

"I never dreamed of having an other-species boyfriend," she told him. "Of course ants don't dream, but you know what I mean." Her mental touch was very like Anthem's, but half a smidgen different. Absolutely feminine, however.

"I do," he agreed. "Nickelpedes don't dream either, but I learned of it when Anthem connected me to a human mind."

"If this universe's Nik is like you, I know I'll want to be with him."

Nik was flattered. "He surely is."

"I never ever thought to have a soul, either. But now that I have one, I want never to be without it. Rhonda has such a history!"

"She does," he agreed. "It was awful for her to lose her lover so mysteriously."

"Awful for him too. But he had to go. At least now they are back together."

"As ghosts and bugs."

"Love is clearly beyond life or species."

"True," he agreed.

They were at the cell. Nik clicked a claw in the standard nickelpede greeting, then entered. "Hello Nik."

The zombie nickelpede stared back at him. "You look like me. Or has my brain gone another stage skew?"

"You are not hallucinating," Nik reassured him. "I am yourself from another universe. I come to cure you, give you a fire ant girlfriend, and a soul."

The other would have laughed, if nickelpedes had any humor. "Now I know I've lost my mind."

"No. I will demonstrate." He selected a pun from the collection Pun had given him. "Have you ever tried drinking expresso? It makes a creature uncommonly good at reading expressions."

Zombie Nik groaned as the rot flaked off. "Have you come to torment me with abysmal puns as well as nonsensical dreams?"

"Look at your pincers."

ZN looked. "They're clean!"

"Because puns are inimical to zombieism."

"And my mind is clear again. Very well, I will try another pinch. What's this about an other species girlfriend?"

Now ZA spoke in both their minds. "I am the former Zombie Anthem Fire Ant. This other universe visitor cured me with awful puns, just as he is curing you. Puns and zombies can't co-exist. His girlfriend is my other universe clone, with the same talent of telepathy. They can't connect romantically physically, but they respect each other's talents and love each other emotionally. You and I can be the same, if you wish."

"My mind is clearing, but this remains apparent nonsense."

"I will kiss you. Put your antennae to mine." Nik put a pincer forward, carrying her on it, so she could come within range.

"If that's what it takes to abolish this bunk, I will do it." The other nickelpede lowered his antennae to touch hers. The two creatures were of far different sizes, but their antennae could make contact.

There was a phantom spark. A little heart floated up from their point of connection.

"I am undone," ZN said, amazed.

"No. you are in love. You will get used to it. Give me your hand."

He slowly extended a pincer. ZA stepped across to it, then walked up his leg to his back. "Now the soul," she said. "Brace yourself; this will impact you worse."

"Now," the local Dane said, taking off.

"Oh my yes," ZN breathed, exactly as ZA had, considering that nickelpedes didn't breathe either. He turned to Nik. "You have not merely cured me. You have utterly changed me. Now my life has meaning it lacked before, on so many levels. There is even music. How can we help you?"

Nik was gratified. "For now, just relax and get to know your new companions. We have other zombies to convert. Then we may have a living enclave here in the zombie universe. Then we'll see about the next stage."

"But—"

"Dear," ZA said, with a melodic chord.

"But this will do, for now," ZN concluded. Marvelous new love had plainly overwhelmed him.

"I will always know where my otherverse clone is," ZA said. "We'll be in touch. Now we have wonderful new histories and emotions to explore."

Nik left them to their discoveries. He knew exactly how it was.

He returned to Noe and Anthem. "We know," Anthem said. "We were attuned."

"We seem to have two for two," Noe said with satisfaction as she stood and walked back toward the tunnel. "We're a bit short of converting this universe, but it's a start."

It was indeed a start. They had verified that they could cure zombies and make significant introductions. Also that the converted folk could be fully functional. But the remaining chore was monstrous. How could a few humans, crossbreeds, and talented bugs transform a universe?

They rejoined the others at the tunnel. But instead of going through it to return to their own universe, they held another conference.

"Gyles and I have been talking," Aura said. "We have an idea."

"As long as it won't make Xenia mad," Noe said, a mixed smile floating nearby. She spoke as one who had been furious when a seeming Aura had seduced a seeming Santo in Hell.

Aura pretended not to see it, or at least to tune it out. "It's this: we should recruit all the zombie alternates to the members of our Quest. Cure them and put them to work mapping Xanth. That way we can not only save them, but work with them, and they will have a reason to associate with each other that doesn't alert whoever or whatever is making the zombies."

"Good idea," Santo agreed. "We already have the local Nik and Anthem and three ghosts. Your clone, Aura, should be here in Thanx. That leaves the two centaurs, and Wanda and Knife."

"And you and Noe," Aura said.

He laughed. "Oops, yes!"

"You are forgetting four," Shameful said. "The Demons. The mapping mission was to enable them to travel Xanth anonymously, studying the details of the mortal realm. There must be their equivalents here."

Which was the difficult truth they had somehow evaded before: their silent observers.

"We can't just summon Demons," Nik said. "You know, sand and galaxies."

"No need; we are here," Andromeda said via the phone. "The local Demons are zombies too, as the ghosts concluded. We have explored privately and verified this. To save this universe we must first save its Demons. But we must be circumspect, because whatever has the power to zombify Demons must be formidable indeed. We Demons do not wish to intervene openly and become direct targets. We appreciate your continued discretion." Her presence withdrew; she had made her point.

The others paused with mixed awe and anxiety. The Demons who governed this universe had become zombies themselves?

"I suggest that you ponder this aspect in the background," Gyles said. "While you tackle the simpler one of assembling the local Quest."

"Yes, let's," Nik agreed. "We can start with Aura, whom we originally found here in the Queendom of Thanx. If she's not here, Queen Apoca may know where she is, as she is a Lips woman."

"I'll tackle her," Aura said. "I am armed with abysmal puns."

They went to Apoca's house. The others stayed back while Aura went to the door and knocked. The queen answered, saw Aura, and paused in surprise. She was a zombie, but fresh enough to be in control of most of her faculties. Her hair still changed colors with her thoughts, though the colors were tarnished.

Aura spoke. "Yes, I am Aura. No I am not a zombie. I am from another universe, here to cure my clone self in this one."

"Thiz doez not make muz senze," Apoca said, her hair turning dirty yellow for doubt.

"When you keep queenly records, do you make type O, type P, or type Q errors?"

Apoca stared at her, her trace rot flaking off her skin as her hair turned orange with annoyance. "Typos. What an abysmal pun! Can't you be serious?"

"And you are cured," Aura said.

"Why so I seem to be," Apoca agreed, her hair flashing plaid for mixed emotions, then green for positive. Then yellow again for doubt, but this time it had no tarnish. "How is this possible?"

"I hit you with an abysmal pun," Aura explained. "Puns are anathema to zombieism."

"They are?" The hair turned plaid. "Who would have thought that such awful wordplay could have such a positive effect!"

"Who, indeed," Aura agreed. "Now I hope my opposite number is here, because I want to cure her and take her with me."

Apoca studied her. "You are one outstanding Lips woman, now that your qualities are not clouded by zombie rot. Yes, the other Aura is here. I will summon her." She produced a whistle and blew a short, sharp blast. "She was converted before the rest of us, so is farther gone. I trained her to respond to the whistle, as that requires less wit. I was afraid she would suffer mischief if I didn't watch her closely, what with her visible headaches and all."

A zombie woman approached. "Yez ma'am," she said obediently.

"Take it," Apoca murmured to Aura.

Aura faced the zombie. "When you have a backlog, is it made of reverse wood?"

Zombie Aura stared at her, some rot dropping to the ground. "Whoo are yeou?"

So one pun was not sufficient, in this case.

Aura was undaunted. "Can a crazy robot get its loose screw tightened and be sane again?"

"Answer my question!" the woman snapped as the rest of her rot flaked off. "Who the bleep are you?"

Now Aura answered. "I am you, from another universe. I just cured you of zombieism by using bad puns. They drive out the rot. I'm sorry I couldn't abolish your migraine headaches too."

The other Aura looked at her own clean hands. "Amazing! I have to believe you. Those puns were stinkers."

"Some stinks are curative."

Then the two Auras hugged. There followed rapid explanations and clarifications, but it was clear that this cure was successful. They decided to call themselves AuraOne and AuraTwo for convenience.

"Now I think it is our turn," Santo said to Noe. "We have been together for years, so we must have gotten zombied together. But where?"

"Probably here," Apoca said. "You two were visiting us when the zombie plague struck not long ago." A smile tugged at her lip. "You made a scene at a dance when a small d demoness tried to freak you out with her potent panties. Every other male succumbed but you. It looked like a disaster area. The girls were furious."

Now the attempted smile crossed to Santo. "Lilith. She and I became friends. She has a long history."

"I'm sure."

"I can locate your opposites," Gyles said from the screen. "I'll check with the local ghost network," He faded out.

In about three quarters of a moment, give or take an instant, he was back. "They're not far from Thanx," he reported. "They liked their visit, despite getting zombied here, and dallied near the border, considering whether to settle in the queendom. I notified them. They are tunneling here now."

The mouth of a rusty tunnel opened a few paces away. The zombie Santo and Noe stepped out, and the tunnel closed behind them with a clank. “We underzand you have a cure for our condition.” Zombie Santo said.

Santo stepped up. “Have you heard about the infernal character who caught hold of a big bat and got carried swiftly out of Hell?”

The zombie frowned. “That’s not even a pun. It’s a mode of transport.” But some rot shook off, and his speech was improved.

“How about the needle-crafter who made a stitch in time to save nine tenths of her thyme plants?”

The zombie groaned, shedding the rest of his rot. “That’s worse. Your puns barely make the grade.” But they had clearly worked.

Now Noe stepped up to her zombie counterpart. “Did you know that wealthy dwarves employ minordomos?”

The zombie groaned away her rot. One pun had done it. Then the two Noes hugged, as the Auras had, and agreed to be NoeOne and NoeTwo. It was another cure.

“I am developing a new respect for foul puns,” Apoca said. “Even unintentional ones, like NoeOne.”

NoeTwo carried Wanda and Knife, who as objects had not turned zombie, and had not transferred to Aura in the course of a Quest they weren’t on. NoeTwo took them to AuraTwo so that she could match AuraOne in this respect. Wanda appeared as a lovely young woman, and WandaTwo matched her. They, too, hugged, though their illusion forms overlapped somewhat. Solidity did have its advantages.

“And the two centaurs,” Nik said, pleased with the progress they had made. “Where are they?”

“On the excluded centaur isle,” Gyles said. “Different parts. They haven’t met. You can introduce them to each other.”

“I can tunnel us there,” Santo said.

They bid parting to Apoca, who still appreciated being cured and having the key to curing others; she would be busy collecting and dispensing puns among her tribe. Then they tunneled to the isle.

First they oriented on ShamefulTwo. They found her, looking bedraggled. She had not been happy as an unpopular centaur, and getting zombiefied had not improved her outlook. Shameful approached her, armed with puns.

“I am bringing you what you don’t want. Awful puns.”

“Get away from me,” ShamefulTwo retorted. “I’ve got problems of my own.”

"Have you tried drinking positivi tea? That gives folk a positive attitude that overcomes any obstacle."

ShamefulTwo stared at her. "Is that supposed to be funny?" But her hide was clarifying."

"Try this: stack two dimes, then step over them. There'll be a pair o' dimes shift."

"You must have something better to do than plague me with your sordid humor."

"And your zombie curse is gone."

ShamefulTwo checked herself. "It's true," she said, amazed. "What is happening here?"

"Puns are the antithesis to zombieism. I smeared you with them, and you have been cured."

ShamefulTwo's hostility evaporated. "Tell me more."

She did. ". . . and elsewhere on this isle is Shameless Centaur, who should be your compatible companion, once we dezombify him," Shameful concluded.

"Let's find him, ShamefulTwo said. "Give me some dreadful puns and I'll do it myself."

Gyles told them where, and soon they were bracing the other centaur. ShamelessTwo was as cynical as ShamefulTwo had been.

"Have you heard about Connor?" ShamefulTwo asked with enthusiasm. "His talent is to trick females into doing his bidding."

"To con her," ShamelessTwo said. "You believe that is humorous?" But rot was flaking off his paisley flank, revealing the animated figures there. The job was not complete, as centaurs had more mass than humans, but it was progress.

"Did you know that night mares wear bridal veils when they marry?"

Now he groaned. "Filly, will you wear a bridal veil when *we* marry?"

"You're cured!" she said, kissing him. "If the example of our opposites in the other universe holds true, we will indeed marry in due course."

"I think our roster is complete," Nik said. "However, challenges do remain. We have the rest of this universe to save."

"Including its Demons," Anthem agreed with a doubtful chord. "And no idea how."

Chapter 8

DANGEROUS KISSES

They got the QuestTwo organized and set to follow a parallel course mapping settlements, nothing all that unusual to others, but with wondrous internal dynamics, they returned to their own universe to work on more basic matters. They camped in the forest not far from the zombie portal, rested a day, then held another conference.

"The problem is larger than we thought," Nik said. "As Gyles suggested, we have been pondering it in the background, but now may be the time for the foreground. Do we have suggestions?"

"Yes," Gyles said. "I suggest that the Demons should now participate directly, not as observers but as the individuals they are. Understanding their need to mask their identities, I further suggest that they speak through mortal members of the Quest, so that we will know who they are but any outside eavesdropper will not. When the session is done they may be silent as before."

"Agreed," Andromeda said. "I will speak through Noe, with a marginally different tone." They were able to distinguish that difference already. "Bang will speak similarly through Santo. You will recognize us, but will not give any indication that we are not our mortal hosts."

"Agreed," Anthem said for them all.

"Ditto for me," Demon Pun said via Shameless Centaur.

"And me," Demoness Entropy said via Shameful Centaur.

"We ghosts will also speak through our associated mortals," Gyles said via Aura. "My otherverse self does, with her alternate, so I can too." His tone, too, differed slightly from hers, having a masculine tinge. "Dane is with Nik, and Rhonda is with Anthem."

"We are," the two other ghosts said together. Their voices were via

Anthem's telepathy, but differed from the mortal bugs' mental tones. There were also faint background chords for Anthem, which echoed "Long, Long Ago" when Rhonda spoke.

"And one more," Gyles said. "The Baton. I'm not sure he anticipated inter-universe interaction, and he may not wish to continue with this particular story."

The phone screen came on, with a picture of the Baton of Protagonism. "Continue," the impersonal phone voice said.

Nik dived in. "There are at least two mysteries. What is the ultimate source of the zombie invasion of at least two universes, and how could it affect Demons, who should be invulnerable to such a seemingly mortal infection?"

"Those are indeed mysteries," Andromeda said. "We desperately need answers. One avenue of investigation may be this: there is a Demoness Zombia, who is sealed off from this universe in the manner Demon Pun was, but far more stringently. The restriction is so effective that few Demons and virtually no mortals even know of her. If her equivalent in some other universe found a way spread zombieism, she would likely have motive. The fact of the zombie invasion suggests that this is the case. She is surely angry." She smiled. "Hell has no fury like that of a scorned Demoness."

There was an uncomfortable silence. Demoness Zombia? That did make revolting sense.

Then Pun spoke, with no hint of levity. "She and I are enemies, because my nature opposes hers. If I were able to get close enough to kiss her, she might implode and no longer exist. At the least, she would lose her ability to make zombies."

"A kiss?" Nik asked. "That is normally a sign of positive connection."

"Kisses have power," Aura said, her tone distinct from that of Gyles. "Especially those performed by motivated females. My kiss can zombify a man, and perhaps a woman." Then she paused. "Could that relate? I was a regular Lips woman with the power to love-slave a man with my kiss. Then I kissed an invisible giant, and it changed. My kiss changed him, and his kiss also changed me. Where did he get the power to zombify?"

"That is interesting indeed," Andromeda said. "There just might be an avenue to Demoness Zombia."

"There just might," Pun agreed. "If my kiss could destroy her, just as my puns destroy zombieism, her kiss might have similar impact on a male. If she hankered for a tryst with a male, and somehow had access to an invisible giant, that could explain some things. Such as how he became a zombie, and how his kiss transferred it to you, Aura. I believe we need to investigate your giant and learn what he knows."

"Yes," Andromeda agreed. "There is where our search should start."

"A thought," Demoness Entropy said. "Perhaps we should first rerun Aura's memory of that kiss. As Demons we have abilities that transcend those of mortals. We may be able to analyze the elements of that kiss, and discover details of what magic it transferred."

"I regret that my memory of the incident is somewhat foggy," Aura said. "It changed my life, as I had no prior experience with being a zombie."

"We can sharpen it," Andromeda said. "You have seen the effects of Demon ambiance when we are stifling our proximity. This would be the effect when we are trying to enhance a mortal quality."

"I don't know," Aura said. Then she sat up straight. "Oh, my! It's like a mundane searchlight coming on."

"Remember that night," Andromeda suggested. "We will follow."

"Put it on the screen," Gyles said.

The giant phone screen appeared. There was Aura as seen by a theoretical observer, rather than looking out of her own eyes. She was a healthy Lips woman, pretty and shapely, except for the aura for which she was named. That aura scintillated near her head, signaling a chronic background headache. Foliage wilted where it touched in passing. It was night, but the aura provided illumination as she patrolled the Thanx garden that was growing rare magical spices.

Then the ground shook with the thuds of an invisible giant, and patches of valuable spices were crushed underfoot. Aura froze in horror. He was raiding the garden, and unknowingly destroying what he didn't harvest. How could she stop this disaster?

Then the giant evidently squatted so as to grab giant handfuls of spices. That intersected her aura, and she saw his outline as a disturbance of that aura. For the moment she could see exactly where he was.

Impulsively, she hurled herself forward at his face, which was larger than her whole body, and jammed her head at his monstrous mouth. She kissed his lower lip, exerting her full power to render him into her love slave. It might not be fully effective with a man this size, but it should at least set him back.

Too late she realized that he was no ordinary invisible giant. He was a zombie! She got a mouthful of rot. She spit it out violently.

And it seemed he carried some reverse wood. Her powered kiss activated it, rendering him both visible and zombie-free alive, and her a zombie.

She stumbled away, her aura tarnishing, while the giant lurched up and fled in the opposite direction. She soon discovered that her kisses now did not love-slave the recipient; they zombied him. She had been unpopular before, because of her hot bright aura; now she was anathema. Only Queen Apoca stood by her, but she could not undo the damage caused by the giant's kiss. She went to the Good Magician, and he told her to join a Quest that was about to start. That was her only hope, and it wasn't much of a prospect. Why should tagging along with someone else's mission help her or them?

The big screen faded. They were now beyond the fateful kiss, and already knew how Aura's contact with puns had dezombiefied her. Except for her kisses, which still zombiefied their victims. The mystery of why remained, as she could not remember what she had never known. How had the giant gotten zombiefied? Where had the awful magic of his kiss originated?

"Still, it's progress," Andromeda said. "We now know what the giant looks like, and we should be able to locate him. He has to know what happened to him."

The ghosts got on it and soon found the giant. He was sleeping beside a snowy mountain, evidently liking the coolth. The Quest members quickly sailed the carpets there, while the two centaurs kept pace, their velocity enhanced. There he was, snoring up a storm that was raining as it drifted downwind.

"We don't need to wake him," Andromeda said. "We can explore his memory while he sleeps. That may be more convenient." The big screen appeared.

They oriented on three days before the kiss, then fast-forwarded the action to zero in on relevance. To Nik's surprise, this turned out to be a little human girl playing among wildflowers in a field. How could this possibly relate to the zombie threat to the universe? But he kept silent, trusting that there was some devious connection.

The giant, who was invisible at this time, lay down near the girl and spoke softly to her, so as not to blow her away. "Hello, child. What's your name?"

She looked around, not seeing him. "I'm Detta. I'm five years old. Where are you?" she asked.

"I'm Gilbert, an invisible giant. That's why you can't see me."

"You are? Wow! Or are you teasing me?"

"No, I really am a giant. Feel my finger." He rested a giant hand next to her and extended his forefinger. The Questers could see it because Andromeda caused a faint translucent outline to show on the screen.

Detta reached out and touched the tip of the finger. "Wow! It's like a big soft rock." She considered briefly, as at her young age brevity was all she had. "Can I sit on your hand?"

"Sure." He turned his hand to lie palm up. "Walk along a bit until you come to the side of it, then climb up."

She did so, managing to scramble up to where she could sit on the edge and dangle her legs down the side. She seemed to be sitting in midair about a foot and a half above the ground. "Wow!"

"Aren't you afraid of me?" Gilbert asked.

"No. you seem nice. Besides, Mom's away, Dad's busy, I got no sisters, and I'm lonely."

"So am I. I like to look at normal women. That makes me a pariah."

"A what?"

He had forgotten that a person as small as she was didn't have big words "It means other giants don't like me. They think I should look at giant women. But they're invisible, except when they glow a little, so what's the use of that?"

"Oh. I see the problem." She giggled. "I can't see you, but I can see your problem. That's funny."

He chuckled. "It is funny. So I'm largely on my own, and lonely."

She giggled again. "Largely. You're a giant. I guess you couldn't be littlely on your own. So we're talking. Do you have a magic talent?"

"Only being invisible, like all the other local giants."

"I just found out my talent. It's throwing kisses."

"I don't understand. Don't folk have to put their faces together to kiss?"

"Sure. But sometimes they pretend throw them. When I throw mine, they go splat on a wall or something. I'll show you." She put a hand to her mouth, kissed her fingers, then threw it toward his face. It splatted against his invisible nose and dissolved.

"Wow!" he said. "That's a nice talent."

"Thank you. But it doesn't do me any good. Like when a bully boy throws dirt at me, a kiss doesn't help. I don't want to kiss him, I want to hit him with a rotten egg."

Gilbert considered. "Maybe you can weaponize your talent."

"Do what?"

"Make it so it can hurt the bully back."

Detta was interested. "How can I do that?"

"I saw an old jar of lip bomb someone had thrown away. There was still some in it."

"Mom uses lip balm to make her mouth soft. I think you misspelled it. Not that I know how to spell."

"Not balm. Bomb. It explodes."

"Ooo, fun! But how does it work?"

"A woman puts it on her mouth, kisses a man, and it blows him away."

Detta considered. She was clearly a clever child. "If I had that, and threw a kiss, would it do that?"

"I believe it would. Let's go find that jar. Hang on."

She wrapped her arms around a finger, hanging on. He got up and walked back the way he had come. "Ooo, wow!" she exclaimed, thrilled by the high ride.

He found the jar, and squatted by it. Detta scrambled down to pick it up. Sure enough there was some bomb goo left in it. She got back on his hand, holding the jar closely. He carried her back to the flower field.

Then they experimented. She scooped out some of the paste and smeared it on her mouth. Then she kissed her fingers and threw the kiss at a nearby rock.

The rock bounced up into the air and landed a foot beyond its original spot, cracked. It had been blown away.

"This will do," the girl decided judiciously. "Thanks, Gilbert."

"You're welcome, Detta. It was nice talking with you."

The giant got up and walked on, leaving the girl to her experiments. He plainly had enjoyed their dialogue as much as she had. Lonely folk could abate each other's loneliness, even when they were quite different otherwise.

"Don't we know it," Anthem thought to Nik privately.

"We do," he agreed, savoring the contact.

The picture froze. "A thrown kiss," Andromeda said thoughtfully. "If you could do that, Aura, you could zombify folk at a distance."

"And so could Demoness Zombia," Aura agreed. "If she got within throwing range."

"I think we are nudging closer to the answer," Pun said. "But we are not there yet."

The picture resumed animation, returning to fast forward toward further relevance. It slowed as Gilbert Giant discovered a stash of reverse wood someone must have forgotten. He picked it up and put it in an invisible pocket, where it became invisible too. He would play with it later.

Then things changed. The trail that had angled up the steep slope of a passing mountain now angled the opposite way, down under the mountain, becoming a tunnel.

"Not one of mine," Santo said.

"It seems to be a phenomenon of the reverse wood," Andromeda said. "Up became down, at least for him."

Somehow the giant fit comfortably in the passage, descending to a fair depth. He came to a boudoir, which confused him as he had no idea what the purpose of such a chamber might be, let alone what to call it. It seemed to consist mainly of an enormous bed so extensive that even he could lie comfortably on it. So he did.

"Hello, Gilbert," a sultry voice said. "Welcome to my bed."

The giant was startled. "Your bed?" He opened his eyes to see an amazingly shapely woman lying beside him, with hair as dark as the deepest void of space and eyes even darker, virtual black holes. She was visible, but seemed to be his size. Her negligee was so insubstantial as to be pointless. In fact parts of it were falling off. Not that this bothered him; he was happy to see more of her.

She gazed at him with the semblance of the thought of a smile, not at all annoyed by the intensity of his stare. "Do you know who I am?"

"I have no idea. But you seem interesting." That was a giant size understatement. Every detail of her was compelling.

"I am a token physical manifestation of the Demoness Zombia."

"The what of who?" His confusion reminded him of Detta's when he used too big a word. This stunning creature had used too complicated a concept. A token manifestation?

She laughed. "A capsule history: the universe is run by a number of essential forces, their personifications called Demons and Demonesses. Some are in better repute than others. I, as the patron of zombies, am in the worst repute extant. I am excluded from participation in any of the interactions of other Demons. This is my prison, whose barriers the reverse wood you carry somehow nullified, so that you were able to come to me. In fairness I must warn you that your association with me will taint you, making you unwelcome among your kind, as I am unwelcome among mine. If you prefer to leave now, untainted, I will let you go, albeit with regret, as you are the first viable male I have seen in some time. But if you are amenable to a closer interaction with me, you may remain long enough to accomplish it. Here is a hint of what I offer."

He gazed at her. She inhaled as the last of her negligee dissolved away. He freaked out, which was interesting because invisible giants didn't freak out.

"Wake," she said, snapping her fingers.

"What happened?" he asked, staring at the sheet she had now interposed between his eyes and her phenomenal bare front.

"I showed you a bit much of me, and you freaked out. Normally giants don't, but I am not a normal woman. I am a Demoness assuming visible human giantess form. I can invoke a spell of trace obscurity to enable you to gaze at me without losing your mind, so we can have a meaningful dialogue. Do you wish that?"

"If it means I can look at you without freaking, yes."

Zombia made a minor gesture. Then she dropped the sheet.

He stared. His equilibrium wavered dangerously, but he handled it. Her image was slightly veiled but still clear enough to take him to the verge of the gulf of freakdom without quite falling in. She was reclining scintillatingly naked on the bed close beside him. He had never even imagined a spectacle like this. That was just as well, because his imagination would have gotten locked in perpetual freak.

"I believe I have your attention," she said. It was an understatement worthy of the comparison of their states, a small galaxy to a large grain of sand. "Would you like to get up and clean with me?"

"Um," he said, confused. "You want me to get up and clean the place?"

She laughed, faintly enjoying his befuddlement. She had not had a chance to play with a man of any type for an eon or three. "Let me explain. I was banished to this subterranean vault in a region where the dread Adult Conspiracy governs. This is mooted as a protection to safeguard mortal children from evil influences, but is actually a scheme to degrade mortal women. Mortal men conquer via physical strength, while mortal women prevail via bleep appeal." She frowned. "It did it again, bleeping out the term for reproductive readiness. It operates on the assumption that there is something evil about the process of signaling the stork for a delivery, and that women are at fault for this. That reduces or eliminates their power in social interaction, leaving the men in charge. That is the real conspiracy that mortals are usually too dull to catch on to. Many unsavvy mortal women actually support it, thus remaining second class citizens, as it were. They are unable to openly flaunt their primary asset, and pay the price in relative powerlessness. Fortunately I am not a mortal woman, despite present appearances. So when I say 'up and clean' it requires some interpretation or even reversal of the meaning of the words. The essence is erotic play." Her upper lip quirked half a notch. "Ha! Got one by the Conspiracy. It's not unduly smart."

"Now I get it," Gilbert said as he figured out the opposite meanings. "Yes, I'd like to get up and clean with you." In fact he was now desperate for it.

"Bearing in mind the taint," she reminded him.

"To bleep with the taint!"

"I must further explain that though I am the source of the zombie infection, I regenerate as rapidly as I deteriorate. So while parts of me, outside and inside, may be slippery from surface decay, my flesh is actually solid. You will get coated, but a good shower will clean you off and you will be clean again. But you yourself will also become a regenerating zombie. That will make you unpopular with others, but you may always return to me for this kind of interaction."

"I'm game." He was actually more than game. He was eager.

She smiled. "Then come to me, you interesting man."

"On my way!" He reached for her.

The screen became a fog bank. The Conspiracy had struck again.

"He kissed Zombia on several parts of her body," Andromeda explained. "Among other actions. Thereafter he was a zombie himself, and his kiss transformed his partners to zombies. That made him unwelcome, so Zombia was his only continuing partner, which more than made up for it. She was obliging and visible and highly knowledgeable. All she asked in return was a collection of herbs or spices for her private garden. He was happy to fetch them for her. Until he inadvertently kissed a Lips woman, whose power, complicated by the reverse wood he carried, transformed him to a visible giant without the curse of zombieism, either in himself or in those he thereafter kissed. But the woman paid a price, becoming herself a zombie with the kissing curse. Until her encounters with puns eliminated part of it."

Aura shook her head. "Apparently garden-variety puns can't get past my power kiss. Fortunately I don't have to use it. But I wish I could be all the way rid of it and be a normal Lips woman again."

"You can be," Pun said. "My kiss would do it."

Aura stared at him. "Then let's get up and clean!" She got up and went to Shameless Centaur, where Demon Pun associated. "This time not to make a centaur into a temporary zombie, but to make a cursed woman normal."

"Do it with power," Pun reminded her.

"Oh, yes."

They kissed. There was a flash of light and Aura fell back. She had not before experienced a Demon kiss. Nik had a notion how powerful that could be.

"Now kiss me," Shameless said.

Aura recovered her balance. "Of course. But if I do it with power, you'll be my love slave."

"No. Pun is shielding me from that. Do it with power, so we'll know."

They kissed again. This time there was no flash. "I'm not zombiefied," Shameless reported. Then he looked at her again. "Your aura is gone!"

"So is my headache," she said, amazed.

"I thought you would be better off without it," Pun said.

"Oh my yes!" she agreed. "And this is my kiss of thanks." She stepped into the centaur's embrace again and kissed them both, this time without power. Even that way it was potent, as her gratitude manifested.

"That was nice," Pun and Shameless said together.

She laughed. "Thank you. Ordinary Lips women are known to be appealing."

"They are," Shameless agreed.

"So this exploration resulted in an incidental benefit," Andromeda said. "But we still don't know how Demons get infected. They generally don't kiss anyone, that being a mortal mode, and certainly they don't kiss Zombia."

Now Demon Bang spoke. "The child Detta has the talent of throwing kisses. They can be weaponized. If she got the zombie kiss infection, she could infect others at a distance. If Zombia got such a talent, or recruited a person with that talent, she could do the same without leaving her vault. In some other universe she must have gotten the equivalent and used it against other Demons, starting a chain of invasions."

"Oh, my," Andromeda breathed. "That must be it."

"We need to locate the source Zombia and neutralize her," Pun said. "But she's too smart to let me get near her."

"We might do better by obtaining her cooperation," Entropy said. "The Demoness Zombias may have an affinity for each other in other universes, and be able to trace back to the source."

"Good point," Andromeda said. "But after the way we Demons have treated her, she will not want to cooperate with us."

"Suppose we offer her release from confinement and association with other Demons?" Entropy asked.

"Then maybe. But it would likely be grudging."

Now Nik spoke. "The finding of a compatible romantic companion can make a huge difference in attitude, regardless of species, as Anthem and I have discovered. Could there be a Demon companion for Zombia?"

"Demons do on occasion romance in the manner of mortals, as an entertaining change of pace," Andromeda agreed. "Bang and I do. Pun and Entropy do. Sometimes Demons even make liaisons with mortals, as Chaos and Squid do, and of course Zombia and Gilbert. So it is certainly possible. But in the case of Zombia, unlikely. Demons don't like her."

"For good reason," Gyles said.

"Sometimes the unlikely becomes possible," Nik said. "Anthem and I are of different species, but we love each other. There might be some Demon out there who, well, would find a sexy creature like Zombia interesting."

"A sexy *dead* creature," Aura said. "A zombie is a dead person given the semblance of life, unless fresh enough to still be close to life. A Demon would be too smart to fall for that. Actually I don't know whether Demons are alive anyway."

"It's an approximation," Andromeda said. "We do seem to be alive, in our fashion."

"It remains a question," Nik said. "An approximation may still have feelings. Even some inanimate objects have feelings."

"Some do. There was once a mortal prince whose talent was to converse with the inanimate," Gyles said. "That is, when he talked to it, it talked back to him. When a girl wearing a skirt in his vicinity stepped over a rock, the rock would cry out 'I see your legs, and that's not all!' The girl would shut it up by stomping it with her heel."

"I understand that some men would like to be such a rock, at times," Santo said, amused.

"They'd get their faces stomped," Noe said.

"It might be worth it," Gyles said.

Nik, having gained recent experience with the interests of human men, realized that such a view up under a skirt might indeed be worth a stomp. Men were very much oriented on one thing, and would suffer almost anything for it.

Anthem spoke. "Demons may not much like Zombia. Unless that Demon's specialty is to encourage life. He might find it a challenge to bring Zombia, who has a start on the process, the rest of the way to full life. Is there such a Demon?"

"Demon Alchemy," Andromeda said. "He has faded from prominence in recent centuries, but is surely still around somewhere. One of his specialties is researching to find the elixir of life. He just might be interested in experimenting on Zombia to ascertain whether she could be made completely alive."

"But would she be interested in being experimented on in that manner?" Aura asked. "Women can be cautious about details like that. I happen to know, being one myself. Just as I'd be cautious about stepping over a smart-mouthed rock."

"Only Zombia would know her attitude in that respect," Andromeda said. "She might deliberately step over the rock, to get its reaction. Some women would."

"And some men would have no reaction," Santo said.

Gyles laughed. "What a waste!"

"We should ask her," Pun said.

"Agreed. Who?"

"I think not a male, as she might just try to seduce him. And probably succeed, if he is anyone other than Santo. Also not a Demon."

"Agreed," Andromeda repeated. "Do we have a volunteer?"

"That would be me," Aura said. "I am experienced with both men and zombieism. I like the one and not the other."

No one argued.

The big screen showed the action. They watched and listened, hoping for the best.

Andromeda took Aura to the entrance to Zombia's prison vault. "I have armored you with a protection against Demon magic, just in case she reacts negatively to your query."

"Thanks," Aura said. "I have gotten used to friendly Demons, to a degree, but have no experience with an unfriendly one. I hope there's no mischief."

"We hope so too. Our interest is in saving the universes."

"Sometimes I do feel like a grain of sand."

"And sometimes I feel like a galaxy. But our emotions relate independently to our scopes in other milieu."

"They do. I heard about how the nymph in that other story saved you from destruction, and I was glad even before I came to know you personally."

"Thank you. Sometimes a grain of sand can make a difference out of proportion to the normal scheme."

Then, Aura walked down the passage the giant had inadvertently made. She was vastly smaller than the giant, but somehow it seemed to fit her much the same. She knew that it was a kind of simulation that enabled Demons to interact with mortals. Otherwise galaxies and grains of sand would have trouble relating.

There was Zombia, lying on her plush bed, clothed in her filmy negligee. She was curvaceous even by Lips standards, a creature who needed no panties or bra or deep breaths to freak out any passing man. That was one reason the Quest had not sent a man on this mission. Aura was unaffected, but appreciated the effect on a practical level. Sometimes a woman needed to get a man's immediate attention, and this was an easy way. Men's reactions could be almost comical on occasion.

The demoness saw her. "Oh, a woman." She knew seduction was off the table, as it were.

"Hello, Demoness Zombia. I am Aura, of the mortal Quest to map the settlements of Xanth and, not entirely incidentally, to save the universes from the zombie threat."

"Aura! The one who nullified my sole human contact Gilbert"

"Yes, inadvertently."

"I will destroy you!"

Lightning flashed around Aura without touching her. Andromeda's shield was effective. "Please," Aura said as if nothing had happened. "I came only to talk with you."

"You nullified my only contact with the outer realm. Now I am alone again."

"I know. I am sorry. I had no idea that my defense of the spice garden would have such an effect. But I have come to make it right, if I can."

"Oh? How?" The tone dripped icy particles that accumulated on the bed.

Aura plunged on into deep water. "I can go out of here, as you cannot. Suppose I recruit a Demon to be your replacement companion?"

"You? A tiny speck on the hide of an indifferent universe? Do you have delusions of impossible grandeur?"

"Maybe." This did not seem to be going well. Had there ever been hope that it would?

"Who?"

The fish was biting after all!

"Demon Alchemy."

There was half a pause. "I know of him. He transmutes base metals into gold, and has been looking for a universal solvent."

"Also the Elixir of Life."

"Yes. He hasn't found that yet." The ice was melting, making a small puddle.

"But your animation of the dead could be the first stage of a process that when taken to its extreme would bring full life to the dead. That might intrigue him as an avenue."

"How could you even think of having a hope that he would have any such interest?"

"I would kiss him with my power, possibly arousing a hint of what female interest can offer a male. I am not bound by the archaic Adult Conspiracy; I can flaunt my assets. I would use full-fledged reproductive appeal to catch his attention. Males of any type are always attuned to that. Then I would tell him that I am hardly the shadow of a suggestion of the kind of assets you have, and that you have a flicker of an interest in him. That you might even be receptive to his romantic or erotic approach."

"As indeed I might be, were he to come within range. I could give him an experience not even another Demoness could." The ice was gone, the water sinking into the bed.

"Yes."

"I am sorry I attacked you before. You did not deserve it. What is your personal opinion of me?"

Aura was startled. "I am here on a mission, not as a person. I am not entitled to opinions."

"Judiciously phrased. You are a woman. You are familiar with the manner females are viewed and treated in certain societies."

"I am," Aura agreed cautiously. What was the Demoness angling for?

"You know that I am not well regarded among Demons."

"I know. But this is peripheral to our dialogue."

"Perhaps. I deal with a necessary part of the living spectrum. Just as there is creation, there must also be dissolution. Old forms must decay to make room for new ones. To a farmer, dirt is good for growing new plants. Rot is the process of the formation of wholesome dirt. Do you agree?"

Where was she going with this? "I see your point. There is a cycle."

"What others may call slime, I call viscosity."

Aura did her best to maintain the dialogue without losing the point of her visit here. "The terms can apply."

"And what others may call sin, I call passion."

That scored. "I like passion."

"I understand that mortal Lips women are much into it."

"We are. We like warmth and feeling." Aura smiled wryly. "Though it seems not everybody does, especially the Adult Conspiracy."

The Demoness abruptly returned to the subject. "Your offer interests me. What do you want in return for delivering Alchemy to me?"

"The universe is being invaded by zombies. We want to abate that threat."

"That is not my doing. I am confined."

"But in some other universe your clone has launched this invasion. We believe that she has found a way to throw kisses that infect other Demons, making them powerless to stop other universes from invasion by regular zombies. We need to locate her and prevent her from launching further mischief."

"This, too, is not my concern. I do not care what my clones may want. I care what *I* want."

Was this a breakthrough? Aura hardly dared hope. "So you will work with us against that clone?"

"Yes. And what do you want of me for this effort?"

"We suspect that you have an affinity for your clones in other universes. That you might be able to point the direction, as it were, to that source Zombia."

"I do have that affinity. I could do this. But direction is not the same as location. She could be an infinite number of universes away. I could not predict the precise one."

"Yes. You would be only one part of a larger effort. But perhaps an essential part."

Zombia nodded. "Deliver Alchemy to me, and I will do this."

"Deal," Aura said, gratified. She turned to go.

"Kiss me," Zombia said.

"But—"

"I don't have to kiss with power any more than you do. I will not zombify you. Trust me."

Aura reversed course and stepped forward as Zombia got off the bed. The two of them turned out to be the same height, in this simulation.

They kissed. Aura felt the immense surrounding power of the demoness, but none of it impacted the kiss. It was just a kiss.

"And if it works out," Zombia said, "I want to be your friend."

Aura was astonished. "But I'm just a tiny speck on the hide of the universe."

"Size makes no difference. Power makes no difference. Character and attitude are what count for this."

Aura was flattered beyond reason. "Thank you, Zombia. If this works out, I will be your friend."

"Thank you."

The Demoness was thanking *her*? Numbly, she ascended the passage.

Andromeda was there. "Zombia is many things," she said. "But she is not a liar. She will cooperate if we deliver Alchemy. She will be your friend."

"I don't know what to make of this."

"I, too, want to be your friend,"

Aura stared at her. "What is happening here?"

Andromeda smiled. "As she said, character counts. You are the kind of woman a woman wants for a friend."

Aura was taken aback, and had to step forward to keep her place. "I had no idea."

"The ideal woman doesn't."

The picture faded.

The members of the Quest looked at each other, mentally. "I think we all want to be Aura's friend," Gyles said. "She is a good woman, apart from being sexy as bleep."

So it seemed. Nik wanted to be her friend too, though he was just a bug.

"Me too," Anthem thought with a sympathetic chord.

Meanwhile, the Demons had located Demon Alchemy. He was engaged in research on a far world. Fortunately it had breathable air and gravity similar to the home region. Andromeda deposited Aura there and faded into the background. It was her turn, again.

The big screen came on. The Quest watched this key sequence of what had become its mission.

Aura approached the scintillating region that was the indication of the presence of focus of a Demon. "Please, I am a mortal woman. I need to talk with you, Demon Alchemy. If you care to assume the form of a human male, this would make it feasible."

The scintillation formed into the semblance of a naked man. When he saw that she was clothed, clothes formed around him matching hers. "Yes?"

"Mortal women normally wear dresses, as I do. Men wear shirts and pants."

"Oh." His dress changed.

"I come on behalf of a Demoness who has a shine for you. Are you interested?"

"No. I am trying to ascertain the secret of the Elixir of Life, and have been too busy to mess with other Demons, who have their own interests."

"They do. But this interest is special. We are trying to save the universes."

"I wish you success. Now if you are satisfied, I will return to my endeavor." He started to turn away.

She almost leaped to intercept him. She flung her arms about him and planted a powered kiss on his mouth. That would have rendered a mortal man into a love slave, but of course hardly affected the Demon.

He was nevertheless interested, having felt the force of the touch. "You are not an ordinary mortal human woman."

"I am a Lips woman. Our kisses have special power."

"So I have discovered. This almost makes me want to do more with you."

Just so. Her physical assets contributed to her mission by attracting his attention. She efficiently stripped away her clothing and stood nude. "You are welcome to do it now."

He gazed at a view that would have come close to freaking out any normal mortal man. "I admit to being intrigued. But you are mortal." He started to turn away again, his interest still minimal. She was not rising sufficiently to the challenge.

"I am mortal," she agreed. "But the one I represent is not. What I offer you is but the hint of a shadow of a suggestion of what she offers. She is a mistress of viscosity and passion. She would love to have you visit her so she can prove it. Please give her a chance."

His eyes focused on her bare upper midsection. He was evidently becoming curious despite his disinterest. "Who is she?"

"She is the Demoness Zombia."

"Oh, the one locked in the vault."

"She is lonely. She wants company. She animates dead bodies, among other things. Your skill might enable her to bring them to full life. Who knows what the two of you might accomplish, working together?" She inhaled, adding to the suggestion of accomplishment.

His eyes widened. Now he was definitely interested, presumably in the subject they were discussing. "Perhaps so. It does seem worth exploring. But she has a bad reputation."

"Her kisses can make males zombify, but she doesn't have to power them, any more than I do. She has a strong libido. She could really do right by a male who returned her interest." She bounced a little on her feet, causing parts of her body to do the same. Lips were not the only asset Lips women had.

That seemed to do it. "Let's go see her," he said, focusing on what was before him.

"Follow me," Aura said, turning around walking away, coincidentally presenting her bare backside. A woman did not lose her appeal when she did that; if anything she increased it.

Andromeda swooped her up invisibly and transported her to the entrance to Zombia's vault. Alchemy of course had no trouble following. "He is here," she called to the Demoness below. "Treat him right."

"Oh, yes," Zombia said.

"Aura tells me you have viscosity and passion," Alchemy said to the Demoness.

There was a breathy chuckle. "How much can you handle?"

"Try me." He sailed past Aura to join Zombia in the vault.

There was an explosion of swirling fog that blotted out the entire screen. The Adult Conspiracy had struck again, barely in time.

Aura found herself back with the Quest. She hastily donned a replacement dress, not that her friends were concerned. She had used her assets well.

They all heard Zombia's final utterance before viscosity and passion overwhelmed her and her new companion. "I will remember, friend."

Chapter 9

DEMON SALVATION

They were back in conference. "So we have made an ally of Demoness Zombia," Nik said, summing it up. "Thanks to Aura. But we still have to deal with the zombies that are already loose. How can we cure Zombie Bang in the next universe?"

"Yes, we want to change that situation," Andromeda said. "While maintaining our Demon anonymity, at least for now, so that we don't get attacked and infected as they did."

"It's a challenge," Demon Bang said with Demonic understatement.

"Can you enhance selected mortals beyond what you have before?" Gyles asked. "So that they can seem to be the ones taking the action?"

A nod of appreciation circled the group, tagging several heads. It was a good idea. The ghost was indeed proving his usefulness to the Quest.

"We can try," Andromeda said. She looked at Anthem, which was a nice effect, because Anthem was perched on the shoulder of the woman the Demoness was speaking through, too close to be seen. "Suppose we try a chord in the other universe?"

"How would a chord accomplish anything?" Anthem asked with a slightly sour chord.

Andromeda smiled in her changeable way. "We shall see."

Nik realized that the Demons were up to something. It was best just to go along with it and find out what it was.

They took the tunnel to the Zombie Universe, then found a private place to camp while they experimented. "I think that you and Nik should go together," Andromeda said. "So that Nik can protect you if you need it."

Go where? Protect her from what? Anthem crossed over to climb onto Nik's back. He now stood alone on the ground, having left Santo's shoulder. He felt her private concern; the Demons' minds were shielded from her telepathy. He also felt her love for him, which he returned.

"Your size and your powers will expand more than they have hitherto," Andromeda said. "Nik's clairvoyance will enable him to grasp the broader situation. Anthem's telepathy will enable her to know the minds of larger entities than before. Together you should be able to handle the situation. Remember, we are watching but will not intervene directly unless it is necessary. Practice and Demon anonymity are the point."

Larger entities than what? Ants and nickelpedes? People and ogres? Or something else?

"On your way," the Demoness said.

Then it started. They rapidly increased in size, becoming the magnitude of mice, then dogs, then humans, then mundane horses. Then trees. Then buildings. Then mountains. Then continents. Then planetoids. Then planets. Then stars. Then star clusters.

They hovered at that size for a Demon moment.

"Sound your chord," Andromeda told Anthem.

What was the point of that? But Anthem obeyed.

The sound reverberated through the ether, penetrating the crannies of the galaxy. In response, a hundred million stars twinkled in unison.

"That is your power," Andromeda said. "Communication and alignment."

Oh. It was hard to believe, but belief was not the point. This was power indeed.

The enlargement resumed. Now they were among galaxies. Nik's expanding clairvoyance was able to handle these concepts, and Anthem's growing telepathy enabled her to assimilate his understanding. The Demons had not been fooling about larger entities.

They drifted clear of what Mundanes termed the Milky Way Galaxy and gazed back at it and its sister galaxy Andromeda. The two were grandly rotating strands of matter studded with glowing stars, and lesser nebulae, a phenomenal sight. Buried within that stately assembly was the Land of Xanth, a haven of magic in a larger array of what Mundanes called Science. Nik and Anthem were coming to realize how small they were, not merely as bugs, but the entire framework of their existence. From the Demon perspective, they were indeed grains of sand, or less.

"Oops," Anthem said.

Nik looked. Something was moving in the space between galaxies. It looked like a weirdly distorted dragon, and it was coming toward them.

"But there's not supposed to be anything between galaxies," Nik said. "It is almost empty space."

"Maybe it is like an invisible giant."

Nik focused. New concepts were clarifying. "Yes. Only this is a creature of Dark Matter, which normal folk can't see. Such creatures infest the galaxies, their mass distorting nebulae and space itself. Most of the realm we think we know actually consists of these unseen monsters. Fortunately they normally can't see us, either, or interact with us on any level but gravitational, so we are fairly safe from them."

"That thing sees us," she warned. "It is opening its mouth."

So it was. Now it seemed that interaction was possible, here in the galactic scope. "Tell it to leave us alone."

She sent out a magnified mental blast, backed by an ominous chord. "LEAVE US ALONE!"

The thing merely gaped its jaws wider as it accelerated toward them. It was evidently hungry.

"Tackle it," Andromeda said. "We have enlisted Nemesis, the Demon of Dark Matter. You have his strength."

Oh? Nik extended a pincer an amazing distance and clamped on the tail of the monster just hard enough to give fair warning. When the monster didn't take the hint, Nik twitched the pincer and flipped the creature back out of the way. It tumbled in an arc and landed on a point of the galaxy. "OwOOO!" it howled as lightning jags of pain speared out from its butt. Then it squirmed away. In a large moment, it was gone.

"We did warn it," Anthem said with a satisfied background chord.

"I am curious about this realm, now that we're here," Nik said. "Suppose we explore it a bit?"

"Let's," she agreed. "I never knew this existed."

"Because it's on a different plane that intersects ours only gravitationally. At present, with Demon power, we are experiencing it."

"I am glad for your understanding."

Now that they oriented on it, the Dark Matter domain clarified into diverse features. There were tree-like plants growing from a ground-like base, and rabbit-like creatures rummaged in the brush beneath them. It was, if not an alternate universe, a different aspect of this one. It was amazing how much more complicated the universe was than it had seemed to them on the ground in the Queendom of Thanx.

There was a sound. It seemed somehow pained. Was it another monster?

"No," Anthem thought. "That's a baby." Somehow she knew, being female. "We need to help it."

Help a gargantuan dark matter creature? Nik did not try to argue the case; feminine instinct was beyond masculine comprehension. They moved toward the sound, and soon found it. A baby dragon had somehow gotten its tail wedged in the split of a divided tree and couldn't escape. It was bawling.

"Help it," Anthem said as she dropped down to the ground.

Nik obeyed, using a pincer to carefully wedge the parts of the tree apart so that the dragonlet could get free. But now it was apparent that its tail had gotten kinked and was still hurting. Further, a bearlike predator, attracted by the noise, was forging toward it, licking its dark chops.

Nik acted without thinking. He jumped between the bear and its prey, lifting a warning pincer big enough to clamp off a nose and maybe even a head. Perhaps news had spread, because the bear heeded the warning and backed off without actually departing. It was reluctant to give up its meal without checking alternatives.

Meanwhile Anthem helped the dragonlet in her own fashion. She drew from her ghost companion Rhonda to telepathically sing a soothing lullaby, or at least the equivalent, "Long, Long Ago." It worked; the baby was distracted by the lovely sound and stopped crying.

It was a weird scene in a weird setting: Anthem singing while Nik held off the bear.

> Though by your kindness my fond hopes were raised, long, long ago, long long ago
> You by more eloquent lips have been praised, long, long ago, long ago.
> But by long absence your truth has been tried
> Still to your accents I listen with pride,
> Blessed as I was when I sat by your side, long long ago, long ago

Since it was telepathic, the baby could hear the melody and understand the meaning, as well as responding to the sympathy. The dragon baby was sitting beside Anthem, blessed.

"I'm going to call you Kinky, because of your tail," she said fondly, "I hope it mends soon."

The dragonlet made a growling purr.

And suddenly there before them was a full-size female dragon, taking in the scene. Was Nik about to have to fight off two monsters at once? He girded his pincers.

Then the dragoness went to Kinky, who chortled in relief to see his mother. All was well again.

The dragoness paused. Then she carefully set down a pellet before Anthem, and departed with her cub. The bear, seeing no further hope of a meal, growled angrily and disappeared into the forest. The crisis was past.

They checked the pellet. It looked like a brilliant disk-shaped faceted diamond, but of a substance like none other, a dark matter gem of inestimable value. Nik picked it up in a claw, as Anthem could not conveniently carry it; it was more massive than she was. This was the dragon's token of appreciation for the way they had treated her baby, protecting and soothing him. A pretty bauble. Anthem's instinct had been on target.

"Next stage," Andromeda said.

They started growing again. The galaxies seemed to shrink, becoming bright disks, then glinting buttons, then points of light in a monstrous expanding firmament. What a spectacle the universe was!

"Now sound your chord," Andromeda said.

Sound a chord again? What could possibly be the point, here in the fathomless depths of the universe, where sound did not exactly exist, having no air to transmit it? But Anthem did it.

The sound was extraordinary, a phenomenal vibration of the substance of space itself, a grand but gentle melodic stroking of the strings of reality.

And a hundred billion galaxies resonated in unison.

"That is your power," Andromeda said.

What could they do except believe?

Then the shrinking began, as they returned to their realm and their size. It was like falling dizzily into an ever-enlarging hole, until at last, it ended. The excursion of the millennium. There they were, back with the Quest.

"We saw it on the screen," Noe said. "That was nice thing you did for that cub." As a young woman she related.

"And what an awesome sound!" Santo said. "We felt the trace quiver even here."

"And that gem," Aura said. "May we see it?"

Nike opened his pincer. There was the dark matter jewel, shining like a miniature star. It had been larger than a real star, but now it was, well, gem size. It had joined them in their reality, maintaining the perspective.

"I have the feeling that's more than a decoration," Aura said.

So did everyone.

"This incident provides you with a hint of the scale at which Demons operate," Andromeda said. "Our interactions with sand grain folk require a minuscule fraction of our attention. You mortals, with your entire focus here, can on occasion pick up details we miss. We hope to take advantage of that soon."

"We are appropriately awed," Anthem said, her background chord echoing "Long, Long Ago."

"Now the Demons," Andromeda said. "Beginning with me."

"With you?" Noe asked, startled.

"I mean my zombie self. We believe we can cure the Demons, to start repairing this zombie universe, but it will require special measures, because a significant part of this campaign is zombie aversion to getting cured. Otherwise, folk would soon be curing zombies as fast as they were made." She smiled with Noe's mouth. "That's surely one reason one of the first actions of the new Demon zombies was to strengthen the confinement Demon Pun suffers here. So that even if folk learn his danger to zombies, they can't use him to fight directly. Only indirectly, stopping them one pun at a time. But if we can cure the other Demons here, we can get Pun freed to guarantee that there will be no subsequent invasion. Meanwhile they eased the restrictions on Demoness Zombia, who is now held in much higher esteem than before. The stakes are high."

"They are," Noe agreed with her own mouth, bemused. "But why start with you? I mean, of course we want your clone cured, but wouldn't it put you in danger if you were seen near her?"

"Yes. That's why I need Aura."

"Me?" Aura asked. "It was all I could do to get Demon Alchemy to go to Demoness Zombia. My desperate flashes barely nudged him. How could I ever have any part in curing your clone?"

"By being your alluring self, and a key part of an intricate deception."

"I'm game. I want to help save you if I can. To cure your zombie clone. To be your friend. But how, in detail?"

"That is the challenge. There is a special private monthly dance, invitation only, where Demons interact with mortals. In fact, it occurs now in the Queendom of Thanx, because Bang and I were married there, thanks to the intercession of mortal nymphs." She paused, remembering. "Nydia Nymph will always be my friend. She had been dismissed as a nonentity, her kind good for only one thing, but she saved me from destruction. Yet that is of only peripheral relevance here. Each participating Demon or Demoness must dance with a mortal person, and kiss that person with greatly muted effect, then change partners and do it again with the new one. Somewhat in the manner of the dance that evoked the passion of Dane and Rhonda, long, long ago. Of course the mortals like it." She smiled obscurely. "It is even hinted that some Demons like it too. Galaxies can find grains of sand fun to play with, on occasion. At any rate, that tradition is being carried on by the zombies, whose interest is to maintain seeming normalcy until the universe has been fully conquered. Otherwise zombie-free individuals, both mortal and Demon, might catch on to the danger and organize an effective resistance. Fully living folk have better minds than zombies, which helps them significantly."

"Living folk have puns," Noe said. "Assuming that counts."

"It counts heavily, among mortals. Not among Demons. To cure a Demon, close Demon contact is necessary. Demon Pun will have some serious kissing to do."

"But he's confined," Shameless protested. "And hiding with me."

"Not in the zombie universe," Andromeda said. "Here he is foreign, and confined only by our need for privacy. It is the clone Pun who is confined."

"Oho," Gyles said. "I think I begin to see the light. The zombies believe he is out of play, but he is not only here with us, he is hidden. So he can do things the native Demon Pun can't."

"Indeed. So he will attend the dance, assuming we can suitably camouflage him."

"Camouflage him as himself," Shameful suggested.

Andromeda frowned. "This is not the occasion for what we don't want to hear,"

"No. I mean pretend he is imitating Pun. Then the imitation can kiss your zombie clone into recovery."

Andromeda paused. "I believe I spoke of mortals picking up details Demons can miss. This might indeed be an effective ruse, considering that I, as a Demon, overlooked it. Let's make him into a seeming Demon imitating Pun, whom everyone here knows is out of the picture. My clone would not try to avoid kissing him, thinking him harmless."

"Then she should have the wit to mask her recovery," Aura said. "So as to be able to join us when we go after Bang."

"Bang will not object to kissing Andromeda," Bang said with a smile about the size of a grain of sand. "But yes, she should hide her recovery." Santo's mouth quirked for him. "But he will not be interested in Kissing Pun."

"This where Aura comes in," Andromeda said. "When the time comes to tackle Bang, she will be the front mortal. What I see is Pun holding the hands of myself and my mended clone, channeling his power through us, who in turn will hold the hands of Aura, who will in turn kiss clone Bang with Pun's power enhanced by our own powers of change. In that manner we hope to change him into another well Bang."

"It will not be enough," Bang said. "My power is equivalent to that of all the other Demons combined. Even my inferior zombie clone will retain enough power to resist the cure."

"You can add your power to Pun's power," Shameful said. "By placing your hands on him from behind while he holds the hands of the Andromedas. Just make sure that the surge does not incinerate mortal Aura during the kiss."

"Excellent caution," Bang agreed. "I will include a protective measure to preserve her wellbeing from literal burnout."

"Thank you," Aura said faintly.

"The dance is tomorrow," Andromeda said. "All of us need to be well prepared for it."

Another Demonly understatement.

* * *

They got on it immediately. Nik and Anthem crossed to Aura, as she was a Lips woman and this was the Lips enclave within the Queendom of Thanx. They greeted Wanda and Knife. Andromeda accompanied them invisibly. "I will change you," she said. "That is my power. I will fragment you into multiple copies for this task, and restore you when it is done. You will not be aware of it, except when you see your other selves. Do not interfere with them or make a commotion; this is business."

"Multiple copies?"

"So you can broach all the Lips women simultaneously. This the most efficient way, since we don't want to call a public meeting."

"This should be interesting," Anthem murmured privately.

First, they went to Queen Apoca, who was startled, her hair turning yellow. "Your aura is gone!"

"That is the least of it," Aura said. "I got kissed by a Demon, who not only banished my zombie lips curse, but also my migraine headaches. It's a phenomenal relief. Now we have an important dance to prepare for."

Apoca's hair turned green. "Of course. We Lips women are catering it."

"Yes." Aura had known about this. "But there's a new aspect."

The doubtful yellow returned. "Aspect?"

"We need to conceal the fact that many of us have been cured of zombieism."

"Whatever for?"

"It is not merely mortals who have suffered zombification. It's Demons."

Now the hair was plaid. "Demons!"

"This universe is being conquered by zombies from another universe. It can't be complete without the Demons being zombified too. Now they are watching to make sure there is no counter zombie campaign. They will be here tomorrow. If all the Lips folk are clearly alive, there will be trouble."

Apoca looked faint, her hair still plaid. "We don't need Demon trouble."

"Exactly. So the caterers need to look like zombies, at least until the Demons are gone."

"Makeup." The hair turned green. "We'll use plenty."

"So will we of the Quest. If we succeed in our objective, we'll cure the attending Demons. Then no more concealment will be necessary."

And plaid again, tinged by blue. "But I have been spreading cures madly for the past day. It will be difficult to get the word out in time."

"We plan to help," Aura said. "We have secret Demon assistance."

"Even with that, I don't see how—"

Andromeda acted. Aura split into two identical women, with identical clothing and companions. Then into four. "We'll spread the word," the four said together.

"Now I think I see," Apoca said with a four-sided smile and multicolored hair. "Do your thing."

There were two more splits. Then sixteen Auras went out to the Lips community residences. They didn't need to visit all the Lips tribe, merely those designated as caterers.

"Are we the originals?" Wanda asked privately.

"I think we're all originals," Anthem replied. "I feel the minds of my other selves. They are just like me, and their companions are asking the same question. It's as if I have thirty-two eyes."

Aura glanced around. Her gaze was met by the others, who were similarly glancing. They nodded synchronously. "Weird," she muttered. "Sometimes I wish I had hair like Apoca's. Then I could mix my emotions for all to see."

"Me too," Anthem said, with a mental array of colors. They all laughed, as ants did not have human type hair.

They knocked on the door of the nearest relevant house. A Lips woman answered. "Aura!" she said. "You look odd."

"Not only am I not a zombie, Mazie," Aura replied, "I have no aura. I have been cured of both. But I'll keep the name."

"And you and your Quest helped us all to get free of the zombie taint. Word spread. We certainly do appreciate it."

"Thank you. Now, ironically, I have an opposite message. We must all fake being zombies at the dance tomorrow, because Demon zombies will be there and we don't want them to realize that now we can fight the plague. We hope to catch them by surprise and cure them. It takes more than puns for Demons, so it's tricky. Then, we will be able to rid this world and this universe of zombieism."

Mazie's full lips pursed. "Oh, I see. I'm for that, of course. I hated being a zombie, even if I couldn't even try to get rid of it. So I'll need to don rot makeup and walk a bit unsteady, as I did before we discovered the pun cure."

"Exactly."

"And now I have the gumption to fight back when one of the molester's figures to have at me. They've been cruising the area."

"Kiss him into submission."

"Can't. They stop that. but I'll find a way."

There were other details, but it was clear that Mazie would cooperate fully. They went on to the next free house. The other Auras were evidently doing the same. The word was being efficiently, competently, and quietly spread.

Between houses, a brute man, not a Lips and not a zombie, cruised through, evidently looking for easy pickings. He spied Aura and closed on her, reaching out as he started to open his trousers. He had a mouth guard on so that she could not kiss him into love slavery, and his arms and legs were shielded so that she could not scratch him into zombieism. He thought that made her helpless.

Wanda and Knife sprang into action. Aura assumed the likeness of an amazon, with a deadly sword in her hand, no bluff. "If I should happen to see any threatening projection," she said grimly, "I will cut it off." The sword made a suggestive twitch, at about waist height, showing its readiness for exactly such action.

The man quickly moved on. That was indeed his best course.

Within an hour the job had been done. The sixteen clones returned to Apoca's house and merged back into one person.

But now Aura's mind, and the minds of her four physical companions, were crammed with the knowledge of sixteen copies of themselves. More than one Aura had brushed off aggressive shielded strangers. Wanda and Knife normally remained quiet, but they were very nice to have around when there was need. The group, now back in one body, had to relax and let it all fade into the jumbled background.

"Good show," Apoca said, her hair green. "We'll be ready for the dance tomorrow."

They walked on to Queen Demesne's residence, as she, too, needed to be notified. This was after all her domain. She met them before they got there, appearing as a ball of smoke that quickly became an elegant woman. She was a small d demoness who liked to keep track of things in the queendom. “I got word. All folk associated with the dance will be apparent zombies. Thank you for your effort.”

“Thank you for your support,” Aura said. “And your support of the Lips tribe.”

“I envy you your close association with Demons.”

Aura laughed ruefully. “I feel rather out of my depth.”

Demesne smiled. “The zombie invasion has made all of us feel that way.” She faded out, literally.

The dance hall was ornate, set up as an ancient royal extravaganza site. The Lips caterers were scantily clad and fresh zombies by the look and feel of them. Refreshments were not served, because zombies didn’t eat when they didn’t have to for politeness. The women were there simply to serve whatever need anyone had, and to clean up any rot that fell on the floor.

The guests, in contrast, were garbed like courtiers and royalty. But they too were zombies. It was clear that they were putting on a show of normalcy, largely for themselves. The whole thing was but a shadow of what it had been before the invasion.

Queen Demesne made the formal announcement to commence the dance. She looked exactly like a well-endowed lady zombie. She was a demoness, so could assume any form she chose, but did seem to be somewhat ragged, and her gown fit imperfectly, as if her body was deserting it. Nik wasn’t clear how demons got infected, but if Demons could be, it had to be easier for the lesser ones. Maybe phantom kisses got them too. “Welcome to our invitational Demon/Mortal Dance. And thank you, Queen Apoca and your Lips women, for so aptly catering it.”

Apoca, to the side, nodded graciously, shedding a bit of decay loosened hair. Her husband, Prince Nolan Naga, stood by her side in his human form. He did not look any better off with respect to zombieism than she. They had both done careful jobs of fakery since their recent cures.

“And now the music,” Demesne said, gesturing toward the zombie orchestra. It started playing, obviously the worse for wear. Even their instruments looked tainted.

Aura was there with a faked-up Demon Pun as her date. He was not posed as a zombie, but, by design, neither was he a very good emulation of a Demon. Everyone knew that the real Pun was not available, so this had to be a fake. Aura was obviously a shapely zombie. Again, everyone knew that she had been zombied before the invasion, so was farther gone than the other Lips women. She seemed barely able to maintain her posture. It was her supposed fortune that the invasion had come, because that eliminated her isolation. There was no sign of her aura, but of course she might simply be between headaches.

Nik, Anthem, Wanda, and Knife were with Aura, as seeming decorations. Strangers who saw her were faintly amused. Faintly was all the humor zombies were capable of. Bugs on her shoulders, clinging to her halter straps? A wand and a knife at her hip? She must be further gone than most. No person of sound mind would think her decorations were appropriate for an occasion like this.

The first dance began. The participants shuffled onto the floor, Pun and Aura included. They did the dance action, concluding with a kiss. It was routine; no little hearts flew out. "This reminds me of how I first danced with Dane," Rhonda Ghost said. "Only we did fall in love."

"It's the same kind of dance," Anthem reminded her.

Then came the partner change. They had arranged to dance near Zombie Bang and Andromeda, so were able to take them as their new partners. Nik, despite the potent lockdown of any mental indication of their talents, felt the phenomenal power of the Zombie Bang as Aura glided into his embrace. Indeed, it would not be easy to cure him.

"I know of you," Bang told her as they danced. "My wife befriended you. I'm not sure why."

"She thinks I have character. She might change her mind," Andromeda said, being the Demoness of Change. But the humor passed him by. He was a zombie, all right. His hand didn't even "accidentally" slide down to her bottom, as tended to be the case with non-zombie males. Zombies were not much interested in that sort of thing, in significant part because they did not reproduce, they just slowly decayed.

Meanwhile Pun danced with Zombie Andromeda. That was the one that counted at this moment. Would he succeed in curing her?

The conclusion of the sequence came. Aura kissed Bang, not with power; that would come later. There was nothing potent about it. Bang hardly noticed it. Nik's attention was mainly on the other couple.

He saw the kiss. He saw Andromeda stiffen in amazement, a flake of rot falling. Then Pun murmured something in her ear. She nodded and went on to the next partner, seemingly unchanged. Zombies might resist getting cured, but once they were healed, they were sublimely glad for it.

"It worked," Anthem said. "Now she's faking being a zombie."

What a relief! They danced on with other partners. Among them was Vol, the human form of the Element of the Void, the powerful figure Nydia Nymph dated. "I love Nydia's iridescent hair," Aura said.

"So do I."

Then they exchanged with Demon Chaos and his partner of the moment.

"Our turn," Anthem said.

Abruptly the immense power of Pun surged into Nik. The Demon seemed to be still dancing with the other woman, a mortal, but his main focus was now on them. Nik relayed it to Anthem, who relayed it to Aura, who was now supercharged. A grain of sand was ready to make like a galaxy. Soon she kissed Chaos with power vastly augmented by the channeled connection. Nik felt as if they were part of a mundane pile driver smashing into the Demon's face.

"Well, now," Chaos said, not at all dismayed. His power was actually far greater than Pun's, but as a zombie he had been relatively ineffective.

"You're cured," Aura whispered. "Fake being a zombie, so as not to make a scene. We have other folk to cure."

"Including Squid," he said.

"Yes. A pun will do for her. It's the Demons that count here."

"Understood. Thank you." They felt his gratitude. Like other Demons he had been caught off guard and zombied before he could fight. That would not happen again. He did love his mortal girlfriend.

They separated, going to new partners. Nik and Anthem were thrilled. It had worked! They were curing Demons.

Pun was doing the females directly, and Aura doing the males indirectly. What was happening here was far more significant than it appeared. They just had to hope that they could continue until the finale, which would be Aura's second kiss of Zombie Bang. Bang had not been exaggerating when he said that his power matched that of all the other Demons combined. It did. She might as well try to move a mountain with her little finger. Or a planet with an eyelash.

In the course of the partners changes, Pun came to dance with Squid, Chaos' mortal girlfriend. She was not human, but looked completely and fetchingly girlish. Nik heard it via Anthem's telepathic connection covering the Demon. "You saved Chaos," she said. "Thank you."

"You saved our universe by taming Chaos," Pun said. "This merely returns the favor."

"Thank you for returning it." The time for the kiss came, and she kissed him, and her rot fell away. He had cured her, as he had Aura.

The dance continued, and the powered kisses. They made it. By the end of the dance, all the attending Demons had been cured except Bang. The zombie's mind was not completely sharp, but he finally realized that something was going on. He stopped dancing, letting his partner go. "What is happening here?" he demanded. The other dancers withdrew to give him center stage. Everyone knew this was the crisis point. As Demon Bang went, so went the universe. The rest was peripheral.

Bang alive stepped forward. He had masked himself as a stage manager, staying out of sight and mind. "We are saving this universe from the zombie curse. You alone remain infected. Now we propose to cure you too."

"You truly are myself from another universe," Zombie Bang said, amazed. He, of course, could tell now that his attention was focused. "But I am not interested in being, as you put it, cured."

"Because part of the curse is to make its victims resist being mended," Live Bang said. "But if you trust the judgment of your wife, as I do mine, who is the clone of yours in my universe, you will accept the need for it. Ask her."

Zombie Bang looked at ex-Zombie Andromeda. "Yes," she said. "I am cured, and I want it for you too, and for this universe. Please accept the cure kiss. You will be much better off for it."

That evidently impressed him. "Whose kiss?"

"Aura's kiss." She indicated Aura.

"I kissed her before. She had nothing."

Aura stepped forward. "Try me now." As if a grain of sand could challenge even an ordinary galaxy, let alone *the* galaxy.

"Very well," he said dismissively. "To get rid of a nuisance."

Aura went up to him. The two Andromedas caught hold of her hands, in the maneuver they had rehearsed. Pun took their free hands. Live Bang put his hands on Pun's shoulders, ready to lend his huge power to enhance that of the other Demon. It was done so quickly that there was no time to comment, let alone protest.

Aura put her face to Zombie Bang's face and aggressively kissed his mouth, this time with power. Nik and Anthem, riding her, felt the monstrous surge of it passing through all their bodies. Four Demons from two universes channeling through one mortal body. Power and change flowed as never before. Never, in the history of the universes, had there been a kiss like this. Indeed, the mortal woman needed shielding, lest she be incinerated. This was no cute little hearts kiss; this was a supernova squared smooch.

The setting of the dance hall, the Lips enclave, the Queendom of Thanx, the Land of Xanth, and the planet on which it clung dissolved into irrelevance. Now surrounding space was manifest. Stars went nova, background ether and dark matter twisted into giant compound pretzels, galaxies wee-wawed crazily and collided, and the essence of the universe imploded into a giant pseudo alternate variant. Reality transformed.

Then it all cleared, and the dance hall was back. "I am cured," Zombie Bang said, taking it in stride. "Thank you." Now that it had happened, he, too, was satisfied.

The chain of people fell apart. Aura sank to the floor in a maidenly swoon as the two Andromedas hugged each other. Pun and Live Bang stepped back, smiling. Nik and Andromeda kissed mentally. So did Wanda and Knife. The universe had been saved. Someone applauded.

It was another Quest conference. "We have saved this universe," Nik said. "But it is only one of a myriad. We need to search out the source of the zombie kisses and end them. Demoness Zombia will help us search, but all she can do is point the direction. We need a way to determine distance so we can go right to the correct universe."

"First we need to stop the existing kisses that are infecting Demons," Andromeda said grimly. "So that no reinfection is possible.

"I agree," Pun said. "It would be pointless to search other universes while our own two remain at risk. We must secure our home base."

"So how do we do that," Gyles asked. "When Demons themselves have not stopped them?"

"The Demons were caught off guard," Andromeda said. "They will be more careful in the future. But those kisses may be savvy enough to catch Demons in moments of inattention; we cannot assume that they represent no further danger. We need to undertake a local zombie kiss hunt and capture. This Quest is prepared to do that." She made one of her changing smiles. "I will magnify the several members and equip you to accomplish it."

Then Nik and Anthem found themselves expanding again. This time so were the others, including the ghosts. They grew into galaxy size, and were back in the dark matter aspect.

"Wings," Andromeda said, and Nik sprouted a set. Beside him Anthem did the same. He resembled a large fly, she a small one. They were iridescently colored, and she was beautiful. The other members of the Quest, human and object, were similarly outfitted. The ghosts didn't need wings.

"Bottles." Wide-mouthed containers appeared at their waists, anchored by light belts.

"Nets." Puffy nets mounted on sticks appeared in their hands, claws, or forefeet.

"Goggles." Each person was wearing appropriately sized spectacles.

"Action," Andromeda concluded. "You will be able to see the kisses as they pass, via the goggles, and hear their buzz. Net them and put them in your bottles, which are designed to lock them in. We'll dispose of the bottles later. When no buzzing remains, the job will be complete."

Nik vibrated his wings and took off. So did Anthem and the others. They had never flown before, but the wings seemed to have their own operating magic. They glanced about. The ghosts were acting as spotters, rapidly crisscrossing the area, searching. Wanda was wielding Knife, who was now a net.

One ghost hovered near Nik, indicating that something of interest was near. Indeed, there was a buzzing ahead. It looked like a mundane butterfly. Xanth butterflies were winged pats or quarters of butter, but this looked more like, well, an insect. The body was like a pair of red human lips, vaguely pursing. He zoomed forward, swinging his net. He caught it and brought it to the jar as he levered up the lid, which was hinged. He plopped it in and closed the cover. The lips were no longer pursing or smiling; they were snarling, realizing that they were being balked. He had made his first capture.

They continued, catching kisses. Then something else appeared. Oops! It was the baby dragon, Kinky. They could tell because of the tail. He had wandered away from his mother again, attracted by the activity. Some juveniles were naturally curious.

Anthem flew down to meet him with a welcoming background chord. "Hello again, Kinky! You need to go home before you get really lost, out here in deep space."

But it seemed the cub was already lost. He appeared to have no idea where he was. He had come out here without paying attention.

"Maybe I can help you," Anthem said. "I'll send out a beacon signal." She flew over to perch on Kinky's head, being so small it was no burden. Then she sounded a sustained chord, the same one she had used as background when she sang "Long, Long Ago" to the baby.

Meanwhile Nik spoke to the others. "There may be a dark matter dragon coming. Give it room. It won't be hostile. It just wants its baby."

"Not to worry," Noe answered. "Remember, we saw it on the screen. Kinky's cute. But we'll stay well clear of Mama Dragon."

The chord had effect. It penetrated the fabric of space, reaching into the galaxies, making them vibrate. Soon the mama dragon heard it and came flying out.

Anthem ended the chord as mother and cub came together. She flew up, in effect turning Kinky over to another adult. The dragon glanced at her, nodded, and went on, making no hostile move against any of them. She understood that they were Anthem's companions and not into hurting babies. The two departed.

"That was almost fun," Noe said. "Now we all know what you two went through, before. Dark matter isn't completely weird."

The kisses chase continued. They traversed the universe as a seeming playground, waving their butterfly nets. The ghosts got really skillful at locating kisses. Their jars were filling with angry lips. No eloquent lips here! Before long there were no more to be found, and the soundless buzz had died away. They had cleared this universe of the zombie threat. At least until more kisses entered it. Preventing that would be their next challenge.

They shrank back to their original size and place. “That was amazing,” Gyles said. “I felt almost alive again.”

“You were alive, in a manner,” Andromeda said. “Dark matter has its own rules.”

Success was wonderful. But Nik knew that larger challenges were ahead.

Chapter 10

GRAV LENS

Nik would have liked to rest, as would the others, but with universes at stake they knew they couldn't relax. But how were they to proceed? His clairvoyance focused on one thing: the gem in his pincer.

"We need to search the universes for the particular Demoness Zombia who is sending out the deadly kisses," he said. "The local Zombia will give us the general direction, but we need to know how far. My talent indicates that the dark matter gem the dragon mother gave us can provide us with that information. All we have to do is learn how to use it."

"This is something even Demons don't really know," Andromeda said. "Our powers are largely confined to our own universes. Travel between them is a rarity for us. The four of us that have done so with the Quest are special cases. So we have to leave this aspect to you mortals. We will continue as observers." Her presence withdrew.

"The queendom has a small collection of similar artifacts to your gem, that turned up in the course of their construction," Aura said. "Apoca mentioned that Demesne had spoken of it once. They don't know what to do with it either. Most folk can't even see or feel them. Just those with special sensitivity."

"More news we didn't need," Santo said wryly. "One dark matter fragment is more than enough."

"It's valuable," Anthem said. "I picked that up from the mind of the mama dragon. She found it on the ground some time back, and liked it because it was polished, so saved it. Then she gave it to us."

"Mothers do appreciate those who save their children," Noe said with about three quarters of a smile.

"So what's next?" Shameful asked.

Now Noe smiled fully. "That's the question we didn't want to ask."

"You want a simple answer that won't be good for you," Shameless said.

"So what answer will be good for us?" Noe asked.

"Go to the Good Magician," Shameful said. "The one in the ex-zombie universe, since you've already been to the one in our home universe."

There it was. The answer they didn't want. They knew it would be complicated, but they were stuck for it. With luck the Good Magician, knowing that they were trying to save universes, would not put them through the three entrance challenges. But his attitude was notoriously unpredictable. The only truly consistent thing about him was his grumpiness.

They went as a party of five apparent individuals: three humans on two carpets, two centaurs on hooves. Plus two bugs, three ghosts, and four observing Demons. Nothing unusual about it, to outsiders.

"And they don't even know about our talents," Anthem said.

"Or our mission to save universes," Nik agreed.

"Or our impossible love."

Indeed. To Nik, that was the most wondrous aspect of the Quest. Their love, amended by the love of Dane and Rhonda. In the gloaming . . . long long ago.

"We agree," Dane said. "The two of you are worthy hosts. You are not like us in body, but you do love as we do. We truly respect that."

Nik appreciated their appreciation, but it didn't lessen the futility of it. How could he ever truly be with Anthem?

"It might have been better to leave me thus, dear," she thought in sad response.

"No!"

"No," she agreed sorrowfully.

They parked the carpets in the care of the centaurs, Aura, and Gyles Ghost in the phone, which would not be serviceable in the Challenges. Santo and Noe walked toward the castle, carrying Nik, Anthem, and their ghosts. The Demons watched passively.

The region around the castle was a dense miasma of ugly bushes, grasses, and vines, buttressed by a green and purple stench mixed with sickly pink stink. There were paths through it, but they twisted around so sinuously that it was impossible to know which one would get them through without pooping out in the worst bog. They did not want to guess. Nik's clairvoyance would not work here, and neither could Anthem read any minds to find out. The ghosts' talents were irrelevant, too, even if they worked. Dropping the other shoe? Scaring the living daylights out of folk? Both talents worthy, but not immediately applicable.

"But somewhere else, we'd love to use them," Dane said.

Ahead of the marsh was a small pavilion where a teen girl sat opposite a decorative wall. "Hello," she said as they approached. "My name is Jade. My talent is to make a spot on the wall. See?" A spot appeared on the wall.

This had to be a Challenge. Spot on the wall talents were shorthand for magic so slight as to be worthless. How could she have any pride in that? She was here for another reason.

"Do you know which of these paths leads safely through the swamp?" Noe asked.

Jade smiled. "Sure." Then she slumped in her seat, her eyes closing. She seemed to have fallen asleep. It would not be safe to disturb her, because that could skew the challenge.

What now? Should they take a path at random, gambling that it would be the right one? It was bound to be wrong, because the challenge was surely to get the girl to tell them the right one. How could they do that?

Nik contemplated the spot the girl had made. It seemed almost alive, its edges moving slightly. It was no ordinary spot. It was almost as if it was watching them.

Then he got a notion. He had Santo get a handkerchief and erase the spot.

The girl woke with a start. "Oh poof, you caught on," she said.

"You transferred your consciousness to the spot," Nik said via Santo. "That's your real talent. Through that spot, you can see what folk are doing here. When I erased it, you had to wake."

"You got it. Now I have to tell you the right path. It's that one." She pointed.

"Thank you, Jade." They took the path she indicated. It wound around as if trying to lose them, and almost succeeded, but finally made it safely out of the mire. One Challenge navigated.

Ahead was a big pond. The path went up to it, then veered to the right, past a pile of wooden planks, to take a long route around. This was too bad, because the loop the path took led around the lake to almost touch the place where it veered. They could see the water wasn't deep here; they could nearly wade across, and save a fair amount of time.

They halted. "There's got to be a catch," Noe said.

Then Santo saw a sign: epilep sea. "We don't want to touch that water."

"We don't," Noe agreed.

"Check those planks," Ghost Dane suggested. "They're not here by accident."

"Still to your accents I listen with pride," Rhonda said fondly.

The planks turned out to be just the right size to bridge the gap between the near and far sections of the path. They laid them in place and crossed, not risking immersion in the Epilep sea. The second Challenge had been navigated.

Next, they came to a nice glade decorated with lovely rare flowers. There was a basin filled with candies. A number of cute vases and figurines were laid out on a table. A sign said tourist trap.

"Beware," Dane said. "It's likely all cheap junk that only tourists will fall for. A waste of money."

"In Xanth things tend to be more literal," Santo said. He could hear the ghost too. "And we don't use money."

Anthem, Rhonda, and Noe were evidently having a similar dialogue. "Stay back," Noe said. She picked up a stone and carefully tossed it onto the table so that it would seem as if a person were touching it, to pick up a figurine.

The stone clattered. Then giant claws rose out of the ground, closing together overhead. Anyone by the table would have been trapped.

"Tourist trap indeed," Santo muttered.

They bypassed the glade. Third Challenge navigated.

There before them was the castle moat. The drawbridge was down. They were free to enter.

They crossed the drawbridge. The moat monster watched them but made no hostile move; it knew the rules of this game.

Dara Demoness greeted them at the entrance. "I am the Designated Wife. I understand you are visitors from another universe. All eight of you."

So she knew about the bugs, ghosts, and Demons. She was after all married to the Magician of Information.

"We are," Santo said. "Our mission is important. We thought the Challenges could have been bypassed, considering that we helped save this universe from the zombies."

"Yes you did," Dara agreed. "I got caught by one of those demonic flying carriers, but the malady dissipated when you cured the Demons and banished the kisses. But Magician Humfrey is a century old, give or take a few days when his dose of youth elixir isn't exact, and is taking longer to shake off the zombie brain rot, so forgot to cancel the Challenges. They weren't meant for you anyway; you are far more sophisticated than ordinary querents. We'll expedite things now. He's ready to see you."

She showed them to the cramped study mostly filled by the giant Book of Answers. "Party of eight," Dara said, and faded out.

The Good Magician looked up. He did look a bit worse for wear. "Nicola Nickelpede, in the punhandle." His sunken eyes flopped back to the book. They had been dismissed.

Dara reappeared. "Nicola is a specialist in dark matter fragments," she explained. "She is also the smartest bug you'll ever encounter. She impressed even a Mundane genius. Here is her address. Your other Quest party will be mapping that mound soon." She handed Santo a slip of paper.

"Thank you," Noe said.

They rejoined the others, and soon were flying toward the punhandle. Their speed was exceptional; the Demons were evidently enhancing it, along with the centaurs. The paper Dara had given Santo turned out to be like a fragment of the map; it showed exactly where to go.

They came to the mound. They landed, and Santo and Noe went to it. The nickelpede guards oriented, uncertain of their intentions, ready to attack if the mound were threatened.

"Peace," Anthem broadcast with a reassuring chord. "We just want to talk with Nicola."

After a generous moment a single female nickelpede emerged. She was quite attractive, with nicely contoured pincers, long antennae, and delicate feet. "I am Nicola. What do you want?"

Nik carried Anthem and went to the ground to meet her. "I am Nik Nickelpede, and this is my associate Anthem Ant. I am clairvoyant and she is telepathic. We have a dark matter lens we need to learn how to use. We understand you know how. Will you teach us?"

Nicola eyed him. "You are reasonably young and you have an excellent talent. My smarts alienate regular nickelpedes. Will you be my male?"

Oops. "I am committed to Anthem."

"An ant?!" she asked, managing two punctuation marks. That was pretty good for an unwritten question.

This was awkward already. "We are in love," Anthem explained. "Completion is impossible, because we are of two quite different species and sizes, but all we want is each other." She sent a burst of feeling.

"Crushed pincers!" Nicola swore as she absorbed the feeling and knew her dawning interest was hopeless. "I find the perfect male, and he loves elsewhere."

Noe spoke, translated by Anthem. "Nik and Anthem reside in the Queendom of Thanx. They have to work together, and their talents mesh—their love just happened. They admire each other's minds, which may be a better relationship than the physical kind. If you want a physical relationship, there are plenty of nickelpedes in the queendom. One caution: they do not gouge humans there. Neither do humans step on them. It is a truce. So Nik and Anthem associate with humans like Santo and me. We all respect each other without fear, and will unite in defense of Thanx. Apart from that, the queendom has a number of dark matter fragments. You will have free access to them, if you come through for us on our gem."

A little phantom pincer appeared over Nicola's head, and clicked. "It's a deal. I hate it here in the punhandle. Puns are everywhere. They squish under our feet. Have you ever stepped on a pun and gotten squelched punch on your foot? The only good thing about it is that the zombie curse bypassed it."

"Because puns destroy zombies," Noe said. "Your residence protected you."

"Oh, I see. Maybe I pundemned them too quickly." She reoriented "Let me see your dark matter gem."

Nik opened his pincer to reveal it.

"Oooo! That's the best I've seen. It's not a fragment, it's a gravity lens."

"Can you teach us its uses?"

"Certainly. Here is a sample." She focused. A beam speared out of the lens. It intersected the branch of a tree looming over them. "This is a projected gravity intensifying field that can make an object implode into a small black hole." The branch shrank where the beam touched, and fell down, hanging from its stump, "But instruction will take time. The details are complicated, and any error could be disastrous."

So it seemed. If the beam had caught a person, that person would be dead. "It's like one of my holes," Santo murmured. "Only different."

"If you are ready," Nik said, "Join me on my human companion, and we will take you to Thanx."

The phantom pincer clicked again. "I am ready."

Santo laid a hand on the ground beside them. Nik and Nicola climbed onto it, while Anthem returned to Noe.

Soon they were on the carpets, zooming back across the Land of Xanth. Nik talked with Nicola, finding her intriguing. It would have been easy to love her, with her intelligence complementing his clairvoyance, had he not met Anthem first.

"She is your kind," Anthem said privately. "If you—"

"No!"

She was silent, but he felt her relief. At least she had made the offer. Their love might be considered crazy, but it was absolute.

They arrived at the queendom and promptly checked in with Queen Demesne. "We have enlisted the expertise of Nicola Nickelpede to enable us to use the Grav Lens we have, so that we can maybe stop the source of the zombie invasion," Noe explained. "She will need a home here, and access to your dark matter fragments."

"The Good Magician messaged us via the magic mirror," Demesne said. "We have the fragments available at need. Here is Nicol, of another mound. His garden variety talent is locating the tastiest seeds. He is looking for a compatible roommate." She lifted a hand bearing a strikingly handsome nickelpede.

"Hello, beautiful," Nicol said to Nicola, clicking a well-formed pincer.

Nicola practically swooned. She might be smart, but she had evidently longed for a physical relationship with a masculine bug.

They combined the lessons with practical tasks, so that Nik, who had an affinity for the lens because of his clairvoyance, could assimilate the nuances as well as the principles. He needed to be thoroughly familiar with it, so as never to make a dangerous error that could affect not only his own welfare, but that of the universes.

Demesne let them know about a construction project. Thanx was still developing, as more women came to settle there, along with their families. It was a good place for men, too, if they were not interested in the politics of government or practicing male dominance. There were more females than males, and the right males of any species could find very nice companions. The surrounding kingdoms were not easy about this business of women having too many rights, let alone power, but there were some quiet supporters there. The nickelpede and ant mounds and bee hives were governed by females, and even the local ghosts haunted matriarchal houses. It was thought that such provocative notions were spreading even to backward Mundania, at least among bugs, where queen bees and queen ants were doing well, and older human women were known as queenagers.

There was a plan for a nickelpede community center, where residents of the several mounds in the vicinity could gather and get to know each other socially. Their presence in Thanx meant less fighting and more cooperation, as the truce applied to all creatures there. But the ideal spot was blocked by a boulder too massive for nickelpedes to move. They could of course enlist the aid of humans, but preferred to do it themselves if they possibly could. It was a matter of species pride.

"This is ideal for a demonstration project," Nicola said. She was with Nicol, who remained in the background per Thanx convention, but seemed quite satisfied with his situation. Anthem was with Nik, being as interested in the use of the lens as he was. "You will use the lens to lighten the rock so that it can be moved out of the way. But first some practice. Try lightening something small, like this pebble." She indicated a stone about the size of the lens.

Nik lifted his pincer to orient the lens and focused on the pebble. His mind surrounded the lens in the way that Nicola had shown him, willing it to project lightness. A beam speared out, striking the ground beside the stone, so that a mini tornado of dust swirled up. Oops. He damped it off immediately, and the dust settled.

"Try again," Nicola said. "Don't change the gravity until the beam is on the pebble. Limit the distance, too."

He tilted the lens slightly, then willed the beam to start. It struck the ground on the other side, but stirred no dust. He aimed it back until it caught the stone. He willed it to go no farther than the stone. Then he willed the lightness.

The stone shot up into the air, slowed, and dropped to the ground nearby. Dust puffed up where it had been. He damped the beam again.

"Too much lightening," Nicola said. "When you limited the range, you forgot to limit the power. Focus on three things in turn: aim, range, power. Do not activate the power until you are sure of all three."

To be sure. He tried again, step by step, and this time managed to make the stone float slowly up. He had done it!

"Good," Nicola said. "Remember, you don't have to make anything float. Just make it lighter, so others can move it more readily. Just make sure they don't intercept the beam."

"Maybe they'd like to float."

"No. Null gravity does odd things to the body, which depends on weight outside and inside to function perfectly. They would get sick, or worse, especially if the beam touched one part of the body and not another. Stay out of the beam!"

"She's making sense," Anthem said. "Suppose your feet were light, and your body heavy? You might flip over and land on your head. Or your stomach couldn't keep your food down?"

He saw it. This was no plaything. It could be worse if the beam got set on heavy, as the tree branch had showed.

He continued practicing until he could get it exactly right every time.

"Now the construction site," Nicola said. "For that, just make the stone light enough to push around. Make sure no one touches the beam."

Noe took them to the site, using the carpet. Anthem broadcast the message. "We will make the rock light enough to move. Take sticks in your pincers to push it. Don't get near the beam, because it could hurt you. Take it slow and easy."

Nik aimed the beam, limited its range, then focused on the lightening. Soon the boulder was wobbling when pushed, then slowly rolling. He kept the beam on it, ready to dampen it the moment anyone strayed too near.

Then a fly buzzed right into the beam, ignoring Anthem's mental warning to all local creatures. It shot upward, spinning, and landed on the ground. It lay on its back, its legs twitching. It definitely wasn't well. Probably the pressure of the surrounding air had badly squeezed its lightened body, doing internal damage. Finally it regained its feet, buzzed its wings, and flew unsteadily away. This was a good lesson: STAY CLEAR OF THE BEAM!

Soon the boulder was out of the way, and Nik shut down the beam. The construction foreman approached and they tapped pincers together in greeting. "Thank you, visitor. Now we can construct our community mound. You made it feasible."

"We are glad to have helped," Nik said. Then he, Anthem, Nicola, and Nicol boarded Noe's hand and returned to their own area.

"I want to thank you too," Nicol said to Nik. "You brought Nicola to me."

"She is invaluable."

"Tomorrow we practice heavying," Nicola said seriously, though her antennae were quivering with appreciation for the compliments. It was clear that she loved having an appreciative male companion. "Later we'll get to the more complicated things."

"Thank you also," Anthem said. She appreciated the expertise that was not only making the lens usable, but adding to Nik's reputation among bugs and humans.

Nicola looked at her. "Your warnings helped keep it safe. Your telepathy is marvelous. I would like to get to know you better."

"Me too," Anthem agreed with an appreciative chord, warming to her. They seemed to be in the verge of the beginning of friendship, maybe. That was a relief, considering their chancy initial relationship: interest in the same male.

The next day they practiced, as Nicola put it, heavying. Aiming and limiting the range of the beam was the same, but now the focus was on making the target object heavier. As with the lightening, the effect was there only when the beam was there; there was no permanent change of weight. A heavier pebble looked just like a normal one. That meant they had to take it to an extreme to be sure of it. That made it more dangerous. They really had to stay clear of the beam.

Nik put a pebble on some straw, then focused the beam on the pebble, gradually increasing its weight until it sank down, crushing the straw.

Then more, until the pebble grew so heavy that it started sinking into the ground.

"That's far enough," Nicola said. "If you want it to make a hole in the ground, you have to carry the lens there and aim down at it. That can be dangerous, because any wobble of the beam will impact the surrounding ground and maybe make it collapse under you. The lens is no toy."

"No toy," he agreed, further appreciating the danger in using it.

The following day they went to the place where Demesne wanted a public well for the humans. The water there was fairly deep underground, a subterranean river, and drilling would be complicated, as they lacked mundane equipment. They would have to use hand tools, which wouldn't work very well when the depth increased.

"We may be able to help," Noe told her. "Nik is practicing with the Grav Lens, making things heavy. If they get heavy enough, they can sink right down into the ground. We might be able to make a hole that way. But it could be dangerous if anything goes wrong."

"I understand," the demoness said. "We'll cordon off the area until it's done."

"If it doesn't work, I will make the hole," Santo said. "You will have your well, one way or another. But we prefer to develop proficiency with the lens."

"I understand that, too. We all know the importance of that mission."

They used a stone ball of the right diameter, which was bigger than a nickelpede and much heavier. Noe put it on the ground in the right place, and stood back with the other humans. Then Nik oriented the lens, got the focus and distance, and started the heavying. It took a while, because the ball was far more massive than the practice pebble had been and they didn't want to push too hard, too fast. But in due course the ball got heavy enough to start sinking. It went a little way and stopped.

Then Noe, guided by Anthem's relay of Nik and Nicola's instructions, carried them to the ball. She knelt by it and put her hand over so that the lens was directly above the ball. Nik oriented, focused, and gave the mental direction for a slow increase in weight. He felt the power as the lens obeyed.

The ball started descending, at first slowly, then faster. They felt the vibration as the earth was shoved aside by the slow force of the descent, heating and melting from the extreme pressure. Smoke rose.

"It smells like a volcano," Noe said, her nose wrinkling.

"Pinatuba, here we come," Anthem said with a volcanic chord.

Was there a distant musical rumble, as of the volcano resenting its name being taken in vain?

Santo used a big hand fan to blow the smoke aside so it wouldn't burn them. Nik kept the focus on, adjusting as the depth increased.

Finally Demesne was satisfied that it was deep enough. Nik reversed the setting and made the ball light again. They were careful not to hover right over it, lest it zoom up and strike them.

The hot ball came up, and Santo pushed it to the side with a solid stick. The hole was complete.

But there was no water, even when they put a pipe down to find it. "Don't worry," Demesne said. "I hate to talk science, but the heat of the drilling vulcanized the sides of the hole so that it is impervious to water. We missed the underground river, so there is no direct flow, but indirect is fine. Fortunately we have a resident whose talent is to make stone pervious. He'll tackle it tomorrow. The water will soon fill in. Thank you for the hole."

"You're welcome," Noe said for them all. "It's good practice."

"We all hope that your larger mission is successful. One zombie invasion is more than enough. How well we know!"

They all laughed appreciatively.

Next day they got serious, as Nicola put it. "We have explored the physical powers of the lens. Now we will get into its observational qualities, which are more sophisticated. First, general principles. The humans have souls, as we bugs generally have not." She glanced at Anthem. "Though I must confess that your Rhonda is appealing, especially when she sings."

"Thank you," Rhonda said. "From long, long ago,"

"This is our gloaming," Dane agreed.

Nicola wavered her antennae in the semblance of a smile, then got serious. "The difference between a live human and a dead human, apart from social implications, is that the dead one has no soul, and therefore weighs slightly less. Anthem with her ghost-soul weighs slightly more than she did without it. This could be verified if there were a suitably precise scale for bugs. The lens can detect it, on the micro scale or the macro scale. Maybe we should verify that now, as we shall need to be certain of it."

"We're game," Anthem said, with an interested chord. She went to stand on a twig with a solid knot on the far end, mounted on a pointed stone, shifting position until she balanced exactly.

"Now leave her, Rhonda," Nicola said.

The ghost did. Anthem slowly rose. She now weighed less.

"Rebalance," Nicola said.

Anthem nudged outward on the twig until she swung back into equilibrium.

"Now return to her, Rhonda."

The ghost rejoined the ant. Anthem slowly sank. She weighed more. The point had been made. Ghosts or souls had weight.

"Zombies are in between," Nicola continued as Anthem and Rhonda returned to Noe. "At least the ones made from living folk. They are not fully dead, so their souls remain, but more loosely attached, so that their effective weight is less. The farther gone a zombie is, the less closely the soul connects, so the weight descends. This generally is not noticed, as far more weight is lost by shedding rot, but the difference is there." She clicked a pincer, indicating a slight shift of subject. "This is the micro scale. The same is true on the macro scale. A zombie galaxy weighs less than a live galaxy. A zombie universe weighs less than a live universe. The Grav Lens can detect that difference, regardless of the scale of measurement. All that is required is the correct use of it, and correct interpretation of the figures."

"Your knowledge of the universe amazes me," Noe said. "We of the fantasy realm seldom get any inkling of it. For us, magic is everything. At least it was until the zombie invasion made some of us reconsider. How did you come by it?"

"For a time a knowledgeable human mundane ghost associated with me. I gave him a temporary life, such little as it was, and he gave me his information." She swayed her antennae. "I suspect he liked that I was an attentive female, truly thirsting for wider knowledge, and pretended to himself that I was human. Finally he tired of living in a mound with bugs and went on to heaven or wherever skeptical mundanes go. But I kept his information about micro and macro things, especially relating to gravity. Not that I had much use for it, until now."

"So you truly understand about bugs and ghosts," Rhonda said.

"I do, and I respect such relationships. I am sorry Albert left me. He would have loved meeting the members of the Quest, though he would have found aspects like instantaneous conjuration somewhat spooky action at a distance." She wiggled her antennae in a smile. "He hardly believed in ghosts, either, despite being one. That may have been another reason he moved on."

"A question," Nik said. "Since the souls, or ghosts, are part of the universe, why isn't their weight registered? The fact that they are no longer alive should not change the weight of the cosmos."

Nicola's pincers clicked. "Apt point. They seem to retreat into a weightless semi-existent state. They can sense each other, and some can make appearances and sounds when they try, but otherwise they hardly exist. It is as if they prefer to become fantasies. Their slight weight manifests only when they associate with a living body."

"Next question," Nik said. "How do I use the lens to weigh universes? I appreciate now that a zombie universe will weigh less than a live one, and that this should enable us to distinguish the zombie ones from the live ones, but the notion of focusing on a universe boggles my little mind. We are after all part of a universe."

"The universes tangle like a four- or five-dimensional cluster of bubbles. Everything is relative. To us, here, all the others seem to be erratically moving. We can send out beams to survey them randomly or systematically. That's not a problem."

"Uh, four or five dimensions? I know of only three."

"We see a rock as existing in three dimensions, height, width, and depth, but that's prohibitively limited. Another dimension is time, as a thing that exists no time does not exist at all. It can endure a short time, a medium time, or a long time, but must have at least some time. Another dimension is mass, as it must have an amount of substance. When we made the pebble float we decreased its mass; when we made the ball so heavy it sank into the ground, we increased its mass. There are other dimensions, such as maybe magic, though I think that's actually a force, but Albert did not explain them to me before he left. I'm not sure he even believed in magic, though he was so smart in other ways." She slicked her pincers in frustration. "He left me so distressingly ignorant!"

"Ignorant!" Anthem echoed with a bemused chord. Nicola was the most knowledgeable bug they'd encountered.

Nik's clairvoyance struggled with these new concepts, but concluded they were valid. A thing did need to have some solidity, and to endure for some time to be real. Magic did seem more like a force than a dimension, as it accomplished things.

Now, the background theory covered, they got practical. "The lens varies in color and brightness depending on the size and distance of the beam," Nicola explained. "It didn't matter when we were limited to the local scene, but it does when we extend to light years or megaparsecs." She paused as Anthem relayed the incomprehension of her audience. "A light year is the distance light travels in a year, used to describe the spacing between stars, often four or more such years. Light seems instant only because we are at the micro end of the scale. Actually it is limited in the manner all energy is, seeming slow at the macro scale. A parsec is about three and a quarter light years. A megaparsec is about three hundred and twenty-six million light years, maybe the distance between galactic clusters. A typical universe is a hundred times that size. That is the macrocosm. There may be no distance between universes; they may even overlap on parallel planes. But there may be considerable traveling to do within universes. So mere location is only part of the problem; you will need to get around within them."

The general incomprehension hardly diminished, but there was a qualification. "We made a hole from our universe to the same place in this one," Nik said. "We had no traveling in space to do."

"Ah. If you can make a similar hole directly to the same place in the zombie origin universe, and the two universes are relatively stable with respect to each other, that will simplify things considerably."

"We'll try," Santo said. "So far all I have needed are direction and distance, but I have not dealt with multiple universes before."

"So location is most of the problem."

"Yes."

"We will see what we can do."

They focused on the lens as Nik held it forth. "The detection beam is neutral until activated," Nicola said. "You must activate it with your mind, as you did its physical mass changing properties. Focus it on an object and think *read*."

Nik focused. A green beam shot out to intersect a distant tree. He thought *read*. The lens went pale.

"That indicates that there is very little mass in that tree, relatively speaking," Nicola said. "Now try a mountain."

He tried a mountain. The lens darkened slightly. "Shouldn't it change more? That mountain is hugely more massive than that tree."

"The scale is exponential." She paused, realizing that they were not going to understand this concept. "It's very small at one end, but very big at the other end. A tree and a mountain both seem small compared to a world. This is a tool that can handle bugs or galaxies. Mortal scale or Demon scale. Now aim it at this world."

Nik aimed the beam down and adjusted its length to Extended. He thought *read*. The lens darkened significantly more.

"Now aim it at the sun."

He did so, lengthening the beam to Amazing, and the color darkened more.

"And at the galaxy."

That took more doing, but finally he got the beam set in the right direction with a length of Wow. The color darkened more.

"And the universe."

That really took more. First, he had to aim it toward the main body of the universe, with a length of Awe, then set it on the maximum power. It was just a reading, not a weight changing; even so the lens heated with the power passing through it. It darkened to almost black.

"Beyond this we will need the help of the Demons," Nicola said. "To orient on other universes and calibrate them. But you understand the principle. The zombified ones will be lighter."

"How will we know which one is the zombie source?"

"The presumption is that that one will be the most thoroughly zombified, thus being the lightest."

"It's a gamble," Santo said. "There could be other factors, such as differing numbers of stars and living creatures."

"Do we have a choice?" Noe asked.

Anthem surveyed the Quest. The consensus was that they did not have a choice. They might simply have to check the lightest universes, and keep checking until they found the correct one. At least Zombia's directional sense should put them in the right vicinity.

"Another thing," Santo said. "I can make a tunnel to another universe, if given the correct orientation and distance. But we don't know that the one we want will be adjacent. I'm not sure that I could tunnel through one universe to get to one beyond it. Even if I could, I doubt it would be safe. We will need to stairstep from one to another until we reach the right one. That could be tedious."

"Also perhaps dangerous," Aura said. "So far, our universes have been very similar, apart from the zombies. But we can't be sure they all will. We could land in something quite different."

"You could indeed," Nicola agreed.

Surveying other universes turned out to be mainly a matter of aiming anywhere and extending the range to Unbelievable. They turned out to be all around, and most of them were lighter than the home universe. That suggested zombie infection to various extents.

It was time for Demon help. "We need to get Demoness Zombia's indication of direction," Nik said. "Then I will try to get the distance to the lightest one, hoping that's it."

"Demoness," Aura said. "We are ready for the direction."

Nik remembered that Demons might assume the appearance of mortals when interacting with them, and seem to occupy a local place, but actually were galactic in scope, or more. Zombia was attuned to Aura, so could hear her anywhere.

A glowing arrow appeared in midair, pointing upward at an angle. Nik quickly oriented the lens and invoked a range of Stupendous.

"Thank you," Aura said to the Demoness. The airborne arrow flashed acknowledgment and faded out.

The universe turned out to be full weight. "That can't be it," Nik said.

The arrow reappeared. Its point lengthened, shrank back, and lengthened again. Oh—go longer.

He reset the range to Ludicrous and willed it so. The lens flickered brightly black as it focused, then gave the reading of the universe beyond the first one.

It was the lightest yet.

Noe applauded, smiling.

"I think we've got it," Nik said, gratified. "It's the second one in that direction. Pretty close, considering how far it might have been. Practically next door."

"But there is a question," Shameful said. "That intervening universe—those zombie kisses had to have passed through it on the way to this universe. Why didn't they take it out?"

And there was the question nobody wanted to address. They would have to go through that universe to get to the key one, using it as a base for the second tunnel. There was something distinctly weird about it. No other universe in the vicinity had escaped the kisses. What was the difference here?

"We'll just have to find out," Noe said uneasily.

They would indeed.

Chapter 11

WEIRDESTINY

The next day the Quest organized. Nik rode with Santo, and Dane rode with Nik. They all rode on the back of Shameless Centaur, the object being to conceal the carpets, which the centaurs carried, and save them for emergency use if needed. Demon Bang observed Nik, and Demon Pun observed Shameless. Anthem, Noe, and Rhonda were on Shameful, with Demoness Andromeda observing them and Demoness Entropy observing the centaur. Aura walked, wearing Wanda Wand and Knife Knight. Plus Gyles Ghost in the Genius Phone. They were a party of sixteen that looked more like a party of five, which was the way they preferred it.

Santo made a tunnel to the same place in the mystery universe as they were here in the ex-zombie universe. The Demons were quietly alert in case there were some problem, like a vacuum or an inferno or an army of zombie robots. There was no suction or heat, no charge of warriors, and there was light at the far end, so it seemed to be safe.

"One question," Shameful said. "Should Nik carry the dark matter lens to other universes? There may be unanticipated risks. We need his clairvoyance, and we need the lens. Shouldn't they be separated?"

Ouch. She was correct, though Nik didn't like it. The assets of the Quest should not be risked with one carrier, as it were.

"Noe's talent is anonymity," Santo said. "Maybe she should carry it, so that it is better hidden."

Anthem's survey indicated that there was general agreement. So Nik turned it over to Noe, who tucked it into the safest place on her body, a pocket in her bra.

They took their places before the tunnel, two apparent mounted centaurs, one Lips woman afoot. Nicol and Nicola Nickelpede waved their pincers in farewell. Demesne and Apoca did the same, only with hands. "Return safely," the demoness said. "We care about you, along with the welfare of the universes."

"Thank you," Noe said. "We'll try to preserve both."

They marched on into the tunnel, Aura walking between the two centaurs. "I'm nervous," Anthem confessed.

"So are we all," Andromeda said. This was a signal that the Demons were watching closely.

They emerged from the other end in good order. The landscape was the same as the one they had left, but there were no folk there to welcome them. That was preferable to an aggressive encounter.

"Things appear to be normal here," Andromeda said. "The local Demons are not infected, and are going about their normal endeavors. There is no sign of any problem on the local or the intergalactic scale." She faded back into obscurity.

That was a relief. But Nik was wary. This was too easy. Also, it did not explain why this universe was unaffected by the zombie kisses. His clairvoyance gave him information but did not help there. It was a mystery that made him nervous.

"Me too," Dane said. "And I think all of us."

A ghost flew up to them. Noe put up her hand, startled, and it touched her fingers. That enabled it to commentate. Anthem relayed the dialogue. "Help! We are captive!"

"Rhonda!" Rhonda exclaimed. "My clone in this universe!"

"Yes," the ghost agreed. "We are locked in a dungeon cell. You must rescue us!"

"Caution," Anthem said, sending a double caution private message to Nik. She had good sense about people, being so much in their minds. So he stayed out of it, merely listening in.

"How can that be?" Rhonda asked cautiously. "Ghosts can't be confined."

"The girl Noe was carrying Anthem Ant, and I was with Anthem. The ant is telepathic, and sensed that a girl had entered an old cell looking for artifacts and the door had closed on her and locked from outside and she couldn't get out. So Noe hurried to help her, finding the cell and opening the door from outside. She went in to help the woman, but she turned out to be a demoness who flew to the door and slammed it shut, trapping Noe inside. We think it's a trap set by a troll who preys on innocent girls with the help of the nasty demoness who is maybe his secret lover. Only the fact that I was along enabled us to get the word out, because a ghost can't be confined to a cell. You must help us before the troll comes and devastates her. All you need to do is go there immediately and open the door, which has a one-way lock, and let her out. It's not far. I can show you. Quick, before the troll gets her!"

It was known that rogue trolls liked to cruelly tease, rape, kill, and eat human girls for passing entertainment. This was dire!

Andromeda joined Bang. "This smells of a trick to make we Demons reveal ourselves. I'm staying here, mum."

"Wait here," Noe whispered as she jumped off Shameful and hurried off after the ghost.

"I don't like this," Nik said. "But I guess we have to let her rescue herself of this universe."

"I am wary too," Santo said. "The way Rhonda found us here seems entirely too convenient."

It certainly did. They had not signaled their crossing. But Noe was already on her way. Worse, Anthem's surrounding telepathy abruptly faded. Nike felt alone in a way he had not since he first met her. What had happened? Had she been killed? That would be the ultimate horror.

"We have to face the possibility," Shameful said. She was on target; none of them wanted to face that prospect. Anthem had been the unifying presence throughout.

"Call Noe on the Genius Phone," Shameless suggested.

But it quickly became apparent that the phone, too, no longer connected. This added to their alarm. The centaur's suggestion had turned out to be no use, per his curse.

"The Demon ambiance has been damped out too," Andromeda said. "We can't investigate that without revealing ourselves. That's suspicious."

Then a ghost came to them. "Rhonda!" Dane exclaimed. "Or are you?"

"I'm the real one," the ghost said. "I mean, from our universe. Feel me to verify it." She overlapped him, and her authenticity was certain; Nik felt it too. *Long, long ago*. "The other is me too, but somehow a spell was used to make her lure the others into a trap. She was real, but her story was fake. I don't think she knew that. Maybe there's Demon involvement, with powerful hidden magic. The nearby cell the Noe clone was thought to be trapped in turned out to be a demoness in her image in a conjure site to a distant cell. Now our Noe really is trapped, and our Anthem too. Not by a troll. We don't know who is doing it. But it's serious trouble. A Demon has to be behind it. There's a field of some sort that damps down Anthem's telepathy, so she didn't catch on about the fake, and she's restricted again to contact mind reading. They were unable to phone out either; that, too, is damped. But at least we ghosts can convey messages."

Nik and Santo reacted together. Anthem and Noe both captive by an unknown party, maybe a Demon? Santo did not love Noe the way Nik loved Anthem, but he did care deeply for her. There was huge relief that the girls were not dead, but also anger that they had been treacherously abducted. Both females had to be rescued without delay. Along with the dark matter gem Noe carried.

"Agreed," Andromeda said. "But do not act impulsively. That risks your falling into the same trap they did, which may be part of the point of this ploy. There is indeed a Demon involved, but his identity is hidden. This is ugly business. We will remain concealed until we can catch him."

"What's going on?" Aura asked. "I seem to be out of the loop."

They quickly explained about the ghost messages and the suspicion of Demon involvement. Then Aura stood up straight, surprised. "Now I'm in a loop of my own. Demoness Zombia just contacted me on a private telepathic line. It seems we are friends in this universe also. Friends can attune to each other in ways others do not."

"Zombia!" Santo said. "As if this isn't complicated enough already!"

"Here is her message. In this universe she supports the other Demons in opposing the zombification of all Demons and living folk. She issued a spell that prevents the zombie kisses from taking effect. The kisses can't touch the folk here, literally. Only she can nullify the spell, as it is in her domain. But some rogue Demon here made a deal with the Zombia of the kisses. We don't know who he is; Demons can hide when they choose to. Somehow, they connected between universes. She will give him, well, what our universe's Zombia gives Demon Alchemy, up and clean, if he can get this universe's Zombia to nullify that protective spell so that this universe, too, will go zombie."

"It's an up and clean deal," Santo said angrily.

"To be sure," Gyles agreed from the phone. "But why abduct Noe and Anthem, who have nothing to do with the spread of the zombie kisses?"

"More from Zombia," Aura said. "In this universe, Zombia had two friends; in all the universe none other liked her. One friend was me. The other was telepathic Anthem Ant. She persuaded Zombia to protect this universe from the zombie kisses, when they started passing through. Because Anthem had other friends, bug and human, she wanted to protect. Then an animal stepped on her and killed her, we think by accident, not even noticing. Zombia mourned her. Then, suddenly, Anthem's clone from another universe appeared. That's us. The rogue Demon saw that and quickly abducted her and her human friend to use as leverage. He will let them go if Zombia agrees to cancel the kiss-null spell. He will give her a month to consider. Thereafter he will kill both hostages, as he maybe got her friend Anthem killed."

"Once we learned the situation," Santo said, "we would have gone on to the next universe to stop that other Zombia."

"Thus depriving the Demon of his up and clean affair with her," Aura said. "So he struck."

It was coming nastily clear. They had blundered into a treacherous situation. Demons opposing Demons.

"How does this universe's Zombia feel about this?" Santo asked.

"She would do anything to save Anthem, despite knowing she is a clone. Any Anthem is precious to her. The universe is less important to her than her friend."

Nik appreciated how that could be.

"But our Anthem won't stay here," Santo said. "She is with us."

"But she will be alive. Zombia would rather have her alive and elsewhere, than dead anywhere."

"Oh, don't we understand that!" Dane said.

"Now we have a question," Shameful said. "Do we yield to this demand, to save our friends at the expense of the universe? Or do we let them die?"

Nik and Santo conferred, which they could do now despite Anthem's absence, as they had gotten to know each other. They quickly agreed, sharing outrage. "Neither," Santo said. "We rescue them."

"This is chancy," Gyles said.

"Neither other choice is acceptable."

"Agreed."

Dane flew up into the sky to reconnoiter. He quickly returned. "There's a dragon coming. It looks aggressive."

"Word spreads rapidly," Gyles said without humor.

"I think you two need to become wizard and warrior," Aura said. "Take Wanda and Sword. They'll know what to do. The centaurs and I will stay out of your way." She gave Santo the sheaths holding the two magic objects, and he attached them to his belt.

"Hello, wizard and warrior," Wanda said. "We'll do our parts."

"Thank you" Nik said.

The dragon hove into view in the sky, flying directly toward them, breathing fire. It was a large one with far-reaching flame. A sword, no matter how aptly wielded, would not defend against that. Neither would the illusion of the wand.

"You need a bit more protection, without being obvious," Andromeda said. "Such as an invisible shield that will make objects and fire guide around you, seeming to miss you. Dodge if you can, to make the misses seem natural, but you won't be hit regardless." She faded back, but the air around them wavered slightly as if there were a force operating.

"Stay clear," Santo told Aura and the centaurs. "We are protected, but you might be struck by what misses us."

"We're protected too," Aura said. "The Demoness is watching. But we'll act as if we aren't."

The dragon came within range, flying low and jetting a searing column of fire. Santo didn't think to draw the sword as he jumped aside, and the flame missed him. Then as the dragon swooped in to bite, the sword leaped out of its scabbard and whipped across and cut off the tip of a wing. More startled than hurt, the dragon angled back up into the sky and flew away. No more strafing; this victim could dodge and fight. That made it inconvenient prey.

"Next time I'll get my hand on the hilt so it seems I'm doing it," Santo said.

"Do that," Wanda agreed. "I covered for you by making it look as if your hand was on it, but it also made it look as if you had an extra limb."

"Good show," Gyles said. "And I do mean show."

All too true. Without the shield they would have been toasted by the edge of the flame, and without the threat of the sword the dragon might have looped about for another run.

"Now all we need to do is find them," Santo said grimly. "Without the phone signal or Anthem's mental light."

"Or open demonic help," Nik said.

"You forgot your compass," Andromeda said.

"I don't have a—" He broke off, because a band had appeared on his left wrist bearing a circular dial. A bright dot was at one edge. When he moved his arm, the dot shifted to continue pointing the same direction. Where Noe and Anthem were, of course. Not exactly a compass, but that was part of its concealment.

Rhonda was hovering. "Tell them we're on our way," Nik told her. "Without using special magic, so it may take a while." She vanished.

Santo faced the key direction. "Let's move."

They did, proceeding afoot, not using the carpet on the theory that the less magic showed, the better. They followed the compass dot.

They came to a river. The dot indicated they had to cross. It was broad and slow with no monsters apparent. But it probably was not safe to wade or swim through.

"Remember the shield," Nik reminded Santo.

"Oh, yes." He glanced at the others. "We are shielded. We should be able to go safely through the water regardless what's there. But we want to avoid the appearance of shielding if we can." They nodded.

They walked along the bank, looking for a relatively shallow place. They found one, but there was a complication. There was a small island midstream on which a mermaid perched. When she saw Santo, she started eerily singing. She was a siren!

Santo smiled. He was immune to the seductive charms of women and pseudo women, sirens included, and Nik was too, for a different reason. So were the centaurs, and of course Aura.

Aura mounted Shameful and they forged into the water, as did Shameless and Santo. They all openly ignored the siren, who continued singing but looked increasingly frustrated, especially as they passed right by her island almost within reach. She slapped the water with her tail. "What is the matter with you?" she demanded of Santo. "You can't be deaf."

Santo laughed. "I fall only for really attractive girls. You don't make the grade. There's something fishy about you."

"Ooooh!" she exclaimed, her fangs flashing. In her rage she was giving her predatory nature away.

Aura smiled. "But I find you appealing, you seductive creature. You've got all the good parts of a woman without the bad parts. Why don't we—"

The siren squirmed off her perch, splashed into the water, and disappeared below, leaving behind a little cloud of fury. Santo, Aura, and both centaurs laughed. They all knew Aura wasn't sapphic, but had not been able to resist teasing the siren. If they had actually kissed, the siren might have been love-slaved, in a nice reversal of the menace.

"That was naughty," Andromeda said, amused.

"I am getting to like you folk," Gyles said. "You have twisted humor."

"But you probably shouldn't have done it," Shameful said. "We face enough mischief already, without aggravating it." As usual, she was negatively on target.

Water monsters appeared. They charged the group, jaws gaping. They didn't care what romantic orientation the travelers had, or whether they had tails or feet; it was their tasty flesh that counted. They pounced, chomped, and somehow missed their targets. They looped about, reorienting, ready to bite more carefully next time.

"My turn," Dane said. As the monsters approached, he loosed his talent.

The creatures reared back, terrified. Living daylight flashed out of them and dissolved into the air. In about half a moment per monster they had all fled.

"That was satisfying," the ghost said.

"You, too, should not have," the centaur said. But half a smile hovered near her.

They forged on through the water and strode out onto the plain beyond. But the hazards hadn't finished with them. Nik's clairvoyance reached out. "There's a storm coming. A bad one."

They looked, and saw it sweeping across the land toward them. The winds were ferociously blowing leaves and small branches about, and swirling rain was blasting down, so that muddy water was already coursing into the river.

"I think our sensible course is to avoid that storm," Aura said. "We could be damaged by flying debris." She paused. "Well, I forgot the shields. But we could get soaked, and there could be nasty things in the water, and there would be the chill."

Indeed, now hailstones were bouncing on the ground. It was cold.

"Is there shelter in range?" Shameful asked.

Nik's clairvoyance reached out again. "Yes. There's an old deserted castle beyond that hill." He pointed. "But it's haunted."

Dane and Gyles laughed. "Ghosts?" Gyles said. "We'll handle them."

The two humans got on the two centaurs, who galloped ahead of the looming tempest and reached the front of the castle just before of the storm did. Santo dismounted and ran to the closed gate. It was locked, so he unobtrusively made a small hole through the lock and yanked the gate open. They crowded through and got into the shelter of the front portico just as the storm struck. Soon the lightning, thunder, hail, and rain were walled off, becoming background effects. The sound of their frustration was the only thing that made it inside.

Then interior of the castle was of course gloomy. "Let's play it innocent, at first," Aura murmured. "So we can learn the situation here, in case it's another trap."

Good advice. The humans and centaurs played along.

"This sure is gloomy," Aura said brightly. "I'm nervous. There might be spooks."

"It's just a deserted castle," Santo said. "Spooks are mainly imaginary."

"Boo!" a ghost yelled.

Aura screamed and clung to Santo in supposed fear. Let the ghosts assume they were a couple.

A faint sinister light manifested in the gloom of the interior. Aura shrank back, every inch the frightened female. Nik realized that she was an excellent actress. Santo drew his wand, which glowed with seeming power. "Show yourself, spook, before I ensorcell you." He was every inch the naive inexpert sorcerer.

This was too much for the castle ghosts. They burst out laughing. They tried to make it sound macabre, but their amusement spoiled it.

Gyles appeared. "Gotcha, castle spooks. We put on our little act to fool you. We have zeroed in all three and a half of you. Give it up. You can't scare us. We have experienced ghosts of our own, as you can see. You are amateurs."

"Oh, yeah?" a spook said. "You're bluffing."

"My turn," Dane said again. He loosed his talent, once more.

This time the screams were by the ghosts as they retreated in terror.

"Come back and talk," Gyles called to them. "We won't hurt you. We're just making our point. Cut the histrionics and introduce yourselves, and we'll get along"

"Bones and tendons," a ghost swore as it appeared as a peon man. "You nailed us."

After that it was easy. The ghosts were of a family innocently touring the landscape that trolls had caught, gruesomely toyed with, and eaten. They had taken refuge in the castle and succeeded in scaring away living visitors. They were united in their desire to gain vengeance against the trolls. Only then would they feel free to move on. They were the father Alpha, mother Beta, ten-year-old son Gamma, and five-year-old daughter Delta. Delta was cute, and Aura soon befriended her, being the only living mortal human female of the party. She arranged to give the little ghost a pretend ride on Shameful Centaur, who was glad to cooperate. Delta was thrilled, and her mother approved. It was turning out to be better to get along with living folk than to repel them. Soon Shameless had to give Gamma a ride too.

The members of the Quest decided to stay overnight in the castle, as the storm was still raging outside, hoping that the ghosts would scare them back outside where they could be properly tormented. The ghost family told them where durable food supplies remained, and Gyles called up a nice ghost story from the children's section of the phone's storage. The big screen appeared, and they settled down to watch it together. It was titled "The Sad Shade" and was in cartoon format. Delta perched on Aura's shoulder as they watched, so they could quietly discuss it when they chose, girl to girl. The little ghost plainly loved the camaraderie with a live adult. Nik made another mental note: Aura was good with children.

Sharon Shade was as pretty as a purple hibiscus bloom, which she often imitated so she could hide among the flowers of the palace garden. It was her job to watch visitors, and scare off any who broke the rules, like dumping trash there or stealing fresh flowers that were reserved for the princess. All she had to do was rise up and yell "Booo!" when they trespassed. Soon the news got around that the garden was haunted, but that folk who behaved themselves didn't get spooked.

Then one night a sinister sorcerer sneaked in to steal rare plants to grind up for an illicit formula he was making. Sharon caught him and yelled "Booo!" so loudly that, startled, he dropped his collection bottle and it shattered on the floor, ruining his prior thefts. He was so angry that he hurled a foul curse at her. "May you never scare a living person again!" Then he stomped off in a swirl of seething sulfurous fog.

After that, Sharon's scare power was gone. Bad folk only laughed when she yelled "Booo!" and retorted "Booo whooo?" It was humiliating, and she was about to lose her job.

Then a little girl about Sharon's age entered the garden. She looked about. "Can I talk to you, Sharon? I'm not here to steal or break anything."

What was this? Curious, Sharon manifested as another girl, herself as she had been when alive. "What do you want?"

"I'm Boobie. I'm ugly and I'm stupid and nobody likes me. I'm lonely. I thought maybe you'd be lonely too, 'cause you have no company, so—" She broke off, tearfully. "Oh, what's the use? Why should you care? I'll go."

"Wait." Now Sharon was intrigued. The girl was plain rather than ugly, and her coming here was clever rather than stupid. "Why does nobody like you?"

"I don't know. I used to be okay, but then it changed."

A faint little cobwebby bulb flashed over the ghost's head. "Did you run afoul of an evil sorcerer?"

"That scary guy in black? He wanted me to steal something for him, a mandrake root from a private garden, and I wouldn't do it. I'm not a thief. Then I ran away before he could curse me."

"I think he did curse you. The curse caught you from behind and you didn't know it. It was to make nobody like you."

Boobie was amazed. "That is when it changed. I didn't make the con-conn—" She was struggling with a word that was too big for her.

"You didn't catch on," Sharon said.

"Yes. How did you know?"

"He cursed me too, when I balked him. He's evil."

"He sure is!"

At that point they became friends. Shades and living folk seldom did that, but they had a common enemy. They weren't lonely anymore.

They did each other favors. Sharon searched around the garden and castle, and found where lost coins had fallen into crevices and under furniture, and told Boobie so she could fetch them and have money to buy snacks and hair ribbons. Boobie found a scary picture of a rattletrap snake she set up in the garden so that some visitors were nervous, helping to restore a bit of Sharon's reputation. It wasn't much, but it helped.

One day they found a lost box of panic patties. Boobie ate one, and said "Booo!" to a boy, and it scared him. But Sharon was the one who needed to scare folk, and she couldn't eat solid food. Then they got an idea. Sharon dived through the box and out the other side, and looked weirdly scary. The panic fumes were clinging to her for two and a half moments. That night when a girl came to steal a flower, Sharon dived through the box again, came up to the girl, and yelled "Booo!" The girl ran away, suitably panicked.

Sharon had her scare back, in a manner. That was enough to save her job. No more plants were stolen from the garden.

The movie paused. "This is the halfway point," Gyles said. "Do you want to see the rest?"

"Yes!" Aura and Delta said together. The others agreed, glad the show was working out better than the prion ones.

The movie resumed.

Boobie grew up as time passed, but Sharon didn't, being locked in to her age when she became a ghost. They remained friends. Then the evil wizard did something that annoyed the king, like putting a stink bug in the queen's perfume bottle, so that instead of smelling like roses she smelled like spoiled garbage, and he got promptly executed and banished to Hell, where he belonged. The evil spells and curses he had made in his lifetime evaporated.

Suddenly Sharon could scare people on her own again, needing no panic patties to help. And Boobie could make friends among living folk. But she remained lean and plain, which made it difficult for her to find boyfriends as she came of age. The boys preferred pretty faces and curvy bodies, regard-

less of personality. That might be considered shallow, but they were the only game in town, as it were. And the king upgraded the security of the garden, so that no spook was needed to protect it. They let Sharon stay, but she had become superfluous. That made her sad.

They commiserated. Sharon wanted to be useful, and Boobie wanted to get social and maybe even have a family. And they got an idea. Sharon had no substance, but could change her appearance to anything she chose. So, she wrapped around Boobie's head and made her skin look fair, her features illustrious, and her hair glorious with subtle little sparkles. She extended downward to make the body look fuller above and broader below, with a waist a wasp would envy. It was illusion, just a thin covering, but there was substance beneath it so that it felt real. Boobie had become a beauty, and Sharon was the essence of it. The shade could not grow older physically, but had done so mentally, learning what it was all about, and could share the experience of her friend. Now to see what they could make of it.

It took them about two moments and half a glimpse to nab a good man. He never knew that his girlfriend was two people, one live, the other dead, nor did he need to. Sharon and Boobie shared the romance. Their sadness of childhood had become their happiness of adulthood, thanks to their friendship and collaboration. And when their marriage brought forth a new little girl, that child was never, ever, afraid of ghosts. In fact she got along with them great, to the marvel of those who didn't know the family secret. The sad shade had become the wonderful wraith.

The movie ended in a shower of credits. Aura and Delta both loved it, and the others, alive and dead, found it reasonably entertaining.

"I'd like to do something nice for these ghosts," Nik said.

"Are those trolls still around?" Santo asked.

"Yes," Alpha said.

"Can you indicate the route they are most likely to be lurking near?"

"Yes. We can point it out exactly. Also the other local pitfalls."

"If I read the situation correctly, the trolls will come after us when we move on." Santo smiled grimly. "When they do, you may obtain your satisfaction. The movie may not be the only case where the living and the dead collaborate."

"He's not fooling," Aura told Delta. "We have a magic sword." The child ghost smiled.

"We'll let you know," Gyles said.

There was one good bedroom in the castle, with a comfortable bed. Santo and Aura shared it, not concerned about personal privacy. They were becoming friends, not lovers. The two centaurs shared a stall. There was no indication that Demons were present. They were truly just observing.

Nik, perching on the bedstead, was quite satisfied to have it that way. His overwhelming interest was to save Anthem Ant. And of course Noe Human, who had brought him into this marvelous adventure. "And Rhonda," Dane said. Because the ghost would not desert her companions, so was in effect imprisoned with them.

In the morning the storm had given up in frustration and departed. The way was clear. They bid a friendly parting to the ghost family and set off for the prison cell by way of the troll path. The two humans rode the two centaurs, acting as if they had not a care in the world.

"They know we're coming," Gyles said. "They are lying in ambush."

"We will give them fair warning," Santo said.

"Which they will ignore," Aura added.

"Fair is fair," Gyles said grimly.

"When the action starts," Santo said, "You other three fleshly folk form a tight huddle as if afraid. I will go forth apparently alone and make a distraction. With luck, they well never catch on about the shields."

"Until it's too late," Gyles said.

"Trolls know no limits except mayhem," Nik said. "Are you up to it?"

"Normally I don't like violence," Santo said. "But these foul trolls need to be eliminated. They shouldn't be preying on innocent families. I can do what is necessary." He could indeed, as they had seen when the Badass Band had attacked. Those holes could be deadly.

They marched innocently on. Right into the ambush.

Sure enough, the trolls pounced from all sides. Santo jumped to the ground and faced them as Aura and the two centaurs formed their frightened huddle. "Fair warning," he said. "I am armed and dangerous."

The trolls bellowed in laughter as they swarmed in to overwhelm him without mercy.

Knife Knight emerged and flashed in the sunlight, Santo's hand barely keeping up. This time there was no defensive maneuver. The sword lopped off the first troll's head, then stabbed the second one through the neck. The third troll came in from the side, and the sword whipped about and cut open his gut. Then the real havoc began as noses and ears few off and arms and legs were detached. In moments a dozen trolls were strewn about together with their weapons and limbs, none of them alive. Nik, watching, at times was unable to see the swift motions of the deadly sword, only the consequences. The trolls never had a chance.

Aura and the centaurs were unhurt, thanks to the shields, but looked somewhat sickened. Yet they had warned the trolls, and the trolls did deserve their fate. This was perhaps an object lesson. Would the trolls learn from it? Probably not. They were what they were, incorrigible brutes. But other predators might take warning.

Santo walked on to the cistern that provided water for the trolls. He plunged the sword into it and swished it about, cleaning it. "Tell the ghosts," he told Gyles.

"On my way." The ghost vanished. The ghost family was now free to move on to Heaven.

Then Santo vomited into the brush. He had done the necessary, but was not immune to its horror. Merciless violence and killing was not his normal style. The others did not comment. They understood perfectly.

They walked on, leaving the battle site for the troll families to find. The trolls were getting a taste of their own medicine. Wholesale preying on innocents sometimes provoked vengeance.

The path led into a dense forest of tangle trees that would normally be impassable by mortal folk. Santo dismounted again and walked to the verge. "Tanglers, I know you understand my words," he said. "I am a warrior who recently fought off a troll ambush. You may have received news of that." He paused, giving the trees a chance to assimilate that news, which surely had spread. Any passing bird could have told them. "I am also a wizard who can shrivel your sap if I get annoyed. Behold my wand." He drew Wanda with his left hand. "We can pass in peace, no damage done, or we can fight. Your choice." Light speared out from the wand, looking like a burning laser. It was illusion, but the trees should not know that. Such a laser could indeed shrivel sap, along with the branch holding it. The hanging tentacles would be severed as if chopped by sharp knives. It could take a tree years to recover from such injuries. No tree would care for that.

There was no response from the trees. That could mean anything from capitulation to Make My Day. "I have given fair warning, as I did the trolls. I really would prefer to pass in peace, but sometimes my hand is forced." Then Santo beckoned the other members of the party. They came up behind him. He strode into the forest, holding the wand aloft menacingly. If the trees called his bluff he would have to use the sword to cut off reaching tentacles, which would be less effective than a laser but would still get the job done. It was a gamble, but not life or death. The shields would protect them. It was just better to avoid a fight if they could. They were not here to tame tangle trees, but to rescue the valued hostages and go on to save the universes.

The trees made no moves. They were heeding the warning that the trolls had not. The party walked on through, and in due course emerged from the other side. This was another green plain. The problem with such plains was the creatures that could run on them.

Sure enough, a pack of wolves was approaching, possibly werewolves, ready to change to man-form once they got close. They would be smarter than trees, less subject to a bluff, though the sword was no bluff. "My turn, again," Dane said. "I will let them get close, then hurl them back."

The pack came close, and some did shift to their man forms, eyeing Aura, who looked good enough to eat, among other things. Then Dane loosed his scare. Living daylight flared as the wolves veered and fled. The pack was soon gone.

"Bleep, this is fun!" Dane said, well satisfied.

Then they came to a wall. It was polished stone, and towered up higher than the tallest of trees. It was featureless, with no doors or windows. How had it come there, and what was its purpose?

Nik's clairvoyance had an answer of sorts. "It wasn't here yesterday."

"The Demon must have put it here to block us," Shameful said. "He's getting tired of our progress." Again, the news they did not want to hear.

"The carpets could not carry two humans and two centaurs together," Aura said. "If we split up to cross over the wall in parts, we might get separated and not be able to reunify." She grimaced. "Divide and conquer, maybe."

"If we try to walk around it," Santo said, "we might discover that it continues endlessly."

"Attempting to climb over it would be hazardous," Shameless said. "There're no handholds, and our hoofs are worse. We should perhaps back off and wait for it to disappear." Which was what they might have wanted, but wasn't good for their mission. Waiting was not an option.

Santo sighed. "All of which seems to leave no alternative but to use my talent and simply make a hole through it. That would be in order if this barrier were not Demon crafted."

"Cut through it," Aura said. "If that alerts the Demon, we may have Demons of our own."

There it was. If the anonymous Demon was determined to stop them without revealing his identity, this would force his hand. Direct intercession would sacrifice his anonymity. Maybe it was time.

The Demons were silent. They would wait for the opposing Demon to act first. They were the counter-trap.

Santo oriented on the wall and focused. He had made tunnels between universes; this was relatively minor. It was the prospect of invoking the active opposition of Demons that made it nervous business.

The hole appeared, its base at ground level, big enough for them to march through. The other side was close by. The wall was tall, but thin.

They went through. In moments they were at the other side.

A silvery sphere formed around them, enclosing them without unduly squeezing them. At its far side stood a donkey-headed dragon.

Nik knew who that was. "The Demon Xanth," he said. "In the form he assumes for mortal interaction." That form had its own history, not relevant here. Demons could take any forms they chose.

"True," the creature said. "You have forced me to reveal myself, within this impervious chamber so that no outsiders are aware. Now that you know what you face, are you ready to return to your own universe and cease interfering with this one?"

No one else spoke. It was Nik's turn, as the leader of the Quest. "We are not. Not yet. Our destiny is elsewhere. Release Anthem Ant and Noe Human, and we will move on without further action in this universe."

"Persuade Demoness Zombia here to terminate her spell, and I will release them."

"No. That would sacrifice this universe to the zombies."

"Then you will lose the hostages."

"I am surprised to see you taking the side of evil," Nik said. "We had more respect for you than to think you would ever betray your land or your universe. I am disappointed."

"You are a bug. Your opinion is irrelevant."

It was time for the hard stuff. Nik emulated Santo's warnings to trolls and trees. "I did not come here alone. Your best course is to back off." It was hard to believe that he was talking this way to a Demon, let alone the Demon Xanth, the source of all the magic in the magical Land of Xanth.

"Your company is two centaurs and a Lips woman? Plus two ghosts? You are deluded."

"Plus Demons." Nik glanced at Shameful, then started the dialogue they had privately rehearsed. "Ennui?"

"Hello, Xanth," the Demoness said, manifesting as a somber human woman past her prime. "I will leach your vigor until my friend Andromeda can change you to support the positive side in this universe."

If Xanth was shaken by her appearance, he did not show it. "Two things, Demoness. First, you can't overrule me here in my own domain. Second, if you could, it would take eons, and the hostages would be long dead."

"No," she said. "It would take seconds."

He was dismissive. "How so?"

"Because my friend Bang will enhance my power a million-fold."

"Bang is far away, and does not know of this discussion. Nor will he know."

"My friend is of my universe, not this one. He knows. In fact he is here."

Xanth did not believe her. "Then let him show himself."

Aura smiled. "He is calling our bluff. He does not believe in our destiny."

"That's one weird attitude," Ennui said. "Bang?"

Bang emerged. The blinding power of his revealed presence threatened to burst the silvery sphere asunder and set fire to the terrain. It was all the mortals could do to keep their feet.

The donkey dragon gazed at him, realizing that the counter-trap ruled. That he had lost his bid to get up and clean with the foreign Zombia. That their destiny was incipient. Then he faded into a cloud as the silvery sphere dissolved along with the wall. From that cloud emerged Noe with Anthem and Rhonda. They looked tired but healthy. The Demon Xanth had capitulated. There would be no deal to loose the zombie kisses.

"Oh, Noe!" Santo breathed in relief.

Noe ran to hug Santo, who accepted it gladly. Anthem, on her shoulder, sent Nik an encompassing kiss. Rhonda flew into Dane's embrace. Little hearts flew out, forming a cloud.

"Noe, if I had to marry you to save you," Santo said, "I would."

"That's weird," Noe said, and kissed him with perfect understanding, "But not our destiny."

"This is one weird destiny," Aura murmured. "And I don't mean just personal."

The centaurs nodded.

Then Aura got another message from Zombia. She repeated it aloud as it came in. "Thank you. You have spared me a cruel choice."

"You're welcome," Santo said aloud for Aura to translate to a mental response. "We are glad to support your effort to save this universe from your clone's mischief."

"However," the Demoness said via Aura, "there is a complication."

"Uh-oh," Shameful said, recognizing an unkind truth on the way.

"The Demon Xanth contacted that other Zombia via Limbo. You have halted his ploy, but she could still influence him or others via that avenue, renewing the threat. It needs to be shut down."

"But Limbo is a realm in itself," Santo protested. "A state of being. Of indecision. It can't be shut down."

"Limbo as we know it is an aspect of Xanth," Zombia said. "Where all its characters exist independently of time. What you need to shut down is free access to it, so that neither Xanth nor anyone else, Demon or mortal, can use it for foul purpose. Only then can you be sure the universes are safe, apart from the present traveling kisses. I don't know how to do that, but I can give you the key to enter it. Perhaps there you will be able to find a way to limit future access."

Santo looked around. "Quest?" he asked.

Anthem surveyed the minds, including those of the Demons, who opened theirs for this question. The consensus was that they should do it. Otherwise their whole prior effort might be wasted.

Now Aura spoke for herself. "*Really* weird destiny."

So it seemed.

Chapter 12

WHY?

Santo oriented on the access to Limbo that Demoness Zombia had provided them. It was an obscure variant of a normal address, with the time factor suppressed, making it timeless. Anthem locked it into her memory for future access, as it represented a way to interact with figures of the past and future that just might turn out to be useful. It hardly mattered which universe they were in; Limbo was mostly independent of space as well as time. As Aura had said: weird.

He made the tunnel, orienting on classical Xanth as the safest way to approach the unknown. It exited near a castle that seemed oddly familiar.

"Castle Roogna!" Shameless Centaur said.

The capital castle of the main human kingdom of the Land of Xanth. Nik had never been there before, and maybe this didn't count, not being exactly real, but it was interesting. He knew it was crammed to the bursting point with Xanth human history. The Queendom of Thanx was a mere instant compared to the centuries of Roogna.

"It would help to know the time frame," Aura said.

"There is no time frame," Noe said. "It is all times in one, or whatever time it chooses to settle on for us as visitors. Maybe it's random. We'll just have to go in and see who's there."

They approached the castle. A horrendous moat monster poked its head out of the water and eyed them. Anthem read its mind, and was reassured. "Just let it know we are friends."

"We are friends!" Noe called. The monster nodded and sank back below the surface. They crossed the drawbridge without incident.

Nik thought of the viciousness of the trolls. This was clearly a less hostile place. But if the trolls invaded, the moat monster would likely show another facet. It surely had a pretty good notion who was legitimate and who was not.

"Sometimes a moat monster is used as a babysitter when a child has to be left at home," Anthem said, reporting a tidbit from her stock of human memories. "A good one can be trusted."

So it seemed.

They went to the front gate. "Is anybody home?"

A devastatingly lovely woman came to open it. "Do I know you?" she asked.

"That depends on who you are and when you lived," Santo said.

The woman's features shifted to show a far more ordinary face and form. "I am Queen Iris, Sorceress of Illusion, about twenty years into King Trent's reign." The loveliness returned.

"You predate us," Santo said. "We are two or three generations after you. I am Santo, Magician of Holes. This is my associate Noe, whose talent is anonymity, and Aura Lips, whose kiss can render a man into a love slave. The centaurs are friends whose talents are to utter unwelcome or unuseful truths. We also have with us Nik Nikelpede, a Magician of Clairvoyance, and Anthem Ant, a Sorceress of Telepathy." He smiled. "Talents are unusual in bugs, but they do occur in our time, and these are the protagonists of this adventure." He glanced up, indicating the Baton, which bobbed acknowledgment. "Also three ghosts. We are on a special mission to save Xanth and the universes from a zombie invasion."

Iris nodded. "You are indeed after my time. Our zombies help guard the castle. Keep the bugs safe, lest local humans misunderstand. Also keep your ghosts invisible, for the same reason." She smiled, evidently accustomed to unusual visitors. "This mission of yours seems worthy. Come in." She opened the gate and ushered them into the castle and to an elegant meeting room where a handsome man and pretty girl stood. "Dears, our visitors are from about two generations hence. They are on a mission to save the universe. The main characters are highly talented bugs. This is a future adventure."

The man strode forward. "Greetings, visitors. I am Magician Trent, with the talent of Transformation, and this is our daughter Irene, who can make plants grow." He smiled. "Show them, dear."

Irene walked to a small potted plant. "This a beefsteak tomato plant," she said. She pointed a finger at it. "Grow."

The plant grew rapidly to full size, flowered, and produced several odd-looking fruits. Irene harvested some and offered them to the visitors. They were hot beefsteaks. Santo took a bite of his, then held it up so that Nik could gouge out a nickel sized chunk to eat. It was delicious. Noe and Anthem were doing the same, the ant shooting a little jet of fire to toast her piece further. Aura and the centaurs enjoyed their steaks too. Irene's talent might not be deadly or spectacular, but it was certainly useful.

Then they settled down to talk. Trent made no mention that he was king, Iris queen, and Irene princess, perhaps because in Limbo such things mattered less. Santo explained about the zombie invasion and how the Quest was out to stop the deadly zombie kisses. "We need to find a way to limit access to Limbo, here, so that no one else can try to corrupt Demons and make new zombie threats," he concluded.

"The problem you face in your day is worse than what we've seen in ours," Trent said. "I think you need to visit the Question Room. This is a special chamber here in the castle where key information can be obtained. But there are caveats. Two minor ones and a more significant one."

"A formidable one," Iris said.

"A doozie," Irene agreed.

Nik's clairvoyance indicated that they were right.

"We will handle it," Santo said.

Trent smiled. "Perhaps. One minor one is that the chamber can be entered only one day a month, so you will have to wait a few days."

"We can do that," Santo said. "Limbo is timeless with respect to the normal realm, so this will not delay our mission."

"The second is that only the castle ghosts know the precise location of the chamber, which seems to move about, or the manner to enter it, which changes, so we shall need to enlist their help to access it."

"We can do that," Gyles said confidently.

"The major caveat is that to obtain the information or favor you require, you must answer a question. We do not know what it is, but you will be unable to depart the chamber without answering. It is a difficult one."

"How can you say that," Aura asked, "if you don't know what it is?"

"Because of the few who have entered the chamber, for their own reasons, none have emerged. They remain there in suspended animation. It seems that they were unable to answer the question, and will remain there until they do."

Nik knew that the Demons could, if necessary, override whatever power the chamber had. But it would be better to leave them out of it, for the sake of their anonymity.

"I think we shall have to risk it," Santo said.

"Then we shall provide you with hospitality for the interim," Trent said. "You may enjoy getting to know the environs. Irene will be happy to show you around."

"Thank you," Noe said. The princess looked to be about her own age, for all that in real time she would be more than half a century older. They might have things in common, such as frustration when dealing with adults.

The following days were pleasant for all, including the ghosts. Sometimes in the background there were the sounds of "In the Gloaming" and "Long, Long Ago" as Dane and Rhonda entertained the local ghosts with their romantic story. But there was something else. Nik extended his clairvoyance, but whatever it was, was vague. It was not a danger; rather it was an opportunity. Maybe more than one. He kept after it, and finally got if not an answer, a direction. In fact it was marked by the compass Santo wore. It indicated a particular way they should go, and it was strongest when Aura was near the compass.

"Check it," Andromeda told Nik quietly. He did not question this; she surely had her reason, which might involve significant change. The Demons were continuing their anonymity, but they acted when they had reason.

"Let's do this," Nik suggested. "Let Aura take the compass, since the direction seems to relate to her. Anthem and I, along with Wanda and Knife, and the ghosts, can follow up on this, while Santo, Noe, and the centaurs relax at the castle. That way we can satisfy our curiosity in the time we need to wait for access to the Question Room, without interfering with the Quest. It should be a pleasant interlude." He glanced across at Anthem. He liked the idea of being closer to her. She glanced back, twitching her antennae suggestively. They both enjoyed pretending.

The others were amenable. It seemed like a reasonable way to pass the time. Santo and Noe enjoyed the company of Irene, and the centaurs were having serious discussions with Trent and Iris. It was good to be able to relax, for a change.

Aura took the compass, along with the rest of them, as suggested. Only Gyles, of the ghosts, remained in the castle, as he was enjoying getting to know the moat monster and ghosts there, and even some of the zombies. He was most comfortable in the original Genius Phone, rather than the insubstantial clone phone Aura carried.

They departed Castle Roogna, following the direction indicated by the compass. It looked like a party of one, which was fine. Aura might seem like a defenseless girl, but that was hardly the case, as Wanda and Knife had demonstrated on occasion. Soon they were trekking through the wilderness.

"So what *is* this little mystery we are pursuing?" Anthem asked for them all once they were private, at least to a degree. "It doesn't seem to relate to the Quest."

"Andromeda made the compass," Nik said. "She told me to check what it indicates. So there has to be something. Maybe it just leads to a love spring."

"Two bugs, two objects, two ghosts," Aura said. "All romancing each other in their fashions. But what about me? I'm alone. A love spring would do me no good."

She had a point. They couldn't blame her for feeling a bit left out. "Maybe you will meet a handsome prince," Rhonda said. "And seduce him with your charm."

"Not to mention your love-slave kiss," Dane said.

"And take him home to another universe? He wouldn't go, and I don't want to stay in a foreign universe or in Limbo."

It seemed pointless to argue the case. She was right. She was emotionally stranded.

"You mentioned romance," Wanda said as they moved. "That may apply to you committed couples, but Knife and I aren't really romantic. I'd rather be with another wand, and he'd prefer a self-powered knife. Since we have not encountered our preferences, we dance with each other, as it were, but it's a bit like Santo and Noe, not quite right."

"That's too bad," Anthem said sympathetically. "Relationships aren't always straightforward."

"Maybe somewhere in Limbo there's an answer," Nik said. But he saw no immediate prospect. It seemed that objects, like humans and bugs, could run afoul of complications.

The route led past an ogre den. A lolling ogre looked down on Aura and licked his lips. Ogres tended to like playing with pretty human girls, though their playing could be lethally violent. “Squeeze she’s,” he said with typical ogre arrogance and dialect as he reached for her with a huge hamhand. He considered her to be a passing plaything.

Dane loosed his talent, and the ogre snatched his hand away so fast it smoked.

“I am getting to like your talent, Dane,” Aura murmured as she walked on unscathed.

A young woman was walking the other way. She was pretty and shapely. In fact she was a nymph. She paused, stepped off the path, squatted, and set something on or in the ground. Then she stood, just as Aura got there. “Oh, hello,” she said. “I’m Jewel the Nymph. Who are you?” There was a smell of curiosity.

“I am Aura, from what I think is a future time compared to this. I am looking for something, but I don’t know what.”

“Could it be a gem?” Now there was an odor of interest.

“I doubt it. I don’t need anything like that.”

“Too bad. My job is to hide the precious stones for others to find.” The smell was of slight disappointment.

Now Anthem made a connection of a memory from one of the many minds she had read. Aura spoke for her. “The miners, the collectors, the lucky finders! You’re the one who plants the gems they find!”

“I am the one,” Jewel agreed with a smell of pleasure. “Someone has to do it. I have hidden thousands, but only hundreds have been found. Maybe I am hiding them too well.”

“Or maybe the finders aren’t trying hard enough. Too many folk are sloppy about their business.”

“Too many,” the nymph agreed, and moved on, leaving the scent of dismissal.

“I found a stray memory. She finally marries Crombie the Soldier,” Anthem said. “Happily, I think. He doesn’t think much of women, but she’s a nymph.”

"Good for only one thing," Dane agreed. "But very good for that."

"Hey," Rhonda said, with a background sniff of amusement.

"You're good too," he said quickly. "Maybe even two things." They evidently liked teasing each other.

"What were all those smells?" Nik asked.

"That's her talent," Anthem explained. "It's like perfume. She smells like her feelings. Much the way Apoca's hair reflects her moods. Mostly positive, like sunlight on flowers. But I understand that when she feels really bad, the smell is like burning garbage."

"Sometimes I wish that I were interesting like that," Aura said wistfully. "Garbage and all. Now that I'm not a zombie, or a zombie maker, my life seems relatively dull."

"I can make you look the way the ghost made Boobie, if that helps," Wanda said. "But you're pretty close already."

"Thanks. But I'd like to nab a man who values me for something other than my appearance or reproductive appeal."

"Few human men qualify for that kind of judgment," Anthem said. "I've seen their minds. They're similar to male ants, only ants orient on smell rather than shape. You'd have to blindfold men to make them be rational."

Nik was silent, knowing that male nickelpedes were similar. Without her phenomenal telepathy Anthem would have been just another ant, literally beneath notice. Dane was similarly silent. His choice had been forced, but in his youth he had taken the money rather than the woman. Interpretations would not necessarily be kind.

"There's Santo," Rhonda said. They all laughed. Santo was indeed different, but not in a way that helped romantically.

They came to a pavilion. The path led right through it, so Aura entered. At which point barricades appeared around it, confining them. It was not a physical trap so much as an indication that they should remain for some event. In fact the stakes turned out to be illusion.

Nik extended his awareness, but detected no danger. This was something else.

There was a puff of smoke as a demon of imposing aspect appeared. "And who is to be married here today?" he demanded.

Anthem read his mind. "Demon Grossclout!" she thought loudly. "The terror of educational classes. Queen Demesne's husband."

The demon focused on her. "The telepathic fire ant. My wife mentioned you. She actually likes you. What are you doing here?"

"We are following a direction. This pavilion is on the way."

"Enough incidental dialogue." Grossclout glanced at Aura. "Where is the groom, Lips woman? Your love slave should be here with you."

"There is no groom," Aura said, startled. "We're just passing through."

The demon radiated a horrendous glower. "This is the Marital Pavilion. Only wedding participants and associated personnel enter here. None leave before the ceremony is concluded. It would not have permitted your entry were you not such a party. I am here to officiate. Do not further waste my time. Produce the groom."

"We're just passing through," Aura repeated with some asperity. She was not a woman to be pushed around by anyone, even the formidable demon professor. "I have no groom. Do I have to kiss you to make you listen?"

The barest hint of a smile hovered in the demon's vicinity, but his stern visage backed it off. "It would be intriguing to try your power, Lips creature. But my wife would make a scene even I would not care to experience. If you are not to be married here, who is? There has to be a wedding."

"Not us," Dane said, laughing. "Rhonda and I are already married."

"Long, long ago," Rhonda agreed, the ghost catching the smile the demon had rejected.

"Not Knife and me," Wanda said. "We're animate objects."

That left Nik and Anthem. Could it be? His clairvoyance coalesced. Yes it could. "Anthem, will you marry me?"

She didn't hesitate. "Yes!" The chord was jubilant.

"Anthem and I will try to emulate the human manner for the ceremony," Nik said.

Grossclout frowned, making his face even more formidable. "And where are your Best Man and Maid of Honor?"

"Not to mention bouquet and rings," Aura said.

Oops. Nik had said they would emulate the human manner. "Um . . ."

Andromeda manifested as a queenly human woman with constantly changing features and outfits. "I will be Maid of Honor."

Bang manifested as a kingly human man, the pavilion shaking with the force of his presence. "Best Man," he said.

Nik's jaw would have dropped, if he had one. "But—"

A bouquet of passion flowers appeared in Andromeda's hand. An ornate little case appeared in Bang's hand, surely containing the rings. That actually hadn't been Nik's question, but he stifled it. Who was he to protest having two of the most significant entities in any universe serve as assistants to two of the least significant?

Even Grossclout seemed taken aback by this development. "Bugs and Demons! Are you sure—"

"Bang and I were married recently," Andromeda said, her hair shifting styles. "Be assured we know the procedure." Which of course had not been exactly Grossclout's concern. He plainly knew who the Demons were. The intimidator was perilously close to being intimidated.

"To be sure," Grossclout agreed as it were routine. He snapped his fingers and a phantom audience appeared. They were ready for the ceremony.

The rest was relatively perfunctory. The Wedding March sounded in the background. Aura held up her right hand with the two bugs on the back of it, the two ghosts embedded as souls, and the two Demons stood on either side. One fragment of one petal of one bouquet flower molded into the bridal dress, and leaves formed the groom's suit. Grossclout asked the pertinent questions, and Nik and Anthem each answered "I do." Then the box opened and the tiny gold rings sailed out, one landing on Nik's left foreleg just behind the pincer, somehow managing to slip on despite being far smaller than the pincer, and the other fastened on Anthem's foreleg, becoming a midget bracelet.

"Kiss."

They touched feelers. A chord of sheer mutual devotion sounded. Little hearts flung out, humming with hugely amplified power as they orbited the couple. Then the bouquet sailed into the audience, where three phantom women fought for it. It was done.

There was one wedding gift, evidently from the Demons: an accommodation spell that would enable them to accomplish signaling the stork together, or the equivalent, and order crossbreed offspring. Ants didn't blush, but Anthem managed one anyway. "We'll use this later," Nik said diplomatically. “We have a continuing route to follow.” Because the compass was still signaling the direction.

“Good enough,” Grossclout said. He snapped his fingers again and the audience disappeared, along with the barricades. Then so did he.

“Congratulations, newlyweds,” Andromeda said. Then she and Bang faded out, returning to their anonymity.

“I believe it is time to move on,” Aura said, and walked on out of the pavilion. If she were disappointed that there had been no groom for her, she was discreetly silent. This was Nik and Anthem’s joy.

“There’s another shoe,” Rhonda said. “I feel it, but it’s not quite ready to drop.” The compass agreed. There remained somewhere for them to go.

They moved on, along with the slowly dissipating cloud of little hearts. Nik and Anthem were now together, physically, emotionally, and socially as she perched on his back and sent rapturous chords through his mind and body. The accommodation spell paced them, ready when they were. Right now they were lost in a mutual dream of bliss.

They came to a fancy castle replete with turrets, parapets, and a moat, though the moat monster seemed to be absent at the moment. The sign said claimless cattle. The compass pointed right at it.

“Something is wrong,” Aura said. “This doesn’t make sense.”

Nik and Anthem were jolted out of their dream, shedding puffs of bliss. “We don’t need unclaimed cattle,” Nik said.

“It changed,” Dane said.

They looked again. Sure enough, now the sign said aimless castigate.

“I can solve it,” Wanda said. “I have a set of ectoplasm figurines. Use me to conjure the spirit of the castle into one, then question him.”

“Why not?” Aura asked. She fished in Wanda’s sheath to pull out the male figurine, which expanded when released from the any-size container and formed into a motionless man-sized figure. Following Wanda’s instructions, she waved the wand. “Spirit of the Castle, I conjure you into this figurine.”

There was an intangible motion. Then the figurine animated, a halfway handsome warrior type. “Who the bleep are you to mess with me?” he demanded.

Aura stepped forward, embraced the figure, and kissed him on the mouth, with power.

"Oh, my," he said, reeling as she let him go. "What did you do to me, you rapturous creature?"

"I conjured you into a humanoid figurine, then love-slaved you with my kiss, you arrogant spirit. All I want is the answer to one or two questions; then I'll let you go. What castle is this, and what's with the changing sign?"

"This is the Nameless Castle, and the sign is suffering from the nature of the prisoner confined here."

"Prisoner? Here in Limbo? Please explain."

He gazed at her with unfeigned adoration. "Since you ask, divine diva, I must answer. He is Dwarf Demon Zanth, confined here because others are endlessly annoyed by his nature. He is the Demon of Typos, and spelling goes wrong in his vicinity. Even his own name is a misspelling of a more legitimate one. No matter how carefully they watch, the errors are made, because a number of them grow on the page after the proofreading. The sign is close by the castle, so is constantly affected." He glanced at it. It now said trainless cassette. "Of course confining him doesn't work, because his influence is universal. It only lessens the effect slightly with distance."

Aura was intrigued. "A Dwarf Demon. That's a lesser creature than a Demon, but still like a fragment of a galaxy compared to mortal grains of sand. Does he have a companion?"

"Of course not. What Demoness or even mortal woman would want to be midst constant errors? Anything she wrote would be fouled up, and sometimes what she spoke. It could be horribly embarrassing. Suppose she tried to say 'I love new friends,' and it came out 'nude fiends'?"

Nik had never seen Aura write anything. She might be relatively unaffected.

"What kind of a person is he?" Aura asked.

"He is actually a good person. He never mistreated anyone, and could have made a fine social match. But that doesn't matter when the print goes wrong." The figure smiled. "Once a local man tried to express his devotion to his girlfriend, here by the castle. He said 'I loathe you. Will you harry me?' She replied 'Guess.'"

"Other Demons have done bad things, like Demoness Zombia or Demon Zanth." Aura paused. "I mean, Demon Xavier. I mean Heman

XXX." She paused again. "I begin to see the problem. But it's minor, compared to the life and death nature of other problems. He should not be punished for it."

"Officially he is not being punished, merely provided hospitality. He has a good if lonely life here." The castle spirit shrugged. "Nevertheless, I'd like to be rid of him, if only so that my sign would be correct."

"Not being punished? Then what keeps him here?"

"The stricture that he can't leave alone. He is locked into human form as long as he is here, so can't just dissolve into smoke and float away, or conjure himself out. Since no person will join him, that prevents his escape. It's a cunning ploy. Unofficial confinement."

Aura nodded. "Thank you, Nameless. Now I will conjure you free, and without a human form you will have no further interest in a mortal human woman like me." She raised the wand again. "Spirit of the Castle, I conjure you out of this figurine and back to your battlements."

The figure wavered and would have fallen had she not caught it in her arms. It has lost its animation. Then she crammed it back into the case.

"Thank you, glorious lady," the spirit thought, duly translated by Anthem. Apparently, the effect of the love kiss had not yet quite dissipated.

They entered the castle without further distraction. The interior was dusty but nice. "Zanth!" Aura called. "Come talk with us."

A handsome man appeared. "I don't get many visitors," he said. "What brings a fair maiden like you here? Do you come to mock me, as others have?"

"No." Aura stepped into him and kissed him with power. He seemed unaffected, being a Demon, but when she let him go, his gaze kindled with interest.

"This suggests that something else is on your mind," he said. "I hope it is seduction."

"I am Daura Lisp," she said. Then she tried again, ferociously concentrating. "I mean Aura Lips. I came here because a compass led me, indicating that there was something of interest. I am a single mortal woman looking for a suitable male companion. Are you interested?"

"I certainly am. You are clearly more than a pretty face and form. But are you aware of my nature and situation?"

"I am. But I have been reassured that you are a good person. I would like to get to know you, to see whether there is a future for us together."

"You wish to be my companion?"

"Yes, without further commitment at this time."

"Then let us be on our way. Take my arm, so that it is clear that we are together and I will be able to leave." He frowned. "One qualification: you must remain my companion. The moment you end that relationship, regardless where we are, I will be snapped back to the Nameless Castle." Half a smile caught him. "The hope may be that a regular associate like you will mute my nature. I doubt it will. There will always be awkward errors in my vicinity."

Aura took his arm. "I would rather suffer awkward errors than an evil nature." They walked out of the castle.

Now the compass pointed back toward Castle Roogna. That was confirmation that its purpose had been accomplished.

The sign said nameless castle. It seemed it was already recovering.

"Let me clarify my own situation," Aura said. "I am part of a Quest to save multiple universes from the threat of zombification. I was at one point zombified myself, but I got over it with Demon help. I have companions with me." She went on to introduce Nik, Anthem, Dane, Rhonda, Wanda and Knife. "They are all worthy folk of their types, and my friends, and we largely share each other's thoughts. There really is no real privacy within the Quest. We are about to enter the Question Room in Castle Roogna, from which it is possible we will not emerge. So there may be aspects you would prefer not to be associated with."

"I have been personally isolated for some time, but I am a Demon, albeit an extremely minor one, and have been aware of significant events outside. I am not concerned about personal privacy, as I have no guilty secrets to hide and my various interests are normal, such as the ones you evoke, you gorgeous lady. But I have not been conscious of a zombie threat."

"That is because it has not occurred in this universe. I am from another universe where it is occurring and is serious." She paused to glance at him. "I propose to take you to other universes. Is this a deal breaker?"

"The way I have been treated in this universe? Not at all."

Aura held him and kissed him, this time without power. "I am glad."

“As I come to know more about you,” he said, “I am glad too.” Then added “Your personal kiss is as potent as your business kiss, in a more individual way. It signals your pleasing private desire.”

That was an oblique but potent compliment. She managed a faint blush as the appropriate response. “Thank you.”

It seemed to be working out. Demons, like mortals, had their nuances.

“The other shoe has dropped,” Rhonda said, satisfied.

They returned to Castle Roogna, where they caught the others up on the details of their excursion, such as the marriage of Nik and Anthem and the recruitment of Zanth as a member of the Quest.

“Bleep,” Noe said. “If I had known it was going to be that interesting, I’d have come along. I missed a wedding!”

“You were the one who first brought us together,” Anthem said with a chord from the Wedding March. “We’ll be happy to share the details with you.”

Then Nik and Aura transferred to Noe, along with the ghosts and Wanda and Knife, in order to give Zanth and Aura the appearance of some privacy, which they both wanted. It had indeed been an interesting day.

But what of the Question Room, soon to come? That was the point of this visit to Limbo, and the main challenge. The rest was incidental. Even the marriage.

The other members of the Quest got to know Zanth, and came to like him despite the annoyance of the typos. “We all have our little quirks,” Shameless remarked. Only the first time it came out “literate jerks.” There was compassionate laughter.

The day came. Nik, Anthem, Knight, Wanda, Dane, and Rhonda were all with Noe for this, together with the Genius Phone and Grav Lens. “You can do this two ways,” Trent said. “Select an individual of your number to represent you alone, or go as a group.”

“I would be the individual,” Nik said. “As the nominal leader of the Quest.”

“Not without me, beloved husband,” Anthem said.

“Not without any of us,” Noe said, speaking for the rest.

“Thank you,” Nik said, unsurprised but gratified.

“Iris, Irene, and I will leave you to it,” Trent said, settling into a couch with his wife and daughter. He was a remarkably steady man, not at all arrogant about either his crown or his Magician level talent of transforming living creatures to other creatures. It was hard to believe that he had once been condemned as the Evil Magician. They all liked him, especially the females.

"But I like you better, Nik," Anthem confided.

"That's a relief," he answered, with a mental smile.

The castle ghost Doris appeared. She was not the same as the woman in the movie; it was a coincidence of names. "I have been selected to guide you to the Question Room. Who is going?"

"All the members of the Quest," Nik said. "I will speak for them, with my wife's telepathic help. You know who they are."

"I do. Especially the ghosts. But I am required to advise you that you may not be allowed to leave the Question chamber, if you fail to answer the Question, and no one has answered it so far. You may not want to put all of your members at such risk."

"And I should advise you that our purpose here is not to ask a question, but to obtain the means to control future access to Limbo, so as to break up the zombie connection. Our assumption is that if we can answer the Question, we will be granted that control. You may not want to risk that."

Doris smiled. "Is that all?"

"Not all. We do not expect to be detained here, because we have significant assistance and our mission is too important to be thwarted at this stage. If we are unable to answer the Question, we will depart without gaining access control; that is all."

"How do you, an assemblage of humans, centaurs, bugs, objects, and ghosts, with one minor Dwarf Demon, expect to change the rules of engagement? The Question Chamber is governed by Demon Limbo."

Demoness Andromeda appeared, with her shifting visage and costume. "I am changing the rules. I am the Demoness of Change."

Doris was unfazed. "You lack the power to overrule Limbo here in his own domain. You and who else?"

Demon Bang appeared, shaking the castle without touching it. "And me. I support my wife." He faded out.

The ghost was evidently jolted, but held on, buttressed by the Demon she spoke for. "Ah. Now we appreciate why Demon Xanth backed off."

"Now you do," Nik agreed. "We're more formidable than we look."

She nodded. "So be it." That meant capitulation, the only feasible course. Their observing Demons had become potent collaborators.

Andromeda faded. Once an issue was decided, by whatever means, Demons did not argue further. It was one of the myriad ways they were superior to mortals.

"This way," Doris said. She indicated a passage that had not been there before. It looked dark and forbidding, but was surely safe. "I will remain here with the family, as I am only an auxiliary." She joined the family on the couch, sitting beside Irene. They knew each other from way back.

Noe, with her riders, led the way. The others followed. The passage seemed far longer than could be accounted for by the dimensions of the castle, but of course the magic ignored such science pollution, especially here in Limbo. The way closed after them, a one-way path. It finally debouched in a comfortable chamber where an indefinite male figure stood. A number of male and female statues stood before the walls.

"Hello, Quest," the figure said. "I am a personification of Demon Limbo. The terms of our interaction have been set. I will ask you one question, and if you answer it you will obtain control of the access to Limbo. If you fail, you will depart without further ado."

"Exactly," Nik said.

"Make yourselves comfortable, as this may take some time."

There were chairs and couches circling the room. The humans sat on them and the centaurs stood beside them.

"Here is the Question: Why is there something rather than nothing? Or to rephrase, why is there a complex of universes, with their substance, energy, dimensions, and rules of operation, rather than mere emptiness? Demons, mortals, souls, ghosts, life, consciousness, Heaven, Hell, justice, humor, grief, irony, etcetera? Logically, existence should not emerge from nonexistence. Our entire complex reality is framed by what appears to be nonsense. How can this be explained?"

Nik's clairvoyance grasped the situation. "You ask this not merely as a challenge to visitors, but because you want to learn the answer yourself."

"Exactly. The ultimate nature of reality is a mystery to me that I wish to resolve. I hope that you will be the ones to accomplish that. Without that answer, my own existence is largely meaningless, and so is yours. You should be as interested as I am."

"We are," Nik said, picking up on the reaction of the others, including the Demons themselves. This Question had not occurred to him before, but now that he had heard it, he knew that his outlook would never be the same. Why, indeed, did existence exist? It was not enough to say that the Demons had made it, starting with Bang. What had made Bang? The mundanes thought that an entity they called God had made it, but then what had made God? What had created creation? There was no answer, and there needed to be.

Nik knew that the others were as mystified as he was. Why? Why was there matter, energy, and time? Rules of the game? Why did any of them exist? None of the folk here could simply let it go.

"First let's explore what there is," Nik said. "In case the larger shape of it indicates its reason for existing."

Nik had organized his resources for possible research into a challenging question. Now he put them into play. He set the Grav Lens on maximum range and oriented the Genius Phone on it. "Where is the edge of all the universes?" he asked. "Start here and go outward until there is nothing." He knew that these tools had been enhanced by the Demons so that they could perform enormously beyond normal.

The big screen appeared, showing the group of them in the chamber. Then the image flung outward, expanding in the manner Nik and Anthem had when they encountered the Dark Matter creatures, and later went after the zombie kisses. The picture showed Castle Roogna, then the patch of landscape and activity that was Limbo, then the stellar system where it hovered, then the local galaxy. It continued to the universal scale, with the galaxies clustering in clouds, and to the multi-universe scale, where roughly spherical universes were expanding their sizes, threatening to jostle each other as the emptiness between them ran out. Then on to an ever-larger sphere of spheres, a seemingly infinite number. A gargantuan ball of balls.

Then came outer emptiness. The super ball seemed to shrink as the perspective continued to enlarge. Finally the pinpoint of it disappeared, a pip in the vastness of the void. There was nothing else.

"Space is not the Answer," Nik concluded. "It's there, but without explanation. Now let's try Time."

The perspective retreated until the ball reappeared. Now the clump diminished as time retreated billions of years, each universe imploding into its origin. The cluster of them became shrinking dots that finally winked out as their Demon Bangs compressed them, in seeming effect. Then the Demons themselves faded into a slurry of uncertainty. It wasn't nothing, but neither was it something. Again, not an answer.

"We are missing something," Anthem said with a disappointed chord.

"Look more closely," Santo suggested. "Sometimes there is news in the obscure details."

Nik played it again, this time tracking a particular stone in the castle back to its origin. It remained until the planet was young, when it formed out of burning slag. That in turn formed out of debris in space, which formed from dust. The dust came from the fluxes around the forming star that was to be the sun. The sun came from a cloud of loose matter that coalesced, compressed by the increasing gravity of its mass. The cloud came from a nebula made of hydrogen gas. The original gas molecules came from radiation that somehow curled in on itself to make tiny atoms.

"Matter comes from energy," Santo said. "Now we have seen it happen."

"But where does energy come from?" Noe asked.

They watched closely as the local universe shrank to its starting pinpoint. Now it was apparent: the energy was from the repulsion of positives and negatives ripped from the neutral fabric of space. Together they were nothing; apart they were opposites.

Yet that, too, was not the Answer. Where had that fabric of space, the ether, come from?

The picture moved through another waver of uncertainty, then formed into a recognizable object: a nickelpede. In fact it was Nik.

"That's what happened to me," Limbo said. "I got my own picture. Investigation either tells nothing useful, or short circuits, reverting to the questioner."

But now Nik's enhanced clairvoyance made a connection. A bulb flashed over his head, startling Anthem, who was close by it. "No. It is the Answer."

They all looked at him. Had his mind short circuited?

"The Answer is the Idea," Nik explained. "Such as the Idea of Nothing" which itself is something, not nothing, paradoxically. That evokes Thought, which in turn evokes Energy, which as we have seen can form into Matter, which can create Life, which can elicit Consciousness, which can produce the Idea. It is a circular progression, a story without beginning or end. But it is indeed Something arising from Nothing. It solves the mystery. Nothing cannot exist without the Idea of it, and the Idea must have the energy of thought behind it, and the rest follows. The Idea is the ultimate reality. All else is the aspects of it playing their roles, to animate it."

Limbo stared at him. "I think you've got it!"

The others applauded, some physically, others mentally.

"Now, about the access," Nik said. "I leave it with you, Demon Limbo, with this stricture: do not allow any zombie entry, or any communications from Demoness Zombia of any universe, to be transmitted through it. That will stop any new zombie threat. We will deal with the old one separately."

"Agreed, of course," Limbo said. "I will now release the prior querents, as there is no further need for their—" He paused, smiling. "Their ideas." He snapped his fingers, and the standing statues came to life. They looked around uncertainly. "I have my Answer," Limbo told them. "You are free to go home."

They didn't argue. They hurried down the corridor, which had reappeared.

The members of the Quest followed them. Soon they rejoined Trent, Iris, Irene, and Doris, who looked bemused, having seen the other querents passing. "Thank you for your hospitality," Nik said. "We shall be moving on now. It has been a productive visit."

"Yes it has," Aura and Anthem said together. "Especially for us."

"That, too," Nik agreed. "And for me."

Chapter 13

GROAN

Back at their staging area in the clean universe, they considered their next step. "Now we have to nullify the malign Zombia," Nik said. "To do that we will first have to catch her. Demons can hide from other Demons, so that may be a challenge, even if she is constrained as she is in other universes."

"What about the compass?" Aura asked. She was sitting on Zanth's lap, making no effort to mask her interest in him, as well as guaranteeing by personal contact that he had a companion. He certainly did! She had been starved for romantic interaction, and was making the most of it. It would be quite awkward if they separated temporally, only to have him zipped back to Limbo. They even held hands when one had a natural function to handle, which required some finesse. "Can it be redirected to point to her, so that we'll always have a line on her?"

"It can be, as it was redirected in Limbo," Andromeda said. "But orienting on a Demoness who doesn't want to be found would be tricky. It would not be reliable. She would simply disappear from its radar, the moment she caught on."

"Maybe we should ask the Zombia of this universe, who is on our side, how to orient on the Zombia of the other universe," Aura said.

"She helped us do the Limbo excursion," Noe said. "I like her."

"Let's do it," Anthem said, speaking for the consensus.

"Zombia," Aura said to the sky. "Much has happened in the interim. May we consult with you again?"

The Demoness appeared as an illusion of herself. "Come into my parlor, friends. There we will have privacy not available here."

Good point. Who knew who might be listening in via magic or talent? They went to Zombia's personal contact area, where privacy was guaranteed. They updated her on their adventures in Limbo, and formally introduced Zanth to her. "Bellow Xanthe," she said, amused.

"Bitto, Bombia." After that he stifled his ambiance, so that their dialogue would not be riddled with awkward typos.

Then they got serious. "We have closed Limbo to her," Nik said. "But she is still sending out zombie kisses, which are infecting other universes. We believe we have the means to stop them, but not if they keep coming indefinitely. So we need to go there and shut her down, probably by having Pun kiss her. We fear that she will know we are coming and hide from us. We have a compass we can orient to point to her, but that may not be reliable. Do you have advice on that?"

"Oh, yes. I know her as well as I know myself. She is a complex and devious creature, much interested in intimate social interactions of the kind the so-called Adult Conspiracy vainly attempts to mask or suppress." She glanced at Aura. "I envy you your committed male, and the manner you will soon be putting him through his paces. You too, Anthem, when you use that accommodation spell. But that's irrelevant to the mission of the Quest. You need to orient the compass not on her apparent location, but on her core essence. That can't be diverted or masked, once it is pinpointed. Set the compass for that and she won't escape you."

"How can we do that?" Nik asked.

"By focusing the compass on me. She is of a different universe, with a different attitude, but her essence is almost identical."

Santo was wearing the compass again. Andromeda reset it to orient on Zombia. When Zombia disappeared, it spun about wildly. Andromeda reset it more precisely as Zombia reappeared. After several tries it got locked on, and no shifts by Zombia could fool it. It had been properly zeroed in. "In her universe, she will be the one it tracks," Zombia said.

"And we will track her," Nik said. "If she's not completely hidden."

"She may not be. I understand she uses the Game a lot."

"The what?"

"All powerful Demons face few challenges other than rivalry among themselves. That's why Demon Bets are so popular; they mostly define status, which is important to those not doing anything useful. They have reserved a section in each universe for challenging entertainment, such as complicated guessing games or puzzles or competitive physical contests or seductions." Zombia smiled. "There is no Adult Conspiracy there, you may be sure. I enjoy my access to it, but my clones in universes where Zombias are banned do not. I suspect that is why this one sends out the kisses; she is getting back at those who limited her. She is a woman scorned, and indeed she has fury. The Game Area will be another challenge, if she is there, despite the compass. Proceed carefully."

"Why is it a challenge?" Noe asked. "If a game is dull or too difficult, why not just skip it in favor of one you like better?"

"The purpose is fairness," Zombia said. "Demons vary in type and power. I am good at erotic games like Female Fascination and Selective Seduction, but poor at intellectual ones like Chess or Go. So participants are limited to mortal type bodies of identical intellect, strength, gender, and appearance. That is, the males can do no more physically or mentally than mortals of that type could do, though they may vary in the details of appearance, and the females have no larger breasts or wider hips or fairer features, though they are free to change their hair styles, apparel, and skin colors as they choose. What counts is the skill they use in those standard bodies to gain advantages. You are mortals, mostly, but you lack the eons of experience the Demons have, so you will lose more games than you win." She glanced at Nik and Anthem. "Many games use the human format, as it is versatile, but there are a number of BEM, serpentine, and bug sections too. Again, if you compete in that arena, you will be at a severe disadvantage."

"Unless our purpose is not to win games, but to blend in as we make our way to our target," Nik said.

"True. But if you lose too consistently, you will stand out as totally inexperienced and arouse suspicion despite your anonymity. So you do want to win some. You should favor games of chance, where skill has less advantage."

"It will be a challenge," Noe agreed.

"Another thing: you can't depend on your anonymity to protect you. You will want limited obscurity, so that while she may know you are coming, she won't be able to pinpoint you. She will have to be active in her identification of you."

"But we want to catch her by surprise," Noe said.

"You can't. If she wants to be hidden, no one in that universe will be able to find her. So you need to give her a reason to place you. Only if she is looking for you, will you be able to find her."

"This surely makes sense," Santo said. "But I am too dull to fathom it."

Zombia laughed. "Artfully put! You are about as smart as mortals come, apart from your formidable talent. Think of the human saying about how a man chases and chases a woman until she catches him. You want Zombia to chase you until you catch her. When she finds you, you will finally have her."

Santo nodded. "I do not chase women, but now I see your analogy. We can never find a hiding Demoness unless she comes out of hiding, so we must lure her out. But how, since her best strategy is to leave us completely alone."

"You now have control of the access to Limbo. You could arrange a leak of information, such as that you have found a mechanism to nullify her zombie kisses, but that you need a lock of her hair, or even a single hair, to analyze to identify the target precisely. She will realize that could be effective, so she must act to prevent it. She cannot afford to gamble that the leak is false, or that none of her hair is to be found loose in the Game Area complex. She could lose her power if she does nothing. All she needs to do is kiss the one seeking her hair, and he will then be a zombie dedicated to her service. So she will kiss any suspect."

"And inadvertently kiss Demon Pun!" Aura exclaimed. "Who will destroy her."

"She will not be destroyed, merely cured of her zombie magic. She will become a Demoness without her power, somewhat the way you, Aura, reverted to your normal state when Pun kissed you." Zombia smiled. "Perhaps she will then go to her erotic interest and make some male deliriously happy. She will still have that power. Regardless, the zombie threat to the universes will be abated, except for the zombie kisses that remain traveling."

"We will see to it," Nik said.

They thanked her, and Aura hugged her, learning friendship with this clone Zombia too, and they moved on. They had another universe to handle.

* * *

Nik had Demon Limbo leak the news about their quest for a hair of Zombia's head, and that the one seeking it would try to hide among the members of one of the human groups visiting the Games. That word would quickly spread to Zombia. She should be looking for someone, but not know which one of which group. So each side was gambling, with the fate of universes at stake.

Santo tunneled to the key universe, the Xanth section, and they set up their camp. It was soon apparent that this universe was in a bad way. Nik used the Grav Lens to spot the Game Area, which was an obscure galaxy near the center of the cluster. Sure enough, the compass indicated that Zombia was there. She would be tracking them as they tracked her, but her tracking would be less specific. They hoped.

Now the members of the Quest needed to hide, because the other local Demons would not approve their mission. The locals were zombies, early victims of the kisses, and would defend the zombie cause.

"Can you hide us the way your hide yourselves?" Nik asked their Demons.

"Yes, in a manner," Andromeda said.

"A manner?"

"Your activity will soon give you away, even if your presence can't be detected. You will be better off with anonymity of the kind Noe involuntarily practices. Folk will see, hear, and feel you, but not take notice, and will forget you when you leave them. That way there will be no assassin team orienting on you."

Noe shuddered. "Assassin team!"

Nik clicked a pincer. "Anonymity is better," he agreed.

"You have it now."

"I feel no change," Noe said.

They all laughed. The change was not in her, but in the rest of them.

"Another thing," Shameful said. "We shouldn't use our magic talents there, because the surest identification of a person is his/her talent. Same as the Demons monitoring us don't use their powers. We have to be just random visitors, nothing special about us." She paused. "Maybe the ghosts, too should not advertise their presence to others. Same reason."

As usual she was telling them what they would rather not have heard. But they agreed she was correct. No talents there, except for the purely mental ones, like clairvoyance and telepathy, and those, too, would be muted.

They organized, rested, applied zombie makeup, and took the next tunnel to the critical universe. They landed in the obscure backwoods of a bordering planet, then went to the Game Area Galaxy Entry Section, Human Division. Andromeda knew the protocol, as there was the equivalent in their own universe. Mortals were allowed to participate, so as to provide increased variety and a better selection of partners for some of the murkier games.

"Males of any type like to get equivalent new females," Anthem said with a sour chord. "Novelty rather than commitment."

Nik didn't argue. There were ways in which males and females differed from each other more than different species did, or Demons from mortals.

They arrived at a side entrance. A passage led inside. Santo shut down the tunnel and they walked on in.

They found themselves on a level platform next to a pile of poles. Beyond it was a narrow chasm separating them from a similar platform on the other side. Behind them was a blank wall. The difference between the two platforms was that the far one had an entrance to the Game Area. Behind them was only an exit to the way they had come.

"I think we are facing the entry challenge," Santo said. "If we can't figure out how to cross the gap, we don't get in to join the other games."

"Thus guaranteeing that no one below a certain savvy can get in to spoil the works," Noe said. "A tacit intelligence test."

"Unless the mechanism of crossing is already known to some entrants," Shameless said.

"No," Andromeda said. "That would be an unfair advantage. No one knows. The challenges change often, randomly."

Obviously, the poles were the key to crossing. They needed to vault across, which seemed dangerous, especially for the centaurs, or to construct a bridge. But there was a problem. The poles were all the same length, with swollen ends on on one side. They were not long enough to span the gap. There was no rope to tie them, or nails, or glue. Nothing to hold a bridge together.

"Like giant matchsticks," Dane said. "We used them in Mundania to light fires."

"And there were games we could play with them," Rhonda said. "Like Nik where players take turns to pick up one or more matches from any pile, and the winner is the one who picks up the last match. Or the reverse, with the loser getting the last match. That may seem simple, either way, but it gets tricky." She looked at the poles. "But that won't help you cross."

"We need a physical way," Aura said. "I don't see it."

"Neither do I," Noe said. "I guess we're failing the smarts test."

"Ah, I know a different game," Gyles said. "It is to make a bridge from loose matches. No glue or string. It took me a while, but I solved it. It's one way I impressed Xenia, the dear girl. I love her still. Folk don't believe that a man and a woman two generations apart can be right for each other, but they can." He took a breath. "Sixteen matches will do." He paused to count the poles. "Seventeen. So that's the answer. One's a spare."

"Let's see your answer," Noe said, a trifle tightly. She clearly doubted that the ghost could do it. Maybe she was slightly jealous of Xenia, with a man so romantically committed to her, and death did not them part.

"The key is dynamic bracing. You form a kind of ladder with the end of one stick braced against another, and you carry it through to the other end."

"That's clear as mud."

"Come on, you living folk," Gyles said. "Put your hands on the planks and I'll spell it out step by step. We'll get our ladder across."

Santo, Zanth, and Shameless took up poles. Gyles directed them stage by stage, and soon they actually had an arcing bridge about six feet high at the center and nine feet from end to end. Its own gravity and the friction of the contacts held it in place, with no fasteners needed. The bridge!

"I admit you made a bridge," Noe said. "That's impressive. But there's one problem. It's all on this side. How do you get it across the gap without it falling apart?"

"Oops," Santo said. "It needs all four feet on the ground, constantly, or it will collapse."

Shameful picked up the seventeenth pole and poked it a little way into the gulf. "Time for another unwelcome pronouncement," she said. "You men just wasted your ingenuity, time, and effort. Those poles are only a distraction. You never needed a bridge."

The three males frowned at her. "Explain?" Shameless asked.

"The gap does not exist. It's only an illusion. Maybe two feet deep. A declivity made to look like a gulf. This is a trick question, in effect, to catch folk who limit themselves to one sense when trying to assess all the aspects of a problem. Check it yourselves."

They did, poking hands down into the evident chasm. She was right. It was only a shallow dip, not a canyon. They had fallen for an illusion.

"Beans!" Noe swore. "I fell for it too."

Zanth considered. "Let's put the bridge across anyway, and leave it there for the authorities to wonder about. It will look as if that was the way we crossed."

"Leave them a mental typo," Aura said, a wicked smile in her background.

Santo and Shameless nodded agreement. The group carefully picked up the bridge, waded across the supposed gulf, and set it firmly athwart the chasm. Let the gamesters figure that one out.

Then the group moved on. Beyond the passage was a chamber with a table on which several cylinders shaped like cones fastened together end to end, or hourglasses, rested, beside several pairs of sticks about a foot and a half long attached to each other by strings on the ends.

"What are these?" Noe asked. They were all mystified.

"I recognize them," Gyles said. "They are Diabolo sets. You rest the diabolo cone on the string, then pick up the sticks and roll it back and forth along the string. When it gets to spinning fast enough it hums. When you get good, you can toss it into the air and catch it again, or even fling it to another player. It was quite the rage when I was young. It's easy to understand, but not easy to play well, but I found it a worthy challenge and worked at it. In fact I got pretty good at it, before the fad passed."

Aura picked up a set of linked sticks. "I'm good with my hands."

"Yes you are," Zanth said appreciatively.

She grinned briefly. "I mean with object coordination. Maybe I can do it with this game. But it would help if you could guide me, Gyles."

The ghost flew across to join her. He put a spectral hand on her head. "Read my mind and skill. Let them flow to your hands. You'll do fine."

She put a blue diabolo on the string, then lifted it as the string tautened between the sticks. Soon she had it rolling and spinning. Then came the hum. Her connection with the ghost, coupled with her natural coordination, was making her good with very little practice. "I am beginning to see why Xenia likes you," she murmured. "You surely make her hum."

"In a different manner," the ghost agreed.

A young woman appeared, evidently a player. There was only a trace of zombie rot on her arms; she was a fresh one. "Ah, you are ready." She picked up another set with a red diabolo and got it humming. "I am Hagar. Who are you?"

"I am Aura."

"Now we exchange diabolos by tossing them back and forth. First one who misses, loses."

"But—"

"You came to play the game, right? Everything is games here. So play it."

Aura paused, evidently listening to Gyles, then nodded. She flexed her string to flip the blue diabolo up, as Hagar did the same with hers. The two spinning cones sailed high, arced down, and were caught on the opposite strings. Now Aura had the red one, and Hagar had the blue one.

They flipped again, exchanging diabolos. And again, this time flinging them higher. And again. And Hagar missed, her diabolo bouncing off the string, dropping to the floor and rolling away because of its spin. "Dang! I lost. The rot is affecting my coordination." She went after the fallen diabolo, picked it up, set it and the string system on the table, and departed, giving no credit to her opponent. While she wasn't a bad loser, she was hardly a good one.

"I won," Aura said, half in wonder. "Thanks to you, Gyles. You guided my hands." She set her equipment down.

"It was fun getting into it again after so long. You did great." The ghost flew back to the phone. Yet again he had proven his usefulness.

"The compass says that way," Santo said, pointing. "But it may be best to go circuitously, so we don't seem to have a destination."

They moved to the next chamber. There was a kind of playing court, with a high net stretched across the center, and a large ball resting below it. "I know this one," Noe said. "It's volleyball. I used to play it with the neighbor's boys. I was pretty good, for a girl, but I lacked the height and strength of the boys." A frown stalked her. "I refused to play for penalty peeks and feels when I lost points, so I wasn't an early pick for a team."

"You did right," Aura said. "Boys can be such brutes, socially."

Noe nodded, appreciating the support.

A group of men and women came in from the opposite direction—more new zombies. Zombies made from living folk were much livelier than those from dead folk, at least when they were fresh. "Ah. Competition," a man said. "I'm Prior. This is my mistress Prisca." He indicated his companion, a girl obviously of the standard stock, but she had set her neckline low, cinched her waist tight, wore a push-up bra, and flared her colored purple hair out high, so as to stand out from that stock. She was also a bright green skin color, in a glowing red dress. She would be noticed in any crowd. As Zombia had said, folk were free to modify such details. Prisca was an example of what could be done to make the ordinary far more interesting, zombie taint notwithstanding. She well might be a Demoness in human form. She was Prior's mistress? That could mean his owner or his girlfriend, probably a purposeful indistinction to make her more intriguing. It was best to be wary of assumptions.

"Hello, Prior and Prisca," Aura said.

"You have a team of six. Get in your court."

"Not all of us know this game," Santo said.

"Hit the ball with your hand," Prior said. "Either directly over the net and in bounds, as in the serve, or to a teammate to relay it. Only three touches and over. Make the other side miss. Fifteen points to a game."

"The strategy is to serve it to a difficult corner," Noe said. "Then when you receive it, bounce it up high near the net so a teammate can smash it down hard, making the other side miss. It's fun."

Four more folk filed in, two males and two females, all standard stock with the zombie taint. Nik realized that some of them might not be zombies, but emulating zombieism to fit in socially, just as was their own case. They took their places in the opposite court while Santo, Noe, Zanth, Aura, Shameful, and Shameless took theirs in the near court. Centaurs counted as humans for this game.

An arrow on the wall pointed to the home court. "That means we get the first serve," Noe said. "That's an advantage. A team can score only when it serves, and holds the serve only so long as it continues to score.

I'll start." She stood just outside the back boundary, tossed the ball up and struck it with the heel of her right hand so that it sailed across and over the net.

As it happened, it went right to Prisca. Noe had probably aimed for her. She put up both fists and bumped it into the air, forward, clearly knowing exactly what she was doing. Another player bumped it higher, barely short of the net. A third one spiked it down so that it crossed the net and struck the floor, untouched.

"And we lost the serve," Noe said. "Next time, someone put his hands up to block it so that the spike bounces the other way and costs them the point. The slam can become a liability against a savvy player."

Prior served the next, and remained as his team scored several points. But then the home team's teamwork improved and they got the serve back and scored several points of their own. Nik was with Santo as he served, and noted how Prisca, opposite him, leaned forward so that her breasts and cleavage showed handsomely, surely a serious distraction for a normal man. But of course Santo was immune.

The scoring went back and forth, but in the end the home team won. It seemed that some of the others really were zombies, whose stamina flagged as the game progressed.

"Good game," Noe said politely. Then, to Prisca, "I like your hair style." She did not mention skin color or cleavage.

"Thank you. It's fun to see what can be done with standard issue."

"It is indeed," Aura agreed. Nik suspected that she was making a mental note. Innovations could be made with natural bodies too, not that she needed them.

There were several passages to new chambers. They took the one that led toward Zombia, as the prior chambers had not been in that direction.

What they found was one labeled "Bug." Nik and Anthem liked the notion. There were plastic sections on a table, showing the various parts of a model bug: body, head, legs, eyes, antennae, tail. The rules indicated that a single die was cast, with the number at the top calling out a particular part of the bug. The assembly couldn't start until the One was thrown, for the body; then legs and tail could be added, but not antennae or eyes, until the head had been found. So it was chancy, depending in part upon the order of the throws. It was luck rather than skill, but readily played by anyone. A children's game that adults could enjoy too, as a novelty.

There were no others in this chamber, so they played against each other, with Santo handling the die and pieces for Nik, and Noe doing them for Anthem. Nik had the first cast of the die. It was a Four. That meant he could place an eye, except that he had no head yet. The others took their turns, and Nik was pleased to see that Anthem got a One, which gave her a body. The others mostly missed, as Nik had.

In the second round, Nik got a One, and Santo put the body piece on the table for him. Anthem got a Three, getting a leg for her body, one of six needed. Again, the others were scattered, as chance would have it.

The third round was a Five for Nik, giving him an antenna he couldn't place because as yet he had no head. Anthem got another leg.

The fourth round gave Nik a Six, which was the tail. Anthem got a head.

The fifth round gave Nik a Two, and a head to go with his body. Anthem got an antenna.

The sixth round was another Four for Nik. Now he could place an eye on the head. Anthem got a Four too, also an eye.

The seventh round was another Five, and this time Nik could place an antenna. Anthem got another leg.

It continued, with most players finally getting bodies and heads to build on. Anthem was finally the winner, while Nik was still short three legs. Second place went to Shameful, who was short one leg, and third place went to Zanth, short one feeler and an eye.

"Congratulations on your handsome Bug, Anthem," Noe said.

"I only wish it were an ant, or a nickelpede, instead of a beetle."

"Maybe the Bug annex has ants or nickelpedes as the models."

They all agreed that this was fun, but that one game was enough. They moved on to the next room.

This turned out to be a larger chamber with a broad green floor formed of soft but firm material marked in lanes. There were bags piled at the near edge.

"Oh, my," Aura said. "I know this one from my childhood. It is Potato Sack Racing. You haul a sack up over waist high and hop along across the field. If you fall, you get up and continue; the ground is soft so you don't get hurt. It's fun for children."

"This doesn't work well for centaurs," Shameful said.

"Or for bugs," Nik said.

"Or ghosts," Rhonda said.

But they had to proceed on the assumption that they, and all players, were being watched, and they had to fit in. So the four in human form took sacks and hopped awkwardly across the floor, while the centaurs acted as referees and called out the winner: Zanth. He was actually a Demon in human form, but managed to make it look like a close race. The whole thing was its own kind of fun.

The next passage led to a lobby with a sign: fun party—free refreshments—admission: one kiss

There was the key aspect: a way Zombia could make more zombies without making a big deal of it. Kisses were part of this game.

There by the several entrances were males and females of many kinds, human and other, such as sylphs, trolls, fiends, and elves. Other players were choosing ones to kiss, with a clear preference by males for alluring females regardless of species, and by females for robust males. But there was no line before one female, though she was a dark haired, shapely, sultry human woman. Why was she being avoided?

Nik looked at the compass. It pointed right at that one. It was Zombia, wearing a different body from the ones they had seen before. The others here must have known, and hesitated to approach the Demoness, whose power in this universe had to be far greater than in others. She was watching for her stalker.

Santo angled the compass so Shameless could see it, though he surely knew already, via his silent companion, Demon Pun.

Could it really be this easy? Or was it an unfamiliar trap?

They played it through. Santo joined the line for one of the human women, and the others selected other entrances. To him, this kiss was business, not pleasure. He had kissed Noe many times in public when he needed to avoid mischief. That was one of the ways she helped him.

Shameless trotted up to Zombia. "I think I know you," he told her. "May I have a hair of your head as a memento?"

She focused on him with sudden interest. Here was her quarry! "You may, for a kiss. I have never kissed a centaur before."

"More than fair." He leaned down as she lifted her face, and their lips met.

There was a surrounding flash as the key quality of one disguised Demon clashed with another. Then Zombia collapsed. Her power had just been terminated.

Shameless turned and stepped smartly into the tunnel that Santo made in that instant. The other members of the Quest walked in behind him. In moments they were back at the zombie-free universe, and the tunnel closed behind them. It had happened so quickly that neither groggy Zombia nor her supporters had had time to react.

"Did really happen?" Noe asked, amazed.

"It really happened," Shameless said, speaking for Pun. "That particular Zombia can no longer make zombies. It seems it never occurred to her that the naive mortal fortune hunter might have a Demon connection."

"Or to the others that anything as silly as a pun might be dangerous," Shameful said. "That was a truth no zombie wanted to hear."

"But we still have to deal with the zombie lips still in circulation," Nik said.

"That is our next chore," Shameless agreed. "Now we have to see whether this universe has a Caprice Castle."

"What castle?" Nik asked.

"It's a castle that travels. There's a vault there where old puns are stored. We'll be needing vast slews of them to make the pun bomb the Demon has in mind."

"Pun bomb!"

"The plan is to assemble it here with half a squintillion egregious puns programmed to pass through the myriad portals between universes so that the skewed wordplay can clean out the zombies everywhere. The puns will regenerate as they enter new universes, so they'll never run out. If that works, all of reality will finally be clean."

"Let's hope it does work," Noe said. "I don't like to seem prejudiced, but I really don't like zombieism."

"I don't like it either," Aura said. "And I have been a zombie, and kissed many folk into zombieism, am friends with one or two Zombias."

"Nobody does like it," Shameful said. "Except the zombies, assuming they have feelings."

"Um, what's your take on this, Nik?" Shameless asked. "I have a feeling that the bomb is what we want, but it isn't complete."

Nik extended his clairvoyance. "You're right! The bomb is useless without a key ingredient it lacks. But I can't tell what that is. Maybe Demon Pun knows."

Now Shameless spoke for the Demon. "You are correct, now that I review the list. It can clear all zombies on one universe, but for multiple ones it needs an ingredient not found in this universe. I don't know what it is. Only my clone in the key universe knows, and he has kept the secret. There has been no hint of it via Limbo."

Aura sighed. "So it seems we have to go universe hopping again. Just when we thought that aspect was winding down."

"Ever thus," Santo said. The rogue smile hovered just out of reach. "Who would have thought that saving universes would be so complicated?"

"Who, indeed," Aura agreed. "Pun, can you give Santo the address of that universe?"

"I can," the Demon said. "But I must advise you that it is a wild one."

"Yet we had better go there," Nik said. "To be sure of our mission."

The others regretfully agreed.

"And we have to do it now."

"Yes," Shameful said, confirming that they would have preferred not to hear.

Pun gave Santo the coordinates, and he made the tunnel. It was intended to arrive in the near vicinity of the Pun clone, where he was restricted for the usual reason.

They walked through, cautiously. The region beyond seemed ordinary, a field with occasional trees. But when they looked around, there was something else.

It was a band of flying knives. They glinted dangerously in the sunlight, but stayed on the far side of a line along the ground.

"They are like Knife Knight," Anthem said. "Conscious and self-powered."

"What are they saying?" Nik asked.

"They are here to keep Pun in and outsiders out. They will slice any intruders to pieces."

"Let me talk to their leader," Knife said, sliding out of his sheath on Santo's hip.

Anthem translated the knives' thoughts to verbal language, as she did for Knife. There was a flurry of words. Then a deadly thin scalpel approached to just beyond the line. "I am Acute," she said.

"I am Knife. We are here to talk with Pun."

"Not here. Not today," she flashed. "He is sequestered."

"Our mission is important. I don't want to fight you, I just want our group to talk with him."

"You look like a strong weapon."

"I am." Knife shifted into sword mode. "But our mission is peaceful."

"I like your look. Here is mine." She became a larger scalpel.

Knife was impressed. "You look sharp." Nik remembered what Wanda had said about Knife's preference for knives and her taste for wands.

"I am." Acute angled in the light, wickedly flashing him.

Knife angled similarly, sharply flashing back.

Nik realized that this was a kind of contest, like trying to stare each other down. "It can also be a kind of flirting," Anthem said privately.

Oops. "Then what of Wanda?"

"When we depart this universe, he'll never see her again," Wanda said on the same private channel. "He can flirt all he wants." She vibrated restlessly. "If only I could do the same."

"We have to talk with Pun," Knife said to Acute. "We don't want to have to use magic to ground you."

"Then talk with the proprietor," she glinted.

"With whom?"

There came a flying baton, like the Baton of Protagonism, only shrouded in darkness. "With me," it said. "I am Banto, the Baton of Antagonism. I will ensure that you fail ignominiously."

"Now wait," the Baton of Protagonism said, appearing. "This is my story, not yours. You can't interfere with what my characters do."

"This my universe, not yours, bird-wing," Banto said. "If your characters get in my way, I will destroy them."

"And we are here to do it," Acute said as her army of knives fell into formation behind her.

Then Wanda flew up to intercept Banto. "Kiss me, you fool!" She formed into a matching baton, only feminine and lovely, and stroked her smooth length along his shaft. It was one potently suggestive maneuver, equivalent to a panty flash among humans, only more so.

Banto quivered in place. He had freaked out.

"We're still on guard," Acute said.

Knife swept across the line and sliced his edge along her blade so firmly that sparks flew. This was not a threat so much as a promise. "Dismiss your minions," he said. "And make sharp coruscations with me."

"Dismissed!" she called, and flew away with him. The sparks had not been damaging; rather they had been exciting, as radiations of passion. She had been blissfully conquered. The army faded back.

Wanda tapped Banto on the bulb, snapping him out of his freak. "Reverse your thrust, you splendid masculine symbol, and I will stay with you and make fabulous fiction. I always wanted to be a story conjurer."

"Reversed," he said meekly. He, too, had been conquered. They flew away together, trailed by a string of little winged hearts.

"Which leaves me in change," the Baton of Protagonism said. "Go meet with Pun Clone."

They crossed the field to the fun house where this universe's Demon Pun resided. Their own Demon Pun flew ahead to consult with him.

"So Wanda and Knife both sacrificed to promote the Quest," Noe said as they went. "That was certainly nice of them."

"But they both got lovers of their own type, as they really wanted," Aura said. "It was a fair compromise. They will surely make many little wands and knives together."

"Not mention livelier stories than this one," Zanth said.

"Not every story can be super heroic," Aura said. "We all have to settle for the hands we are dealt." She lifted a hand and dealt him a pat on the backside.

"We do," he agreed, returning the pat with interest.

Demon Pun flew back. "He gave me the secret. Jalapunos! The hottest puns ever. There's a field of them growing beyond his house. We can take what we need."

They found the field and harvested a baker's dozen minus one. They had their final ingredient.

They returned to the tunnel. "Knife and Wanda certainly came through for us in the end," Noe said.

"And for themselves," Santo said. "It's a step up in the fantasy realm."

"They did help us significantly," Nik said. "We were lucky to have them along."

They emerged back where they had been. Now they were ready for business.

"Where were we?" Aura asked. "The big pun vault?"

"At Caprice Castle," Shameless said.

"If there is one in this universe," Shameful said. "There may not be."

"There is a Caprice Castle here," Shameless reported, relaying more information from the Demon. "It was built by a version of Demon Pun, the Dwarf Demon Pundit, to store puns, and is run by a man named Piper. Not the same person as the woman we met before. We have put in the summons. It will be here soon." He smiled. "Piper must suffer from the Punic Curse. I understand that was really bad in Mundania in the time of the Romans, and they weren't laughing."

Indeed, the castle appeared in the adjacent field, forming out of the mist, setting down roots as it were, looking as if it had always been there. A basement door opened and they walked in. There, around a central hall, were several huge vaults. They were tightly sealed; no one wanted any awful puns to leak out.

"First we must construct the bombshell," Shameless said, still speaking for the Demon. "We will use punk wood, which cushions the puns while holding them firmly in place. The castle has a supply."

They found the pile of punk, and the group of them carried the curved sections out to the adjacent field. Then they assembled them, fitting one dovetailed edge into another, though that did spook the doves, until they had a ball shaped container as tall as a man, with a hole in one side.

Next came the puns. These were in tight balls bound in comic yarn. They filled buckets with them and hauled them out to the bombshell and dumped them into the hole. There was a funny odor, as of a punball cracking open to release part of its story, but no real stink. Until one rolled out of a bucket Noe was hauling and dropped to the floor. It split open with a musical tune and the pun burst out. "Do you like the music of the sea? Here's a Nep Tune." A small cloud of smoke looked like the sea god.

"Oh, vinegar!" Noe swore sourly.

Then a second ball dropped and cracked apart with another spot melody. "Do you like musical sea life? Here's a Tune Na Fish." The dissipating smoke looked like a big swimming fish.

"Horseradish!" This time the nearby grass wilted.

No one else commented. Noe obviously had been put into a very bad mood, and would surely regret her intemperate language when she cooled off. For some reason the Adult Conspiracy did not bleep it out, maybe because she was just at the edge of adulthood and mostly anonymous.

At last the bomb was full. Shameless put on fireproof gloves and added the jalapuno peppers and set the final panel in, closing the hole. The bomb was primed. The puns would be really hot.

"Now it is time to detonate it," Shameless said. "That requires a good punt. Hold your noses; there'll be some blow-back."

Then the centaur faced away from the bomb, planted his forelegs, and delivered a two hoofed back kick to the shell. It exploded in a burst of moaning miasma, and filthy patches of dreadful puns radiated out.

One of them struck Nik. The foul cloud was shaped like a fowl. "Do you watch birds on the weekend? Here's a Sat Tern." He groaned. What a stink! It smelled like rotting bird droppings.

The others were suffering similarly. But in half a moment the punburst had passed them by and the pungent odor was dissipating. The worst was over, at least for them.

"That was a pain in the bleep," Santo said, rubbing his neck, or wherever.

The local Demoness Zombia appeared. "That was some commotion! It burned my rotten clothing right off, along with some excess flesh, and scorched my hair." Indeed, she was spectacularly nude, with wisps of smoke rising from her sightly body, and her hair was smoky. "But I'm glad to do it, to save the universes." She faded, smiling.

"Now it is done," Shameless said. "We can go home."

They tunneled back to their own universe. There was no sign of any zombies.

"Tomorrow we will resume our Quest to map Xanth," Nik said. "But tonight I think we have earned a rest."

The others agreed, including the Demons. They went to the queendom, where Queen Demesne was glad to give the Quest members accommodations for the night. She had already noted the decimation of the local zombies. She also congratulated Nik and Anthem on their marriage. As a demoness among humans and other species in the queendom, she was not concerned about differences in species. What counted was how well they got along.

Noe took them to the Bug section, and put her hand down to the ground so they could descend. A young human couple was walking by. "Ooo, bugs!" the girl said, shying away.

"Remember, there's a truce," the boy said as they moved hurriedly on. "We all leave each other alone."

"But what use are bugs to anyone or anything?"

"Back to the ignorant realm," Noe muttered as she stood.

Nik and Anthem retired to his old apartment at the nickelpede mound. If other nickelpedes noticed his companion, they did not comment. They, too, had an inkling what the Quest had accomplished. "My only regret," he said, "is that I am not quite certain that the Pun Bomb was universally effective, even augmented by the jalapuno peppers. How can we be sure it didn't just fix a few local universes?"

"I have the same concern," she said with a downbeat chord. "We all do; I read the other minds. One universe is one thing; several universes is another. But there may be an infinite number. How can we ever be sure of them all?"

They agreed that they could not be perfectly certain. The proper response to a bad pun was a groan, but that was just one person to another. They could not be sure, and that doubt would haunt them indefinitely.

It was time to invoke the accommodation spell, which would enable them to consummate their relationship in the way they both ardently desired. Such spells allowed widely divergent participants to come together physically in size and type to make meaningful love. To Nik, she would seem like a lovely lady Nickelpede; to Anthem, he would seem like a handsome, virile fire ant. Their minds had no problem; love was supreme. At least they had that to be sure of, at last. Their marriage was about to be complete, despite the background zombie doubt.

But there was a distraction. It was a very faint but persistent sound that nagged them both. What could it be?

They realized that it might be a confusion they should ignore, but they decided to use their powers to seek the answer. Nik extended his clairvoyance, and Anthem her telepathy, both of which remained enormously enhanced by the Demons. They linked them together, as they had sometimes done before, augmenting their powers to make them dimensionally more effective. Perhaps no one else would be able to resolve the mystery of the sound, but at least the two of them would. Maybe.

Then they got it, and gazed at each other, amazed. Suddenly they knew that the Pun Bomb had been truly effective for a much wider reach of reality. Their effort was a success. Because it was a sound like no other, ever, with truly phenomenal significance. They listened to it, awed.

It was the sound of a hundred trillion universes groaning in unison.

Author's Note

This is the forty-ninth Xanth novel, with at least one more to go, and it's a bit different from the others, as you may have noticed. For one thing it's more adult. Let's do a capsule review of the series. This gets ugly, so if you don't like that, skip to the next paragraph or three. Way back in the 1960s when I was getting started as a published story writer and novelist, after trying since the 1950s—yes I was always a slow beginner; I even took three years and five schools to make it through first grade, because I couldn't learn to read—it wasn't until my daughter was diagnosed with dyslexia that I realized she had the same symptoms as I had had, only in my day there was no dyslexia, only stupid kids—I protested getting cheated, by a publisher, for which I was blacklisted six years, until a new editor at that publisher discovered that he had been similarly cheated, and invited me back. He was the fantasy editor, so I wrote a fantasy novel. In effect I turned local geography into the magic land of Xanth, where every person had a magic talent of great or small potency, and went on from there. That was A Spell for Chameleon, and it concluded with the Evil Magician becoming the new King of Xanth, ushering in what turned out to be a golden age. He was actually a good and highly talented man, unfairly condemned until he was vindicated. If you see a parallel to my own situation of the time, shh, my illustrious critics don't see it that way. In fact they object to my even writing about it. I continue to annoy them, not shutting up about it as a docile writer should, being incorrigible. Now you know.

The book won the British Fantasy Award as best fantasy novel for the year 1977. The story features one man, Bink, in this magic realm, who lacked a magic talent, so was exiled from the Land of Xanth, which by a weird coincidence is a peninsula shaped just like Florida in dreary Mundania, where I lived. Obviously, no originality there, confirming the judgment of the critics. In exile Bink meets Magician Trent, and returns to Xanth with him. It finally turns out that Bink is not talentless, but has powerful but hidden magic, and was wrongly exiled. Again, if you see a parallel to a kid too stupid to learn to read finally becoming a successful novelist, ignore it; obviously it's an ignorant dream. Ask any critic. I discovered that I couldn't take fantasy seriously, which is why the humor and parody came in. Soon fans were sending in puns and ideas for subsequent novels, and I used them. So I can answer the question of where do I get my ideas? From my readers who obviously have more imagination than I do.

Because of its lightness, the editor was afraid the novel would be taken as a juvenile, so he had me upgrade the language. Thus a phrase like "a high place" became "a lofty promontory." It didn't work; the kids loved it anyway. So in later novels I had to avoid the taboo subject of sex, though obviously it exists. I had folk perform a secret ritual that signaled the Stork to deliver a baby in a few months, storks being notoriously inefficient. Instead of men being sexually attracted to women, they freaked out at even a glimpse of a girl's panties. The dread Adult Conspiracy forbade children from knowing the secret of Stork Summoning. Even so, there have been protests about the sexuality of the series. I have pretty much given up trying to please the critics, who I think really don't want to be pleased anyway. As for the upgraded language, we finally did a simplified language edition of *Spell*, which is the ebook version you can find online.

So this novel, *Knickelpede Knight*, is a maverick in ways. It starts smaller than any of the others, with a bug as the protagonist, and ends larger, with multiple universes. It touches the horror genre as they watch a mundane murder movie. It acknowledges the seduction of sexuality, especially when Demoness Zombia gets up and clean. It paraphrases Einstein's Theory of Relativity as the dread pollution of science infests this supposedly pristine fantasy, yet another no-no. It glorifies the realm of Dark Matter, something I regard as fantasy that astronomers invented in an effort to explain why whirling galaxies don't fly apart. Folk, gravity ain't the only game in town. It features miscegenation, as a Nickelpede and a

Fire Ant seriously romance each other. And it exalts the nefarious Power of the Pun. If you ever fear that the zombies are after you, now you know how to set them back. Your universe can be forever free of such rot, if you can stifle your groans. Critics may protest it's not worth it, being largely humorless.

So what's going on here? Have I lost what little mind I ever had? Am I trying to alienate both critics and readers? Maybe. My relationship with genre fandom has been mixed. I was accused of being an ogre at fan conventions, before I had ever even attended a convention. That shows the way of it. So I made an ogre the hero of my next novel, *Ogre, Ogre*, which became my first national bestseller. After that I made ogres my theme. An ogre is justifiably proud of his stupidity. Later I did attend conventions, but was never nasty. As I write this I am pushing age eighty-nine, and there are those who are concerned that I am far from the brightest bulb on the chandelier. Here's one example of my recent craziness: after living over sixty-two years in Florida I abruptly moved to California with my wife MaryLee. From the backwoods of the Sunshine State to the seashore near Los Angeles. I wrote this novel in my new office on the tenth floor of a nine-story building; actually it's fourteen stories if you count them all, including the three parking basement levels. As I pondered my text I gazed at the clouds above and the people below. The clouds travel mainly north, sometimes south, but not eat or west, and they never rain; I'm not sure what governs them. But of course we've been here only four months; maybe cosmic law sends them different directions in other seasons. There is one cloud that forms over the area I think is Hollywood, you know, the movie industry. Maybe there's extra hot air there. When the writers' strike started, that cloud faded. How's that for proof? I'm a writer; I hope the writers prevail. In Parnassus, which is the New York publishing scene, the income of the average writer puts him/her at poverty level. But story and novel writers don't have leverage to force fair terms, or even honesty in accounting, as my own bitter experience shows. The arts are in thrall to the money moguls, a sad state.

To the northeast some days I can see the San Gabriel mountains, which were snow-capped in spring but dull gray now. There are all manner of palm trees and exotic vegetation. There are multiple solar cell panels; I love the evident dedication to nonpolluting power. Also the trees on the horizon, that look like the outlines of a small herd of buffalo, with the bull humping a cow, and a mountainous pile of poop farther behind. Probably only a window this high, in this region, can see it, so the folk there don't know the kind of neighborhood they have. I can see a round house near there; one day I walked there and verified that it really is round, not my imagination. Our city is Redondo Beach, which means round, so that house is where it belongs. I also see a tilting orange roof in another section of town, but when I walk there to verify it, it doesn't exist. Maybe my imagination is displacing reality; that may be a liability for fantasy writers. Also visible from here is the steeple of a small Episcopal Church that really is there. I wish it well. I am a lifelong agnostic, but am not against religion; my first wife was a UU minister's daughter, and our marriage lasted until death did us part. It has been said that an agnostic is a gutless atheist. If I had ever encountered whoever said that, I might have had news that would puncture his certainty. I have no belief in the supernatural, despite earning my living from it; that annoys it, so it messes me up in unprovable ways, such as growing typos on my manuscripts after the proofreading, as mentioned in the novel. So what's my take on Jesus? I do know him, in my fashion, as I had him as a character in a novel, and I am closer to my characters than I am to most mundane folk. If Jesus existed, and visited this contemporary world, and saw the violence and greed, the hate and hypocrisy preached in his name, his tears would flow. He was a man of peace and poverty, of love and truth. But if he tried to do anything about it, to reform this corrupt world and make it a truly Christian place, the powers that be would crucify him again. They're not ready to give up their money or their power, any more than the Romans were. So no, he's not coming back, at least not at this time; he's not stupid. I speak not as a believer, but as an independent friend who does not like to see Jesus' message abused. That's part of what agnosticism means to me.

On the other side of our apartment is the view of the beach and the broad Pacific Ocean. The weather can be different on the east and west sides, an intriguing phenomenon. One day I looked out of our balcony and saw a wedding taking place on the beach. The bride looked nice in her flowing white gown. But usually it's just folk walking their dogs, or bicycling, or skateboarding. On the sea it's sailboats, speedboats, and passing ships. On July 4th they had a drone light show, with the drones forming various shapes like a giant five pointed star, an American flag, a rocket with moving exhaust flames, or the words rodondo beach backwards, as we were evidently behind it, an unintended audience. Regardless, it was an impressive display. Sometimes we hear sea lions barking. On my exercise days I walk on the paths abutting the beach, going north one day, south another day. I have been exercising for decades. First, I ran, then I jogged, now I speed walk. Or so I thought, until a young woman pushing a baby carriage with a baby in it passed me by, not even looking as if she were hurrying. I suspect I'm not as fast as I used to be. I admire the sights along the way, such as the local piers and parks, the lovely beds of flowers, the cyclists, the joggers, and yes, the occasional buxom babes in bikinis on the beach. I may be old, but I'm not dead, and a nearly nude nubile nymph is a sight warranting some attention. If you disagree, don't look; her annoyance will pass.

Overall, I like it here. We have not driven our cars since we arrived here at the end of the Month of Marsh (you know, the Ogre Calendar: Jamboree, FeBlueberry, Marsh, etc.); instead we have ordered groceries and meals via Smartphone and eaten well without leaving the building. Yes, I now have a smartphone, and am slowly learning how to use it. It is not quite as versatile as the Genius Phone in the novel, and seems to like to pull odd stunts like going dark in the middle of use, or adding gibberish to my letters text, but will do for now, at least until I can afford a magic one. Most deliveries have been good; some not. Luck of the draw, there. We are considering retiring from driving and using the Uber services to get around, as that is feasible here in the metropolis. Our apartment is on the top floor, so we hear the constant grinding of the elevators, as their mechanisms operate from the top, right next to us. Our building is near the local firehouse, so we regularly hear sirens and complicated beep tunes as they hurry in and out. We also hear the melodic honking of what I think is the harbor foghorn. And of course the constant crashing of the waves at the shore. Sounds are much a part of our new life. It is a secure building, so we need keys to get in, which is fine; we'd rather not have strangers with unknown agendas pounding on our door. We are occasionally meeting the neighbors in other apartments, all of whom seem nice. We are also slowly unpacking the two hundred big boxes of clothing, books, DVD videos, and household furnishings shipped from Florida and Tennessee, where MaryLee hails from. Slow because I have been frittering away my time writing a novel—ask any critic—and MaryLee is suffering sieges of long covid that exhaust her and make her what she calls a Covidiot. I had covid in Florida once or twice but threw it off like the ogre I am reputed to be. We do use masks in public.

Why the move? As readers of these author's notes may remember, I lost my first wife of sixty-three years, Carol, in 2019. She was eighty-two. I didn't want to live alone, so I remarried, though I am not sure my second marriage will last as long as the first. MaryLee is a quarter century my junior and a writer herself, under the name of Muri McCage. She likes older men and I like soft women, so we must have been made for each other. She tolerated being sequestered in the backwoods tree farm during the Covid-19 pandemic, but after three years of that she wanted to go live on the beach. One place off the coast in Florida looked good. Then a hurricane crossed right over it, forcing an emergency evacuation by boat. That dampened that interest somewhat. So she continued looking, and finally found the ideal condominium on the coast of California, where hurricanes are rare. I was ready to move on, as my prior personal life at our home in Florida was gone, and here we are. To stay, I believe. Any residence where I can write a provocative novel is my kind of place. The local intellectual climate is liberal, as I am, in contrast to the MAGA clime of central Florida. So if this novel seems crazy, blame it on the environment.

Now the credits: my wife rates early mention, as you can see. But no, you don't have to marry me to rate a credit. The move disrupted my notes, so I didn't use all the ideas I meant to. Maybe I'll catch up with them next novel.

The Nikipedia map; swamp gas; arabesque; ghost in the machine; webbed toes; jalapuno peppers; Wanda and the Baton—MaryLee Jacob

Sphinx and nickelpede ancestors; Helena Handbasket; blood vessel—Misty Zaebst

Night and Day mares on a stream of consciousness; zombies take a dirt nap; D Mentia's lost marbles; pussy willows; crazy robot with loose screw; character rides bat out of Hell—Robert Blaut

Cold Medicine; flu medicine for clogged chimneys; three toad sloth—Emmery Chrisco

A-Lot-A; expresso—Andra Genius

Aura, as a zombie Lips woman; conjuring tunnels; fee mail; robot ticks; boring drone; pan teas; Mun Danes, Tues Danes, etc; flip pants with flip flops; Liber Tea and Democra Sea; peace of cake with war of cake; Zom A, B, C etc; Lesson and Less Daughter; Conjuring coats of any kind; dropping the other shoe; scaring the living daylights; Type O, P, Q errors; Backlog made of reverse wood; Nep Tune; Tune Na Fish; Sat Tern—Timothy Bruening

Towelette becomes wet blanket—Alexander Sellers

Nickelpedia—Jim Loy

Zombies need death support systems; Absinthe makes the heart grow fonder; minordomos; pair o' dimes shift; night mares' bridal veils—Richard Van Fossan

Humbull—David D. Stanton

Elm elves use reverse wood—Tim Davenport-Herbst

The Tangle Elf tribe—Kenneth Adams

Shameful Centaur—Dakota Unlauf

Meteor—Jeff Brown

Muddle Puddle—Sandi Bateson

Magician of Puns which became the Demon of Puns—James Blakeney

Hal E Tosis; Positivi Tea;—Thomas Pfarrer

Stitch in time—David Seltzer

Connor tricks women—Gabe Tsui

Spot on Wall consciousness—Jade at Quasar Nebula

Epilep Sea—Kimberly Johnson

Tourist trap—Mary Rashford

And my credit to my proofreaders, [Scott M Ryan, Doug Harter, Kate Brooks, Avi Ornstein, Charles Schuman]. They help me avoid otherwise inevitable embarrassment of typos.

If you enjoyed this novel and want to know more of me, you can check my website at www.HiPiers.com, where I have news of my career, a character database, do what has become an irregular blog-type column and maintain an ongoing survey of electronic publishers for the benefit of aspiring writers. I do try to help others in my fashion.

I don't know much about the next novel, Xanth #50, except that it may occur in Limbo and feature characters from the prior forty-nine novels. Just in case it's the last one. I don't expect to live forever, and doubt I would want to, but as an agnostic who has no belief in any afterlife I find the prospect of my life's conclusion daunting.

About the Author

Piers Anthony is one of the world's most popular fantasy writers, and a *New York Times*–bestselling author twenty-one times over. His Xanth novels have been read and loved by millions of readers around the world, and he daily receives letters from his devoted fans. In addition to the Xanth series, Anthony is the author of many other bestselling works. He lives in Inverness, Florida.

THE XANTH NOVELS

FROM OPEN ROAD MEDIA

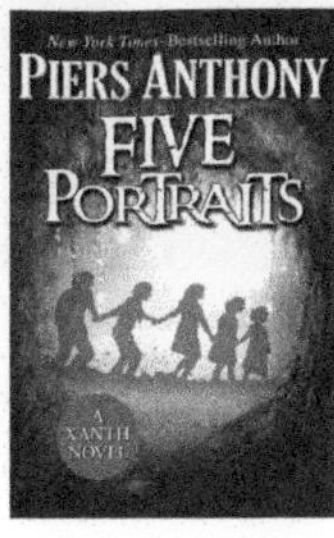

OPEN ROAD
INTEGRATED MEDIA